offside
shay savage

D1474105

Cover Design: Mayhem Cover Creations

Interior Formatting: Mayhem Cover Creations

Editing : Chayasara

DEDICATION

This book is for all the die-hard soccer fans out there who watched the World Cup along with me, cheered for the teams, and are currently suffering through withdrawal while counting the days to World Cup 2018.

As always, huge thanks to the team of people who are always there to encourage me and occasionally talk me down from the ledge: Adam, Andrea, Chayasara, Heather, Holly, Kandace and of course, everyone on my street team!

TABLE OF CONTENTS

CHAPTER ONE
red card

"Hiya, Thomas!"

Ignoring Heather Lones' grating voice coming from behind the goal, I tried to wipe the sweat from my eyes with the back of my glove, but I think all I really managed to do was to rub mud across my face. I tipped the ball with the toe of my cleat to the right and then to the left, keeping it close and within my control. The opposing team's striker jogged up, trying to put a little pressure on me. I waited until the last possible second before bending over and grabbing the ball off the ground.

I had six seconds.

I tossed the ball up into the air, and then gripped it a little tighter as I ran to the top of the box. I could see Jeremy Martin, the central defender, heading left and drawing one of their midfielders with him, which left our striker, Mika Klosav, wide open. I punted the ball straight to him with a second to spare.

"Oh my God! That was so awesome!"

Damn, that chick was annoying.

With the score tied at one-to-one, I couldn't afford to make any mistakes. It was only the first game of the season, but it was also the one that would set the pace for the rest of the year. Having what had to be the single most obnoxious cheerleader in the history of cheerleading right behind my goal was not helping the situation. I didn't think I had ever even given her the time of day. No, definitely not. I might have taken her virginity when we were both drunk during the end-of-year bonfire down at the beach, but I definitely never told her what fucking time it was.

Seven minutes left in the game. I caught an easy one when it came straight at me, rolled it to Jeremy, and he took off down the side of the field. I signaled Klosav and midfielder Clint Oliver to head right, and when Jeremy belted an incredible cross to the far side of the box, Clint was there with the header.

Heather's screech was enough for me to turn around and glare at her.

"Will you shut the fuck up?" I snapped. She just giggled and linked arms with some girl I hadn't seen before. She was small and wearing a hoodie drawn up over her head. If I were hanging out with Heather Lones, I'd be hiding under a hood, too. The two of them skipped off toward the corner where the tunnel to the locker rooms was located. Well, Heather skipped and dragged the other chick with her. I shook my head and refocused on the game.

The forwards were moving up on me—jersey number sixteen on the right and number four on the left. The one on the right was offside by at least six feet, so I turned my attention to the other one who was currently blocked by Jeremy. The ball flew over the midfielders' heads and number sixteen on the right trapped the ball and started to swing his leg back. I straightened up, waiting for the offside flag to go up and the whistle to sound as the ball flew past my right shoulder and into the goal behind me.

The ref blew the whistle and signaled a goal while I looked from him to the line ref at the side and back again. He was taking his booklet out of his back pocket and scribbling on it.

"You're kidding, right?" I snapped. "He was offside by a mile!"

The ref shook his head from one side to the other as he marked the score two-all. I stomped up to the top of the box until I was nose to nose with him and tossed my hands in the air.

"This isn't a Pee Wee game, you idiot!" I yelled. "We aren't children! Are you fucking blind or just smoking crack?"

"Get back in position," he said quietly as he shoved the book back in his pocket.

"Are you a fucking moron?" I clenched my fists. "Have you read the fucking rule book?"

The next thing I knew, I was seeing red.

A red card, that is.

I stomped off the field and through the tunnel to the locker rooms, staring at the ground and ignoring the cheers and jeers from the crowd. As I got to the mouth of the tunnel, Heather was babbling some bullshit, but I didn't listen to her words. I was still looking at the ground, fuming and not watching where I was going, which is how I managed to slam right into Heather's new friend.

"Get the fuck out of my way!" I bellowed before I even looked at her. When I did look down, I saw bright, wide blue eyes as they stared up at me in shock. I watched her lower lip disappear behind her teeth and felt my cock get hard.

Fucking great.

Like I needed that shit.

Not during my last high school season.

I needed focus.

I pushed past her and stormed out of the bright sunlight and into the dark hallway. Inside the locker room, I stripped, showered, and started dressing again without even bothering with a towel. I shook the water from my hair and watched droplets land on the mirror in front of me. I tried keeping my hair pretty short on the sides at least, but the top was just all over the place. I couldn't seem to do much with my light brown hair even when I grabbed a glob of styling putty out of the jar and went to work on it. I turned to one side, examining the bruise running up my bicep that appeared to have a distinct hexagon shape to it.

For a moment, I stared into my own eyes. The hazel-green orbs looked angry in the harsh fluorescents, which fit my mood perfectly. I took a deep breath and dropped to the bench in front of my locker—locker number one, just like the number on my jersey. I was the fucking star, and everyone knew it.

Everyone except that fucking ref.

I wondered where he was from and who brought him to our field. I'd never seen him before. He had to be from out of town, or the fucker never would have carded me. The refs around here just knew better.

Grabbing my bag out of my locker, I fished out my phone and started going through contacts. I found the name I was looking for and hit the send key.

"Hey, Malone!" the voice said. "What can I do for ya?"

"Find out who was reffing my game today, and have the fucker's credentials revoked."

"Name?"

"No idea. Five foot five, bald, and blind as a fucking bat. If this had been a World Cup game, he'd have to be quietly removed from the country just to keep him from ending up with a bullet in his skull. Fucking idiot."

"Center ref?"

"Yeah."

"You get a yellow?"

"Red."

"Damn!" I heard a low whistle through the phone's speaker. "Gotcha. I'll find out who it was. You won't see him again."

"Better not, or it's your ass," I told him.

"Nice. Going to the dance tonight?"

"Probably." I ended the call and threw my phone back in my locker. Swiveling around, I leaned against the locker door and stretched my legs out far in front of me, pointing my toes in the air and loosening my ankles.

Motherfucking ref.

Red carding *me*.

Doesn't he know who the fuck I am?

I closed my eyes and felt my jaw lock up as I started grinding my teeth tightly together. My fists clenched, and I kind of wished the ref *would* decide to come and "talk to me" after the game—so I could get the chance to fuck up his face. I heard the band start playing outside and knew the game must be over. I wondered who might have stepped up as goalie for the last couple of minutes. We had already used all our subs, so our backup goalie, James, couldn't even get on the field.

Poor bastard—might have played in the first game of the year but couldn't.

Ha!

Fucker.

I continued to stretch as my teammates walked in, some of them grumbling a little but not much. Not with me there, anyway. I learned pretty quickly that the game ended in a two-two tie and that Jeremy had stepped up as goalie for the last three and a half minutes of the game. I leaned back against my locker and continued to stretch out with my eyes closed.

"What's wrong with you, Malone?"

I opened my eyes, and I looked at the new kid…um…whatever the fuck his name was. Tony, maybe? He was a freshman player who happened to make varsity though he didn't get played today. I didn't think he was from the area, and he had just moved here from… wherever.

Who gave a shit?

"Excuse me?" I looked at him and raised one eyebrow, wondering just how stupid he was.

"You don't stop looking at the ball just because you think a foul will be called! And you sure as hell don't drop f-bombs in front of the ref!"

I tensed everywhere. For a brief second, I considered just decking the little shit. I quickly forgot that idea for one that was much, much better. I stood slowly and took a step from the bench.

"There is no fucking way you are talking to me," I smiled a half smile at him, but narrowed my eyes. Several of the guys snickered.

"Who else let a goal right by him without even trying to go for the ball?"

No snickering now. Actually, the whole locker room went pretty damn silent. There was the sound of water from the showers and some mumbled voices over that way but nothing else.

"Who the fuck do you think you are?" I asked as I nodded toward Klosav and Oliver. They walked slowly up to either side of him.

"I'm part of this team!" the little shit exclaimed.

"And as part of this team, you do realize I am your team captain."

"I know that," he said. His voice trailed off as he noticed the two bigger guys coming up beside him.

"And as the team captain, I do get certain…*privileges.*" I smiled wider and took another step closer to him.

"What? Like acting like an asshole on the field?" He looked from side to side as if he wanted to back away, but there was nowhere for him to go.

"No, like getting blowjobs from the youngest player on the team." I watched his eyes get wide as he froze in place.

"You're fucking insane or something," he mumbled.

"Seriously? I'm thinking you need a little lesson." I motioned toward Klosav and Clint, and they each placed a leg behind the kid, forcing him to stay where he was. "You need to understand that what I say goes. I'm always right. And you don't fucking question me."

I took another step closer.

"Ever."

Mika and Clint moved quickly, and they grabbed Tony by his shoulders and arms. My teammates wrenched his arms behind his back as they shoved him down to his knees in front of me. I reached to the front of my jeans and undid the top button.

"Don't worry," I said in a low voice. "It really is an honor to suck me off. You'll probably like the taste."

Tony's chest started to rise and fall rapidly. He moved his eyes quickly from my face down to my crotch as he pushed back against his captors. I reached for my zipper like was I going to drop it down but then stopped and leaned toward him instead.

"Lucky for you, there are a dozen girls still up in the stands who would beg for the opportunity," I told him as I stepped back and smiled again. "I'm not about to stick my cock in your mouth, but that isn't the point, is it? The point is I could have, right?"

He nodded quickly, and I could see his Adam's apple bob up and down as he swallowed.

"My dad owns this town," I reminded him and everyone else in the room, "and I own this school, and I sure as hell own this team. Don't fucking forget it."

I buttoned my fly and grabbed my bag, tossing it over my shoulder before I walked out of the locker room and back out the tunnel. I didn't even look back. There were only a half-dozen girls still waiting around for me in the stands, and I gave them all a good smile and picked out one to walk into the school with me. She was a cute little junior, and she'd been practically salivating over me during practice this summer. She would get her thrill tonight.

The high school gym was a freaking zoo. You would think being out in a small town an hour away from Portland, Oregon, it would never get that crowded, but it was. Some DJ from the city was spinning some decent metal tunes, and the place was too loud to hear anyone talk. That suited me just fine. I smiled and nodded a lot when people tried to talk to me about the game.

I grabbed Lisa—the chick du jour—by the hand and pulled her over to the table with the refreshments. She was all smiles and rubbing up against my shoulder like she was marking her fucking territory or something. Mostly she was sneering at the other girls. Whatever. As long as she gave me a little something later, all would be good, and I probably wouldn't trash-talk her too much at school next week.

I grabbed a cup and immediately went over to Jeremy to add a bit of "fun" to the punch. I dumped a bit from his flask into Lisa's drink, too. It couldn't hurt to loosen her up a bit. She asked if I wanted to dance, but I had to have her repeat it four times before I could even hear what she was saying.

"Go ahead," I suggested, pointing to the dance floor.

"With you, silly!" she squealed back.

"Dance by yourself," I told her. "I'll watch."

She scowled and went out onto the floor, wiggling her hips around and holding her hands up over her head to make her tits stick out as she danced. My cock noticed at least, and I figured it was about time to find a place that was a little more private. I downed my punch, got another one, and chugged it back, too. I was feeling pretty good at that point, so I went out onto the dance floor and grabbed her waist from behind.

"Let's go dance somewhere else, baby," I murmured into her ear. After shouting the same words a couple more times only to have her stare at me blankly, I finally just pulled her off the dance floor and out into the hallway. At least I could hear myself think out there, but my ears were still ringing.

"Where are we going?" she asked as I pulled her down the hall.

"Locker rooms," I said.

"Won't they be locked?"

"Nah."

I turned the corner and pushed the door open. Lisa pulled back.

"I don't think I'm supposed to go in there," she said. She glanced up and down the halls, but there wasn't anyone around. I turned around and grabbed her waist, pulling her close and pressing my mouth against hers. I could feel her moaning against my lips and knew she was going to do anything I asked her to do. I kissed her a few more times before I let my hand creep up and cover one of her tits.

She didn't protest, so I gripped her a little tighter, running my thumb over her nipple and feeling it get hard under my touch.

"Come on in now," I whispered into her ear. "I have something to show you."

"What is it?"

"My cock, baby." I wasn't playing around here. Either she was going to get me off, or I'd go find someone else. "He'd like to get to know you a little better."

It took about five minutes of coaxing before she was on her knees in the shower room, opening up and trying to take my cock in her mouth.

"You haven't done this before, have you?" I smirked a little as she shook her head. "It's all right, baby. Just use your tongue a bit more. Yeah…that's it."

I tried not to push with my hips too much, but she was only taking about half of me, and I really wanted a little more. I put one hand on the back of her head, just to encourage her a bit, but she gagged and backed off.

"It's all right, baby," I said, trying to sound reassuring, "just try again."

She nodded and sucked me in again, swirling her tongue around my cockhead.

"That's it, baby…good girl…yeah…"

I took one of her hands and had her wrap it around the base so I could get a little more friction. I moved in and out of her mouth pretty slowly, just letting her get used to it as I reached down and slipped my hand into the top of her shirt and under her bra. I rubbed at her nipple as she kept sucking away.

"Oh yeah," I moaned as I leaned my head back against the tiled wall. "Good job, baby…you're a natural."

I could see her eyes light up at that one, and she sucked a little harder. I looked down at her and saw her close her eyes like she was really concentrating.

"Look up at me, baby," I told her, and she complied. "There ya go...good girl. Just like that. Fuck yeah...I'm gonna come, baby—you try to swallow it, okay?"

I didn't wait for an answer but held onto her head as I thrust a little faster. I felt my balls tighten, and I groaned as I spurted into her mouth. She clenched her eyes shut but kept me in as I felt her swallowing around the head.

"Oh yeah...baby...so good! Keep it up now...get it all...yeah, that's it."

She obediently sucked on me until I went soft in her mouth. I pulled out and reached down to wipe a little cum off the side of her mouth before I helped her back to her feet.

"That was awesome, baby," I told her. She smiled and blushed a little. I kissed the back of her hand and led her back out to the hallway and into the gym. It was getting late, and things were not quite as loud as they had been. There was a slow dance song playing, and when Lisa asked if I'd dance with her, I figured I at least owed her that. I took her out there and danced for about half the song before I told her I needed to head out.

"Where are you going?" she asked.

"Home," I replied, rather deadpan. "I gotta train in the morning."

I walked off, leaving her there on the dance floor. She'd done all right, but I'd had better, too. I didn't want to piss her off because I could probably get her to do more later on, but I also didn't want her clinging to me. I had to focus on my game.

Shakespeare coined the phrases "fair play" and "foul play." Somehow, I was pretty well-versed at both.

Now how was anyone supposed to compete with that?

CHAPTER TWO
first touch

My ears were still ringing a bit from the loud music when I walked through the front door of the largest house in the whole community. I turned around and shut the door slowly and softly before I locked it. Slipping my shoes off, I tiptoed toward the coat closet. Apparently, I didn't need to worry about the noise—Dad was still awake and in the living room. I heard him get up out of his chair as soon as I hung my jacket and tried to mentally brace myself. He hadn't been able to make the game due to some meeting. Maybe he hadn't heard yet. I could be lucky sometimes, couldn't I?

"What the fuck, Thomas? Red card?" I glanced up at his glaring blue eyes. His arms were crossed over his broad chest, and his thick, blond hair hung over his eyebrows as his eyes narrowed further.

Shit.

No luck here.

I was kind of hoping I'd at least make it until morning when I could be sure everything was taken care of before having to deal with Doctor Lou Malone, Chief of Surgery at Memorial Hospital and mayor of our little community. He didn't really care if the shit

I did was right or wrong, but I had gotten caught, and that just wasn't supposed to happen. Ever. Forgiving was not exactly in his nature.

"Um…yeah," I mumbled. "I took care of it."

"I should fucking hope so," Dad snapped. He stood up and walked into the foyer where I was depositing my soccer bag in its designated spot beneath my jacket. I held my breath. "You better not have any game suspensions."

"I don't think he got the chance," I said. "I'll look into it tomorrow."

Without warning, he shoved me in the shoulder—hard. I spun around and tried to brace myself with my hands against the wall, but my head smacked against one of the coat hooks. I saw little white spots dancing in my eyes, and I squeezed them shut as I waited for another blow.

It didn't come.

"I'll fix it," I said as I slowly opened my eyes but kept my gaze to the floor.

"You better. Here." He thrust an envelope into my hands. "You know what that is?"

I looked at the printed envelope with my name on it and a return address that said Real Messini.

Holy shit.

"Did you read it?" I asked.

"Of course I read it."

Figures.

I opened it up and glanced down at the letter. Wayne and Andrew Messini were coming here to scout me personally. Real Messini was one of the best freaking teams in the world, up there with Bayern Munich, Manchester United, and Barcelona. And they were interested in me—saw my video, checked out my stats. Their goalie turned thirty-five earlier this year, which was practically ancient for soccer, but Manuel Mario was still one of the best keepers ever to live.

"I'm counting on you," Dad said. He put his hand on my

shoulder and gave it a squeeze.

Reflexively, I flinched and held my breath. Even though I knew I was too built up now for him to really do any major damage to me, such habits die hard. Dad continued on as if there wasn't blood running down around my eye.

"You know the plan. Now you just have to focus, Thomas. Don't lose your focus. Classes okay so far? I don't want anything distracting you."

"They're okay," I told him. I shrugged a little, hoping it would get his hand off me. It worked, and I took a deep breath. "It's only the first week of school, but they're all okay so far."

"I never should have let you sign up for those AP classes," he grumbled.

I really, really didn't want to have this fight again.

"It's only two of them, Dad," I reminded him. "Just Biology and English. It'll be fine."

"Well, if one of those teachers gives you a B on anything, you let me know."

"I will," I promised.

"And no girls," Dad added. "If you want pussy, I'll fucking buy you some pussy."

"Geez, Dad," I turned my head away, cringing. "Not a problem, okay? Seriously, I need to get to sleep soon."

"Running tomorrow? Six AM?"

"Yep."

"Good."

He turned and walked into the kitchen, depositing his empty mineral water bottle in the recycling bin. I took the opportunity to get to my room as quickly as possible. Once the door was shut and locked, I could breathe properly again. I stripped down and grabbed some lounge pants before I went to brush my teeth in the hall bathroom. I checked out the cut on my forehead in the mirror. It wasn't bad and certainly didn't need stitches or anything like that. I washed it off and put a dab of antiseptic cream on it before I returned to my room and sat on the edge of my bed.

I reached down and pulled out a sketchbook from the bottom shelf of my nightstand and turned it to the last page, a black and white drawing of the US national team's goalie making a save in the last World Cup qualifying game.

I'd been working on this one for a while, even before classes started. When Ms. Mesut, the art teacher, said there was going to be an art show next month…well…fuck. I thought it might be a good one to give to her and to see if it could get into the show. They were only picking ten pieces, and I didn't have a lot of hope that mine would be picked. It wasn't really very artsy or anything —it was a fucking soccer drawing—but I wanted to show it to her. I didn't know why. I never showed anyone anything I drew.

I pulled out my charcoal pencil and started adding a little bit of shading off to the side, giving the ball a little more depth. The goal turned out pretty well, I thought, though it took freaking forever to get all the netting. I knew the angle on the right side wasn't perfect, and I had ended up placing the keeper about half a foot away from where he had really been in the goal.

I closed my eyes for a second, picturing the game in my head as the striker approached and kicked. I could see Tim Howard as he moved to his left, bending at the knee at just the right angle before he jumped to get his hands on the ball. The imaged paused in my head, the ball just barely touching his fingertips, and I carefully looked over the placement of each of his gloved fingers before I began to draw.

I drew, and I drew, and I drew.

When I glanced up again, it was nearly four in the morning. Shit. I had to run in two hours. I placed the sketchbook and the charcoal pencil in their hiding spot under a few copies of *Goal* magazine. I rolled over, switched off my overhead lamp, and dropped onto the pillow.

In my head, the day replayed—every single moment from the time I woke up, through my classes, to warm-ups, to game time— in extreme fast-forward. Every single motion, every image, every sound. I remembered my morning piss had taken twelve seconds longer than the day before and realized I had drunk one extra glass of water with dinner's spicy salsa. There was the book in my locker with the crushed edge that wouldn't line up correctly with the others. I remembered the forward player—clearly offside—as his leg swung. I could have stopped it if I had tried. I remembered the angle of the ref's eyebrow as he wrote me into the book. I remembered the feeling of terry cloth as I slammed into a girl in a hoodie and the slight indentation of her teeth in her lower lip as she stared up at me.

I shoved the palms of my hands into my eye sockets and rubbed. My head hurt. I rolled over onto my stomach and wrapped my arms around my pillow, burying my face into the Egyptian linen case.

<hr />

I downed my homemade lunch with a big bottle of Gatorade before heading out to the practice field to kick the ball around a bit. There wasn't anyone else out there, so I focused on juggling and ran a couple of laps before hitting the shower. I shook out my hair, yanked my jeans up over my damp legs, and threw on a muscle shirt. The second bell had already rung when I walked out of the locker room, but I didn't rush. I sauntered into AP Biology and ignored the glare from Mister Bucher as I turned down the aisle to go to my seat.

The empty seat in front of me where I usually placed my feet was strangely occupied.

Long, light brown hair covered most of her back and shoulders. She had smooth, porcelain skin, an athletic build, and deep blue eyes. She looked up at me, her teeth sunk into her bottom lip, and I knew immediately who she was. It was the girl I slammed into after I was kicked out of the game on Friday, and she was sitting right in front of my seat.

I dropped down behind her and leaned forward and to one side so I could look at her better. She tilted her head down, which made her hair drop over her shoulder and hide her face. It kind of pissed me off, actually, though I wasn't sure why. I reached over and pushed her hair away from her face and back over her shoulder. She looked up at me, eyes wide and sapphire blue.

"Hey," I said as I smiled at her.

"Um…hi," she replied. She pulled back a little, and her hair dropped away from my fingers. At least it wasn't hiding her from me anymore.

"I'm Thomas," I told her.

"So I've heard," she said. Her eyes flashed up to Mister Bucher, who was beginning his lecture on blue-green algae.

"Have you now?" I smirked. I wondered just what she had heard and from whom. "You got a name?"

"Yes." She turned to look toward the front of the classroom and narrowed her eyes. She crossed her arms over her chest and stiffened her shoulders.

I had to laugh.

"Want to tell me what it is," I asked, "or do we get to play Rumplestiltskin?"

A few other games I could play with her flashed through my mind.

"Malone?" Mister Bucher snapped. I looked up at him. "You care to answer my question?"

The fucker thought he could trip me up. I blinked a couple of times, hit the mental rewind button in my head, and glanced up at the whiteboard.

"Oxygen production," I said with a smile. He huffed and growled something about keeping my eyes up front.

Whatever.

I glanced back to the girl in front of me and saw the corners of her mouth turn up a little as if she was holding in a laugh. I shifted my desk forward with a scrape, moving a little closer to her and extending one of my legs so it was right next to her. She looked back at me and then quickly looked away.

I didn't reach out to touch her again though it was a little tempting. I kept my leg just about three inches away from hers, shifting my foot when she moved so I could keep the distance constant. She had long, slender legs, but I could tell they had some muscle to them as well. I resisted the urge to immediately get out of my chair and run my hand over her thigh. No need to move too quickly on a chick that was obviously new. Maybe even a challenge.

I could feel that she was a little nervous—either because of my proximity or just because I kept leaning forward to stare at her throughout class. Bucher tried to catch me up a couple more times, even to the point of asking me where my book was and why I didn't have a pencil. I told him I didn't need them and noticed the girl in front of me glaring a bit.

I just smiled and winked at her. She rolled her eyes.

Yeah…definitely a challenge.

After class I sat there at my desk as she gathered her stuff and shoved it into her book bag.

"So…Rumplestiltskin," I said. "Where are you from?"

"Very funny," she replied as she stood up. "Minneapolis."

"You must love the warm weather here," I said with a friendly smile.

"Not really." Totally deadpan answer. She didn't offer anything else either. I followed her out of the classroom and down the hall.

"Enjoy it now—rainy season is on the way," I added. She ignored me, so I pressed on. "What class do you have next?"

"Calculus."

"Do you know where the math hall is?"

She stopped in the hall and looked up at me.

"Is there some particular reason you are being nice to me?" she asked.

Damn.

"Straightforward, aren't you?"

"You were a complete jerk on Friday."

"You caught me at a bad time," I replied. It was at least partially true. She narrowed her eyes at me then turned and started walking away. "Hey, Rumple!"

She glared back at me.

"The math hall is this way." I pointed over my shoulder, the opposite way she was going. She stopped in her tracks and sighed. "Come on. I'll show you."

She paused and seemed to consider before she finally started following me.

"This map is useless," she mumbled as she shoved a paper into her book bag.

I just smiled and led her down the hall.

"So, Rumple," I said, "why weren't you here for the first week of school?"

"I just moved here," she replied. "It was kind of a last minute thing."

"Why did you come here?"

"My dad lives here," she said.

"A little more info?" I prodded. I turned the corner and started down the next hallway, watching her the whole time. She gave me another big sigh.

"My mom got a new job as a journalist, and she's going to have to travel a lot. It just made sense for me to come here. She's very career-minded."

"Sounds like a blast." Sarcasm is a beautiful thing. I brushed my hand against her arm…accidentally, of course.

"I'm very happy for her," she explained. "It's exactly what she wanted."

"Yeah, I can see how thrilled you are," I noted. Her expression told me I was right.

"It's only for a year." She shrugged, and we turned another corner. My arm touched hers again. The first bell rang, and she glanced around as other kids started scrambling into classrooms. "Don't you have to go to class?"

"I've got practice last bell," I told her.

"Will you be late?"

"Maybe." I smiled and watched her lip disappear behind her teeth again. Damn, that was hot. I started imagining other things I could do with that lip.

"What happened to your eye?" she asked.

I raised my hand up to my forehead and lightly touched the cut above my right eye. It wasn't a bad one but certainly noticeable.

"Ran into a door," I said with a half-grin.

"That's a lame story," she replied.

"How about underground cage-fighting, then?" I suggested. She continued to glare at me. It wasn't like I was going to tell her what had actually happened, so I went with the ridiculous. "Actually, I was wrestling bears."

"You are so full of shit."

I turned the conversation to other topics as we went around another corner, peppering her with questions, and then turned back toward the math hall. She looked around quickly, and her eyes went wild.

"This is where we started!" she exclaimed.

"Yeah, I guess it is." I tried to keep in a laugh as the second bell rang. I pointed to the end of the hall. "Calc is right there."

"What the hell?" she shrieked. "Now I'm late!"

"Just tell Miss Jones you were with me," I said as I raised an eyebrow at her. Her eyes were still full of fire as she stared up at me.

"You *are* a jerk," she exclaimed, turned on her heel, and disappeared into the calculus room.

I chuckled and headed out to the field.

Nothing like practice in the pouring rain.

I shook my head, sending water everywhere, but it didn't make any difference. Coach Wagner was yelling at Mika Klosav, and Clint Oliver was taking potshots at the goal. He wasn't really trying too hard, and I hadn't missed any of them.

"You suck!" I finally screamed at him through the downpour. "Why don't you at least try?"

It worked, and he almost got one past me. The new guy—whose name apparently *was* Tony—jogged up after talking to Wagner.

"Coach wants you," he said to Oliver. Tony eyed me warily as Clint ran off.

"Quit with the freak out," I told him. "You didn't swallow my cock, so you're still going to grow up to be a man. Now just kick the fucking ball, all right?"

He glared but then nodded. He took a couple warm-up shots, and I had to admit, the kid did have a decent leg on him. In a couple of years, he'd be pretty good. I watched his legs move—the angles, the tension in the muscles of his thigh and calf as he kicked.

"Come here," I said. Tony paused for a moment and then walked up to the goal slowly. "Your knee's bending right before you get foot to ball, and you're losing leverage."

I showed him what I meant, had him try a couple shots, and he gave me a nod and admitted he was getting more power now. Coach Wagner called us all together, and we did a quick scrimmage before calling it a day. I headed back to the locker rooms, but Lisa approached me before I could get there.

"Hey, Tom!" she beamed.

"It's Thomas," I replied. I didn't really care for the shortened version of my name and definitely didn't like chicks thinking it was somehow endearing. I kept walking.

"So, you know the next dance is the Sadie Hawkins dance, right?"

"Is it?"

She had to practically run in the rain to keep up with me. She giggled and told me to slow down. I took a deep breath and turned to look at her. She was still smiling up at me with rain cascading off her face and hair and mascara running under her eyes. She looked like she came right out of a zombie movie.

"Well?" She fluttered her eyelashes at me.

"Well, what?"

"Do you want to go to the dance?"

"With whom?"

"Well…with me…" Her voice dropped, and I had to shake my

head a little. Poor thing. She really was clueless. I'm not sure how she could have grown up around here and been in this school for over two years without understanding how things worked around here. I pay attention to you. You put out. I find someone else. End of story. Well, usually. I hadn't actually seen her naked, so there was still some potential there, and maybe that's what she was really offering—a chance to really fuck her.

My mind flashed backwards—the feel of warm, soft skin brushing against my arm and the look in Rumple's eyes when she realized I had walked her in a big square around the school—and I smiled. My mind returned from its musings and back to the blonde next to me. I had planned to pull her along for a while, at least until I got into naked and riding my cock, but I really didn't want to right now.

"Sorry babe," I told her. "I've got a game the next day."

I turned away from her and headed from the rain shower to the locker room shower, Lisa's disappointed face already a thing of the past. I warmed up in the shower, talked to Clint a bit, grabbed my bag, and headed home. As I sped out of the parking lot, I noticed a beat up old Hyundai with a cute little brunette in the driver's seat and decided to follow her home.

Holy fucking shit!

The Hyundai pulled into the driveway of none other than the town's sheriff, Greg Skye. I didn't know if I should laugh or laugh harder. For one, the guy absolutely hated me, not so much because I got in trouble, but because I always got out of it on the few occasions I had been caught. Whether it was a speeding ticket, illegal parking, or a noise violation—I'd never had to pay for anything I had done. Not when Daddy was the sheriff's boss. Definitely not. For the other...well...the guy did have a gun.

This was going to be interesting.

I didn't stop but just drove by a couple of times before heading home. My house was quiet and empty when I got there, so I cooked and devoured a pizza from the freezer, quickly finished up my homework, and then pulled out my sketchbook. I had a couple hours before Dad would be home, and I was almost done with the goalie picture. Just a few changes here and there—deepening the shades, softening the angles. When I was done, I pulled it out of the book and neatly trimmed the edges.

It actually looked pretty good, I thought. I narrowed my eyes at the paper, looking at it from different sides for a minute. I wondered if Ms. Mesut would like it…I mean, it was still a fucking soccer picture. Is that art? I shook my head a little before sticking it into my homework folder and placing everything into my book bag. I hauled the bag back downstairs and deposited it on the floor in the kitchen.

My phone started ringing, and I glanced at the name before answering.

"All fixed?"

"Yeah, he'll never ref in Oregon again, at least."

"Good thing. Suspensions?"

"Wiped."

"You rock."

I hung up just as I heard the front door open.

"You fix your shit yet?" Dad called out from the foyer.

Good timing.

"Yeah, all good—no suspensions."

"Good." He dropped the mail on the kitchen table and started flipping through a carryout menu. "Homework?"

"Done."

"Did you have a bunch of extra shit from those college prep classes?"

"Nah," I said, "it's all good. I've already read the first book we're doing in English, and the biology stuff is mostly going to be lab work in school."

"When the hell did you read a book?" he snapped. "You don't have time for that shit. I don't know why you're bothering at all. You aren't going to college. Pros or bust, asshole."

"I know," I said. I tried to walk out of the room, but he grabbed my arm.

"I asked you a fucking question," he said. His cold blue eyes stared into mine. "I expect an answer. What book?"

"It's a Shakespeare class," I mumbled.

"What the fuck, Thomas!" His grip on my arm tightened. I tried to keep my arm from flexing in order to ease the pressure because I knew that shit would just piss him off. I didn't need him angry.

"I figured it would be an easy A," I told him.

"Little shit," he grumbled. "Next, you'll be playing the fucking piano again like a pussy."

My hands started to shake a little, and the tension crept up from my gut and down my arms. He released me, and I headed straight to the solace of my room. Along the way, I tried not to glance at the piano in the living room, but I couldn't help it. It sat there, lid down, as it had for the past six years. I locked my bedroom door, but the relief didn't last.

"Thomas! Get down here!"

Shit! What now?

I unlocked the door and headed back down the stairs.

"Yeah, Dad?" I asked as I walked into the kitchen where he was chowing down on Chinese food. My book bag was open, and my homework folder was sitting in the middle of the table.

"What the fuck is this?" he asked, shoving the sketch I had just finished over toward me.

Shit! Shit! Shit!

"Um…"

"That's not a fucking answer." He smacked his hand down on the table, and I jumped a little.

Might as well get it over with.

"I went for the art class instead of study hall," I told him. I tried to brush it off. "Another easy A for my senior year…ya know?"

"Goddammit, Thomas!" He slammed his hand down on the table, and I cringed. "You should be out on the fucking field during that time! What the hell is wrong with you?"

"My last period is open," I told him, "and I go to the field at lunch. I figured—"

"Bullshit," he snapped. I started to reach for the sketch, realizing too late how big a mistake that was. He grabbed it, tore it up, and crumpled the pieces in his hand. "You don't focus on this shit. Soccer, asshole. You focus on *soccer*, and that's it, you hear me? You think Real Messini is going to want to look at your fucking coloring?"

"No, Dad," I admitted. He shoved the torn paper into the bag of empty soy sauce packets and fortune cookies before tossing it in the garbage can.

"Drop that fucking art class tomorrow."

My stomach tightened as if there were big balls of pizza dough in it, but I swallowed hard and replied.

"Okay."

Shakespeare phrased destruction as "dash'd all to pieces." Somehow, that line from *The Tempest* came to mind though I wasn't sure why, so I tried to think about something else.

Now how was I going to get Rumplestiltskye to tell me her first name?

CHAPTER THREE
out of play

"Hiya!"

Heather Lones plopped herself down beside me at lunch just as I was finishing up and about ready to head out to the field.

"Hey," I responded, not really wanting to talk to her.

"So, you know the dance is coming up next weekend, right?" She popped her chewing gum in her mouth as she bounced up and down in the plastic cafeteria chair.

"Yeah," I said. I knew where this was going and didn't want to hear the rest of it.

"So, do you want to go with me?"

"Busy," I told her as I stood up to leave.

"Do you already have a date?"

"Not the point." I started walking away, but she followed.

"Thomas!" she whined. "You don't have to spend all your time on the field, you know."

"Yeah, actually," I said, "I do."

I walked faster, leaving her behind pretty quickly. I took a few shots on the goal—not my position, but every once in a while you have to branch out, and there was no one else outside to kick a few at me. It was only misting, so at least I wasn't soaking wet when I went back into the school, changed, and headed to biology with my hair still dripping from my shower.

As I walked down the hall, my mind flashed through my interactions with Rumplestiltskye from the previous day. I couldn't help but smile to myself; she had been so ticked off at me, and it was seriously fucking cute. When I entered the classroom about ten minutes late, she glared at me before I even sat down. Bucher didn't even bother saying anything to me; he just went on with his lecture.

"Hey there," I said, shifting my desk forward and into the aisle a bit to make sure I could look right into her face. It was hot today despite the misting, and she was wearing a short-sleeved shirt with a V-neck. I quite liked the deep blue on her, which was fucking hot against her pale skin and brought out the color in her eyes.

She only gave me a slight nod in response and kept her eyes up front. I watched her as she stared at Bucher, taking copious notes as he rambled on. I kicked the side of her leg under her desk, and she glared at me.

"So sorry," I said with a wink. She rolled her eyes and went back to trying to ignore me. I reached out and bumped her arm, causing her to smudge her notes, and then shrugged apologetically when her eyes shot a handful of daggers at me. She flicked her hair over her shoulder and glared at her paper. I tapped her arm again, and she shifted her whole body so it was angled away and continued her note-taking.

I reached over and swiped her pen.

"Hey!" she snapped under her breath. "Give me that!"

"You didn't say please," I whispered, holding the pen out of her reach.

"Give me my pen," she snarled. I smirked.

"Come to practice," I said.

"What?"

"You come to my soccer practice after school today, and I'll give you your pen back."

"You're crazy."

"You'll come, then?"

"No!"

I twirled the pen around in my fingers. Bucher stared over at our table, and I could hear Rumple take a deep breath and sit very still until he looked away.

"Come to my practice," I repeated.

"Are you going to give that back to me?"

"Are you coming?"

"Fine!"

"Fine," I repeated and handed her the pen.

"Such an ass," she mumbled.

I honestly didn't think she would actually show up but was pleasantly surprised to see her sitting with Heather, Lisa, and a handful of other girls at the sidelines while we warmed up with some drills. After a while, Coach Wagner put me in goal to do some PKs.

Fucking A.

My specialty.

Klosav came up first. He was too easy—always leaning in such an obvious way, contrary to the direction he would kick—it was easy to know which direction to jump. I caught it without much effort. Clint was next and not a lot harder. Jeremy was a little more difficult and would try to fake me out. The thing was, he always faked out in the same way, so I knew the direction he would kick based on the tension in his leading thigh.

Out of twenty-seven PKs, I missed three.

"All right—hit the showers and get out of here!" Wagner yelled. I ran over to the sides and grabbed a water bottle. I looked up at the bleachers and saw Rumple still sitting there. She had her arms crossed and was eyeing me though I wasn't too sure about her expression. I walked up to her as Heather and Lisa stood up and started gushing over my saves.

"What did you think, Rumple?" I asked her, ignoring the other two.

"About what?" she asked.

27

Oh yeah, she was definitely going to make me work for it. No problem, baby. I knew this game as well as I knew soccer.

"About the ending of the movie *Castaway*," I said with a smirk.

"It was awful," she responded. "I can't believe he was screeching over that stupid ball."

I laughed.

"I'm going to get a shower," I told her. I barely restrained myself from asking her to join me. "Want to head over to the diner later?"

"Not unless you have another one of my pens," she said as she stood up. She brushed past me and headed toward the school parking lot and that horrible piece of shit Hyundai. She didn't even look back. I still smiled and continued to ignore the other girls as I walked to the locker room.

I was heading back to her house tonight. Definitely. I wasn't completely sure why. Maybe it was the challenge, and maybe it was because she was the new girl and a little mysterious. I liked that I didn't know her name though it frustrated me at the same time. I considered all of this as I finished up in the locker room and headed back through the school.

"Thomas?"

I stopped and turned, surprised to see Ms. Mesut in the hallway. She walked up to me, her expression concerned.

"Yeah?"

"You weren't in class today," she stated as if I didn't already know that. "I thought maybe you were ill."

Why do teachers always say "ill" instead of "sick"?

"I was practicing," I said with a shrug.

"Isn't soccer practice after school?"

"Yeah," I answered. This conversation was obviously going nowhere. She wasn't going to get it; I could tell from the tone of her voice. When people dropped the timbre down a half step, then raised it back up on the last syllable, it was always because they were trying to help you *understand* something.

I looked down at the floor near my feet and waited for her to get on with it.

"Can I at least assume you'll be in class tomorrow?"

"No, not really," I sighed and looked up at her. "I thought it was going to be something different. It's stupid and a waste of my time. I'll get around to dropping it later."

I turned and started to walk away.

"Thomas!"

I took a deep breath, stopped, and turned around to meet her gaze again.

"Earlier this week, you mentioned the art show," she said. "I thought you might have something for it."

"You must have misunderstood," I responded. "I don't do that shit."

I didn't turn back when she called after me again.

I rode home past Rumplestiltskye's house, saw that her car was there, and kept going. As I drove past this time, I looked up and saw a second floor window and a flash of long brown hair. I felt the corner of my mouth turn up as I wondered if she closed the curtains when she got undressed at night so no one could see in.

Maybe I should check...you know...just to warn her in case she didn't think of such things.

I decided to come back later if I could get out of the house. I checked my odometer and figured once I got home that the round trip would be a twelve-mile run, a bit much for my normal jog, which was only five miles. Dad always thought I should run in the mornings and wouldn't buy into me jogging at night. Once I got home, I realized I had the perfect excuse when I looked in the freezer and noticed we were out of just about everything. I decided to make a box of mac and cheese and ate a can of pears while I waited for the water to boil. By the time Dad got home, I had my grocery list and my excuse to get out. He just grunted his acceptance of my plan and added that he would go out to eat while I was at the store.

"Don't forget the banquet on Saturday," he reminded me.

"I remember," I told him. "I checked and my tux still fits."

"I thought you were bulking up," Dad said with a scowl. "You haven't worn that for three months. Haven't you put on any muscle? You know that trainer said you were going to have to bulk up so you could take a bigger hit."

"I have, Dad—"

"Bullshit. Go to the fucking store, and get a bunch of raw eggs and meat or something. You'd better put on muscle before the holidays come around."

"All right," I said as I escaped out the door. I had bulked up, just mostly in my legs. I could take a bigger hit than I would have been able to three months ago. I shook my head as I started the car, almost laughing to myself that I had actually thought he'd be pleased he wouldn't have to buy me a new tux. My mind flashed to the last time he seemed pleased with me—when the first scout came up to me after a game in Seattle last fall and started talking about the Sounders. Dad had smiled and tossed his arm lightly around my shoulder as he spoke to the guy.

Gotta keep up appearances.

I turned into the parking lot of the Thriftway and parked up front. Both the scent and bright colors of the mums in the front of the store triggered another memory and not a welcome one. My eyes squeezed shut, and I felt the warmth of long fingers reaching around my hand and pulling me from the back seat of the car.

The mums had been on display in the same spot though there were fourteen more pots than there were at present. I had pointed at the brightest red ones, and Mom had placed them in the child seat part of the cart next to where I sat.

Dad joined us and looked at me as I held the flowerpot in my hand.

"What the hell is that?"

"Mums, sweetheart. We can plant them near the front porch."

"He's not a girl, Fran," Dad had said. "You're always making him do girly stuff."

"He's a wonderfully well-rounded little boy," Mom responded.

She reached up and touched the side of his face, and his expression calmed. "He would still rather be in front of the goal with you than on the piano bench or reading with me."

I picked up one of the potted plants and put it in the cart.

It wasn't Dad's fault—I knew that. He had a lot to worry about between the hospital and coping with single fatherhood, not to mention dealing with the whole fucking town. That was a lot for a guy to deal with, as he reminded me fairly regularly.

I was going to have to figure out how to get this thing planted without him noticing. As I finished shopping and jumped back into the car, I considered various places in the yard he might not detect.

I didn't head home.

I kept driving past *her* house.

I did the same thing the next day—figured out a plausible reason to leave home and drove around her neighborhood.

One certainly could have argued that I was displaying some obsessive-compulsive behavior, which I was known to do, but I would have argued right back that her house just happened to be on my way to a lot of different places…or at least, not too far out of the way. Regardless, I only did it two times during the day and maybe once at night just to make sure she remembered to close her curtains.

She always closed them, but I was hoping at some point she might forget…just so I could let her know about it. You know— like a Good Samaritan kind of thing. Once I saw her and her father sitting at the kitchen table, eating enchiladas or something that looked like them. I wondered if she could really cook. Sheriff Skye seemed to be enjoying them.

The mums I had left on her front porch had been planted by the mailbox.

I drove by before school and after school just to check to see if she had either left already or was home yet. I never stopped or anything—just drove past. When the sheriff's car was there, I drove past a little faster, not over the speed limit, though I wouldn't have had to pay for it, but I still didn't want him pulling me over while I was right by his house, checking out his daughter.

Rumplestiltskye.

After four days, I still had no idea what her first name was. She wouldn't tell me, and I refused to ask anyone else. I just kept calling her Rumple because it seemed to annoy the shit out of her, which made her glare and take out her verbal claws. She reminded me of the kitten I hid in my room for a week before Dad found it and took it to the shelter: little tiny claws and lots of yowling for such a tiny thing. Rumple was like that, too.

She was bringing extra pens to biology class now, so I needed some way to get to her.

Friday, I walked into the cafeteria and saw her sitting at the end of one of the long rectangular tables. I smirked to myself and strode right over, dropping down across from her and plopping my sack lunch to one side. I crossed my arms on top of the table and put my chin in the middle of them.

"Hi there, Rumple," I said with a smile and a raise of my eyebrows.

She closed her eyes and took a slow breath through her nose. She picked up a bag of chips off her tray and tore into it as she stared off into space and refused to look at me. I reached over, grabbed her sandwich, and bit off the corner.

"You are unbelievable," she finally said.

I knew she wouldn't be able to ignore me forever.

"You're adorable when you're angry," I told her. I meant it— she was.

She growled something under her breath and looked away from me again. I reached over to her tray and grabbed the plastic spork out of the bowl she had for her fruit cup. I started spinning it around my fingers like a drummer with a drumstick, but I wasn't very good at that. I kept dropping it and starting all over again.

"You should come to practice again tonight," I told her.

"Why would I?" she asked, still not meeting my gaze.

"To watch me," I said with a shrug, as if it was obvious. It *was* obvious. Most of the girls there were coming to watch me or one of the other guys. "Why else?"

"Is that supposed to be the point of the game?" she asked, finally looking at me. "Watching the guys play? I thought there was some sort of objective about getting the ball in the net or something."

"Well, yeah!" I laughed. "That's during a game, though. If you come to watch practice, you're just there hoping I end up on the team playing skins in the rain."

Her eyes widened and then narrowed, but I picked up on her quick breath. She tried to let it out slowly, tried to calm herself, but I was pretty damn sure she was thinking about what I had said.

"You want to see me without my shirt?" I winked at her. "I'm only too happy to oblige."

"I most certainly do not!" she snapped and glared at me. She started to grab her tray, but I put a hand on it and held it against the table.

"Am I annoying you?" I asked with a half-smile.

"Undoubtedly!" She pulled at the tray, but I slid it to the side and grabbed both her hands in mine. She started to pull away, but I held on. She leaned back a little but didn't keep trying to get away from me.

"Let me just make a quick observation," I said as I looked into her blue eyes. "You do want to see me practice, and you do want to see me with my shirt off. You'd probably like to see more, too."

"Oh, yes, because you are such a charmer." Her voice was dripping with sarcasm, and she rolled her eyes, but her pupils were slightly more dilated than they had been, and her lips were darkening in color.

"Yes, you do," I insisted.

I lifted my head off my arms, pulled my legs up and got on my knees on the bench seat. Then I leaned over the table, getting right up next to her. I moved forward until I was only a few inches from her face.

"There are several ways I can tell," I informed her, keeping my voice low and soft. I let my tongue dart out and lick my lips, noting her distraction as her eyes flickered to my mouth and back again. "Like right now, I know what you're thinking about."

"Oh, really?" she said, trying to sound snarky but not quite pulling it off.

"Yeah," I responded. "You're breathing faster. Your heart's pounding in your chest. Right now you're thinking about how it would feel to have my mouth on yours. You're wondering if I'd kiss you hard and rough or soft and gentle. You're thinking about just how it would taste to have my tongue in your mouth and where I might put my hands on you…I bet you're even getting wet, aren't you?"

Even as her eyes went wide with shock, and she seemed just a little bit paralyzed by what I had just said, I leaned forward a bit more and moved my mouth close to her ear. I was pushing my luck…I knew I was. Sometimes I just couldn't help myself.

"Are your panties wet, Rumple?"

She gasped, and I watched her hands tighten into fists as she yanked them out of my grasp. Her eyes narrowed, and Rumple's little kitten claws came out, tearing at me.

"You are the most conceited, narcissistic, obnoxious jerk I have ever met in my entire life!" She swung her legs around to the other side of the bench and stomped off.

"She is right, you know."

Taking my eyes from Rumple's retreating backside, I looked to my left to find a barely five-foot tall, dark haired and dark eyed girl dressed entirely in black. She had dark, smudgy eye makeup, and her hair was stuck up in spikes all over the place.

Amy Cutter, the school freak.

"Fairly certain I wasn't looking for your opinion," I told her. I sat back down in the seat, hoping she'd get the hint and go away when I didn't look at her again. It didn't work.

"I know you aren't looking for anyone's opinion," she said. "That's kind of the point. The thing is, I've never seen you actually try to pursue a girl before, and it's just sad."

"What the fuck are you talking about?"

"I've seen you grab a girl by the hand, whisper to her, and then take her to the locker room for fifteen minutes," Amy said, "but I've never seen you actually trying to get the attention of a girl who's just not falling for it."

"Shut up and go away."

"Unfortunately," Amy went on, "she's straight. I did have my hopes up for a minute, but I guess I'm going to have to continue to stick to the city nightlife. No one else in this part of bumfuck is out of the closet yet."

I guess the rumors of Ms. Cutter's sexual orientation were accurate.

"Let's try this again," I growled. *"Shut up and go away."*

"I'm just a little too intrigued," she continued. I put my head down in my hands and tried wishing on my PB&J for her to just disappear. It didn't work. "...partially because you are actually trying harder than ever, and even more so because it isn't working for you. Have you ever gone after a girl and not been successful?"

"Of course I have," I grumbled. "You ought to know that."

"You consider the lame pass you made at me an actual courting attempt?"

"Courting?" I snorted. "What the fuck century do you live in? Yes, I count that. You did turn me down."

"Your anatomy is seriously underwhelming," she stated. I sat up straight in my seat.

"The fuck it is—"

"Not *your* anatomy *personally*," Amy clarified. "I just mean boys in general. The penis is a ridiculous looking thing. I never understood the appeal. The new girl, though—she has beautiful, round breasts, though she doesn't show enough of them, and a nice perky ass. I bet the rest of her is just as luscious."

I couldn't argue with that.

"But if you want to have any better chance of seeing that than I have, you are going to have to try tactics that didn't die out in the fifth grade."

With that, she stood up and sauntered away. I quickly shoved down lunch, practiced, showered, and walked into biology late.

"You'll be working in your assigned teams…" Mister Bucher was saying as I walked in, still dripping wet from my post practice shower. He eyed me, took in a long breath, and huffed it out as he stopped and looked down at the paper in his hand.

"Who's my partner?" I called out.

"Miss Skye will be working with you," he informed me without looking up from his list.

I waggled my eyebrows at her.

"In what way are we partnering up?" I asked Rumple as I dropped down onto the desk behind her. There were quite a few ways of "partnering" I could think of that I'd like to explore with Rumple, and this was a biology class, after all. I gave her a little wink.

She sighed heavily and didn't look up at me as she spoke.

"Organism research," she said. "We are supposed to pick any organism we want, do a research paper, and present it."

"Orgasm research? Fabulous!" She rolled her eyes and looked away from me. As class continued, the grin on my face wasn't to be stopped. Working with Rumple meant we would have to spend some time together outside of class, and I was all for that.

She wouldn't have a choice about it either.

"Are you coming to the game tonight?" I asked her as the bell rang.

"Why would I?"

"You have to," I told her as I tried to come up with a reason why.

She looked over to me, her expression one of disbelief.

"How did you discern that?"

Good question…oh yeah!

"Because we have to work on the project after school," I surmised. "I'll have a couple hours free once I'm done with practice and before I have to be back for the game.

"As if," she mumbled.

"What is that supposed to mean?" I asked. She ignored me.

"I'll be in the library after school," Rumple stated matter-of-factly. "You do what you want."

"I'll meet you there after last period," I told her. Knowing that she had to be in my presence and talk to me in order to complete a project put me in good spirits, and I headed out to the field with a smile that seemed to scare my teammates.

Hanging out in the library to get our project going was definitely going to give me all the advantage I needed. Once she realized that there was no resisting me—since she wasn't striking for the other team—she'd have to give in, and then…well, we would just have to see what happened then.

Maybe like Shakespeare's Othello, I denoted it a "foregone conclusion." Somehow, in the back of my mind, I had the feeling it wasn't going to be quite so straightforward.

Now it was time to focus again.

rounding the keeper

I needed to get laid.

I wasn't sure if it was because I had spent most of the last five days thinking about the same girl without making my usual progress, because I hadn't had my dick in a girl's *anything* for a week, or because there was a game tonight, and I always felt a little tense afterward until I got off.

Dad's offer of store-bought pussy was actually sounding appealing.

Well…not when I really thought about it, but still.

It might have had something to do with looking forward to my little study date with Rumple and not being able to find her anywhere. She definitely wasn't in the library, and her car was absent from the school grounds. When I drove to her house, the car wasn't there, either.

Dammit.

She had to have had something horrible happen to her, because why else wouldn't she be there? The more I thought about it, the more worried I became. I started driving around town, then back toward her house and then around the school again. By that time, her car was in the parking lot along with about five hundred other cars. I looked at the clock on my dashboard.

"Shit!"

I should already be in the locker rooms.

I parked next to the picnic tables on the grass since there weren't any close parking spots and ran to the locker room. Everyone else smirked at me, and I just gave them a bit of a raised eyebrow and started pulling stuff out of my locker.

"Get a little pre-game action, Malone?" Robin Stephens, one of our strikers, asked. "Was it any good?"

"You ever have pussy that wasn't good?" I asked him. I didn't give him time to answer. "No wait…let me rephrase that. Have you ever had pussy?"

That one got a big laugh from everyone except Robin. He didn't respond at all, which made me pretty sure I was right about his virginal status. He was only a sophomore, though. If he didn't get some action by the end of the year, I'd have to help him out.

Yeah, I definitely needed to get laid.

I pushed the thoughts from my head as I put on my uniform and stretched. When we walked through the tunnel and onto the field, the noise from the crowd was just about deafening. We did the usual lineup and handshaking with the refs, and I shook hands with the captain of the team from Eugene before heading to my goal. I tossed a bottle of water and a towel off to the side then turned and faced the field.

I took several slow, deep breaths. I gazed over the lines of the box, making sure the repainting had been done right and nothing was screwed up. I checked out the center ref and the line refs, and I knew them all. I could hear the yelling of the crowd, but it became background noise in my head as the whistle blew.

Soccer was big in our community—much bigger than in most high schools around the US—and had surpassed American football in recent years. A lot of that had to do with me, and I knew it. Hell, everyone knew it, and they pointed it out on a regular basis. It brought money to the school and made my dad happy. Well, happy for him, anyway. When the ball was at the other end of the field, I glanced over at the area in the stands where my dad was sitting and saw a couple other people also in his area. I couldn't tell who they were from the goal, though. One of them almost had to be a scout though.

I directed my eyes back to the ball and watched the left wing bring it up the field. He got past Jeremy and ended up being tackled by Robin Stephens. The problem was, Robin got a lot more of the opponent's ankles than he got ball, and he was in the box at the time.

Penalty kick.

I watched one of the players come up and recognized him immediately. I didn't know his name, but I knew his face and his number—ten. He'd taken one penalty shot against me last year, kicking to my left. I watched his legs as he walked up, noticing he definitely favored the right, though I remembered him kicking with the left the year before.

The ref shoved a few players back behind the line and walked over to one side of the box. Number ten tapped the ball with his foot, and then took a few steps back. He was kicking with his right foot, no doubt. I guess he didn't favor his chances as well this time.

I crouched, tensed my fingers, and kept my eyes on his legs as the whistle blew, and he ran up to kick. He was going for the left again—but top corner, not low. His toe was pointed up at too great an angle for a low shot.

Before he actually made contact with the ball, I was already jumping for the left corner, hands out. I felt the impact as the ball bounced off my gloves and dropped to the ground. I jumped on it and curled it into my chest as the screams erupted around me.

We won the game, 2-0.

As soon as the team started to walk out of the locker room, all the usual girls crowded around us. Jeremy was leaning against the rail to the bleachers, smiling at Rachel Becker and waggling his eyebrows at her. Mika had made his way up to Heather as soon as he saw her, and I heard someone say she had ended up asking him to the dance next weekend. Thank God. Maybe she'd leave me the hell alone now. Lisa was there as well, along with a girl I hadn't seen before. Apparently, she was Lisa's cousin from Portland and had come along for the game and was spending the weekend with Lisa. The way they both looked at me definitely gave me pause and gave my cock a reason to stand up and take notice.

Lisa's cousin's name was Lucy, and I was all about a double pair of Ls and was about to start talking to them about maybe heading to the beach for a while when I looked over Lisa's shoulder.

Shit.

Dad's eyes were narrowed, and he was heading straight for me.

"Sorry ladies," I said with a smile. "Duty calls."

I walked away from them a little disappointed, but there was always later. Dad was walking with one of the men that had been sitting with him in the stands—a big burly guy with a beard and a black rain jacket.

"Thomas! Fantastic game!" Dad called out. He came right up and put up his hand for a high-five. I smiled and smacked his hand.

"Thanks, Dad," I replied. "The team played really well. Seth's cross was perfect, and giving us the two-point lead so soon in the second half really clinched the rest of it for us."

"No doubt!" he agreed with a big smile and a nod. "But you didn't let a single one past—not even the PK! Nice work!"

"I thought that last play was going to get through you," the man with him remarked. "It was the perfect opportunity to round the keeper, but your timing was spot-on."

"Thanks," I said. "He was quick but unbalanced on his left."

"Definitely," Dad's companion said. He stuck his hand out and introduced himself as Nahuel Ruiz, scout for the Seattle Sounders. Next thing I knew, I was heading to dinner with Dad and the scout. As we walked toward Dad's car, I saw Rumple getting into her Hyundai. We made brief eye contact, and I almost called out to her but not with Dad there. I didn't need him suspicious and couldn't exactly use the biology project as an excuse, or I'd be out of that class as well.

It was my only class with her, and I wasn't going to take the chance, so I didn't even wave. I could see her eyes narrow a little as she pulled herself up into that ugly car and drive off.

"It would be nice to have him stay on the west coast," Dad was saying, "and the Sounders have certainly proven themselves as such a young team."

"Schmidt's been a major asset," Nahuel said. "Thomas is not going to find a better coach in the States."

"That may be true," Dad said with a nod.

Always the politician.

I did a lot of smiling and nodding and rewinding inside my brain so I could answer questions. Mostly Dad and Nahuel talked though. Nahuel ordered some import beer, which Dad politely declined. My mind wandered.

Rumplestiltskye.

I wondered if she went home or if she went to one of the post-game parties, like I would have preferred myself. I wondered if she went to one of the parties out at the beach, because now that I was thinking about it, her car did sound a little rough when she started it. She could get stranded out there.

I tapped my fingers against the table until a sharp look from Dad got me to stop.

Dad set up a visit for me to go and fly up and train with the Sounders for a day next month, which seemed to make both of them pretty happy. I was mostly glad to be getting out of there because I wanted to make sure Rumple got home all right.

Dad dropped me off at the deserted school so I could get my car. I told him I needed to go to the locker room for a bit, but as soon as he drove off, I got in my car and headed for Rumplestiltskye's house.

Her car was in the drive, thankfully, because there was no way Dad wouldn't notice if I ended up spending another couple hours looking for her. I did slow down a little as I drove by. Well, actually, I slowed to a stop and looked up at her window. I could see her hair piled up on top of her head and her face illuminated by a computer monitor. I started wondering if she used any kind of instant messaging system and if I could manage to find her that way.

I started counting in my head and made myself leave after three minutes. At least I knew she was home and didn't have some drunken motherfucker harassing her somewhere. I drove home, managed to avoid Dad as I got myself a bottle of water, and headed to my room. I locked the door, set the alarm for five-thirty, and changed into some lounge pants.

As I lay back on the pillow and replayed the entire day in my head, I listened to the sound of Rumple's breathing as I licked my lips and spoke quietly to her. I considered the minute movements of her tensed muscles when I said the word "orgasm" during class.

Morning came far too quickly.

I tossed on a pair of sweats and my running shoes before I headed out the door. I stretched and warmed up a bit and then put on my pedometer before I started to run. It was still dark, but at least it wasn't raining at the moment as my feet pounded against the driveway and past the trees. Once I got to the road, I turned left and picked up my pace.

Rumple invaded my thoughts.

Actually, it was starting to annoy me for several reasons. Even though I had been trying a hell of a lot harder than I ever did, she still barely answered me when I asked a direct question.

And did she stand me up? For a study date? Did that actually happen?

My pace had slowed, so I picked it back up again, sprinting for a minute before dropping back to my normal pace. I could feel a trickle of sweat sliding down between my shoulder blades. It wasn't raining, but it sure was humid. I wiped my forehead with the back of my hand and trudged on.

The thing that annoyed me the most was not knowing what I should do next. Usually all I had to do was show up and smile, and chicks would line up. They still did, as evidenced by Lisa and Lucy last night. Hell, I probably could have walked right up to Heather when Mika's arm was around her and gotten her back in the locker room with me. So what the hell was wrong with Rumple?

I sped up again. My meandering thoughts apparently were affecting my feet. I wondered if the freak chick, Amy, knew what she was talking about but dismissed it almost as quickly as I thought of it. I mean, it's worked on everyone else, hasn't it? Maybe I just needed to dial it up a notch.

I got home a little late, and Dad was up and glaring at me as I came through the door.

"You didn't get up on time?" he spit out at me.

"I was out the door at six," I told him.

"Give me that," he said as he reached over and grabbed the pedometer. "You really want to show these averages to the scouts? You want Wayne Messini to see your first mile is almost six minutes? Seriously?"

"Sorry," I mumbled. "I guess I'm tired this morning."

"What are you thinking about?" he asked.

"Nothing, really," I said. I had to look away from him because lying to his face was too hard.

"Schoolwork?"

"No, really, Dad," I said. "I'm just tired."

"Do extra on the bike," he insisted. "I want your averages under five-thirty tomorrow."

"Okay."

"And lay off the pizza."

I nodded and went downstairs to the stationary bike, then did the weights, and then went out in the back yard for some juggling practice.

———————

I fiddled around with my bow tie until the damn thing was straight. There appeared to be a little spot of something on the jacket that didn't come out when it was at the dry cleaners, but I hoped no one would notice. I checked myself in the mirror, evaluating my unruly, gelled hair—short sides, slightly longer on top, and basic brown. I'd gotten a haircut two days earlier, so I was looking more polished than usual. My hazel eyes shimmered in the light from the bulbs above the sink.

Deciding I was as perfect as I was going to get, I walked out into the hall and heard Dad cursing in the master bathroom.

"Need help?" I asked as I stuck my head around the corner. He was standing in front of the sink, leaning over and looking into the mirror with his bow tie wrapped around his wrist and fingers. His blond hair was perfectly groomed, quite in contrast to my own. He turned his blue eyes on me and glared.

"Goddammit, yes!" he snapped. Then he sighed and pulled the bow tie off his neck altogether before handing it to me. I smoothed it out and started tying it around his neck. His voice softened. "I used to wear the damn clip-on ones."

"You did?"

"Yeah, until..." He paused and took a deep breath. "Your mom said they were 'undignified'. She kept trying to teach me, but I never could tie the damn things right."

I tried not to meet his eyes or even breathe. He didn't talk about Mom. Not ever.

"She said she'd help me..." His voice trailed off.

"I can do it," I said as I wrapped one end around the other and looped it through. He pointed his chin up at the ceiling.

"Yeah, and where the fuck are you going to be next year?" His jaw clenched, and I saw his hands clench into fists. I tried to tie a little faster. "Who is going to tie it for the city banquet then, huh?"

"If I played for the Sounders, I'd be—"

"You aren't playing for the fucking Sounders!" he screamed. I tried to step back, but it wasn't enough. His hands pushed against my chest, knocking me backward into the bathroom counter. Pain shot up from the small of my back as it made contact with the edge of the counter, and I winced. "You are going to Europe to play football! Real Messini! *Real football!*"

I started to move to the side to get out the door, but he shoved me back again. I tried to hold my muscles still, but I was starting to shake.

"Maybe if I hadn't been stuck with you, I wouldn't have made it *that* big," he snarled low, "but there's no way I would have ever settled for what was *convenient*. You are not going to settle for anything other than the best, you hear me? You won't settle for anything but *being* the best!"

I didn't answer. I had no idea if I should or not, but chances were if I answered him when he didn't want me to, it would be worse than if I didn't answer and he had to ask again.

"Doesn't fucking matter anyway," he said as he stood up straight and started brushing non-existent lint off his jacket. "Like you would come back here even if you were close. You probably can't wait to get away from me."

"I'll still come home, Dad," I said quietly. My hands gripped the edge of the counter, but I could still feel the shaking in my arms. "If I'm in Europe, you could move there, too…or I could—"

"Get the fuck out of here," he interrupted. Not about to argue, I moved fast—out the door and into the hallway.

"Maybe with you out of the way, I'll finally find someone else," I heard him mumble as I left. "Who wants a guy with a fucking teenaged kid?"

I went down to the kitchen and splashed cold water on my face, careful not to get any on the tux, and tried to make my hands stop shaking. I rubbed at my back, which was bruised just a little, and then ran my hands through my hair again.

I paced and glanced at the clock. We had to be out of here in four minutes, or we were going to be late. If we were late…well, shit. I didn't want us to be late. I was just about to head up to get him when I heard his footsteps on the stairs.

"Come on!" he yelled. "Let's get going before we're late!"

The car ride was silent, and when we pulled up to the city building, there were a massive number of people there, so I started calming down before I even got out of the car. I looked around at the gathering—the small-town politicians, people from the hospital and the school board—all dressed in their finest as if they were trying to relive prom or something.

Time to start playing the role for which we were dressed.

Dad tossed his arm lightly around my shoulders and laughed heartily at nothing as we walked across the sidewalk and up the stairs to the giant double front doors. He greeted everyone with a smile and at least a chuckle, shaking their hands, kissing their babies—the whole nine yards. Several people mentioned my PK save, and he beamed and clasped me on the back as he told them how proud he was of me.

I tried not to wince when his hand made contact with the bruise on my lower back.

"Ah, there you are, Greg!" Dad beamed again. His eyes were brighter than LED headlights. I turned my eyes to where he was looking and caught my breath.

It was Sheriff Greg Skye in his tux, and on his arm was Rumple in a light green, shimmery dress. It was extremely tasteful, covering her from her neck to her knees, and absolutely fucking gorgeous. Her hair was curled and loose around her shoulders, and the fabric of the dress was flowing over her arms and body as if it could be completely removed by a strong breeze from the wrong direction.

Thank God for the length of this tux jacket because parts of me were definitely taking notice and trying to poke out to get a better look.

"Thomas, you remember Greg." Dad smiled, showing all his teeth as I reached out and shook the sheriff's hand.

"Of course, Sheriff Skye."

"And this is my daughter, Nicki," the sheriff said. "She just moved here for her last year of high school. She's only been here about a week, but I sure am glad to have her. I forgot what real food tasted like!"

"Dad!" she growled under her breath, but I could only think about her and her father sitting in the kitchen and eating dinner together.

I locked eyes with her.

Nicki.

I felt the corner of my mouth moving up a little.

"A pleasure to meet you, Nicki." Dad reached out and brought her knuckles to his lips for a moment.

Very smooth.

"It's Nicole," she said as she smiled at him. "I keep telling Dad that, but he still seems to think I'm ten instead of nearly eighteen."

Dad laughed, and Sheriff Skye joined in.

"Teenagers, huh?" Dad continued to chuckle. "Well, Nicole, this is *Tommy*."

Dad and the sheriff both laughed again.

"Very funny." I nodded and looked at Rumple…er…*Nicole*… as I rolled my eyes. "No one's called me Tommy since I was four."

Her lips smashed together as she held in a grin. I watched as she bit into her lower lip as I took her hand and copied my father's motions.

"A pleasure to meet you, Miss Skye," I said with a smile. My lips brushed the back of her hand for a moment, and she apparently couldn't hold in the laugh anymore. It literally exploded out of her, and her eyes went wide. Her hand quickly covered her mouth as a few other people looked over in her direction.

"Nicole…geez…" Her father patted her on the back. "You all right?"

"I'm fine, Dad," she insisted. "It's just…well, Thomas and I have biology class together. We're partners on a project, so we already know each other."

"Oh good!" my father said with a smile and some more beaming. "Thomas, why don't you take Nicole over to the refreshments and maybe show her around a little?"

"My pleasure," I responded, and I completely meant it. Nicole's eyes widened again as my father put his hand on the sheriff's shoulder and walked him toward another group of people. I held my arm out for Nicole. "Shall we?"

Her eyes narrowed a bit, but she accepted my offer.

"Would you like something to drink?" I asked as we walked over to the banquet tables. Nicole had her hand around my arm, loosely holding on to me. I felt giddy. "The iced tea is pretty good."

"Sure," she said. She looked up at me with slightly narrowed eyes. I poured two glasses and then led her over to one of the balconies. I held the door for her, and she walked through, still eyeing me kind of warily.

"You look exceptionally lovely this evening," I told her.

Nicole's eyes went wide for a second.

"Um…thank you," she said. She gave me another strange look. "You look really good in a tux."

I gave her a half-smile.

"Thanks," I replied. "I only wear it to this banquet and the occasional wedding."

"And a real bow tie?" she noticed. "Do you even know how to tie it?"

My mind flashed through my altercation with Dad before we got here. I allowed it to flow because sometimes trying to push it back was just too hard.

"Yes, I do."

"That's kind of cool."

"Mom insisted I know how to do it," I heard myself blurt out and immediately wished I could take it back.

"So, is your mom here tonight?" Nicole asked. She took a sip of her tea.

I stiffened a second. My throat tightened up on me. I wasn't used to anyone asking about her. We lived in such a small community, and everyone knew the story, so I was never questioned about it.

"Um…no…uh…my mom's dead."

"Oh shit!" Nicole spit tea and tried to catch it dribbling down her chin. I couldn't help but smile a bit as she pawed at her face and her dress to get it off while simultaneously nearly spilling more of it as she tried not to drop the glass at the same time. "I'm so sorry, Thomas! I had no idea!"

"It's all right," I replied. Her messy display had lightened the mood but couldn't completely stop the lingering memories. "It's been a while."

"Still...wow...I'm really sorry." She wiped the liquid from the front of her dress. For a couple of minutes, we just stood there in an awkward silence and looked out over the balcony rail at the river beyond. My mind was going at top speed, trying to figure out what I was supposed to do in this situation. What was my part? What were my lines? Was I supposed to tell her more?

I couldn't keep it in, and eventually some of the overflow spilled out.

"It was a car wreck," I said. I couldn't call it an accident. If it weren't for me, it never would have happened, so it wasn't a fucking accident. "I was twelve at the time."

"What happened?" she asked quietly.

Too much.

Reaching down and grasping the railing to steady my hands, I looked out over the river. I tensed inside, trying to keep the memory from coming back—literally squeezing it out of my head until my temples began to throb.

"I'm sorry," Nicole said. "You don't have to talk about it."

I swallowed past my clenched throat. I didn't want to think about it—I didn't want to trigger the memory—but I still wanted her to know. I didn't know why I wanted her to know, only that I did.

"She hit a tree," I said through clenched teeth. I didn't look at her—I just kept staring at the water and listening to it cascade over the rocks. My head was really throbbing, and the effort to keep the scenes out of my conscious mind was excruciating.

I felt a cool touch against my arm and glanced down to see Nicole's fingers slowly running up and down my forearm. The muscles in my arm were hard and tense as I squeezed the railing, but as she touched me, my grip loosened and I started to relax. I watched her slender fingers as they brushed over the hairs on the top of my hand.

"I didn't mean to pry," her soft voice sang up to me. I shook my head slightly, unable to find any words. She must have misunderstood, because she pulled her hand back, running it nervously down her side.

I didn't want her to let go of me.

I wanted her to touch me again because the pain in my head was gone, and the memories weren't still trying to push through. I wanted to touch her to see if her skin was really as soft as it looked. I wanted to feel the coolness of her hands, still moist from the condensation of her glass in contrast to the warmth of her body.

Inside, music began to play as couples joined on the dance floor.

"Would you like to dance?" I asked her suddenly.

"Dance?" She took a step back. "Ah…I don't dance."

"Why not?"

"Um…I don't know how?" Her words came out as a question.

"You don't need to know how," I told her. "I'll show you."

"I don't think—"

"Please?" I asked as I held out my hand. I just wanted to touch her again…just for a few minutes.

"Okay," she finally said as she placed her hand in mine. I led her out to the dance floor and placed my hand at her waist.

"Put your hand on my shoulder," I instructed, and she complied. I took her other hand in mine, feeling the coolness of her fingers. "That's it."

She was tense at first, stumbling a little, but it was only a few measures before she relaxed, allowed me to lead, and really began to look stunningly graceful as I twirled her around. She smiled up at me, and then her eyes went abruptly dark.

"What's the deal, Malone?" she asked suddenly.

"What do you mean?"

"I mean…are you even the same guy I've seen at school?"

"Well…yes, obviously!" I laughed.

"You are going to make my head explode," she mumbled.

"Excuse me?" I questioned back.

"You are a total jerk at school," she pointed out.

I laughed through my nose.

"Don't hold back," I advised. "It'll give you ulcers."

"You are an ass on the field."

"That's a whole different costume," I replied without thinking.

"Costume?" Nicole stopped her rant long enough to look up at me with her brow furrowed.

I glanced down and tapped the lapel of my tuxedo jacket with my thumb.

"This is a whole different costume from my team uniform," I explained.

"So what," she exclaimed, "you become a whole other person because you are in a different...*costume?*"

The Bard's words rolled off my tongue without permission.

"All the world's a stage, Rumple," I said with a wink.

"And all the men and women merely players," she continued. She smiled and raised her eyebrows at me.

I spun her around in a slow circle and then brought her back close.

"They have their exits and their entrances," I quoted. "And one man in his time plays many parts."

Her smile broadened, and she was stunning. My chest clenched, and breathing became more difficult. I lost my step in the dance.

I wanted to know her.

I wanted her to know *me.*

Not the jerk at school.

Not the guy in the tux.

Not the goalie on the field.

Just *me.*

But I didn't know who that was.

As my mind raced, the idea of spending more time with her and just...*talking* to her became more and more appealing. At the same time, it terrified me. I could see myself telling Nicole quite a bit—maybe far too much. What would she think of my drawings? Did she like classical music? Would she think it was all just a stupid waste of time? What if she found out how messed up my head was? She already thought I was an ass, and I couldn't really deny the fit of the name—I was certainly no sweet-smelling rose. What would she think if she knew even my own father couldn't stand me? What if she found out why he hated me so much?

What would she think if she found out I killed my own mother?

In Shakespeare's *The Merchant of Venice*, Launcelot said, "but at the length truth will out." Somehow, I would have to keep her in the dark about how horrible I really was.

Now how could I do that?

CHAPTER FIVE
hooligans

"You gonna pop that little cherry?" Dad asked as we drove from the banquet.

"Fuck yeah," I replied automatically.

"Damn," Dad laughed, "that would seriously piss off her father."

"Heh," I smiled a little and wet my lips with my tongue. "Yeah, it would."

"Well, get her worked up so she'll do your biology work," Dad said. "You need to keep your focus, but string her along a bit if it doesn't get in the way. Greg was going on about how smart she was, so if you play the game right, maybe she could take care of your other homework, too."

"Yeah, that would be good," I said. I nodded in agreement as my mind relived every moment I had experienced with her.

Seeing her in the hoodie, behind my goal.

The warmth of her touch when I ran into her and the deep blue of her eyes as they looked up at me.

Trying to ignore me during class.

The smell of her hair as I leaned close and asked her if she was wet.

The look of incredulity as I held the door open and asked her to dance.

"Just keep the focus on the important stuff, son," Dad said. "You know how cherries are. If she gets clingy or something, ditch her before she becomes a distraction."

"I don't do clingy," I heard myself respond, "but a little cherry sounds appetizing."

"Damn straight." Dad chuckled a bit more but didn't mention Nicole again.

Thankfully.

I relaxed a little since Dad seemed to be in good spirits. It was pretty late by the time we arrived home, so I headed straight to bed to watch the day's re-runs. I closed my eyes and felt the cool slickness of her fingers as they curled around my shoulder. I felt her initial resistance and eventual relaxation as she let me guide her body on the dance floor. I saw her smile and detected a faint hint of some kind of perfume…flowers or herbs…I wasn't sure until I went back further.

Lilac.

Mom planted one of those shrubs at our old house.

I opened my eyes and reached my hand across the bed and down to the nightstand. I pulled out my sketchbook and started to draw. First there was the angle of her head as she tilted it slightly to the side, exposing her neck to me as I held her in the proper waltz position. There were the curls of her hair, flowing softly over her shoulders as she spun in a circle. Of course, there was also the vision of her teeth, partially embedded in her lower lip as she looked up at me in contemplation.

I didn't stop until it was time for my morning run.

As I ran, I pushed…hard. When I checked my times, my average mile was five minutes forty seconds. Good deal. I tried to keep my eyes peeled as I ate some cereal for breakfast and tried to gauge Dad's mood. He glanced at my pedometer and gave me a nod, so at least that was good.

"I'm heading to the hospital," he told me. "I probably won't be back until late."

"No problem," I replied.

"You do your weight training this morning?"

"It's my off-day," I said. "No weights until tomorrow."

"Oh, yeah." He grumbled something else, but I couldn't hear what he said. I wasn't going to ask.

After he left, I got the laundry going and went grocery shopping. The mums were still on sale, so I bought two pots of them. As I drove past Nicole's house, I saw both her dad's cruiser and her car were gone, so I left one of the pots on her porch and headed home.

A few hours of FIFA 2013 on the Wii and several loads of laundry later, I did my homework and finally thought about the biology project again. I wondered if Nicole had actually waited for me at the library and I had missed her, or if she really did just stand me up on purpose. I hadn't thought to ask her last night. I pulled out my laptop and started looking for interesting organisms. I was tempted to look up orgasms but contained myself. Vertebrates were boring, so I discounted those altogether. Maybe something weird like euglena or sea cucumbers or something would be good. I wondered what Rumple would want to use for the project subject, which made me realize I didn't even have her phone number.

I'd have to fix that.

I pulled out my phone and dialed.

"What's up, Thomas?"

"Hey, I need some info," I said. "Sheriff Skye's got a daughter named Nicole. I need a cell phone number and any online accounts you can find. Twitter, Facebook—whatever."

"Sure."

I hung up with a smile.

Yeah, sure I could just ask her, but she could also refuse to tell me. Shit, I couldn't even get her name out of her, so the chances of learning anything more personal were just about nil.

I went to bed before Dad got home, woke up for my morning run, and then got ready for school. I left early so I could take the long way—that is, so I could drive past Rumple's house. Usually by the time I went past, she was either getting into her car to go, or she was already gone. This time, she was sitting in the driver's seat and beating the dashboard with her little fist.

Kitten on steroids, not something I could pass up.

I swung my Jeep around and pulled into her driveway. She looked up at me and narrowed her eyes as she opened the door and climbed out of the car. I couldn't help but notice how nicely tight her jeans were and wished the weather was a little warmer so she wouldn't be in long sleeves. I turned off the car and got out, too.

"Having problems with that piece of shit, Rumple?"

"Nice," she replied with a smirk. "It won't start."

"Need help?"

"Yeah, if you could," she said.

I went around to the front of the car and propped open the hood, looking around for a while before I figured out the damn thing just stayed up on its own and didn't have one of those little stick-things to hold it up. I looked inside and wondered what the fuck all the shit in there was and what it did.

"Try turning it on," I suggested.

She got back inside and turned the key. It made a lot of noise, but nothing seemed to be going anywhere. I poked at a big round metal thing in the middle.

"Try again!" I called out. No difference. "Hold on. Let me try something."

I looked around and found a little round piece to pull on. A stick came out and was all greasy and shit, so I figured that was okay. I found a belt that looked loose, but for all I knew, it was supposed to be loose. There was a big blocky thing with two bolts on top of it, which I thought was probably the battery. Could it be dead?

Fuck if I knew.

"Okay, Rumple!" I called out. "Give it another shot!"

She did, and nothing happened.

I started poking around again and heard the door to the car

open and close.

"What do you think it is?" she asked as she peered over my shoulder.

"Could be a few things," I replied, tapping my chin. I turned my head to look at her and smiled when I saw her biting her lip. "The battery could be dead," I pointed at the blocky thing. "Or maybe a fouled fuel caliper. Could be the sparks or this—" I pointed at the big metal round thing "—which isn't spinning right."

"What is that?" she asked.

"Ah, that's the…um…the manifold destiny."

Her eyes narrowed again, and then her lips twitched before she busted out laughing.

"Manifold destiny?" she squealed. "Thomas Malone! Do you know anything about cars at all?"

"Well…no…" I admitted, "but this is a Hyundai!"

"Do you know anything about Hyundais?"

I couldn't keep it in anymore, and I started laughing too.

"I don't know shit about any of this," I confessed.

"You brat!" she yelled as she slapped me on the shoulder.

"Sorry," I shrugged, though I wasn't. Not at all.

"We've been standing out here for fifteen minutes!" she exclaimed. "I'm going to be late for school."

"Most definitely." I tried to hold my laughter down, but it wasn't really working.

"You are such an ass," she said, but she was still smiling a bit.

"Want a ride?" I asked her. I refrained from adding *on my cock.*

"I don't think I have much choice," she said. "Let me get my book bag."

I had to stop myself from bouncing in my seat as she made her way from her car to mine and got in. I was definitely going to stay under the speed limit for this ride. I wanted to spend as much time with her as possible, and the more time I could spend with her alone, the better. If I could just keep this up, eventually she'd fall for me. She'd have no choice against the Malone charm.

"So what's your favorite number?" I asked as I pulled excruciatingly slowly out of her driveway. I crawled along at twenty-four miles per hour.

"Um…seriously?" She glanced over to me with a puzzled expression.

"Yeah."

"Why?"

"I figured it was a get-to-know-you kind of thing," I replied.

"Shouldn't you ask my favorite color then?" she finally said.

"Nah," I said with a shrug. "I prefer numbers."

"Eight," she said.

"Eight?" I repeated. "That's a weird favorite number."

"It is not," she retorted. "It's very symmetrical."

I couldn't really argue with that, but still—eight?

"What kind of music do you like?"

"Lots of different things," she said. "I like some of the trendy stuff, but I also like jazz and classic rock. Mostly I listen to heavy metal."

Interesting.

I continued to pepper her with questions all the way to school, trying to figure her out. I didn't really make a whole lot of progress until I asked about her favorite flower just as I was pulling into the school parking lot.

She turned full on to look at me, her expression both curious and accusatory.

"Mums," she said bluntly.

I pushed my lips together, trying to hide the smile.

"Really?" I asked. "Why is that?"

"Well, they are very magical flowers," she said, the look on her face not changing as I parked and turned off the car.

"Magical?"

"Yes," she said with a nod. "They just appear out of nowhere."

"Do they?"

"They do."

"Interesting."

"I think so."

"We're late for first bell," I told her. I jumped out of the car and grabbed my book bag from the back seat. I was pretty sure she said something else, under her breath a bit, but I only caught the word *deflect*. "What's your first class?"

"History," Nicole replied.

"Well, you missed about half of it," I said with a smile.

"What class are you missing?"

"Trig," I replied.

"Are you going to be able to get caught up?" she asked.

"Not a problem." I laughed through my nose.

She looked at me with a strange expression before she looked away again.

"Well, I hope I didn't miss too much," she said, and she started walking faster. "See you in biology!"

"Oh yeah!" I called out as I quickened my pace to catch up with her. "What the fuck was with the blow off last Friday? Are we doing this project or not?"

She slowed and looked at me sideways.

"Don't feel as if you have to put yourself out," she said. "If you want, we can meet in the library after school."

"I have weightlifting."

"How long is that?"

"Just a half hour."

"I'll still be there."

"Promise?" I asked.

"Promise." She smiled.

"Okay." I returned her smile as she turned down the hall. I called out, "See you later!"

She waved and kept going.

Classes were extremely slow that morning.

When lunchtime finally rolled around, I jumped right out of my chair and grabbed my lunch out of my locker. As I walked into the lunchroom, I saw Mika and Jeremy waving frantically at me. They were at a table with about half the starting team. I made my way over to them after I grabbed a Gatorade.

"Hey T—you fucked Heather, right?" Frankie Ronald, one of the team's midfielders, asked.

I smirked, rolled my eyes, and nodded.

"Yeah," I acknowledged as I plopped down in the seat next to Jeremy. "So?"

"Thomas has fucked every cheerleader on the squad," Robin spat out.

"Jealous," I shot back at him. "Besides, that's not true. Some of them only gave me blow-jobs."

"But you fucked Lones, right?" Frankie asked for confirmation.

"You want me to draw you a fucking picture?" I tossed back at him. "My cock, her cunt. Cum *everywhere*!"

I lifted my arms up and out in a grand gesture, and raucous laughter ensued. I leaned back in my chair until the two front legs were off the floor and tipped back my bottle of Gatorade.

"So, Klosav needs advice," Jeremy said as he continued to laugh. Clint snickered, too. "She asked him to the dance and he wants some *ac-tion*!"

Within about thirty seconds, the whole group had sunk into near-hooligan mentality. I was surprised they hadn't managed to start a food fight or at least flip over a couple of tables. Jeremy stood up on the chair and started thrusting his hips back and forth in time with some goofy arm movements. Frankie started making noises that may or may not have been his attempt at singing.

"Bow chicka bow-wow!"

"You guys are oh-so-much-help!" Klosav whined.

"I told you not to worry about it," Clint said. "If she asked you, you're in there."

"You fuck her, too?" Jeremy asked Clint.

"Sure," Clint said with a shrug. "Malone isn't the only asshole around here that gets laid."

"Yeah," I said as I reached over and punched Clint in the arm, "but when I fucked her, she was still tight. You got the sloppy seconds."

"Thirds!" Paul said as he took one of the empty seats at the table. It was becoming a regular party. "I got her on the '*Thomas's not talking to me after he took my cherry*' rebound two weeks later!"

"Hey, that's how I ended up with Crystal!" Clint laughed. "I let her cry all over my shoulder then showed her one of my 'special tricks'."

He waggled his eyebrows.

"Lones has fucked half the team by now." Jeremy pointed out. He was still standing on his chair, and he leaned over and started tapping people on the head as if he were playing duck-duck-goose.

"Only half?" Mika laughed. "I thought she'd fucked us all by now! In jersey order number!"

I had to laugh at that one. Paul's jersey was number two and Clint's was number three.

"Who?" New kid Tony came over, holding a tray of food, and hovered near where I was sitting before he walked around to the other side of the table. He dropped into the chair across from me.

"Heather Lones," Frankie said. "She'll probably be your first piece of ass."

Tony glared at him.

"You guys are sick," he said with a shake of his head. He started popping open a can of Coke.

"Nah, he doesn't want her," I said. "Tony's still pining after my cock."

His evil eye flipped over to me.

"It's okay, kid," I told him in a soft, reassuring voice. I reached over and patted him on the hand. "I know I'm hard to resist. If you want, just crawl under the table and suck me off. No one will see you."

The laughter at that one pretty much engulfed the cafeteria. One of the teachers yelled at us to keep it down. I glanced over my shoulder to see which teacher it was and was met with a stare from deep, beautiful blue eyes.

Aw, fuck it all.

Rumple was sitting about three feet behind me, turned most of the way around in her chair to point toward where I was sitting. She stood up, grabbed her tray, and walked out of the cafeteria without looking back. I wondered what she had heard. Shit! She could have heard it all.

Considering the look on her face, she probably had.

Shakespeare popped into my head: *I wonder men dare trust themselves with men.*

I considered going after her and trying to explain it was just a bunch of talk, but I didn't get the chance.

"New chick's got a fine ass on her, hey Malone?"

I felt myself tense just a little. It was Jeremy, though, so I let it slide.

"Yes, she does," I said quietly. I didn't look at him, but I thought I heard him huff through his nose.

"The things I would do to that ass…" Frankie let out a whistle.

"What?" I snapped as my head swiveled around. He didn't look at me—he was too busy watching Nicole walk away.

"She's got the kind of thighs you just know are going to hold you tight."

My chair crashed to the floor, and I was over the table and punching the shit out of that motherfucker a second later. I could hear people yelling around me, including Frankie, but I didn't pay any attention. Someone grabbed my arm from behind and started pulling me off of him, so I kicked Frankie in the shin instead.

"Jesus, Thomas!" Jeremy said with a snarl as he yanked me away. "Calm the fuck down!"

He kept dragging me backwards as I continued to kick out at Frankie.

"You stay the fuck away from her, you hear me?" I screamed at him.

"Shit! Yes! I hear you!" Frankie yelled back as he held his bleeding nose. He looked up at me. "I didn't know you were after her, Tom—I swear. I didn't mean anything!"

"Don't fucking touch her!" I screamed again. "Don't you ever fucking touch her!"

"Come on, Thomas," Jeremy said as he tightened his grip on both my arms. "Let's go hit the field. I'm feeling lucky today."

I let him pull me out of the lunchroom and to the lockers. I threw on my practice jersey and shorts without thinking. I couldn't think. I knew some of Frankie's ways of getting chicks were less than scrupulous, even by my standards. Worse than that, all my mind could do was conjure up visions of Rumple wrapping her legs around Frankie, and it made me want to go right back out there and finish beating his ass.

Out on the rain-drenched, muddy field, Jeremy pelted me with free kicks until all I could do was concentrate on defending. That asshole could put some serious power behind the ball, and I was bound to be bruised before we were done. He delivered another one at close range, and I caught the ball at my chest and curled it inward, securing it before I ran to the top of the box and rolled it back out.

"So," Jeremy said as he tossed the ball on the ground and started to position himself for another kick, "you want to explain that shit in the lunchroom to me?"

"Don't know what the fuck you're talking about," I replied. I bounced up and down on the balls of my feet, getting ready. I watched his leg muscles, but he didn't seem like he was going to kick yet. I stayed in position.

"You were out of control, dude."

"So?" I snapped. Way too defensive, and I knew it. "I don't want anybody chasing after the girl I want. Not until I've had a piece of her."

The words didn't even feel right coming out of my mouth. They flowed easily enough because I'd said these lines before, but they didn't *feel* right.

Jeremy took a step back and prepared to kick.

"Thomas, when you and I were both checking out Rachel last year, you didn't do that." His foot slammed into the ball heading far left and down. I jumped for it and got enough of my fingers on it to knock it to the left of the net but ended up in the fucking puddle in front of the goal.

"Shit!" I was covered in mud.

Jeremy laughed. He walked up to me and held out his hand. I took it, and he pulled me out of the puddle.

"Perfect shot," he said, "even if it wasn't a goal!"

"Nice," I replied. I rubbed my hands on my shorts to try to get some of the mud off.

"Seriously," Jeremy continued, obviously not letting this drop, "when I said I was looking for more with her, you just shrugged at me and backed off. I think you even told her to fuck off and leave you alone. So what's the deal with Nicole?"

"There is no deal," I said. "I just don't want Frankie fucking up my plan."

"That's what it is?" Jeremy raised his eyebrows and looked at me sideways. "A plan?"

We started walking back to the building. I tapped the ball repeatedly, keeping it no more than five feet in front of me.

"Admit it," Jeremy said.

"Admit what?"

"You like the new girl."

"She does have a nice ass," I replied.

"You'll be bringing her flowers next."

"Fuck you," I said as images of mums flooded my head. Jeremy just laughed, so I threw the mud-covered ball at him. "Asshole."

There was no way, no matter what else happened, that I was going to let any of the fuckers on my team get anywhere near my Rumple. Every single one of them would treat her like shit, and I wasn't going to let that happen.

I knew I shouldn't let the comments of others about Rumple bother me, but I couldn't seem to let it go as I showered off. It took forever for me to wash all the mud out of my hair, so I was really late for biology. I was also a little nervous walking in and paused for a bit outside the door before taking a big breath and making my way to my seat. Nicole didn't look up at me at all, and when I glanced at her, I could see her jaw tensed and her eyes tight. Bucher was droning on about what exactly constituted "life," and Nicole was taking copious notes with her pen. I tried reaching over and grabbing it, but she jerked away.

"Don't you touch me!" she snarled under her breath.

I backed off, not knowing what to say. She didn't look at me again, and when class was over, she practically bolted out of her seat.

I took off after her.

"Hey, Rumple!"

"Don't call me that!" she snapped. She continued to walk as fast as she possibly could toward the gym. I caught up and matched her strides.

"I'll see you in the library after class, right?"

"No."

Damn.

"Why not?" As soon as I asked, I knew I should have kept my mouth shut.

"Because you are the biggest dickhead I have ever had the misfortune to encounter!"

Damn again.

"We need to work on the project," I reminded her, trying to appeal to her academic nature.

"*I* need to work on the project," she corrected me. "*You* can go roll around in the mud with your asshole friends!"

"It is a team project," I said.

She stopped right outside the math hall and turned her glare at me.

"Look, Malone," she said with venom, "I know how the whole jock thing works. You don't do shit, and you still get an A because you're the star player. I get it. You don't have to fake anything with me. I know you aren't going to do any work on this at all, and there is no point in you showing up just to pretend. I promise

I'll add your name to the top of the paper."

"Hey!" I reached out and grabbed her arm but released it immediately when she—quite literally—growled at me. "I can do my own work!"

"Oh, whatever!" She took a step back and rolled her eyes. "You show up to class late every day, but Bucher says nothing. You don't take notes—you don't even bring a fucking pencil!"

Hearing her use the word *fucking* stuck with me for a few seconds, and I had to mentally replay the rest of what she said.

"You obviously don't care about anything other than soccer and getting laid. Well, I'm not interested, Malone! I don't know what you think you're trying to prove or to whom, but stay the hell away from me!"

I swallowed hard, but any words that would make any difference just weren't converging in my head. I couldn't even think of a fucking Shakespeare quote. I went with desperate instead.

"You still need a ride home," I said quietly. Hopefully.

"I have a ride home," she barked. "With my *friend*, Heather."

With that, she marched into the calc room and slammed the door in my face.

I stood there just staring at the closed door for a long time. The scene replayed in my head over and over and over again. I tried to come up with something to say to her when she came back out, but I had nothing. I had no idea what to say. Every time I heard her words in my head, it felt like I was being punched in the gut.

No, it was worse. I'd been punched in the gut. I'd take that over this.

"Malone!" I turned my head to see Clint walking down the hall toward me. "Coach is looking for you!"

I took a few steps backwards before following Clint to the locker room, tossing on my muddy shirt and heading out to the field. Coach yelled at me for punching Frankie, and I told him if Frankie learned to keep his mouth shut I wouldn't have to bust his face. He wanted details, so I told him to fucking forget it. He told me to play nice on the field. I told him to kiss my ass.

Practice was…tense.

Afterwards, I went to the library without even taking a shower first…just in case.

She wasn't there.

I reached up and rubbed my aching temples as the scene continued on a perpetual loop. I still had no idea what I could have done to make it any better.

Hamlet had his issues, but Shakespeare even has him ask, "Where be your gibes now?" Somehow, I didn't think I could come up with a joke to make this better.

Now how was I going to get her to talk to me again?

CHAPTER SIX
assist

My phone rang as soon as I sat down in the car. I pulled it out of my soccer bag and answered.

"What?"

"I got that info for ya."

Fucking fabulous. Too little, too late.

"The cell number is a Minnesota area code. Does that make sense?"

"Yeah, it does." What the hell? I dug a pen out of the glove box and found a receipt to write on in the center console.

"Okay, no Twitter or Facebook, but I got two IM accounts—one for Gtalk and another for AIM. It doesn't look like the AIM account has been used for a long while. She logs into Gtalk most days, though."

"Good to know."

"I emailed you something that might be helpful as well."

"Oh yeah?"

"Yeah. Let me know if you have any trouble running it."

"Okay."

He rattled off the phone number and IM account information as I jotted it down.

"Got it."

"Good luck!"

Yeah, I was going to need it.

I went home and ate. Dad was in the living room, and I was avoiding him like the plague, which would go on for at least the next week. He didn't even acknowledge me, and I wondered if he was drinking yet. He obviously hadn't gone to work since he was just hanging out in the same bathrobe he had on when I left for school. I snuck off to my room, did a little homework, and then sat in front of my laptop. I opened my email and found the one I was looking for. Inside was a link to an executable object, which I placed on my desktop and double-clicked. When it popped up, it asked for an IM account number.

I entered Nicole's and clicked OK.

A few minutes later, my own Gtalk account beeped at me, and informed me that *BlueSkye17* was asking to befriend me.

I smiled and accepted.

Then I sat there, staring at the screen with a small, blank box in the center of it, having absolutely no idea what to do.

Eventually, I closed it and shut down the computer. My head was still aching, so I popped a couple of Tylenol PMs down my throat and gulped a Dixie cup full of water from the bathroom tap. I lay down and watched the day go by…repeatedly. I managed to fall asleep just before midnight, but it wasn't very restful.

Nicole completely ignored me the rest of the week even when I spoke directly to her. She didn't come to the game on Friday, either. It was probably best because I played like shit, letting two goals get past me. Thankfully, both my dad and the scouts were absent since it was an away game. On the bus ride back, Crystal Lloyd sat down next to me and practically crawled onto my lap so she could stick her tongue down my throat. It was a nice distraction, but by the time we got back to town, I just wanted out of there despite her promises of additional entertainment.

The week hadn't been the greatest under any circumstances, and it wasn't exactly the very best time of year for us, regardless.

My chest was starting to tighten up, and even though I hadn't really forgotten, I had put the exact date out of my head. That didn't seem to keep it from creeping up on me, though. Once I got home, I told dad about the game, skipped some of my bigger blunders, got chewed out anyway, and then headed for the shower.

Afterwards, I locked the door to my room and turned on my laptop. I sat in the desk chair in my boxers as I had for the past four nights and stared at IM, a little empty box with *BlueSkye17* written up in the corner.

There was a green dot next to her name, indicating that she was online.

I reached out and pressed the "H" key, followed by the "I".

I deleted them both.

Then I typed them again.

Then I deleted them again.

I let out a long sigh, shut down my laptop, and got into bed. I lay there and stared at the ceiling, but nothing happened.

Damn it, Malone!

I got out of bed, booted the pissy laptop back up again, typed "Hi," and hit enter before I could stop myself. I closed my eyes and sat back in the chair, waiting for the little chime that would tell me someone had replied to my message.

I waited.

And waited.

I opened my eyes again.

And realized she wasn't online anymore.

Fuck my life.

After tossing back a couple of Tylenol PMs—which had become a regular routine at night—I threw myself back on the bed and covered my eyes with my hands. I needed to get to sleep, and before the date changed. Tomorrow would be bad enough, but if the clock hit midnight before I fell asleep, I wouldn't get any rest at all.

"You may my glories and my state depose, But not my griefs; still am I king of those."

As the clock approached midnight, the king of all my own griefs began to demand attention. I fought it as hard as I could and eventually just closed my eyes and refused to look at the clock again.

I had no idea what time it was when I finally drifted off.

━━━━━━━━━●◦●◉●◦●━━━━━━━━━

I woke up, wide-eyed and staring at the ceiling.

September twenty-third.

I sat up and wrapped my hands around my knees. I could feel it coming just like it did every year, and there was nothing I could do to stop it. The images were always crystal clear, just like every day since, but in sharper focus because of the number of times I had watched it all play out in my head. I closed my eyes and just tried to wait it out.

I woke up and pranced down the stairs in my pajamas to watch cartoons in the living room. Mom was making pancakes, and Dad was reading the paper. When she called me over for breakfast, I noticed my pancake had fourteen blueberries in it, and Dad's only had twelve. Mom got them at the farmer's market, and they were big and juicy and fresh. The maple syrup was in a ten-ounce glass bottle.

My game was early that day, so as soon as breakfast was over, we all piled in the car. I was already dressed for the game—cleats and shin guards and jersey—and I was bouncing the ball on my knee in the backseat.

We got to the field, and I started looking around the back seat, but I couldn't find my gloves. I remembered they were on the bench near the front door. I left them there after practicing with Dad in the back yard the night before.

"How can you forget your damn gloves, Thomas?" Dad snapped. "You're a keeper, for God's sake."

"They didn't get back in my bag," I said. "I thought they were in there."

"You have to check these things!" Dad growled as he shook

his head.

"Don't yell at him, Lou," Mom scolded. "I'll go back and get them. We're only five minutes from home, and there's plenty of time before the game."

And so she left.

And we waited.

And waited.

And waited.

The coach called us to the center of the field. We all shook hands, and the ref blew the whistle, so I started the game without gloves.

When I stopped the ball, I had to rub my hands on my legs to get rid of the sting. That's what I was doing when I heard Dad's phone go off. At about the same time, Sheriff Skye showed up on the edge of the field. He headed for Dad.

The game went on, but I lost focus as the sheriff went up to him and put his hand on Dad's shoulder.

The ball went into the net behind me as I watched Dad jump out of his folding chair and start running back to the parking lot. Sheriff Skye went over to talk to my coach and then the ref before the whistle was blown to start play again. Coach called me over to the sideline and said I needed to go with the police officer. While in the cruiser on the way to the hospital, Sheriff Skye told me about the wreck.

I put on a button down shirt with a pair of dark colored Dockers. I pulled my black tie out of the closet and in front of the bathroom mirror, I tied it in a full Windsor knot. I pulled a warm sweater on over my shirt in case it was cold outside. After I was dressed, I headed past Dad—who was passed out on the couch—and slipped outside. Back behind the garage, I picked up the pot of bright yellow mums.

Gripping the key to the Jeep, I slowly turned it, and the car started smoothly. I made sure the mums weren't going to tip over on the floor of the passenger seat and started heading down the drive. It didn't take long to get there—it wasn't that big of a town

—and the city cemetery was on the same side of town as our house.

I pulled into the parking lot and got out of the car, carrying my potted mums and a small hand shovel. I walked through the trees and around a couple of large stone monuments. There was a little mausoleum in the center of the cemetery, and I walked to the left of that. Near the edge of the path, there was a large, rectangular stone of mauve-colored marble.

Francis Malone

Beloved Wife and Mother

Getting down on my knees in the damp grass, I used the little shovel to dig a hole big enough for the mums, pulled the flowers out of their plastic pot, and planted them in the ground next to the headstone. Leaning back on my knees, I took a deep breath as I ran my hands through my hair. I shifted a little and dropped my ass down next to her headstone and then pulled my knees up close to my chest.

"Hi, Mom," I said softly. "I, um…I brought you some flowers. They were on sale."

I cleared my throat and wrapped my arms around my legs.

"I'm sorry for what I did," I whispered. "I'm still keeping my promise, though. I'll never forget anything again—I swear it. I haven't forgotten anything since that day, Mom. Nothing."

For a while I just sat, reliving the day over and over again… the ride to the hospital, sitting in the waiting room for hours before someone comes to take me back to another room where I sit for hours again. Dad finally coming in, freaking out, taking me to the room where she is—hooked up to a dozen noisy machines that are the only things keeping her alive. Saying goodbye. Being taken away by the nurse who tries to give me coloring books to occupy myself while Dad is switching off the machines. Going home. The look in Dad's eyes as he hits me over and over again. Knowing it was my fault. Knowing I deserve all of it.

He told everyone I was too torn up to come to the funeral. He didn't want them to see the bruises.

It started raining, of course, but I only barely noticed.

"School's pretty good this year," I said to the slab of marble beside me. "The team is doing well. Oh, yeah—Real Messini is actually checking me out, too. That made Dad happy."

I reached over and yanked one of the mums off the plant. My fingers slowly shredded the petals from the flower. The rain poured down a little harder, plastering my hair to my forehead. I needed a haircut.

"I'm taking a couple of AP classes. Shakespeare is one of them, which I thought you would like. Biology, too. There's a girl in there…a new girl. She's from Minnesota. It's Sheriff Skye's daughter. She, um…she's really…interesting. I think I kind of like her, you know? Not like the other girls…but I never told you about them. I don't think you'd really approve, you know? Well, no you don't, but anyway…"

I took a deep breath and wiped some of the rain from my face.

"I think I really like her," I continued. "She's just different. She's smart—I can tell that, even though we only have one class together. The thing is—I kind of pissed her off. She heard me saying some stuff…it wasn't very nice stuff…and now she won't talk to me. I don't know what to do."

I reached out and ran my finger over and over the letter "F" carved into the marble.

"I wish you were here so you could tell me what I should do. I've never really had to…well, to do anything to get a girl to like me. I don't know how to do that. I'm not really sure what there is to like. She said I was a jerk…but she danced with me at the city banquet. She's so pretty, and she smells good."

I closed my eyes and leaned my head against my knees. My clothes were soaked through, and there was a breeze that was sending a chill through me. I leaned over and placed the side of my face against her headstone. I could feel the indentation of her name against my cheek. When I opened my eyes again, my vision was all blurred from pressing against the stone.

"I miss you," I whispered. "Dad misses you, too. I know he

doesn't come here and tell you that, but he really does. I helped him tie his bowtie again this year. He's afraid of being alone when I'm gone. I told him to come with me, but I don't think he really wants to. I just remind him of you, and it hurts him too much to have me around and to know it's all my fault. He's stuck. He doesn't want me around, but he doesn't want me gone, either."

I closed my eyes again, trying not to think…not to remember.

It didn't work.

I listened to the rain.

I listened to my heartbeat.

I listened to the bass, choking sounds as I tried to breathe deeply.

At some point, the rain stopped.

I blocked out the sounds altogether, and listened to the sounds inside my head—the sounds of the machine that was keeping her body alive even though she was already gone. I listened to my Dad's screaming and the steady thump of his fists on my body.

"Thomas?"

I didn't move.

"Thomas?" This time, the sound was accompanied by a soft touch against my hand. I opened my eyes to long, muscular legs encased in red running shoes. I licked my lips and thought about how I might respond, but I didn't know what to say.

"Come on, Thomas."

The first hand was joined by another, and they started to work together to pull me up by my arm. I obliged, pushing myself first to my knees and then to my feet. As my eyes managed to focus a little more, I saw Nicole at my side, wrapping her arm around my waist and leading me away.

"Rumple?"

"Yes?"

I sighed and leaned my head on top of hers. She kept her arm around me as we walked toward my car.

"Give me your keys," she said.

"Why?"

"I really don't think you should be driving."

I tried to process the information.

"You want to drive my Jeep?"

"I think that would be best, yes."

"It's a stick."

She turned her head to look up at me and raised her eyebrows.

"I can drive a stick."

"Oh yeah?"

"Yeah."

I reached into my sodden pocket and pulled out my keychain. She took the keys from my hand and clicked the fob a couple of times before opening the passenger door and pushing me inside. I looked around a bit—I'd never seen my car from this angle before. It was strange to see someone else getting into the driver's seat and turning the key.

"What's your address, Thomas?"

"Not going home."

"You should go home."

"No," I replied.

"Where is your dad?"

"He's home."

"You should be with him."

"No…it's too soon." I looked over to her. My eyes hurt, but I tried to keep them open anyway. "I can't go home yet."

She sat there and looked at me a minute and then huffed a breath through her nose.

"Do you want to come back to my place?"

I began to focus again as I realized just what she was saying, and more importantly, the fact that she was speaking to me at all. I could only nod in response, afraid any actual words would remind her that I was a jerk.

She turned her head to look out the back window as she shifted into gear and headed out of the cemetery while Shakespeare echoed through my head.

"In the course of justice, none of us should see salvation: we

do pray for mercy."

⇒➻➸⦿⦿⦿⦿⦿⦿⦿⦿⦻⦺⇐

I knew what was happening as Nicole pulled me from my car and led me up to the front door of her house, but I was still in a daze. Undoubtedly, I would remember it all later with crystal clarity, but while it was happening, everything was sort of a blur.

Nicole held open the door while I stood on the porch and just watched her. She continued to watch me as she tilted her head toward the foyer.

"Are you going to come in?" she asked.

I looked down at myself.

"I'm all wet," I said.

"Yeah, you are," she agreed. "Come in anyway; take your shoes off here by the door."

I did as she said, but even with my shoes and socks off, I was still dripping a bit.

"You are soaking wet," she said. "Is that a wool sweater?"

"Um…I don't know. Maybe?"

Her fingers ran down the sleeve.

"Well, I'd say it's pretty much ruined," Nicole said. She pursed her lips together and looked up at me again. "Let's get it off, okay?"

"Okay." My head was still pounding as I stared at her, unmoving.

Nicole took a deep breath and sighed, then reached up and unbuttoned my sweater. She pushed it off my shoulders and hung it on a hook next to her father's police jacket. She pulled at the knot of my tie, loosened it, and I bent my head down so she could loop it over and off. She tossed it over the same hook as the jacket. Her fingers brushed over the front of my button-down shirt once, and then she began to release the buttons one at a time.

"You're freezing," Nicole said quietly as she finished with the last button. Her fingers pushed my shirt open. I couldn't do anything but watch her hands in seemingly slow motion, trailing up my chest and easing my shirt off my shoulders and down my arms.

"Come on upstairs. The towels are up there, and I'll find you something else to put on."

I followed her blindly up a flight of stairs to a small landing. There were three doors—two leading to bedrooms and one to a bathroom. She grabbed two towels from the cabinet under the bathroom sink and placed them on the counter.

"Dry yourself off a bit, okay?"

"Okay."

She walked into one of the bedrooms and left me in the bathroom. I dried my chest and arms a bit, but I started shivering anyway. I used the towel to rub my hair, but it just flopped back over my forehead again. Nicole walked back in holding a plain white T-shirt and a pair of sweatpants.

"These should work, I think," she said. "I can put your other stuff in the dryer, but I'm not sure there's any hope for the sweater. Go ahead and put these on, and I'll see what I can do."

"Okay."

She looked up at me again.

"Thomas?"

"Yeah?"

"Can you get yourself changed, or do you need help?"

Her words finally penetrated, and I glanced down at the towel still in my hand and the clothes she had placed on the counter.

"I can do it," I replied quietly.

She nodded and closed the bathroom door.

I pulled the button of my Dockers open and dropped the zipper. I had a hard time getting the wet fabric down my legs but managed to do it without falling over. I yanked the sweats and T-shirt on, but the sweats were falling off my hips. I found a drawstring inside and tightened it a bit. I picked up my wet pants and boxers but wasn't really sure what I should do with them. I didn't want them dripping all over the place, so I just hung them over the edge of the bathtub. I opened the bathroom door and wandered out to the little hallway.

I glanced into one of the rooms and knew right away it was Nicole's. I recognized the window because of the little desk and chair right under it. There was an old desktop computer with a CRT monitor sitting on top of it. On the other side of the window, where I wouldn't have been able to see from the outside, was a full-sized bed with a blue comforter over it, a dresser with a lamp, and a nightstand containing an MP3 player, and a stack of dystopian-themed books.

"Thomas?"

My head kept pounding, and I couldn't bring myself to answer. I felt her come up beside me, and her hand touched my elbow.

"Geez, Thomas—you're absolutely freezing," Nicole said as her hand brushed up and down my arm. "Your skin feels like ice."

She looked me up and down, and her voice softened.

"Come here," she said as she took me by the hand and led me to the edge of her bed. She pulled back the comforter and the sheet under it and placed her palm on my shoulder blade, pushing me forward. "Get in."

"In your bed?" I asked.

"You need to warm up," she said, "and you look like you're about to fall over."

I didn't have any energy to argue with her even if I had been so inclined. Once my head made contact with her pillow, and I was completely encompassed by her scent, there was no way I was going to protest. I inhaled deeply as my eyes closed and my body sank into the warmth of the blankets Nicole pulled over me.

"My mom died today," I heard myself say and then corrected myself. "I mean…on this day."

"I know," Nicole told me. "I saw the date on the stone."

"What were you doing there?" I asked.

"Running," she said. "I usually run in the morning, but it was raining too hard. When the rain stopped, I decided to go. My route takes me past the cemetery, and I saw your Jeep there. I looked around, and I saw you on the ground. I thought you might be…hurt or something. I didn't know about the day…"

Her voice trailed off, and I nodded. It made sense. I felt the bed drop a little and opened my eyes. Nicole was sitting beside me with her eyes full of concern.

"Is this okay?" she asked. "I mean, if I sit here?"

I looked up at her and nodded again. She was quiet for a minute, and I just kept basking in the scent that was all around me as I stared blankly toward her bedroom wall.

"Thomas? How long were you out there?"

"What time is it?"

"Almost three."

"In the afternoon?"

"Well…yes."

I turned my eyes into the pillow. I had left the house shortly before eight in the morning.

"A while," I finally said.

"You were soaked," she reminded me. "It hadn't been raining for a good hour when I saw you."

I shrugged, which made the blanket shift off of my shoulder. Nicole reached up and fixed it again.

"Do you want anything?" she asked. "Are you hungry? Or I could make some hot chocolate. That might warm you up."

I shook my head and closed my eyes. I sank further into the pillow and finally started to feel a little warmer. At least I wasn't shivering anymore. The mattress shifted again, and I opened my eyes to find Nicole standing to walk out the door.

"Stay!" I reached my hand out from under the blankets, toward her.

Nicole turned back toward me and slowly returned to the edge of the bed. I relaxed again as her fingers ran down my arm. When she got to my wrist, I flipped my hand over and wrapped my fingers around hers. I looked up to her just to check her expression, but she didn't seem to mind. I closed my eyes again. Soft fingers brushed over my temple and began tidying the hair that was plastered to my forehead. Her fingers continued up and over my head, pushing the longer strands back over the top of my head as my consciousness faded into the background.

I felt as if I were floating—my mind only barely comprehending the images in my brain.

Nicole's hand still stroked my hair, but we were sitting out on the cliff near the ocean with the wind blowing across our skin. I had my legs pulled up against my chest, and Nicole's were sticking straight out. She was pivoting her feet back and forth at her ankles.

"Is this it, Thomas?" Her voice was a low whisper over the wind and the waves. "Is this the real you, without the costumes?"

I looked down and realized I was sitting on the rock, naked. I looked back up at her, trying to figure out if I should be embarrassed by my lack of clothes, but she was only looking at me inquisitively as she awaited my answer.

I didn't have one for her.

I was disoriented for a moment when I finally woke up, but I didn't feel at all concerned about where I was.

The light in the room was dim, and the clock on the nightstand said it was twenty after eight. I was warm and comfortable, and the smell all around me was just glorious. I couldn't describe it, but I could definitely name it—*Rumple*. It just smelled like her. I closed my eyes and inhaled deeply before opening them again and focusing on what was around me.

Nicole was on the floor with a reading lamp beside her along with a bunch of books and papers. She kept going back and forth between one of the large textbooks and a notebook, where she furiously scribbled notes and then to a worksheet. Every once in a while, she would stick the tip of the pen in her mouth and nibble the end of it. As I shifted in the bed, she looked up at me.

"Hey," she said quietly.

"Hey," I replied hoarsely. I cleared my throat and tried again. "Hi."

She smiled, but it didn't reach her eyes at all.

"How are you feeling?"

Dying…empty…dead…revitalized…cold…warm…unsure…

I didn't know, so I just shrugged.

"Hungry?"

I shrugged again.

"It's getting late," Nicole said quietly. "Do you want to call your dad and let him know where you are?"

I shook my head.

"He might be worried."

"He's not," I said. I didn't think Dad had ever really worried about me in the way she meant. He'd be pissed if I wasn't at my next practice or if I didn't show up for a game, but it was Saturday, and I wasn't missing anything. I didn't think he would be too concerned with my workout schedule right at the moment. It did make me wonder, however, what her dad would think of me being here in her bed.

Shit.

"Is your dad here?" I asked, my eyes going wide with a bit of panic, now that I was thinking about exactly where I was—in the sheriff's house, in his daughter's bed.

And he had a gun.

"No." Nicole bit down on her lip to keep from smiling. "He's on a fishing trip. He won't be back until tomorrow."

"Oh." I relaxed again. My vision blurred into the pale off-white pillowcase. I inhaled again, letting the scent of her overcome all my other senses for a moment.

"Don't you want to go home?" Nicole suddenly asked.

I shook my head emphatically.

"You really should."

"No."

"Why not?"

Her blue eyes looked over me, and I wanted to tell her. I wanted to tell her everything, but I knew I couldn't. How do you say that on this day—of all days—going home is the very last thing I want to do? How do you explain to someone how much your own father hates you? How much he would prefer that you had died on this day instead of her?

I would have preferred it that way, too.

"I'm not going home," I said. "I can leave though. I don't want to be…in the way."

"You're not," she said. He voice was still soft and warm, and I was reminded of my dream, which was odd. As much as I remembered everything else, I rarely remembered my dreams. "But I do think your dad would want to know where you are. He has to be worried—"

"Trust me," I said. I licked my lips, feeling how dry they were. I hadn't had any water or anything to drink all day. "He's not worried, and he's not looking for me."

She seemed to contemplate this for a while.

"Do you want to stay here?" she asked.

My heart started beating a little faster.

"Can I?" My voice was just barely above a whisper.

She nodded and put her pen down on her notebook before looking up at me again, her brow furrowed. She collected her legs underneath her and gracefully stood without using her hands for balance. She took two steps toward me and sat on the edge of the bed. She reached out and ran her fingers through my hair, and I closed my eyes to the feeling.

"Will you tell me about her?" Nicole asked softly as her hand traced around my ear.

I looked up at her, staring into her eyes and searching for something though I didn't know what. No one ever asked me about my mom, which was probably because almost everyone in the town had known her. I never talked to anyone about her before, and I realized I actually *wanted* to tell Nicole about her.

"She played the piano," I told her. I tucked my head back into the pillow. "And she wrote plays. She wrote musicals and even wrote the music to go with them. None of them were really popular or anything, but lots of different theatre groups performed them. Everyone always liked what she wrote."

"I'd like to see some of them," Nicole said. I looked back up at her.

"You would?"

"Yes, I would." She smiled a little, but it didn't last.

My mind swirled around and tried to come to terms with... well, with everything. I was having a really hard time just not staring at her. I was trying not to think too much about how I was in her bedroom, lying on her bed with her hand touching me, and how her dad apparently was gone until morning.

"She really liked plays, then?"

"Yeah."

"Is that why you can quote Shakespeare?"

I nodded.

"She loved Shakespeare," I said quietly. "She'd read it to me all the time. When I was little, we would act some of it out with the other kids in the neighborhood."

"That sounds like fun."

"It was." I found myself smiling a little as I remembered a kid from down the street. I couldn't remember his name, but he was so funny when he started singing the *Hamlet* lines he had heard on an old episode of *Gilligan's Island*.

My eyes closed again as her hand trailed lines through my hair. Her fingers were warm, and I could feel exactly where they touched, even when she didn't take the same path every time. I opened my eyes again and found her looking down at me. I didn't understand her expression, and I wondered if she was regretting her decision to let me be here with her.

"I can really stay?" I asked for clarification and also to give her an out if she wanted it. I didn't *want* her to want it. I didn't want to leave.

"You can stay," she said with a nod, "on one condition."

"What's that?" I asked, as if I wouldn't agree to absolutely anything she requested. That knowledge didn't stop me from being a little worried about what she wanted though.

"You have to eat something," she said with a completely

serious expression. "I have the feeling you haven't eaten all day."

I smiled a little and nodded.

"I made Mexican," she said, and I watched her cheeks turn a little pink, and she bit down on her lip again. "Do you like enchiladas?"

I laughed through my nose, trying to hold it in, but it wasn't quite working.

"Yeah," I said, "I do."

"Mexican rice and beans?"

"Definitely." As if I needed an exclamation point, my stomach rumbled in appreciation of the whole idea. More amazing than the return of my appetite on this day was the realization that I was also strangely relaxed in her presence.

Shakespeare's words flooded my head: "Her voice was ever soft, gentle and low, an excellent thing in woman." Somehow, Nicole had managed to calm my mind.

Now how did she do that?

CHAPTER SEVEN
penalty

Damn.

Nicole could cook.

Maybe I just hadn't eaten anything really homemade for a long time, but the Mexican feast she concocted was the best thing I could ever remember eating. When she had said rice and beans, I assumed it would be from one of those boxed dinners, but she had obviously made everything from scratch right down to using fresh chili peppers.

It was phenomenal.

Even though my head didn't seem particularly interested in food, my body clung to the taste and feeling of the warm sauces and vegetables. I filled my stomach with three helpings along with extra rice.

"When did you last eat?" Nicole asked with a smile as I shoveled in the last of my third serving.

"After the game," I replied.

"There was a game today?"

"No," I said, "last night."

"So I was right—you didn't eat all day today?"

I shook my head.

"No wonder you're so hungry." She smiled.

"I think it's just that good," I replied.

"Thank you," she said. "I'll box some of it up, and you can take it home."

"Really?"

"Yes, really."

For a moment, I thought about the kind of questions having homemade leftovers in our refrigerator would spark. Dad seemed to have no problem with getting Nicole to do my homework, but I had the feeling he would consider cooking, crossing some kind of line.

"Probably not a great idea, really," I said.

"That's a pretty quick change of mind," Nicole remarked.

"Well…" I said, my mind racing to come up with something plausible, "if my dad saw it, he'd want to know where it came from. Your dad does work for him, and he might end up mentioning it. You know…"

"Yeah, you're probably right," she agreed. She started putting the leftovers away and gathering up the dishes. I grabbed our plates off the table and took them to the sink. She didn't have a dishwasher, so I dried everything as she washed it. My head was starting to fog up again—images of Mom danced around in my head, cooking and washing dishes while I sat at the table eating warm cookies from the oven or just reading the comics from the newspaper.

After the dishes were put away, Nicole asked if I wanted to watch TV or something. We sat on the couch in the living room, but I was barely able to keep my eyes open as she flipped through channels, trying to find something worth watching. Something about sleeping away most of the afternoon actually seemed to make me feel more tired than I would have been if I hadn't slept at all. Though it was only ten-thirty on a Saturday night, and I had slept for at least four hours already, I was wiped out.

"You should go to bed," Nicole said. She turned off the TV and led me back up the stairs. She poked around in a tall, narrow closet in the hallway and came out with a green toothbrush still in its package. She also handed me a little tube of travel-sized toothpaste and a purple washcloth. "Do you need anything else?"

"I don't think so," I said. I blinked a few times as the day started over again in my head. Mechanically, I went into the bathroom, washed my face, and brushed my teeth. I looked into the small round mirror and tried to figure out just who was in there. I didn't get any answers from my reflection, so I tried to tame my hair a bit, failed, gave up, and went back to Nicole's room.

She had changed into sweats and a T-shirt and was typing away at her computer. She glanced up at me and bit down on her lip and then clicked with her mouse a couple more times before shutting the thing down. I stood in the doorway, not really sure what I should do. Nicole looked agitated. I wondered if I had done something to piss her off again, but I couldn't come up with anything.

"Is something wrong?" I finally asked.

Nicole gave me a tight smile.

"No, not really—just feeling a little guilty."

"Guilty?" I asked. I had no idea what she could have been feeling guilty about.

"Yeah, well…" she took a deep breath and blew it out of her mouth. She stood up and motioned for me to get into the bed. I obliged, and she sat down next to me.

"Tell me?" I asked quietly as I settled back down on her pillow. She took another breath and started playing with her fingers before she started talking.

"I'd been feeling really sorry for myself all day today," she said. "I talked to my mom last night, and she was telling me about all the things going on with her and her travels, and I was just pissed off about being here and not there with her. I really miss her."

She turned her head back to me.

"But then I found you," she continued softly, "and I realized that my complaints were kind of trivial compared to yours. At least

I can call her…or send her an email."

"Why don't you just text her?"

"I don't have a smart phone," Nicole said. "I have a regular one, but all it can do is make phone calls. I stick with email."

She nodded over to the computer, and I wondered if that was what she was doing every night when I saw her at her window. I felt her hand brush through my hair before she stood up.

"I'll be on the couch downstairs," Nicole said, and she started walking to the door. "Let me know if you need anything."

"Nicole?" I called out. My stomach and chest tightened up. "Will you stay with me?"

Her eyes narrowed a little. I knew how my request must have sounded, and I didn't mean it that way. I didn't want to be alone. It was strange because I had always been alone on this day and never really thought about it before. But now I just wanted Nicole here.

"I swear I won't try anything," I told her. "Nothing at all—I promise."

"You want me to lie down with you?"

It was too fucking ridiculous for words, and I wondered why in the hell I thought she would consider it. I nodded anyway, figuring it wasn't going to be any worse. If she said no, she'd still be on the couch, and she was going to do that anyway.

Except it would be worse, because it meant she'd said no.

I closed my eyes, not wanting to actually remember seeing her say the words for the rest of my life even if I would continue to hear it forever. The next thing I knew, she was sitting on the edge of the bed again, but this time she was pulling the blankets back and tucking her feet underneath them.

I scooted back to make room for her and followed every movement with my eyes as she lay down beside me and placed her head next to mine on the pillow. I watched her gather up her hair with her hand and hold it to the back of her neck to get it out of her way. I saw the way she meticulously smoothed out the top blanket until we were both completely covered and how she kept glancing down—away from my face—as she settled in.

I had never been in a bed with a girl before. Locker rooms, backs of school buses, behind bleachers, backseats of cars, yes, but never in a bed. It felt really strange but not in a bad way at all. What was particularly weird to my mind was that I wasn't the least bit turned on, though looking back, it was probably at least partially due to the date. My mindset was not exactly normal. Regardless, the whole situation wasn't the least bit sexual. It was warm and comfortable and safe.

Tentatively, I reached out and found her waist. I watched her eyes widen a little as I wrapped my fingers around her back and pulled her a little closer to me. Her expression remained wary.

"Is this okay?" I asked. Again, I felt everything inside my body tense, waiting for the rejection.

"It's okay," Nicole said, and she placed her hand on the top of my arm, near my shoulder. It was almost as it had been when we were dancing at the banquet.

With my head back on the pillow and the warmth of Nicole's body lining up with mine, I closed my eyes. Visions in my head paraded through again—blueberries, gloves, police car, fear, pain —but when I flinched at the memories, Nicole's hand was there, running over my skin and up into my hair. She stroked my head, and as the long-ago images of September twenty-third scrolled through my head for the final time that day, I opened my eyes.

Her eyes were on mine, and she offered me a small, sad smile. My fingers tightened on her skin, holding her closer as my mind memorized everything it could see. When I closed my eyes again, the day repeated, ending with visions of deep blue irises and a feeling of warmth and security.

<hr />

I woke from the most peaceful sleep I could ever remember having.

Enveloped in her scent, I slowly opened my eyes as I turned up my mouth in a smile. My nose was buried in her hair as Nicole lay with her back against my chest. My arm was still woven around her, and her arm lay on top of mine with her fingers gripping the back of my hand. I closed my eyes, inhaled through my nose, and then blew the breath out of my mouth.

Tilting my head a little, I opened my eyes and tried to get a look at her sleeping face. The angle wasn't really right for it, though, so I looked down her body instead. My fingers twitched against her skin where the hem of her T-shirt had ridden up a little, and I tried not to pay too much attention to how her breasts were rising and falling with her slow, steady breathing.

Go away, morning wood…

There was light coming through the window, and I realized it was pretty late in the morning, at least by my standards. At first, I felt a wave of panic, but I pushed it back. For one thing, there wasn't anything I could do about it. For another…

Well…

Whatever might happen because of my missed morning run, it would be worth it just to stay here a little while longer.

I closed my eyes and settled back against the pillow, content to just listen to her breathe and enjoy memorizing the feel of her body along mine. Every once in a while, I would move my fingers, just to feel the electric tingle I got when my skin touched hers. Her hair was tickling my nose, but I didn't move.

As much as I might have wanted it to, I knew it wasn't going to last forever.

The numbers on the clock went by far too quickly as I absorbed the feeling, the sight, and the smell of her all around me. Eventually Nicole stirred, tickling my nose some more as she shifted and stretched her neck against the pillow. From my angle, I could see her eyes flutter open, and I felt her grip my hand as she turned around to face me.

Even with sleep in her eyes and a yawn on her lips, she was beautiful. Her hair was scattered all over the place as if it were some crazy, wild animal that had been attacked by first-year beauty students, and she was still the most gorgeous sight I had ever seen.

I just stared at her, taking it all in, until I realized what I was doing.

"Hey," I said, suddenly embarrassed. I looked away from her eyes quickly but couldn't stop myself from looking back.

"Hey," she answered. She smiled slightly. "How are you?"

Good question.

I shrugged.

"Better," I offered. I felt a little tense again because I wanted to be able to give her a better answer than that. She had done so much for me yesterday, and I hadn't even...

Fuck.

"Um...you didn't...I mean...shit." I turned my head to the side and pushed my forehead against the pillow. I took a couple of deep breaths before looking back into her eyes. "You really did a lot for me yesterday."

She flashed me another Mona Lisa kind of smile.

"You didn't have to do that," I continued. I turned my head away and closed my eyes for a second before looking back to her. "Thank you."

"You're welcome," she said softly.

My hand moved up her back, over the top of her shirt to the middle of her back, realizing for the first time all night that she wasn't wearing a bra. Did girls usually take them off to sleep? They probably did. It didn't seem like they would be comfortable otherwise.

I tried not to think about how her body was pressed against mine and how I was pretty sure her nipples were up against my chest. If I thought about that...well...I just didn't want to push my luck. Not now.

If nothing else, Sheriff Skye was supposed to be home today.

"I should probably go," I said, hating the words as they came from my mouth. "I really don't think I want to have your dad walk in right now."

I watched Nicole's pale cheeks turn crimson.

"No, probably not," she agreed. "He's not supposed to be back until noon, though."

I glanced back at the clock on the nightstand, which indicated it was just a quarter past eight. I wondered if Dad was hung-over enough to still be in bed. I took a deep breath. If I got home before he woke up, I could get my run in, and he wouldn't even know.

"I should still go," I said softly.

"Do you want breakfast first?"

God yes.

"I should just go."

She nodded slightly.

I didn't move.

My fingers fluttered over her skin again, and I felt my heart begin to pound in my chest as I looked into her eyes. My face was only inches from hers, and my eyes were drawn to her lips. Nicole's hand was splayed out against my chest, and I could feel a slight increase in pressure from her fingertips. I reached out with my tongue and wet my lips.

There had been many, many times I'd looked at a girl and had wanted to feel my cock in her—in her mouth, in her pussy—I didn't care. I'd kiss her because it was a means to an end—the end being me getting off. I'd get her off, too, because it just seemed like the polite thing to do, but the main goal was still the same.

But this… This was different.

I just wanted to kiss her.

Be closer to her.

Keep touching her.

Stay here with her.

Never, ever leave.

If someone told me I could stop time—stay right here where I was, feeling exactly how I was feeling, but I would never get off again—I wouldn't even hesitate to agree.

"I have to go," I said, and though I was sorely tempted to give up and stay where I was or take her up on her offer of breakfast and damn whatever consequences may come, I knew I had to leave while I still had my sanity intact. I slowly brought my hand from her waist and pushed myself out from under the blankets and excused myself to locate my clothes.

My shirt was all crispy-feeling from air-drying on the coatrack. I didn't even bother buttoning the damn thing up. I pulled the still-tied tie over my head in a loose loop just so I wouldn't have to carry it. With my shoes in my hand, I cringed as I walked in bare feet over the gravel drive to my car.

At least my pants were dry.

I tossed my likely-ruined sweater into the back seat of the Jeep along with my socks and shoes and then walked around to the driver's side door. A car horn beeped, and I looked up to see Clint Oliver cruising by, waving and smiling broadly at me. I gave him a half wave, got into the car, and drove home.

I didn't think anything of it.

My focus was on getting home and trying to get into my room without being noticed. I parked the car and walked up to the door, looking around as I did. Dad's Mercedes was in the garage, and it was nearly nine in the morning. The chances of him still being asleep weren't great, but it was possible. Taking a slow, deep breath, I opened the door as silently as I could and peered though.

Silence.

So far, so good.

I peered around the corner to the living room but didn't see him. He wasn't in the kitchen, either. I tiptoed down the hall, up the stairs, and right to my bedroom door.

"Where the *fuck* have you been?"

Shit.

I froze.

I was close, so close, to my bedroom door. He was already pissed. How much more pissed could he get if I just made a run for it and locked the door behind me?

It wouldn't work.

I'd never get it locked in time. Even if I did, I would have to come out sometime, and that would just be worse. He might even just break the door down, and then I wouldn't even have that normal barrier between us.

Shit.

"I asked you a goddamned question, asshole!"

I closed my eyes for a second before I turned around to face him.

His hair was plastered to one side of his head and sticking out the other. His normally clear blue eyes were bloodshot and narrowed, and his hands were tightened into fists. His face was contorted and his jaw clenched, and he breathed heavily through his mouth.

Not good.

Not good at all.

Taking a step backwards, I felt the edge of the door against my shoulder.

As Shakespeare's *Hamlet* gave me the words: "*A countenance more in sorrow than in anger*"—I knew well that Dad was not angry with me for coming home late; his grief over what I had done was just more than he could handle. Somehow, lashing out at me for causing that pain was the only thing that made it bearable for him.

Now to buckle down and take it.

CHAPTER EIGHT
dive

"Hey, Paul!" I cringed and tried to breathe a little deeper while trying to keep my voice from sounding weird over the phone.

"Wassup, Malone?"

"Let's scrimmage," I said. "Get a few guys together—play over at the school field?"

"Yeah, sure," Paul replied. "What time?"

"I can be there anytime," I told him. I swallowed hard. "Half hour?"

"Sure, I can get people together by then."

"Cool—see ya there!"

I dropped the phone on the floor and tried to lie back against the pillow. I couldn't breathe deeply enough, and I was having a hard time trying to keep myself from hyperventilating. I ran my hand over my ribs and winced even though I had taken a half dozen Motrin tablets. I tried taking a deeper breath, but sharp pain rippled through the left side of my body.

I need to get to the field quickly.

I told Dad I was going to go practice, but he ignored me. He usually did for a while afterward. I would be seeing him again soon enough, no doubt. I drove over to the school, but there wasn't anyone else there yet. Bending over to lace up my cleats was difficult, to say the least, and took forever. By the time I was done, other cars started showing up, and we started playing six-v-six.

Paul wasn't nearly as good a player as he thought he was, but he was a damn big guy with a temper that just wouldn't quit. He was exactly what I needed on the opposing team. I stood up as straight as I could and didn't pant, no matter how tempted I was. It didn't take long for Paul to come barreling down the field at me. His ball control was all right, but he didn't play smart—always going for the goal instead of making it harder on me with a quick pass to a teammate.

It didn't matter now. I didn't care if he scored or not; I just needed his temper.

As soon as he got to the top of the box, I ran up, dropped shoulder and rammed him—taking the ball at the same time. He dropped to the ground right at the top of the box.

"What the fuck, Malone?"

"Get off your ass, you pussy!" I screamed at him. "You were offside anyway! If you can't take a hit, I hear we need a new water bitch."

I tossed the ball over to Paul, who started running in the opposite direction, passing to Jeremy and then to Klosav. I tried to breathe again, but it just wasn't working. I was only going to be able to take one more hit. I had to make it look good. It didn't take long for Paul to get another breakaway and start heading for me. His eyes found mine, and I knew I had gotten to him. He didn't care about the goal anymore, either. He just slammed right into me.

Perfect angle.

I flew into the air and landed on my back inside the goal. I rolled quickly to the left and cried out as my breath left me.

"Malone! You okay?"

"Hey, man!"

"Shit, is he hurt?"

"Fuck," I groaned. "Can't breathe."

"Shit—I'm sorry, man!"

"Call 911!"

"No, let's just get him to the hospital," Jeremy said, his voice calm. "Tom, can you walk?"

"Dunno," I said. "Maybe."

He helped me to my feet, and I stumbled to his car. A few minutes later, I was in the emergency room getting my cracked rib taped up. Dr. Shepherd wrapped the bandages around my side as I winced and bitched.

"Do you have to make it so tight?"

"Do you want a punctured lung?" she retorted. "We've been through this before. You know the drill. I'm sure your father will remind you of everything you need to do until it's healed."

"No way," I said. "I've got a game on Friday."

"If you get hit again, it's going to be a lot worse. You should stay away from contact sports for three weeks."

"You know that's not going to happen."

"Thomas? Thomas! My God, what happened?"

Right on cue.

"It's nothing, Dad," I told him as he walked over and started shining a penlight in my eyes. "Paul went for the ball; I went for the ball. You know how it is."

"Are you dizzy?"

"I didn't hit my head," I told him. I glanced at Dr. Shepherd, who had an amused smile on her face as she wrote some shit down on my chart.

"No headache?"

"No headache."

"Well, thank God for that." Dad took a step back and tilted his head so he could look at me straight on. "You have got to be more careful, son. You know if you get hurt too bad, you won't be able to play pro. Isn't that what you want?"

"Of course it is," I said. I tried to keep my eyes up toward his as we said our lines. It was hard, though, because my side was still aching.

"I was going to write him a script for the pain," Dr. Shepherd said. "Do you want me to send it down to the pharmacy to be filled here?"

"That will be fine, thank you," Dad responded. "I'll pick it up on my way out. Thomas, why don't you let Jeremy drive you home? He's still in the waiting room. I'll pick up your script and be home right after you."

"Sure," I replied. I found Jeremy in the waiting room, and we walked back out to his car.

"Thanks for sticking around," I said. "Dad will probably be here a couple more hours. I hate hanging out at the hospital."

"No problem," Jeremy said. "Paul and Mika went and got your Jeep and took it back to your house. I got the keys out of your bag. It's in the back seat."

"Cool." I hadn't really thought about my car. I tried to breathe a little deeper, but it still hurt a lot. I wondered if Dad would actually let me have the pain pills or if I was going to need to stock up on Motrin. I leaned my head against the cool window as the mist turned into rain.

"Thomas?"

"Hmm?"

"You landed on your back," Jeremy said.

"Yeah? So?"

"You didn't fall on your left side—not even on your stomach. How did you crack a rib on your left side?"

I glanced over at him and saw that he was looking at me out of the corner of his eye.

"Maybe it was how we collided," I said with a shrug.

"I thought about that, too," Jeremy replied, "but he didn't hit you there, either."

"You obviously have the eyes of a ref," I told him as I turned back to the window. "Blind as a fucking bat. The x-ray says I have a broken rib, so you must have missed something."

Jeremy didn't respond but turned the wheel sharply to move us from the highway to my driveway. He gunned the engine and took us up the hill and through the trees. When he stopped near the house, I opened the door and jumped out—not thinking. I winced and held my side for a minute until I could breathe right again.

Jeremy came around from the other side of the car to help, but I waved him off.

"Hey, Thomas?"

"Yeah?" I replied as I opened the door.

"I didn't miss anything," he said. When I looked over to him, his eyes were focused on mine, and for a moment, we just stood there looking at each other. Jeremy finally inclined his head a little and opened up the car door as I went into the house.

My head was feeling a little wonky after the pain pill Dad let me take. He didn't say anything about it at all; he just brought one of the pills with a glass of water and a sandwich and told me to eat first. I knew he felt bad about it—he usually did when I actually got hurt. That hadn't really happened since last year, though.

Dad knocked on my door, and I pulled myself out of bed to go and unlock it.

"You doing all right?" Dad asked.

"Yeah, I'm good," I told him.

He stood in the doorway while I went and sat down on the black leather couch under the window. He was fidgety, and that could only mean one thing. I didn't want to hear it. It didn't matter.

He started saying it anyway.

Babbling…barely understandable.

I knew he was sorry. I knew he didn't mean it. I didn't need to hear him say it.

"I never really thought…I mean…when she was here…I never thought I'd have to do this on my own." He looked back at me. "I get a little carried away sometimes. I know that…but I don't mean it. You know that, right?"

"Sure, Dad," I replied. I needed him to just stop and move on. I didn't want to talk about this. "It was my fault. I shouldn't have been out all night."

"Right," he agreed, though I kind of wondered if he even remembered that bit of it. "Yeah…we'll have to talk about your curfew."

"Sure," I said with a nod. I knew he'd never actually come back and talk about it. I'd never had any real rules, not that kind, anyway. Play soccer. That was my only real mandate.

He walked over and sat down next to me, and I tried not to flinch.

"I'm not going to do that again, son," he said quietly. "I just… I had too much to drink. You know how it is…on that day."

"I know," I replied. I didn't look at him and focused all my energy on being completely still.

"You're a tough kid, though," he said. "So…you're okay, right?"

"Sure, Dad," I said again. "I'm fine."

"Good kid," he said as he patted me on the back and stood up. I didn't exhale until he left the room, and I could lock the door again.

I crawled into bed, careful not to bump my left side too much. The pain was down to a dull ache at least. As I slipped off into that state of mind where you're not quite awake and not quite asleep, my brain recaptured the day's events. I slowed down the images as the morning scrolled by, reveling in the memories for a bit and then tried to ignore the rest of the day as it spun through my mind.

The next day at school was…awful.

It started off okay—I got up and did my run. My time sucked because my side fucking *hurt*, but Dad didn't say anything about it. I gathered my stuff together, threw on a jersey, and headed off to school.

So far, so good.

As soon as I got out of my Jeep, the comments started.

"Hey, Malone!" Some other senior walked up to me and raised his hand for a high-five. "Nice job!"

"Thanks," I said, having no idea what he was talking about. I had played a mediocre game at best last Friday.

"You've got balls, dude!" Another guy clapped me on the back as he walked into the building. I shook my head a little and headed in.

All morning long, the remarks continued. Random guys coming up repeatedly and making some comment to congratulate me. They were always just rushing past me—people trying to get to their classes and shit, so it wasn't until lunch that I figured out just what the hell was going on.

"Holy shit, if it isn't king stud himself!" Mika smacked my shoulder as he walked past me.

"What the fuck, Klosav?"

"You, my man!" he cackled as he plopped down in the chair next to me. "You have to have balls the size of Texas!"

"Are you going to tell me what the fuck you're talking about?" I asked, "or do I need to beat the living shit out of you first?"

Klosav laughed.

"I'm talking about you, dude!" he yelled. "Who else spent the weekend boning the sheriff's daughter while he was out of town? In the sheriff's house, too! Leaving your Jeep right out front and everything? Holy shit!"

Oh no.

Oh, fuck no.

"Who the hell told you that?"

"Clint," Mika said with a shrug. "He said you were fucking her all night while her dad was out of town. Said he saw you coming out of her house with only half your clothes on, looking like the cat who ate out the pussy."

"That didn't make any fucking sense," I told him. Inside, my head was reeling. I had completely forgotten about Clint, but when I thought about how I must have looked as I walked out of Nicole's house first thing in the morning—shirt unbuttoned, shoes in my hand—I knew exactly what he had assumed.

And had obviously told everyone else as well.

Shit, shit, shit.

"You gotta tell me." Klosav leaned over conspiratorially. "Did you fuck her in the sheriff's bed? Because if you did…holy shit!"

Had Rumple heard any of this?

Oh shit! How could she not have?

"And you were there the whole fucking weekend? 'Cause Paul said he saw your car there on Saturday afternoon, and Clint saw you…"

Shit, shit, shit.

Fuck, fuck, fuck.

What was I going to do?

I looked all around the lunchroom, but I didn't see Nicole anywhere. I did see Heather Lones.

"Hey, Heather," I called. I shoved myself out of my chair and left Mika still babbling. She stopped and turned around though her expression was not friendly.

"What?" she asked. Her tone was even less friendly.

"Have you seen Nicole?"

Her eyes narrowed.

"She left," Heather finally said.

"Left? What do you mean she left?"

"She left the school," Heather said. "Went home, I guess. After having fifteen guys practically jump all over her this morning and then finding out why, she took off."

"Shit."

"She's not like that," Heather said quietly, "and you made her sound like she was."

She turned and walked away from me as Mika walked up behind me.

"So, since Nicole's free game again, I was thinking of asking her—"

My fist hit his face before he could finish his sentence. He went sprawling to the ground.

"Hands OFF!" I screamed at him. "You don't fucking touch her, you piece of shit!"

As temped as I was to finish beating the shit out of him, I had to find Nicole.

I drove all over fucking town, trying to find her with no luck whatsoever. Where could she hide an ugly-ass car like that? It was obviously running again since it wasn't in her driveway anymore, so she had to be in it somewhere.

Deciding she had to come home eventually, I parked at her house and sat myself down on the front porch. Everything that had happened over the past few days started running through my head. What could I have done? Even if I had stopped Clint and threatened him, someone else had obviously seen my car at her house on Saturday. I should have thought about it when she drove me to her house. I should have just told her to take me home.

No…I couldn't bring myself to regret that.

For the first time in a long time, I dug into the bottom of my soccer bag and pulled out a pack of Camels. Unfortunately, smoking a cigarette only agitated me more and didn't calm me down at all. It made my lungs hurt, too. Smoking also didn't make her appear.

My side was starting to ache, and I probably needed another one of the prescription pills, but they were at home, and I didn't want to leave without seeing her. I leaned forward and dropped my head into my hands, closing my eyes and just trying to figure out what the hell I was going to do or say. My mind spun, and I lost track of time. When I heard the crunch of tires on the gravel drive and looked up, it was not the vehicle I wanted to see.

It was a sheriff's cruiser.

Shit.

Sheriff Skye eyed me as he got out of the car and walked over to the porch.

"Thomas?"

"Um…yeah," I stammered. "Hi."

"I didn't really expect to see you on my porch," he said.

"Well," I said, "I didn't really expect to be here."

"You want to tell me why?"

"Not really."

He tilted his head to one side to look at me.

"Why don't you explain it anyway?" It wasn't really a question.

I took a deep breath. I had absolutely no idea what to say.

"I was just…looking for Nicole."

"She doesn't seem to be here," he remarked.

"Yeah, I noticed that."

"Maybe you should wait to see her at school tomorrow."

"I'd rather not," I said.

"What's going on, Thomas?" Sheriff Skye asked in a very police officer, no-nonsense tone.

"She's pissed off at me," I told him. "I just wanted to…talk to her."

"What did you do?"

I really didn't like the way he leaned back and put his hand over his gun. I swallowed hard and tried to come up with something I could actually say.

"It was all a misunderstanding," I started to explain.

"If you touched her…" he said with a snarl, "I don't care who you are…"

"I didn't!" I yelled. "That's just it! I didn't do anything—I swear! But…well, someone thought I did…and told someone else, and…shit!"

"Don't swear," he growled again. "Do you think I don't know your reputation?"

I was tempted to completely lose it and start screaming. In the back of my mind, I knew he wasn't going to do anything to me even if I came out and said I'd fucked his daughter on the hood of his patrol car. He couldn't touch me, and he knew it, too.

But that wasn't going to help the situation.

At all.

Against my better judgment, I opened my mouth and told him the truth.

"She helped me," I said quietly. "Last Saturday was…um…the same day as…"

I couldn't finish. Sheriff Skye's voice softened.

"I know what day it was."

I nodded.

"Um...Nicole saw me...at the cemetery." I put my head back in my hands and pulled at my hair. "I wasn't doing that well. She...she brought me back here. She made me dinner."

I didn't think he needed to know all the gory details.

"And?"

"And...um...someone saw my car here. They just assumed..." I looked back up at him. "I didn't do anything, Sheriff. I swear I didn't. But people talk, and Nicole heard it. Now she's mad, and I just wanted to tell her I didn't say anything."

"That explains it," he said with a bit of a smirk.

"Explains what?" I asked.

"All the Mexican food," he said. "I couldn't believe she ate that much of it."

I chucked a little.

"I hadn't eaten all day," I told him.

We both looked up as the rattle of the Hyundai met our ears, got louder, and then was joined by the sight of Nicole pulling into the driveway. I could see her eyes go wide as she took in the scene before her.

I stood up off the porch and took a few steps forward. For a moment, she just stayed in the driver's seat, looking out over the driveway at the two of us. Sheriff Skye reached up and scratched the back of his neck. A minute later, Nicole's eyes narrowed as she slowly opened the door of the car and climbed out. Her hands were balled into fists.

"Oh boy," Sheriff Skye mumbled under his breath. "You just might be on your own here."

He actually took a couple of steps away from me as she approached, kitten claws out and sharpened.

"You son of a bitch!" she yelled. "What are you doing here? Bragging to my father, too?"

"Nicole, I didn't—"

"Do you have any idea how many people came up to me today?" she continued. "How many guys came and asked me out? Because suddenly I'm another chick who puts out for Thomas

Malone, and now that's he's had me, I'm fair game to everyone else!"

"Ouch," Sheriff Skye said with a whistle. "You know, since I already got the short version of this, I'm just going to excuse myself…"

"No!" Nicole and I both yelled at the same time.

"What the hell did he tell you?" Nicole said as she glared at me.

"I'm gonna let you two work this out…" He tried to escape again, but Nicole told him to stay. Then she glared at me again while I tried to figure out how to form words.

"There is nothing you could possibly say that I would want to hear." Nicole turned and started to walk toward the door. "And I really don't have anything to say to you."

"Please, Nicole!" I said as I finally found my voice again. "Just let me explain!"

"Explain? Explain how I've been trashed all over school because I felt *sorry* for you? Explain how all any of you jocks care about is bragging to your friends about what you've done with which girl? I'm really not interested!"

"If you would just listen for a minute—"

"Go away!" she screeched.

"You really should at least give the boy a chance…" Sheriff Skye started to say, but the kitten claws dug into him, too.

"Are you serious?" she screeched. "This is why I left Minneapolis, Dad! Or had you forgotten that? I left because of this kind of bullshit, and now, because I tried to help this jerk, it's all happening again!"

"Don't swear, Nicole…"

Now I was lost. I looked back and forth between them and watched the sheriff cringe a little.

"What's happening again?" I asked. I couldn't have been more confused. Sheriff Skye shook his head a little.

"None of your goddamn business!" Nicole yelled at me.

She might have been yelling, but the façade was broken. I

could see it in her face and focused on her eyes enough to see that they were red and swollen. She wasn't just angry, and she wasn't just hurt. Not by this. There was something else.

"Rumple?" I questioned. "What is it?"

"What the heck is a *Rumple*?" her father asked as he looked at me from the corner of his eye.

"Never mind, Dad," Nicole said with a sigh. "I just want to go inside and make dinner."

"Please listen to me," I said again. "I never said anything to anyone—I swear. I spent most of yesterday in the hospital and hardly talked to anyone! It wasn't me. Someone just saw my car parked here…"

She looked over to me with deep furrows across her brow.

"Oh my God," she muttered, and she dropped down to the porch where I had been sitting and covered her face with her hands.

"*Good luck*," Sheriff Skye mouthed to me as he slowly opened the door and slipped inside.

I walked up to her and slowly sat down on her right side. I was in completely unchartered territory here. Aside from never actually trying to comfort a girl before, I had never really apologized to one, either. I had no idea which one I should do first.

I decided to try comfort, but I didn't really know how to accomplish that. I remembered what she had done for me and reached out to tuck her hair behind her ear.

She punched me.

"Oh fuck!" I gasped as breath left me and pain shot down my side. She didn't actually hit my ribs, but just below was close enough.

"Are your ribs taped up?" she exclaimed.

"Umm…yeah," I admitted as I tried to keep my eyes from watering.

"You really were in the hospital yesterday?"

"Yeah."

"What happened?"

"Nothing," I said with a shake of my head. "Don't worry about it."

"*What happened to your ribs?*" She accented each word, and when I looked at her eyes, I knew she wasn't going to let it drop.

"I got hit during a scrimmage yesterday," I told her. "Just cracked one—no biggie."

"During a *scrimmage?*"

"Yeah—you know, just a quick, friendly game."

"Doesn't sound too friendly," she remarked.

"Well...shit happens." I looked away, unable to meet her eyes. I felt her hand on my arm, and I looked over at her scrunched up face.

"Sorry," she said.

"It's okay," I told her. "I deserve it."

"Deserve a broken rib?"

"Yeah...um...no, I mean..."

Shit.

"I mean, I deserved you hitting me."

"Hrm." Her eyes narrowed at me again. She took a big breath and huffed it out. "Who saw the Jeep?"

"A couple people saw it Saturday, I guess," I told her. "And Clint saw me leaving in the morning. He just assumed..."

I turned to her and leaned closer.

"I swear, Rumple—I didn't say anything to anybody. I didn't even tell anyone I *saw* you. I never would have done that, not after..."

I looked away for a second and then looked back at her.

"Not after what you did for me."

There were tears in the corner of her eyes.

"I hadn't even gotten into the building yet," she said, "before Clint came up and smacked me on the butt and told me he was ready when I was. By the time I got to the door, Mika grabbed my waist and asked what I was doing for dinner. I had four more offers before my first class was over."

"Shit..."

"And then Crystal Lloyd called me a slut," she said. "She told me only the really stupid girls spread their legs for you the first time, and I should have at least held out until the second date."

I balled my hands into fists. I wouldn't hit a girl, but I might go smack her brother around for having the same last name.

"Next thing I know, I find out the whole school is talking about how you fucked me in my Dad's bed."

The tears slipped out of her eyes and rolled down her cheeks. I felt my chest clench and wished I could do something about it, but I knew there was nothing I could do.

"I'm sorry," I said quietly. "I had no idea...I mean, people were saying shit to me, but I didn't even know what they were talking about...not until lunch—but you were already gone."

She nodded.

"I looked all over for you," I told her. "Where did you go?"

"To the trailer park on the other side of town," she said with a shrug.

"Why the heck did you go out there?"

"Just to see a friend."

She didn't seem interested in elaborating, so I let it drop.

"What am I going to do?" she whispered as she finally looked over to meet my eyes. "No one is going to believe nothing happened, even if you tell them. Now I have a bunch of guys chasing me because they think I'm going to put out and a bunch of girls hating me for the same reason. I can't believe this is happening again."

"What's happening again?"

"Forget it," she grumbled, and she started to stand up.

I reached out and grabbed her arm.

"Tell me," I insisted.

"It's really none of your business," she said again.

Taking the chance, I reached over and put my hand on top of hers.

"Tell me what happened," I said.

Nicole looked over at me with narrowed eyes.

"How about I make you a deal?" she said as she pulled her hand away from mine. "We go out to the soccer field at school, and if I can't get a penalty kick past you, I'll tell you the whole story. If I do get one past you, you have to answer one question completely truthfully—anything I ask."

I couldn't help it—I laughed.

"You think you're going to get a PK past me?"

"I don't know," she said with a shrug. "I've never tried. It doesn't look that hard, though. Besides, you're hurt."

I shook my head.

"If that's what you want," I said.

"So we have a deal?"

"You got a deal, Rumple," I snickered. "You're an idiot, but you got a deal."

"Now?"

"Sure."

Shakespeare wrote, "Ambition should be made of sterner stuff." Somehow, I still had to admire her tenacity.

Now to get this over with so I could figure out what had happened to her.

CHAPTER NINE
golden goal

Nicole leaned over and double knotted her tennis shoes as I juggled the ball around, only half paying attention to what I was doing. Mostly I was watching her bent over, tying her shoes, wearing red short-shorts. She really did have gorgeous legs, and I didn't think I had really appreciated them before. Firm…shaped… must be from all that running she does. I could see the flex in her calves and thighs—she had some muscle there. I was very tempted to run my hands over them.

I shook the thoughts from my head.

The girl had to be just a little bit crazy, I figured, or maybe she was just looking to lose the bet. Anyone would have to be damn good to get past me, and from the very beginning, she obviously didn't know what she was doing. Maybe it was her way of saying she wanted to tell me whatever this dirty little secret was but without just coming right out and saying it.

I didn't know; girls were weird.

I smirked as she walked toward the goal. I popped the ball up in her direction with my knee, and she squealed and batted it away from her face. I laughed as she glared at me, picked up the dirty ball with her fingertips, and placed it at the top of the box.

"You're making it a lot harder on yourself!" I chuckled.

"What do you mean?"

I pointed to the white circle in between us.

"That's the PK spot, baby."

"Oh." She mumbled something else that I couldn't hear and then took a few steps forward to place the ball on the right spot. "Here?"

"That's it, Rumple." I winked at her as she glowered at me.

She stood right behind the ball, looking back and forth from one side of the goal to the other. I crouched down a little, bouncing on my knees a bit.

"How many tries do I get?" she asked.

"Normally, one," I explained, "but you can have three because I'm such a nice guy."

She snorted.

I might have let her kick all afternoon, but eventually I'd get tired. It was still a little hard to breathe, too.

"Okay."

She brought her foot back with bended knee and kicked. The ball glanced off her toe and rolled at about the same pace as a toddler's plastic truck. I jogged over and picked it up before it hit the side bar.

"Rumple, Rumple, Rumple," I teased. "You gotta get some power behind it!"

I walked over to her with the ball, placed it down on the circle, and started explaining the physics of kicking to her.

"Use a running start to give yourself more power, but the main thing is to keep your leg as straight as possible. You gotta use those beautiful thighs."

She whipped her head up from the ball to me as she narrowed her eyes.

"Just calling it as I see it," I said with a shrug, but I walked back to position anyway.

Her next try was a little better. She did take the running start but still bent her knee too much. The shot was on-goal but had nowhere near enough leverage to get past me. I jumped left and easily trapped it in my hands. I settled into position and rolled the ball back to her.

"One more try, Rumple," I said, "and then you're gonna have to spill it!"

She smashed her lips together and scowled at me before taking a deep breath and placing the ball back on the white circle. I was still standing straight up—not even close to being ready to jump—when I watched her take a couple of steps back, and her thigh muscles tightened deliciously. I may have been a bit too focused on the shape of the muscles instead of what she was doing with them. The angle was more firm, her quadriceps more sure of what they were doing—something that only occurs when muscle repeats a movement often enough to create long-term muscle memory.

She took two steps forward, curled the toe of her foot back toward her, which would make for a higher angled kick, and straightened her leg like a fucking pro. Straight, long, lean, and enough leverage to fling the ball right at the top left corner of the goal.

It flew up fast. My balance was off—I hadn't even been trying to bother jumping since I thought it was obvious she wasn't going to get enough power to kick it fast enough. A goalie has to know which direction the ball is going to go before it's kicked to have a chance at stopping a penalty. You already have to be moving before your opponent's foot touches the ball. I wasn't ready, and I would have had to jump in exactly the right direction long before I realized it was too late. I dived anyway, landing on the ground too low to be of any use. She nailed the top corner.

Score one for Rumple.

Holy shit.

I looked up from the dirt to her smirk.

"Varsity striker," she said with a raise of her eyebrows and a thumb pointing back to her chest.

"You bitch!" I yelled out, but I couldn't stop laughing at the same time. I rolled to a sitting position and reached behind me to grab the ball out of the net. I cringed a little as I stretched to reach for the ball, and my ribs ached from the movement.

Nicole raised her eyebrows at me.

"You conceited little bastard," she retorted. "Always thinking you're better than everyone else. It's about time someone took your ego down a peg."

I smiled and shook my head at her.

"You did that on purpose," I accused. "You conned me."

"And you fell for it."

I couldn't argue with her there. I snickered and dribbled the ball between my legs. She continued to stand over me with her hands on her hips and a smirk on her face.

"All right," I sighed. "What do you want to know?"

I figured it was going to be something about my past conquests with the girls in this school, and I wasn't looking forward to talking about it with her. I mean…I didn't see her that way, and I didn't want her to think I did. Or maybe I was going to have to confess about the flowers—I could cope with that. I kind of wanted her to know.

She hooked her thumbs into the little decorative pockets on her shorts and leaned back on her heels a bit. I looked up to see her biting on her lip, her smile now gone.

"What happened when you went home Sunday?" she said as her eyes grew dark.

"I don't know what you mean," I replied, but at the same time, I felt my stomach drop. There was something in her tone… something I didn't like. Not at all.

"Tell me how your rib got broken," she said.

My body went cold.

No.

No fucking way.

"I told you," I said quietly.

"You told me you got it cracked in a scrimmage," Nicole said. "And that's bullshit. I want to know what really happened."

"I told you what happened," I repeated. I stood up, popped the ball into the air with my toe, and grabbed it before I started heading back to my Jeep, taking long strides through the damp grass.

"Hey!" she called out. "We made a deal!"

"Fuck you!" I yelled back over my shoulder. My hands were shaking, and my breathing was quick, making my side hurt. I tossed the ball to the ground and walked faster.

"Tell me what happened!" she continued from behind me. "Why didn't you want to go home, Thomas? Why?"

"Shut the fuck up!" I yanked open my car door, fully intending to just fucking leave her there. I didn't need this bullshit—some bitch conning me and then pulling this kind of shit. No fucking way.

She managed to wrench the passenger door open before I could lock it, and I tossed the ball into the back seat without looking in her direction.

"I won," she said. "You have to tell me."

"Shut the fuck up," I said again, my voice lowered, "or you can fucking walk home."

"We had a deal." Her voice didn't sound quite as forceful now. "Are you backing out on me?"

"I told you what happened," I said again.

"The deal was for the truth," she countered.

As if I needed the reminder.

I started the Jeep and gripped the steering wheel, trying to decide if I should just get her home quickly and never speak to her again or dump her ass in the school parking lot right now. I was still panting, and my head was getting swimmy. I needed a pain pill…or maybe a drink.

"I won't tell anyone," I heard her whisper. "I swear I won't."

My foot tapped the accelerator, revving the engine but still not going anywhere. I just stared straight ahead, trying to silence that tiny piece in my brain that wanted to tell her everything. No fucking way.

I continued to grip the steering wheel even as I watched

Nicole reach over to turn the key back to the off position. The engine whirred for a moment before dropping back into silence.

Out of the corner of my eye, I saw her get up on her knees in the passenger seat and crawl partway over to me. Her hand slid around the back of my head, and she pulled me close to her. That's when I could smell her, and as I inhaled, she threaded her fingers through my hair and pushed it back behind my ear.

No fucking way…

No way…

No…

I can't…

Please…

I turned my head toward her, something inside of me letting go…giving up. I didn't know what this was, but I couldn't stop it. I buried my face against the skin of her neck and wrapped my arms around her waist. I heard myself scream over and over again—my throat going raw from the force of it—until my body just collapsed against her, and she held on to me.

Just like she had before.

"It's not his fault," I whispered against her skin. "It's mine… it's always been my fault."

Oh shit.

Oh no. No, no, no, no, no, no…

My mind continued to scream even though my voice had failed.

There was nothing I could do. The words were out.

My mind was empty.

Or it was full, and I just couldn't see past the fog inside to know the difference.

The warmth of the girl holding me in my car in the middle of the school parking lot was the only thing keeping me grounded, keeping me from completely going over the edge. I was still close, and as the tension throughout my muscles slowly released, the spring inside my head just wound tighter. I closed my eyes as her fingers brushed across my temple in their seemingly endless task of pushing my hair away from my face.

My head was now in her lap, and my arms were wrapped tightly around her waist as she held me, comforted me, and hummed quietly. The emergency brake was uncomfortable against my side, but at least it was my right side. My left side ached. My throat ached. My head ached.

But it was so, so easy to forget about all of that because I was wrapped up in her arms and her scent. I clung to her as if she were the railing of a balcony on the top floor of a hotel, and my drunk ass had just stumbled over it. It hurt to try to hold on to her, and part of me just wanted to let go and let myself fall—be done with it.

Rain started plopping against the roof of the car—slowly at first but then harder. I still didn't move, and Nicole didn't seem to be going anywhere, either. The inside of the windows fogged up, making it hard to tell just how late it was. I wasn't sure if the dim light was due to the cloud cover or if it was really that late.

I needed to get home.

I raised my head a bit and ended up with my forehead against her shoulder as I finally met her eyes again. She looked so *worried*. I couldn't keep my eyes on hers, so I looked away again, focusing out the window though there was nothing to be seen.

My shoulders tensed as I thought about what I had just done and said. What the fuck was I going to do now? She knew. Somehow she knew even before I said it, but she didn't understand why he had to do it. I'd taken everything that mattered from him, and he had every right to be pissed about it.

"It's not his fault," I said again, my voice barely loud enough to be heard over the rain. I coughed, my throat still hurting.

"What happened?"

"He was drinking the night before," I said. "He had too much. He doesn't usually drink at all…just that day. He was angry, but he didn't mean it. I just fell."

"You *fell?*" she repeated. "How did you fall?"

"He only just…pushed me away," I told her. "There's one of those vanity table things—some antique—in the hallway. I cracked my rib on that. It wasn't his fault; it was mine."

"He pushed you," Nicole said, "and you hit a table, and that's when your rib broke?"

"Yeah."

"How exactly is that your fault?" she asked quietly.

"It's *all* my fault," I said. My arms tightened around her, and I ducked my forehead into her shoulder. "It's my fault she's dead."

"My dad said it was a car accident."

"But she wouldn't have been there if it weren't for me." I proceeded to tell her about my forgotten gloves and how Mom went back for them.

"It was an accident," Nicole insisted when I was done. "Everyone forgets things sometimes…"

"I don't anymore," I mumbled.

"What did you say?"

"It never would have happened if it weren't for me," I growled under my breath. "Would she have even been in the car then if I hadn't forgotten my gloves? Huh?"

"That's not the point, Thomas. You were just a kid…"

"That didn't stop it from happening," I said, "and it doesn't change the fact that if I hadn't been so fucking stupid, she'd be alive now."

"You are not responsible—"

"Yes, I am!" I yelled as I pushed away from her, wincing and grabbing my side. Moving away didn't work, so I just dropped my head back on her shoulder again. "Tell me she still would have been on that road if I had remembered all my shit! Go ahead. Tell me she would still have had a reason to drive back home! You can't, can you? And you know why? Because *it's my fucking fault!*"

Nicole leaned back against the seat and tilted her head to look at me, her expression pained.

"Even if it was," she said, "and I am *not* agreeing with you, but even if the accident was your fault, that doesn't mean he gets to treat you like this now. It happened six years ago."

"It's six years later, and she's still gone," I said, repeating Dad's words to me from the previous day. "Nothing changes."

"It's supposed to change," Nicole insisted, "but you guys are stuck."

I closed my eyes and thought about the word *stuck* for a while. I had to admit it did kind of fit.

"Thomas, you need to tell someone about this," Nicole said softly. "My dad could—"

"No!" I turned my head to hers and gripped her waist. "No, Nicole! You promised! You said you wouldn't tell anyone!"

Nicole shook her head.

"I won't," she said. "I just think *you* should."

I tried to take a deep breath, but between the uncomfortable position in the car and my rib, it wasn't working well. I didn't want to let go of her, though. Even if I couldn't breathe at all, holding her and feeling her hands in my hair was good. I didn't want to ever let go.

"No one can know," I whispered into her shoulder. "No one."

I thought maybe having someone who knew about it might make it just a little better, but I didn't know what that was going to mean to Rumple. I also didn't know where we were supposed to go from here. Even though Jeremy had his suspicions, this was entirely different.

"What now?" I asked quietly.

I had turned the car back on, but we were still sitting in the school parking lot. I leaned back in the driver's seat, my fingers clutching the center of the steering wheel. I felt strange—nervous, embarrassed, empty—and I simultaneously wanted to get the hell away from this girl and also hold her tightly and never let go. It was freaking me out.

"I still think you should tell my dad," she responded—again. "But I'm not going to push it—not now. He has no right to treat you like that."

"Going to your dad is pointless," I said—again. We'd gone over a lot of this in the past hour. "I'm over eighteen. What's he going to do? Even if I was still underage, you obviously haven't been around long enough to understand my dad's hold on this community."

"Then move out."

"I can't do that."

"Why not?"

"I just…can't," I said with a sigh. "I can't do that to him. He needs me. Besides, I don't really have anywhere to go."

"That's what I thought a couple of months ago," she responded. "I never would have considered coming to live here before then. I didn't think I had anywhere to go, either."

"Why did you leave?"

"You lost the bet," she reminded me.

"I don't care about the fucking bet," I said, my voice a little harsher than I had intended. "I want to know."

She glared at me and then looked back toward the passenger window. Her fingers twisted around themselves in her lap.

"You know all my dirty laundry now," I said. In truth, she only knew a portion of it, but whatever. "Tell me."

Nicole pulled her legs up so her tennis shoes were on the edge of the seat, which I tried not to let bother me too much. Anyone else and I would have flipped out at the thought of mud on my leather. She took a deep breath.

"This goes nowhere, right?"

"Of course."

She sighed again.

"My high school in the suburbs of Minneapolis was just like this town—no girls' soccer team," Nicole said. "I played just for my club the first couple of years, but I wanted to play for the school, too. There weren't enough girls to form a team, so I decided I was going to try out for the boys' team."

She laughed dryly.

"I honestly thought I'd have some kind of battle on my hands, you know? But they were okay with it. A lot of varsity players had graduated the year before, so they were a little low, and I guess I impressed them. So I made the team, and not too long after the season started, the team captain, a midfielder named Dennis, asked me out. We seemed to hit it off really well and started dating pretty seriously."

She paused and ran her hand through her hair.

"I'd never really had a serious boyfriend before," she continued. "He was my first...you know? I mean, we had been dating a couple of months, and it did seem kind of natural. He was really sweet...at least, I thought so."

I held on to the bottom of the steering wheel, gripping it tightly.

"He said he loved me, and I thought I loved him, too." She stopped again, and I heard her sniff. I looked over and could see her tearing up a bit. I released the wheel and reached over to grab her hand, and she didn't protest.

"Go on," I urged.

"We won our division championship," she said. "There was a big party afterwards at this other guy's place. His parents were out of town, I think. At least, there weren't any adults there. We were drinking, and I had quite a bit. But then...then Dennis asked me if I wanted to try something else."

One of the tears escaped and dropped over her cheek. She wiped it away quickly with the hand I wasn't holding.

"It was stupid. I know it was, but he and Alex—the guy who was throwing the party—they took me to one of the bedrooms and gave me something. They told me it was ecstasy and that it would make me feel really good. It did, too. I remember it all, but it's kind of fuzzy. I know I agreed to it...to what they wanted to do... but..."

I closed my eyes for a second because I had a pretty good idea of what was coming, and the dread that was beginning to rumble around inside of me was numbing. I didn't want to hear this. I didn't want to know she had been with someone else, but I had asked for it. I wanted to believe what my father had believed, that she was innocent…

…and potentially mine.

I pushed my hormonal thoughts away.

"I think they planned it," she whispered. "I think they planned the whole thing. They took pictures of each of them…with me. I remember agreeing to all of it, but I wasn't in my right mind, you know? And then the next Monday…at school…"

She grabbed her hand away from mine and covered her face before she blurted out the rest. I knew everything that was coming as soon as she mentioned the drug—Frankie was into that shit. I still didn't want to hear that I was right.

She blurted it out anyway.

"I let them both fuck me, take pictures of it, and then the pictures were all over the school. I went from pretty happy with a boyfriend, a starting position on the soccer team, and a fairly active social life to nothing in the matter of a day. Dennis dumped me, the pictures got back to my Mom—which is a whole other story— and every time I walked into school, I had to pull copies of them off my locker. Every guy on the team—and most of the rest of the school—started asking me out then. Every one of them stating very clearly that they were looking for someone to fuck, and they knew I was obviously willing to do anything with anyone. I won't even get into what the girls did."

Nicole wiped off her face with her hands and dropped them back in her lap.

"During the summer, I didn't make the club team I'd been playing on for years. The rumors had gotten that far. I pretty much stopped playing altogether, and I definitely didn't have any kind of social life anymore. My friends had always been guys for the most part, and none of them wanted to have anything to do with me if I wasn't going to put out for them, too."

"So, I left and came here," she said after a moment, "vowing to never date again, at least not until high school is over. I thought

I could start out again here…fresh. I guess that was stupid."

When Nicole finished her story, I didn't know what to do. I wanted to comfort her like she had done for me, but I really didn't know how. All I could think about was how she was in the same situation now, which was why she left Minneapolis.

I didn't want her to leave.

What I really wanted to do was to fix it. I wanted to fix it all. I wanted to find both of these guys and rip their fucking heads off for starters. Then I wanted to beat the shit out of anyone who passed those pictures around. I wanted to destroy every copy in existence and tell her everything was okay now—that I would take care of it for her. I wanted to take care of her.

I had a lot of influence in our home state because of my dad, but that didn't really extend past our area. If it had happened here, I could have fixed it, but there was nothing I could do for her now.

"Going to school tomorrow is going to suck," she said quietly. "I thought I left all this shit behind me."

Wait a minute. Maybe there was something I could do…

"What if…" I sat up a little straighter, trying to form the right words in my mind before I said them. "What if I could take care of that?"

"What do you mean?"

"I mean, what if I could keep it from happening again?" I asked. "What if I could make sure no one said shit to you, and no one bothered you at all?"

"How would you do that?" she asked warily.

"What if…" I took a deep breath. "What if you were…my girlfriend?"

"I told you, Thomas—I'm not dating anyone. Maybe ever again. I might become a nun."

I knew she was joking…at least I hoped she was.

"I understand that," I said, trying to reassure her, "but no one else needs to know that, do they? If they all think you're mine, the guys will leave you alone. No one will think you're a…a…"

"A slut?"

"Um…yeah," I stammered. "No one will think of you that way if you're just with me, right?"

"They already think I slept with you," she said.

"I know…but it wouldn't matter so much if we were together, right?" The more I thought about it, the more the idea appealed to me. "No one would dare bother you. No one is going to touch you if you're mine."

"*Yours*?" she snorted.

"Well…um…as far as anyone else knows…"

"So what, we pretend to be dating?"

"Yeah."

"But we wouldn't be."

"Right."

"That's fucked up, Malone," she said with a humorless laugh.

I felt my stomach drop.

"But it beats the alternative," she said.

"Beats the alternative," I repeated, trying to make sure I got her meaning correct. "That's a yes, isn't it?"

Her hands went back to her face and she rubbed at her eyes.

"We can give it a try," she said. She turned toward me with an expression on her face I had not seen before. She looked wary, distant, and frightened.

"I didn't try anything when we were in bed together," I reminded her as I tried to understand the meaning in her look. "I still won't."

She nodded and wrapped her arms around herself.

"Do you want to go home?" I asked.

"Yeah, I do," she said.

I put the car in gear and headed out to the street.

"So how is this going to work?" she asked.

"Well," I said, "I guess I'll pick you up for school tomorrow?"

"My car is fine now," she said.

"Yeah, but then we'd arrive at school together, you know?"

"I guess." She seemed to think about it for a minute.

"You don't have to," I said quietly, sounding defeated.

"It's all right," she replied. "I just need to get my head wrapped around this. And Dad is going to flip."

"What are you going to tell him?"

"I'm going to tell him the truth," she said succinctly. "I don't lie to him. I don't lie, period. I may refrain from saying something. I may even twist my words around, but I don't lie. That's one of the reasons this isn't going to be too easy for me."

"What about that shit in front of the goal?"

"That was totally different," she said. "Besides, I never lied."

"You acted like you didn't know where to put the ball for a PK!"

"But I never said I didn't know, did I? I placed it at the top of the box, and you corrected me like I knew you would."

I smashed my lips together to keep from smiling. My mind quickly whirled through everything she had said, and I couldn't argue with her point—she hadn't ever lied about it. Even when she said she had never tried, she could have meant she had never tried getting a PK past *me*. Twisting her words. This *was* going to be interesting.

"So, I have to be able to give you things you can say that will be true, right?"

"I guess that would help," she agreed. "What did you have in mind?"

"Well, if I took you out for dinner, you could say we were dating, couldn't you?"

She eyed me again.

"I need to get dinner for Dad," she said.

"Fries and Cokes at Mickey D's, then?"

She sighed.

"Fine."

I turned the car around and headed back toward the center of town. I hoped Dad's work schedule was back on track now, and I was right that he wouldn't be home for another couple of hours. I was pretty sure about it, but he hadn't said a lot to me in the past couple of days, so I wasn't positive.

I pulled into the fast-food place, glad to see it wasn't very busy. Nicole seemed glad of that as well. We entered, grabbed fries and drinks, and then took a booth over in the back corner so we could talk privately.

"So, you're going to drive me to school?"

"Yeah," I said, "if that's okay?"

"It's okay," Nicole said with a sigh. "What else?"

"Well…um…" I racked my brain for any romantic comedy movies I had ever seen, but there weren't that many, so I wasn't really sure what to do. "I'll open the car door for you?"

Nicole laughed.

"Thomas Malone? Turning into a gentleman? No one will believe it!"

"Well, I could give it a try," I said. I rubbed my chin with my hand and tried to think of what else I could do to make it look like I was her boyfriend.

I sipped at my Coke and pondered.

"I'll walk you to your classes," I told her.

"You really are going all out, huh? How many girlfriends have you had?"

"Um…none," I admitted.

"I kind of thought so," she replied with a nod and a harsh look.

"I'm playing this by ear," I told her. "How about a little help?"

"I should probably plan on doing my homework while you're practicing."

"You'd come watch me practice, then?" I couldn't help my grin.

I grabbed a handful of fries and chowed down.

"You really like that, don't you?" she accused.

"The fries?"

"The idea of me watching you practice."

I shrugged.

"Yeah."

"Why?"

"Because you'd be watching me," I said.

"You want me to watch you?"

"I want everyone to watch me," I replied. "It kind of goes with the territory."

"So you are an attention whore?"

"Pretty much." I shoveled more fries into my mouth—they were damn good—and wiped my lips with a napkin. Nicole ate hers in little bites, tearing each one in half before dunking it in ketchup.

"At least you admit it," Nicole said as she sat back and gulped down the rest of her drink. "Okay, if this actually counts—we've been on a date now. I guess that means we're dating."

"Yes, we are," I said with a smile, "and tomorrow everyone will know you're mine."

Nicole rolled her eyes.

"I belong to *me*, you jerk." She shook her head, but she was smiling, too.

Perhaps Shakespeare would have considered us "woo'd in haste," but at least we had something of a plan together. Somehow, I thought it would be easy to convince the student body of our high school to see us as a couple.

Now, how was I going to keep my dad from hearing about it?

CHAPTER TEN
caution

After I dropped Nicole off, my mind began racing to come up with some sort of explanation that would work on Dad. Obviously, I couldn't be like Nicole and tell my dad the truth—that would just be stupid. I needed a plausible reason to have him see her around me and not flip out. As far as I could discern, there was really only one way.

Dad's car wasn't in the drive when I got home, which was good. I did my homework, lifted some weights in the basement—which didn't last long since my ribs started hurting—and toasted a bagel. When I heard Dad's car come up the driveway, I took a deep breath and tried to remember my lines.

"You missed practice," he said as soon as he walked in the door. He looked tired, which was also a good thing.

"Um…yeah," I stammered. I wasn't expecting that from the get-go, but it actually made for a good cue. "I know, and it won't happen again. I've got it all worked out now."

He dropped his briefcase near the door and stalked into the kitchen. He glared at me as he pulled the stack of delivery menus out of the drawer by the refrigerator.

"You have what worked out?" he demanded.

"Well, you know that little cherry-girl, right?" I asked. "Sheriff Skye's daughter?"

"Yeah?"

"Well, let's just say she'll be taking care of my homework assignments this semester," I laughed and shook my head a little.

"Oh yeah? Were you fucking her instead of practicing?"

"No," I said. I swallowed hard. "Not yet. But I've got her worked up enough that she'll do anything I ask. I know I missed practice, but I think it will save me a lot of pointless work in the long run, you know? And I did some lifting when I got home, and I did go out with another…um…another player and did some practice PKs afterwards."

"Any get by you?"

"Just one."

"Good boy."

Cue major sigh of relief.

"I think if I can kind of play nice with her for a while…you know…string her along...be all boyfriend like…"

"Fuck her when you're done with this semester," he concluded. "Then dump her and move on, though—okay?"

"Yeah!" I agreed. "Exactly!"

"Sounds pretty good," Dad said with a nod. He picked up the phone and started dialing. "But don't miss another practice."

"I won't," I promised. "She's already going to do our whole biology project."

"Good, good." He nodded and started ordering his dinner.

Holy shit, that went about as well as it possibly could have. The timing was good because he was usually a little easier on me after…well, just *after*. When he was at games, I'd be able to hang out with Nicole, and he wouldn't question it, and if word got back to him, he wouldn't be blindsided by the news.

Perfect.

Actually, Dad was a little on the buddy-buddy side after he ate some dinner. He asked about my running times, practices, and which team we were playing in the next game. He even called me into the living room and had me sit with him while he flipped through channels with the remote.

"How's your side?" he asked.

"Not too bad," I replied. "It hurt a bit when I was lifting."

"You didn't take any more of the Percocet, did you?"

"No," I replied, "I took four Motrin."

"Good," he said. "I don't like you taking that strong stuff. It's not good for you, and you're a tough kid. Tell me if you think you need one, though, okay?"

He wouldn't have let me have one. I knew that. I was kind of surprised he gave me one the first night. Suffering through pain was more aligned with his values.

"Sure, Dad."

He reached over and patted me on the shoulder. I tried to hold still as he left his hand there for a minute while he kept channel surfing. He finally stopped on the World Cup game.

"Is the US going to win this one?"

"They better at least tie," I said. "If they don't, they might not make the round of sixteen."

"One of these days, I'll be watching you in that goal," he said with a flick of his wrist. Tim Howard filled the screen, the ball grasped between his gloved hands. He ran to the top of the box and punted it nearly to the other side of the field. "Play club overseas, but I want you taking his place on the national team when he retires."

"He's awesome," I said with a nod. It had been a while since we had just sat and talked soccer—not since the last World Cup. "I wish Hejduk was still on defense, though. With him there, Howard's job would be easier."

"He was always fast," Dad agreed. "Who is he playing with now?"

"Retired," I replied. "He's some kind of fan-relations guy with the Columbus Crew now."

We chatted about soccer for most of an hour, even cheering together when the game ended with just enough points to move the

US forward. It was weird, but in a good way. Rare times like these made me think the other shit was sometimes all worth it.

It was late by the time we went through all the World Cup teams' stats and determined each one's potential for getting to the final. I finally started getting ready for bed. After a shower, I took a couple more Motrin, and Dad retaped my side. Once I was in bed, the day began again, flowing quickly through my head. I smiled at Rumple and how she had gotten a PK past me and then cringed as I heard her story again. I remembered the way Frankie talked about her in the lunchroom, and I recalled stories about him using similar tricks on girls at parties. It never made sense to me; he could have gotten pussy anyway. I didn't understand why he did that shit.

The thought that he could try that on Rumple just fucking pissed me off. I pushed the thought away. If I thought about it too much, I'd never get to sleep, and I had to pick Rumple up in the morning.

I closed my eyes as the game replayed in my mind in full color HD, and I watched Tim Howard make another fantastic save. I wanted to capture it on paper…but I didn't. I didn't want to take the chance right now because I had other, more important things to keep hidden.

⟫••◦◖◉◗◦••⟪

I didn't know why I felt nervous when I left my house to pick up Nicole. I mean, I had already taken her to school once though that hadn't been planned, so I guess I hadn't had a chance to get nervous. We had also been late, so there hadn't been anyone to see us. This time was different. We were going early with the sole purpose of making sure everyone who was hanging out around the parking lot saw us come to school together.

It was a bright and sunny day, and I pulled a pair of Ray-Bans out of the glove compartment before I got out of the car and knocked on Nicole's door. I fidgeted from one foot to the other and glanced down to the side of the porch. The second pot of mums I had left her was planted in the flowerbeds there. I smiled and wondered if I should say anything about them as Sheriff Skye answered the door.

Not what I was expecting.

"Oh…um...hi," I blathered. "I'm here to pick up Nicole."

"Yeah, I've heard," he grumbled. He opened the door wide and signaled me in with a grand gesture of his arm. I walked into the little foyer and heard Nicole's footsteps on the stairs. "For the record, I think your little 'plan' is a little 'insane'."

He used finger quotes. Huh. Who would have thought?

"Oh…she….she told you about it?"

"Yep."

"Oh." I was in complete loquaciousness fail.

"Come on," Nicole said as she hoisted her backpack over her shoulder. "Let's get this over with."

"It's not that bad, is it?" I asked. I thought it was a pretty good plan, really.

"No," Nicole said.

"Yes," Sheriff Skye said.

"Shit," I grumbled.

Nicole rolled her eyes and walked past me and out the door. I followed, remembered what I was supposed to do, and ran around her quickly. With a bright smile, I opened the passenger side door and gestured her inside.

"You're really serious about this, aren't you?" she said.

"I don't want anyone bothering you," I told her. "They won't as long as they think we're together."

"We'll see."

We drove in silence. As we approached school, there were kids all over the fucking place. I pulled around to one of the front spots and put the car in neutral before turning it off.

"Ready?"

"No," Nicole replied, "but let's do it anyway."

"Stay there," I reminded her. I pushed my door open, got out, casually stretched my neck and nodded to a couple of people as I walked around to the other side of the car. I could feel their eyes on me as I opened up Nicole's door, reached in, and took her hand to help her out.

I could even hear the gasps. I could practically hear what they were thinking.

"Come on, baby," I said quietly—but not *too* quietly.

Nicole stood, bit down on her lip, and started walking slowly. I placed my Ray-Bans over my eyes, tossed my arm around her waist, and smiled at everyone around me as I escorted my Rumple into the school. Nicole pretty much stared at the ground, only occasionally glancing up at those around us.

"Why are they all looking at us?" she asked under her breath.

"Malone doesn't *date*," I told her. "Everyone knows that. I sure as hell have never brought a chick to school in my Jeep before. Well, not in the front seat."

I snickered but quickly silenced myself when I saw her glare and realized how prickish I sounded. I offered her an apologetic shrug, which was met with eye rolling. Hoping I hadn't blown it already, I pulled her a little closer to my side as students began to fill the hallways.

"Where's your locker?" I asked.

"It's number 8420."

"Okay," I said. "Mine's 7289—right over here. Stop here first?"

"Okay."

Nicole fiddled with the strap of her book bag while I twisted the combination lock. I opened the locker and carefully hung my bag on the back hook, pushing it against the back wall so it didn't stick out too much. I pulled out the green folder where I kept my homework and then straightened the books lined up at the bottom.

"You have got to have the most organized locker I have ever seen," Nicole said.

"I don't like things out of order," I said with a shrug. I pushed against the twisted up edge of one of the books. It still kind of bugged me. I should have gotten a new one. While I was doing that, Nicole reached around me and pushed at the spine of one of the books, leaving it askew.

"Hey!" I exclaimed. I grabbed the book and lined it up again. "Don't do that."

Nicole giggled. *Giggled.*

I glared at her.

"Oh, this is going to make things interesting," she said softly.

"Don't push your luck," I said with a growl, but I couldn't glare at her for long when she looked up at me all innocent-like and bit down on her lower lip. "I'm being the nice boyfriend. You have to be the nice girlfriend, too."

"I don't recall agreeing to specific terms," Nicole said with a raise of her brows. She leaned close to me. "You are a fool, dear Thomas."

I smiled down at her, closed my locker door and wrapped my arm around her shoulders as we went down the hall. I noticed the looks some of the guys were giving her, but a stern glare from me had them staring at the ceiling pretty fast. I was going to have to put a clear end to that kind of shit. No touching, no talking, and no looking at my Rumple.

Mine.

I was going to have to keep the wolves at bay.

We rounded the corner and Nicole flipped the combination lock until it opened. Inside, her locker was a total disaster. It hurt just to look at it.

"How can you even find anything in there?" I asked as she dug around in a pile of papers, shuffling things from her book bag, which I realized was equally catastrophic, to the locker and vice versa.

"I have my ways," she mumbled with her head still inside the metal cabinet.

"It's a fucking mess!" I said.

"Fuck you," she snapped back.

I felt an involuntary twitch as I turned up the corner of my mouth a little bit, and my head cataloged other times people had uttered the same phrase to me. It had always been met with either indifference or violence. Rumple, though—she just amused me.

When she was done orchestrating the movement of disaster one and disaster two from one place to another, I wrapped my arm back around her and led her down the hallway to her literature class. People continued to stare with open mouths, and Nicole continued to hide behind her hair. When we got to her classroom door, I pulled her over to the side and backed her up against the wall. I held her hips and she looked up at me with wide eyes. She was definitely a little nervous.

I leaned close to her ear.

"Relax," I whispered. I reached up and pushed her hair back behind her ear. She tensed a little but then seemed to take my advice to heart.

"Easy for you to say," she mumbled back.

I looked down at her, trying to ignore the throat-clearing from some of the students as they walked close to us. My eyes dropped to her mouth for a second, and I remembered again the feelings I had when I woke up with her—primarily, the desire to kiss her. My tongue darted out over my lips, and my eyes met hers again.

"Everything is good," I told her. "I'll be here right after your class is over, okay?"

"If you say so." She sounded about as convinced as a collection agent talking to a guy about his back child support.

"I do," I replied. I tried to keep my eyes off her lips as best I could. I wanted to kiss her. It seemed natural, like I should have kissed her right then.

But we hadn't talked about anything like that.

Fuck.

"See you soon," I finally said. Nicole nodded. I released her, and she walked into the classroom.

Once I saw she had settled down toward the back of the class, I started heading for my Shakespeare class. Before I got very far, I felt a hand on my shoulder and looked up into Clint Oliver's face.

"Malone!" he said with a smile.

"Wassup, Clint?"

"I was going to ask you the same thing, man!" he said as he leaned in toward me like a co-conspirator. He was talking way too fucking loud for anything to be secretive.

"Don't know what you're talking about," I said. I sped up a bit as I pushed his hand from my shoulder.

"You and the Skye girl!" he yelled. As if I didn't know what he meant. He quickened his pace to keep up with me. "I thought you already tapped that bitch! Since when do you go back for seconds on pussy?"

I froze in the middle of the hall, stopping dead in my tracks and bracing myself as some freshman plowed into me and then backed away with wide, frightened eyes. I barely noticed him. I clenched my hands into tight fists and barely resisted the urge to just turn around and beat the living shit out of Clint right there where he stood.

I had a better idea.

"Come with me," I said coldly.

"Where are we going?" the idiot asked.

"Locker room," I replied as I took off again. There was no first period gym, so it would most likely be empty.

"What for?"

"I need some practice," I replied.

"But it's first bell..."

"So what?" I turned to him and leveled my eyes with his. He nodded slightly and followed me as I knew he would.

He'd follow me after today as well.

We entered the locker room and found Mika Klosav in there, smoking a cigarette by the showers.

"Hey, Thomas!" he called out. "Did you really bring Nicole to school?"

Actually, his presence was fucking perfect.

"Shut the fuck up," I said with a growl toward Klosav. Then I turned to Clint, but I didn't speak to him.

I grabbed Clint's shirt by the collar and threw him against the lockers. I didn't let go but pulled him back and slammed his head against the metal. I punched him twice in the stomach, causing him to double over, but more importantly, taking the wind out of him so he couldn't fucking talk. I reached over and opened one of the tall lockers, shoved him inside of it, and then slammed the door in his face. I could hear him yelling, but I didn't give a shit about the words, so I didn't really listen.

Pain seared down my side, but I didn't fucking care.

"Malone…what the fuck?" Klosav dropped his smoke and took a few steps toward me. I turned and snarled wordlessly at him, and he stopped in his tracks.

I fished a padlock from the bin, twisted the key to open it, and returned to the locker, flipping the lock through the little ring by the handle while Clint continued to yell. I backed up and kicked the center of the door, denting it slightly with my heel.

"Shut the fuck up!" I screamed at him. I twisted the lock and clicked it shut. "You keep your fucking mouth shut, you hear me, you little piece of shit? If I hear one more fucking SOUND from you, I'm going to rip your fucking throat out!"

I kicked at the door again, leaving another mark.

"I want to make one thing *absolutely…fucking…clear…*" I accentuated my words with continued kicks to the door. "Don't you ever…*ever* speak about Nicole like that! You don't talk about her. You don't touch her. You don't fucking *look* at her without my permission!"

I took the little key to the padlock and balanced it on the bench next to the row of lockers—right at the edge. I jumped up on the bench and placed my foot right on the edge and on top of the key. I pushed hard, leaning into it while trying to keep my balance. Once it was bent enough to be useless, I picked it back up, jumped off the bench, and threw it toward the showers.

Mika ducked to keep from losing an eye.

"Do you fucking hear me, Clint?" I slammed my fist into the damaged locker door.

"Fuck! Yes! I hear you!" he screamed back.

"You hear me, Klosav?" I turned and snapped at Mika. "Is it perfectly fucking clear to you, too?"

"I got it," he said quietly, his eyes wide.

"Make sure everyone fucking gets it!" I turned on my heel and stormed off.

I was only five minutes late to class, and the teacher was going over *Hamlet*. I ignored her glare as I walked to the back of the room and dropped down in my seat. I rubbed my bruised knuckles against my aching side. I couldn't concentrate on the teacher's flowing words. Inside my head, there was nothing but violence.

It scared me.

News about Clint spread pretty fast, maybe a little too fast. The first half of the day, I walked Nicole to all her classes, and everything went well. I had calmed down. No one was bugging Rumple. I had my arm around her, and by third bell, she was relaxing and not hiding behind her hair so much.

Lunch was a little different.

I was waiting for her outside of her calc class, but instead of walking over to me slowly and sliding up next to me as she had done during her previous classes, she stomped right past me with fire in her eyes. I turned and followed her, ignoring a couple of snickers behind me. She went straight into the lunchroom and stood in line. She didn't even turn back to look at me.

She was obviously pissed.

And it was just cute as hell.

"Something wrong, Rumple?"

"Don't call me that!" she snapped. She grabbed one of the orange plastic trays and slammed it down on the silver steel rails.

"Why do you always say that when you're pissed about something?" I asked. I moved up close behind her—not quite touching her but knowing she could feel my presence. "You don't usually mind me calling you that."

"I don't really want to speak to you at all right now, Thomas."

"Well, I haven't seen you for the last hour, and everything was good up until that point," I said. "Want to tell me what's gone wrong since then?"

"What did you do to Clint Oliver?"

"I shoved him in a locker and padlocked it," I said.

"And you hit him?"

"A couple times." I shrugged. "Not really hard or anything. It was mostly to shut him up. I did more damage to the locker."

She turned to me with a look of complete disbelief.

"What the fuck is wrong with you?" Nicole used that sort of whisper-yell thing that only girls seem to be capable of doing. "You beat him up and locked him in a locker? Why would you do that?"

"I didn't like the shit spewing from his mouth," I replied. "He was disrespectful. I reminded him to show me some respect."

"Christ, Thomas!" Nicole looked down at the banana on her lunch tray as she shook her head. "You beat a guy up!"

"He deserved it," I told her.

"Did you beat up Frankie Ronald and Mika Klosav, too?"

Oh shit. Forgot about them.

"Um…Frankie, yeah," I admitted. "Mika—not really."

"Not really?"

"I punched him." Again my shoulders went up and down. "Only once."

"Is that what you do all the time, beat people up when you don't like what they say?"

"Not always," I said. I pulled away from her a bit. I didn't like this…this having to justify myself. I never justified my own actions. I did what I fucking wanted to do at school.

"Why, Thomas? What did Clint do that was deserving of all that?"

"He was running his mouth," I said. "I already told you that."

"What did he say exactly?"

Well, I really didn't want to tell her the specifics. I promised to protect her from all that bullshit, and that's exactly what I intended to do.

When I didn't respond, Nicole grabbed a yogurt and a bagel

and slid her tray to the cashier. I dropped a Gatorade on Nicole's tray and slammed a twenty-dollar bill on the cash register. Nicole turned to glare at me as she put her wallet back in her book bag, shoved the Gatorade back at me, and stalked off with her tray.

She was actually starting to make me a little hard.

I followed her to a table and flopped down next to her. She leaned forward on her arms and turned her head away from me. I leaned forward, too, placing the side of my face on my arms and peeking up at her through her curtain of hair.

"Would it matter if I said I was defending your honor?"

"Not in the least!" she snapped back at me. "You can't just do that, Thomas! You can't just attack someone because they say something you don't like! They had to take the lockers apart to get him out!"

"That was the idea," I said. "How is he going to learn a lesson if he gets out right away?"

"What?" She turned to me with her eyes full of fire. "That's your idea of a teaching lesson, is it?"

"You're cute when you're mad," I told her.

"You have been, and continue to be, a total jerk," she replied. "I don't think I have ever met anyone who is as self-centered and obnoxiously egotistical as you are."

I moved closer, raising myself out of the chair a little so I could get close to her ear.

"Teach not thy lip such scorn, for it was made for kissing, lady, not for such contempt."

She glanced at me quickly, and I heard her breath stop in her throat. Her skin tone darkened for a split second before she scowled.

"Do you think quoting Shakespeare is going to make any difference?"

"A guy can hope, can't he?"

"You're incorrigible."

I had to smile.

"A little," I admitted with a shrug.

Nicole's look softened, and she turned toward me a bit. She looked at me quizzically for a moment as she took a bite of her bagel. I stole the spork for her yogurt and started tapping it against the side of her tray.

"Were you?" she suddenly asked.

"Was I what?"

"Defending my honor?"

"Maybe."

"What did he say?" she asked, and I could see the hurt in her eyes. That's exactly what I didn't want to see. I tucked the spork into the pocket of my jeans. I'd put it on the top shelf of my locker with the other one. I reached up to push her hair over her shoulder.

"It doesn't matter," I told her. "I said I would take care of it, and I did. No one is going to say anything about you again. I'm going to…"

I thought about it for a moment, trying to make sure I chose the right word.

"I'm going to protect you," I finally said.

She looked at me thoughtfully for a moment, nodded slightly, and then sat back in her seat with a sigh. I sat back, too, and then scooted my chair closer to hers. I slipped my arm around the back of her seat, and I leaned my chair back until it was casually balancing on two legs.

Maybe I had been out of line in barricading Clint inside the locker. Maybe Shakespeare would have said I was one to "imitate the action of the tiger." I wasn't sure, but at least I seemed to be forgiven at the moment.

We made it through the rest of the day and off to my soccer practice. Jeremy pounded me with free kicks from inside the box along with questions about Nicole.

"Since when do you kick ass for a chick?" he asked as he slammed another ball toward the goal.

I jumped and tapped the ball with my fingers, sending it far left of target, but landed on my left side in the process. I winced and pulled myself up to my hands and knees.

"Sorry, dude," he said.

"It's okay," I said as I tried to control my breathing. "It's really not bad...just when I hit it in a certain spot, you know?"

"I don't know," Jeremy said. "No one's ever broken my ribs."

"Rib," I corrected him. "Only one."

"Whatever." He looked at me for a minute as he dusted off the ball and tossed it back to the ground. I positioned myself just right of the center of the goal and crouched—watching the tension in his legs and hips...calculating which way he would move...which way he would kick.

"Okay, boys—let's scrimmage!" Coach Wagner's voice called out from the sidelines. Everyone started lining up in the center, and I looked over to the stands to see Nicole walking up and standing near the fence by the bleachers.

"It was an interesting little display this morning," Jeremy said quietly as we approached the rest of the team. "Want to explain that one?"

"Clint's an ass who needed to be smacked down," I replied with a shrug.

"Over a girl?

"Fuck you."

Jeremy just chuckled in response.

We lined up, and I ended up on the skins team. I jogged over to the fence, toward Nicole, and pulled my practice jersey over my head.

"Why don't you hold on to this for me," I said with a wink as I tossed my shirt in her direction. Nicole rolled her eyes.

"It smells godawful," she remarked.

I smirked as I stretched my arms behind my back and then leaned to each side in turn.

"Your rib okay?" she asked suddenly as her eyes moved to my taped-up side.

"It's all right," I answered. I raised an eyebrow. "You worried about me?"

"You wish," she snarked right back at me, but her tone was

teasing.

I glanced at the other girls lined up on the bleachers, looking over me and the other guys on the team. They huddled together, whispering and giggling.

"You could join the other groupies," I said to Nicole as I nodded my head toward the crowd.

"That's okay," she said. "The high school soap opera news of the day was not completely in my favor, you know."

"What do you mean?"

"Well, your overzealous behavior may have kept the guys at bay," she said, "but the girls are a whole other story. Or are you planning on beating them up, too?"

"Do any of them need it?"

"For goodness' sake, Thomas…"

"Just kidding," I said with a smile and a half-grin.

"They all want you," she said quietly, "and by default, none of them want anything to do with me now."

"I told you I wouldn't let anyone hurt you," I reminded her. "I meant that. If any of them bother you, you let me know. It won't happen again."

Nicole looked into my eyes for a moment and seemed as though she was going to say something before the coach's voice interrupted us.

"Malone! Would you mind getting into position?"

I ignored the coach and leaned against the fence a little harder.

"We'll be done in about a half hour," I said. "We can talk about it then, okay?"

"I guess," she said. She glanced quickly over her shoulder to the group of girls, who were now watching us intently.

She turned toward me again with a defeated look on her face. I reached out and touched her cheek with the back of my knuckles—just skimming her skin quickly from her cheekbone to her chin and leaving a tiny, muddy mark on her face.

"Soon," I said softly, and then I turned and jogged back to the goal.

Shakespeare might have wondered, "For why should others' false adulterate eyes give salutation to my sportive blood?" Somehow, she had to eventually understand that what I did was for her and her alone, and that I didn't care what anyone else said about it.

Now, how do I convince Rumple of that?

relegated

The scrimmage had to be cut short because of a fight.

Not on the field—in the stands.

I had the ball in my hands and was just about to kick it downfield when I heard the yelling. I glanced up and saw Rumple and some of the other girls up on the bleachers, screaming at each other. I threw the ball out of bounds, ran up, and jumped over the fence, ignoring the coach's words to get back on the field. I had to scale two rows of bleachers before I could reach Rumple.

She had gone all "lioness" on Crystal Lloyd.

Meow.

"Maybe he just prefers someone who isn't quite so skanky!" Nicole was yelling as I got there. She had her fingers curled into claws, and her jaw was clenched. I was pretty sure there was a little sparkle of a tear in the corner of her eye, too. I didn't know what to think of that.

"One reason and one reason only," Crystal was saying as her head bobbed around on her neck. She jutted her chin out at Nicole and put her hands on her hips. "Is it still sore, or were you already used to it?"

"You little bitch!" Nicole suddenly screeched, and she started scrambling over the bench to get to where Crystal was sitting with Lisa and Heather.

Thankfully, I got to her first and wrapped my arm around her middle, effectively capturing her and pulling her back against my chest.

"Let me go!" she screamed. Claws out, she grabbed at my arm around her waist. I wound my other arm across her arms and chest, holding her tighter and keeping her from being able to use her arms effectively. I took a step backwards and over one of the benches, pulling her with me. "Dammit, Thomas! Let go of me right now!"

"Not just yet, kitten," I told her.

"Is that about the right position?" Crystal yelled.

"Fucking bitch!" Nicole screamed back. "Jealous little skank!"

"Whoa there," I said as I tried to calm her down a bit. I wasn't the least bit successful, and she continued to struggle against me. I had to get her away from the other girls before she actually hurt me.

"Oh, she definitely let him," I heard Crystal saying to the other girls.

"It does explain a bit, huh?" Lisa said with a giggle.

"Innocent little act of hers didn't last long, did it?" Heather nodded in agreement.

Wasn't she bitching at me yesterday for talking smack about Nicole?

"Klosav!" I yelled out. Mika jogged over and reached us just as I got Nicole out of the stands and back down on solid ground. She kept struggling and trying to punch my arm, but I held tight. "Go shut your girl up. Get Jeremy and Clint, too."

"No problem."

He'd been hanging all over Heather since she asked him to the dance, so I figured he could do a little something to help out. The rest of the team was just standing around watching and trying to figure out what they were supposed to do next. Coach Wagner was trying to get them to pull it together, but everyone was focused on what was going on in the stands.

"Dump her ass if she won't play nice!" I called back up to Mika as I kept pulling my kicking, screaming kitten backwards away from the field. I didn't wait for his answer because it was right about then that Nicole managed to land a kick to my shin, which nearly took me down.

That shit *hurt*!

"Holy shit, Nicole!"

"I told you to let me go!" she yelled with another snarl.

"We'll figure that out later," I told her. I placed her feet on the ground just long enough to get a better grip on her, spun her around, and tossed her over my shoulder. It made it a lot easier to hold her legs, which really were pretty damn strong.

I carried her across the field, into the parking lot, and to my car despite all her protests. Dropping her ass down into the passenger seat, I blocked her way so she couldn't get back out. Eventually, she stopped screaming at me and started to calm down.

"You want to tell me what that was all about?"

"Just what I said before!" Nicole snapped.

"What did she say to you?"

"It doesn't matter!" She pulled her legs up to her chest and covered her face with her arms. Her shoulders rose and fell as she took deep breaths. I was pretty sure she was trying to stop herself from crying.

"Obviously it does," I replied. I crouched in front of her and touched the edge of her knee with my finger. She pushed my hand away.

"Take me home!" she finally yelled.

"I will," I said, "but my keys are in my soccer bag, which is back at the field, so you're going to have to wait a minute. Will you stay right here for two minutes while I go get my shit?"

Rumple huffed and crossed her arms over her chest, lioness turning back into a kitten. She still had her claws out, but at least she wasn't screaming for blood anymore.

Meow.

I took my own deep breath. Her display was kind of turning

me on, and I was pretty sure that was a bad idea right at that moment. I stood and placed my hands on the roof, leaning in close to her. She looked up at me, and I could see the tears in her eyes.

"I'll take care of it," I promised. "Let me take care of it, okay?"

"I'm not coming back to your practices." She was adamant.

"I'm going to fix that, too," I said. "I should have thought of it before, but that will be fixed before tomorrow. You'll have someone else to sit with who won't give you shit, and those bitches aren't going to bother you again."

"Are you going to play another round of locker stuffing?"

"No, I have other ideas, though."

"Like what?"

"I'll tell you on the way home," I told her, "as long as you tell me what Crystal said to get you so fired up."

Nicole promised to stay in the car while I went back to the field to grab my soccer bag and my practice jersey from the ground. I looked up in the stands and was glad to see exactly whom I wanted to talk to at the moment. But first, a quick call.

"Hey, Malone."

"Everything you can find on Harry Lloyd in the next five minutes. Call me back."

"Will do."

I hung up and stared at my phone for a minute as I collected myself. I tapped the app store, found a set of ringtones that sounded like meowing kittens, and set my phone to use them. I tested it out, snickered to myself, and then took a few leaping steps up into the bleachers.

The scrimmage was obviously over, and everyone was either milling around the field with Gatorade bottles in their hands or had moved off to the bleachers. Mika and Jeremy had Heather and Lisa off to one side, and Crystal was standing near them with her hands on her hips. I couldn't hear what they were saying, but I wasn't looking for them right now anyway.

"Hey, Ben!"

He looked over at me with his eyes narrowed a little. Ben was a midfielder, and though there was nothing flashy about him, he was a decent player. He was a quiet guy with a quiet, shy girlfriend. She was in the bleachers with him, silently reading a book while he rehydrated.

"Hey, Thomas," he said with his usual, soft tone.

"I need a favor."

Just like Shakespeare wrote in *The Merchant of Venice*, I was going to have all of this fixed "in the twinkling of an eye." I'd promised Rumple everything was going to work out, and I intended to keep that promise. I just needed a little assistance from my teammates. I hoped this would get Nicole to trust me—this *was* my school, after all, and I was in charge. I only needed to secure some backup.

"Ben, you and Maria are about to get some steady company."

<hr />

My phone rang on my way back to the parking lot, making little kitten sounds that were realistic enough people were looking at my soccer bag like it had a litter in it. I snickered again, dropped my soccer bag to the ground, and fished the phone out.

"What do you have on Lloyd?"

"A couple things. One, he's trying to get a school loan."

Ah, yes…I had a pretty good idea who would need such a loan, too.

"That's a good one."

"He's also on heart medication—sounds like he had a mild heart attack last winter."

"Okay—anything else?"

"That's all I got for now. I'll see what else I can find."

"Good deal."

I hung up and turned back around, searching. No time like the present.

"Hey, Crystal!" I yelled. She was walking back toward the school with Heather and Lisa. Mika and Jeremy were still near the stands, watching them walk away. "Get over here!"

She turned her head toward the other girls, who snickered, then tossed her hair over her shoulder and walked toward me.

"Ready to see some reason, Thomas?" she said with a sly little smile.

"Funny," I replied with a hint of sarcasm, "I was going to ask you the same thing."

"It's not my fault if she can't handle the truth." The snarky little bitch bobbed her head at me as she raised her eyebrows, challenging.

She was going to regret all of this.

"Come over here," I said softly, and I took her arm and led her over to the side of the building and out of sight of anyone else wandering around. I leaned my head close to her and spoke sternly. "Let's get something perfectly straight between us, and I am by no means talking about my cock. You aren't coming near that."

She snorted, and I gripped her arm a little harder.

"Ow!"

"Shut up."

"What the fuck, Thomas?" she snapped at me. "Are you going to shove me in a locker, too?"

"No, I have much more interesting plans for you," I informed her.

"You aren't going to hit me," she said with conviction. She narrowed her eyes at me. "You can't do anything to me!"

I leaned into her, pushing her body back against the brick building. I tilted my head and placed my mouth right up to her cheek.

"You know what would be a damn shame?" I purred against the edge of her ear. "If your dad's credit report ended up with a bankruptcy on it—and some really bad credit card debt to boot. I bet he'd have a hard time trying to pay for your college then, wouldn't he?"

"What the fuck are you talking about?" Crystal pushed against the bricks, twisting her body and trying to get a little distance, but I wasn't going to have any of that. She glared at me.

"I mean with one phone call and about ten minutes, I can fuck up your dad's credit score so bad, he'll never get the loan he wants. Never. It won't ever go away, because even if he gets it cleared up as a mistake, which wouldn't be until you're twenty, I'll just fuck it up again. You hear me? That little 'get out of the small town' dream of yours would be dead on arrival."

Her face went a little pale.

"Not to mention how much it would suck if the pharmacist screwed up his heart pills."

"What the hell?" she said in a breathless whisper.

"Don't fuck with me, Lloyd," I warned. "Consider yourself relegated – you no longer play in this league. If you try, you'll lose, big time. And by don't fuck with me, I mean don't fuck with my girl. You stay the hell away from her because if she hears one more thing from your mouth—directly or indirectly—I'll fucking destroy your family. Got it?"

Her body tensed, and she nodded. I released her arm and gave her a little push back toward the school entrance.

"Get the fuck away from me!" My nostrils flared as I glared at her.

She didn't need to be told twice. I retrieved my bag and continued on my way.

Nicole had calmed down a little by the time I got back to the car. She was sitting with her feet up on the seat again, and I tried not to cringe. I remembered what her locker looked like and decided I was going to have to do something about it. I settled into the driver's seat and turned the car on before I looked toward her.

"You okay?" I asked.

"Not really," she replied. She stared out the window.

"What did she say?"

"I really don't want to repeat it."

"You said you would," I reminded her.

"I didn't agree to anything," she snapped as she turned her head to look at me. "Besides, even your own conditions included you telling me what you were going to do. You go first."

"Fine," I said, grateful for the out. "Forget it, then. She won't say anything else to you."

I backed up and pulled out of the parking lot and onto the street. I still kept my speed at twenty-four miles per hour, crawling along and enjoying just being in the car with her. Nicole leaned her head back against the seat and sighed.

"You know, it's bad enough just coming to a new school during your senior year," she said. "Now I have to deal with all this shit, too? Seriously, Thomas—I don't know if I can handle all of this."

She held her hands over her face again, which I really, really hated. Aside from not being able to see her face—which I quite liked to look at—she was obviously upset, and I didn't know what to do about it. She had taken care of me when I was a mess, but I didn't know how to return the favor. All I could cook was mac and cheese. So I did the only thing I could think of, which was to try to convince her I would take care of it without actually giving her any details. I didn't think she would care for the details.

"I'm going to work something out, okay?" I said, trying to reassure her. "Please, just let me work it out. It's going to be okay, and you don't have to worry about it. Tomorrow will be a thousand times better. I just didn't know what to expect today, and I didn't prepare so well. I'm fixing that now."

At least she didn't argue.

Nicole stayed silent the rest of the way to her house. I pulled up into her driveway and had a nice mental debate about whether or not I should turn off the car and walk her to her door, plan to stay awhile, or just leave her alone. I didn't want to leave her, but I also hadn't checked Dad's schedule for this week.

For the chance to spend more time with her, I was willing to risk Dad's beating me home. I turned off the car and came around to her side, but she had already opened the door and was starting to get out.

"I thought I was going to open your door for you," I reminded her.

"We're not at school, Thomas," Nicole said. "There isn't any reason to pretend here."

I nodded, but I didn't like it. I wanted to open her door for her even if there wasn't anyone looking. I wanted to take care of her. I came up with an excuse instead.

"It's good to stay in practice," I said, hoping she would believe me. I had to move quickly to follow her up to the front door. "You know, so we don't forget when there are other people around? This won't work if it's not convincing."

"I think everyone is convinced," Nicole said dryly.

"For now," I said, but my mind was starting to spin a little bit with the other sorts of things people were going to expect. I mean, I would expect to end up with at least the threat of detention for PDA or something, not an actual detention—which no teacher in his or her right mind would give me—but at least the warning. The whole idea reminded me that I never did hear what Crystal's exact transgression was.

"What did she say to you?" I asked.

Nicole didn't respond for some time and then finally let out a long sigh.

"Are you going to tell me what you said to her?" Nicole asked.

"That conversation is not on my bucket list," I admitted.

At least that got a bit of a snicker out of her.

"Let's just leave it like that, okay?" she suggested.

"If you want," I replied. I wasn't really worried about it; I could always find out from someone else.

My pocket meowed.

"What the hell is that?"

"My new ringtone," I said with a shrug. I checked the screen and saw a text from Jeremy but decided to ignore it for now.

"I'm going to finish my homework and get dinner ready," Nicole said. She opened the front door and then turned to face me. "Thanks for driving me. See you tomorrow morning?"

"Yeah, of course," I said. I had kind of hoped she would ask me to stay, but I reminded myself that this was all pretend. There wasn't anyone watching her now, so there was no reason for her to be around me. The façade could continue again tomorrow.

The phone meowed again, and I pulled up the message app.

Took care of the girls—Jeremy

Good I don't want any more shit from them

I shoved the phone into my pocket, not feeling any better about any of it. My stomach felt like it was turning to stone as I walked back to my car by myself, started the engine, and headed for my house. All the way there, I tried to figure out why it was getting me down. Even after fucking girls, I never felt bad about leaving them in the dust afterwards, and I had hardly touched Nicole.

I kind of wanted to, though. Maybe that was the problem.

Dad had beaten me home, so I mentally prepared myself as I approached the house.

"Why are you fucking with Harry Lloyd?" Dad asked as soon as I walked in the door.

I had to play this cool, so I just shrugged.

"His daughter is being a bitch, and I'm sick of it," I told him. "I needed something to shut her up. I'm pretty sure just the threat was enough."

"Make sure you talk to me before you actually do anything," Dad said. "I need some shit from him, and I don't want you fucking him over until I get it."

"No problem."

I put my soccer stuff away and started digging around for dinner. Dad sat at the counter in the kitchen and watched me.

"Got any homework?"

Yeah…not falling for that one.

"Well, I have to pick up Nicole Skye on the way to school tomorrow so I can sign my name," I said with a smirk. "Does that count?"

He laughed.

"Nice job." He opened up his phone and started scrolling

through the screen. "How was practice?"

"Good," I said. "Cut a little short, but we'll make it up before Friday's game."

"Hmm." He obviously wasn't really paying attention, so I got myself some food, finished it up, and headed up to my room without further conversation. Once I was up there, I locked the door and decided to quickly finish my homework. I was obviously going to have to make sure he didn't catch me doing it, or there would be hell to pay.

As soon as I turned my eyes toward the room, I knew he had been in here.

There was a CD sticking out a little, and it definitely hadn't been when I left. My pillow wasn't straight on the bed, and the drawer to my nightstand was open just a tiny bit. My skin felt cold. Dad had obviously been in here, looking around—looking for *something*. What? What could he be looking to find? What did he suspect?

I went over to the nightstand and knelt down near the stack of *Goal* magazines. The one on the top was two months old. They were out of order, and they weren't stacked up as high as they were before. I picked them up, started sorting them again, and discovered quickly what was wrong.

My sketchbook was gone.

I closed my eyes and tried to keep my breathing slow and steady. It didn't work, though. I could feel the tension in my muscles and the quickening of my pulse throughout my body. My fingers were trembling, and I had to set the magazines down on the floor. I couldn't stand that, though, so I quickly sorted them again and stacked them back on the nightstand shelf.

Maybe he only moved it.

I quickly scrutinized the room, looking for other changes. It was getting harder and harder to take a deep breath, and my chest hurt.

The bookshelf—I straightened out the six books that weren't parallel anymore.

My dresser—two of the soccer trophies on it weren't level with the others.

The leather couch up against the window—it was sticking out a little farther, and I could see the slight dent in the carpet from the legs. I moved it back into place.

What else? What else?

I couldn't stand it. He wasn't supposed to come in here, and he wasn't supposed to touch anything. Everything was wrong now, and I just couldn't handle the disorder. Nothing was right. Nothing. *Nothing.*

I needed my sketchbook back.

I opened the door and headed back down the stairs, trying desperately to keep my calm. I couldn't ask him for it—there was no way—so I just had to find it.

I failed.

There wasn't any sign of it in any of the trashcans—inside the house or outside.

I went back to my room, but I couldn't stand to be in there. It was just wrong now. There were too many things to fix. I moved the clock back into its position on top of the nightstand, noting that it was nearly ten-thirty. I didn't realize so much time had passed.

What else was wrong? What else was missing or out of place?

I glanced around the room. I couldn't focus. I needed to go to bed, but I wasn't going to be able to sleep here. No fucking way.

Tip-toeing back down the stairs, I shuffled through my soccer bag for my keys, opened the front door as quietly as I could, and got into my car. I didn't really think about where I was going though my destination was completely clear to me.

I had only one place to go.

The light from the computer monitor created a soft glow from the other side of Nicole's window. I had parked where there was an old logging road, and my car wouldn't be visible from the street, and now stood on the grass right below her window.

Looking around, I found a handful of pebbles on the ground and tossed them one at a time at the window until Nicole looked out.

"What the hell are you doing?" she asked.

"Can I come in?" I called back.

She let out a sigh as she rolled her eyes.

"Go around to the door," she grumbled.

I made it to the porch just as Rumple opened the door. She was dressed in a gray T-shirt and shorts and was obviously about to go to bed.

"What are you doing here?" she asked.

"I can't be in my room right now," I said, begging her with my eyes not to ask. She must have heard my silent plea because she looked me over, sighed, and then motioned me inside the house.

"Be quiet," she whispered. "Dad's a heavy sleeper, but if he saw you…"

She really didn't have to say anything else. Every time I thought about Sheriff Skye, I pictured him with a gun bulging out from his belt. I knew he'd never risk doing something to me in a premeditative way, but if he thought he was protecting his daughter, I'd be shot before he thought about it at all.

We crept upstairs and into Rumple's room. She turned off her PC monitor and motioned toward the bed. I watched her as I tried to decide exactly what I was supposed to do now. It felt like I was suddenly playing on offense, and I couldn't remember how to handle the ball with my feet. I had no idea what to do.

Thankfully, Rumple seemed to know.

"Come on," she said with an exasperated sigh. "Get in."

Perhaps Shakespeare would have said I "should suffer salvation, body and soul." Somehow, I thought Nicole could be my salvation.

Now what if she didn't want to be?

CHAPTER TWELVE
practice

After I took off my shoes and socks, I climbed into Nicole's bed and put my head on her pillow. Even before she lay down next to me, just the scent of her surrounding me seemed to calm my nerves. Once she was there beside me, and I wrapped my arm around her waist again, my world came back into focus. When her hand came up to my face, and her fingers tangled in my hair, I felt like I could take a deep breath again.

"What did he do, Thomas?" Nicole whispered. With the lights off in her room, I could only just make out her features in the dark.

Somehow, that made it easier.

"He was in my room," I said quietly. "I just… It's stupid, I know, but…"

My voice trailed off.

"What?" Nicole pressed.

"He moved stuff…took stuff. Everything was out of place."

Nicole was quiet for a moment while she seemed to contemplate what I said.

"That really does bother you, doesn't it?"

"Yeah," I admitted. "Your locker just about gave me a heart attack."

She laughed quietly through her nose and stroked my temple.

"But you aren't freaking out being in my bed even though I never make it?"

"Yeah…it's okay," I said and realized I meant it. "It smells good."

"It smells good?" she raised her eyebrows.

"Yeah," I replied. "It smells like you."

I felt my face get warm, which was strange. The darkness probably hid the fact from her, and I was good with that.

Nicole was quiet for a few minutes, and I closed my eyes halfway, just lying there and thinking about how it felt when her fingers curved in a little, and her nails lightly scratched my scalp.

"What did he take?" Nicole asked after a while.

"It was nothing, really." I shrugged. "Just my sketchbook."

"You draw?" The shock in her voice made me tense. I never talked to anyone about my sketchbook or anything I had ever drawn, and I didn't want her to think I was a pussy about art or anything.

"Not really," I said, trying to backpedal. "I mean, not seriously or anything. I just kind of…doodle, I guess."

"Why would he take it?"

"He doesn't want anything to distract me from soccer," I told her. "He's just looking out for me—I know that. He just wants to make sure I keep my focus, but there were some sketches…well, I just didn't want them gone. I don't know what he did with them."

"How is *that* looking out for you?" Nicole said with her voice full of venom.

"I want to go pro," I said, shrugging again. "If I let other things get in the way, then my chances of getting on the right team aren't as good. If you are going to be the best, be the fucking best. I'm not going to settle for anything else."

Nicole scowled at me.

"What team is the *right* team?"

"Real Messini."

"Really?" Nicole scoffed. "Thomas…they don't even scout in

the US."

"They do now."

There was a long pause before Rumple spoke again.

"What do you mean?"

"They're coming to watch me play in two weeks," I said.

"Are you serious?" The pitch of her voice increased, and she sat partway up in the bed, looking down at me. "They're looking to replace William?"

"Yeah, eventually."

"Holy shit," she mumbled. "Thomas, that is huge."

"That's why he doesn't want anything else getting in my way," I explained. "He just wants what's best for me."

"Taking your sketchbook and breaking your rib are what's *best* for you? How well are you going to play with a broken rib?"

I cringed, feeling my muscles tighten all over. I closed my eyes, as if squeezing them shut could force the images out of my head.

"He didn't mean to," I said. "It was an accident."

"Bullshit," Nicole mumbled.

"Please…don't." I'd beg her if I had to. I couldn't talk about this.

She lay back down and traced her fingers over my cheek, down to my jaw, and then up into my hair again. She started pushing the stray strands behind my ear, and I felt my body melt into the mattress.

"All right," she said.

"It will be better by then, anyway." I shifted a little to get into a more comfortable position, and my hand slid down her side. My fingers grazed over her bare skin where her shirt had ridden up a bit. I probably should have moved my hand on top of the material again, but instead I slowly traced little circular patterns on her skin with the pads of my fingers.

I looked back to her eyes, and even in the dim light, I thought she was about the most beautiful girl I had ever seen. She might not have the glamour of some model-types, but she had something more natural—more undeniably *feminine* about her. She also had strength—not just in her body but in her spirit.

And her skin was really, really soft, and it made me wonder if her lips were as soft as the skin on her side. That's when I remembered something I had been thinking about earlier in the evening on my way home from dropping off Nicole.

"Hey…um…Nicole?"

"Yes?" she replied. "I am the only one here, you know."

"Heh…yeah." I felt one side of my mouth involuntarily turn up a little. I licked my lips and took a breath before continuing. "I was just wondering….um…"

I paused.

"Spill it, Malone," Nicole said with a grin.

"Um…you know," I started and then stopped again. "I mean, um…I was thinking…you know people are going to expect us to… well…to act like boyfriend and girlfriend, right?"

"Yeah," Nicole said with wary eyes. "Quit stalling. What do you mean *exactly*?"

Turning my head back against the pillow, I stared up at the darkened ceiling for a second before I rolled over and just looked at the pillowcase instead.

"Well, I was thinking at some point…I mean…it would only be natural…" I stammered on, unable to complete an actual sentence.

"Thomas, will you just spit it out?"

Why was this so hard? I usually just fucking grabbed the girl and kissed her when I wanted. What was it about Rumple that made everything so different?

"We ought to kiss…you know…in front of people," I finally blurted out. I looked back at her, and Nicole's eyes widened a little. I just hoped and prayed she wouldn't tell me to get the fuck out.

She just lay there staring at me, so I kept on babbling.

"So…I was kind of wondering if we should…um…practice."

"Practice?"

"Yeah," I said. I moved my eyes away from hers again and stared at my hand at her waist then back at the pillow. "Like, we should try kissing…so it doesn't look awkward if we have to do it in front of other people."

I kept my eyes trained on the pillowcase, wondering if it was more of a tan or beige and mostly just trying not to meet Nicole's gaze at all. I was tensing up again, but only a little bit because she still had her hand in my hair. She hadn't moved away from me yet.

"Okay," she whispered.

The pillowcase was definitely losing its appeal, so I looked back at her.

"Now?" I asked.

"Um…yeah."

I tried to keep my heart from leaping right out of my broken ribcage.

I ran my fingers against the skin at her side, gripping her lightly as my gaze danced involuntarily from her mouth to her eyes. I shifted my head, rubbing my cheek against the pillow a little before I rose and moved a few inches closer. I looked at her eyes, dilated in the darkness, but clear and bright…beautiful. I looked back at her lips…ever so slightly parted and releasing her breath just a little quicker than before.

I traced my tongue over my bottom lip and focused solely on what she was going to taste like. I grasped her side just a little bit tighter as I pulled her slightly toward me. Nicole's hand slipped behind my head.

I moved closer, and I could feel her breath against my mouth. I could even taste it. Inhaling through my nose, I let her scent wash over me as my eyes closed, and I eliminated the final, minuscule distance between us.

My lips met hers.

So, so soft.

My head was spinning in circles. My skin rose in goose bumps, and everything around us faded and disappeared from the senses. There was no sound, no sight, no feeling outside of the slight contact between our lips.

Warm.

She tasted like she smelled…heavenly.

Pushing just a little, I molded my lips around hers, kissing her again. Her fingers tightened their grip in the hair at the back of my head, pulling me tighter against her mouth. I heard and felt her muted gasp.

I didn't stop. I kissed her again, softly and slowly, moving my lips in sync with hers. It was as flawless as when we danced together. It was as flawless as the ripple of her thighs as she swung her leg, contacted the edge of the ball, and pinned it in the corner of the net.

Nicole shifted, pushing herself up a little, pressing my head down against the pillow. Her mouth wrapped around my lower lip, sucking on it gently, and it was my turn to moan. My fingers slid up her back, under her shirt, and teased along her spine. I felt the arteries in my thighs start to pump more blood to my cock as it pressed against her leg.

So, so good.

Nicole pulled back, breaking our contact, and I had to stop myself from whining. For a long moment, we just looked at each other. Both of us were still breathing quickly, and my heart continued to race in my chest. She was still very, very close…I could have reached out with my tongue and still touched her mouth.

"Do you think that was good enough?" Nicole's whispered words brushed my lips with her breath.

"I'm convinced," I said. I closed my eyes, mentally cataloging the last thirty seconds under the best fucking seconds of my life. I went over and over it…again and again. Every touch, every breath, every beat of my heart, every twitch of her fingers...everything. When I opened my eyes again, I looked into the deep, beautiful blue irises next to me, and I knew I didn't want to pretend anymore.

I wanted her to feel it.

Really feel it.

This wasn't any old game anymore; it was the fucking World Cup to me.

I don't know how long we lay there just looking into each other's eyes. I actually lost track of the time. Nicole's hand stayed against the back of my head, and my fingers continued to trace lines up and down her lower back. It wasn't awkward or strange just to be looking at her in the darkness of her room. It felt natural and right to me.

"It's late," Nicole finally said.

I nodded but felt a slight sense of dread, too. Was she going to send me away? It was nearly midnight after all.

"Dad usually gets up around six, and I don't really want to have him walk in here and see you before I have a chance to talk to him, so I'm going to set the alarm for five, okay?"

"Yeah, that's good," I agreed. "It's not like I brought a change of clothes or anything."

I tried to laugh it off.

"Well, remember that for next time," Nicole replied.

"Next time?" I felt my heart rise into my throat, and I swallowed before speaking again. "You mean...I could come back?"

Her fingers flipped my hair off my neck.

"Anytime you need to," she said quietly.

One of her fingers began tracing back and forth over my jaw, and I felt my eyes start to close. I felt tingly and warm, as if I were nearly asleep already. Nicole's hand left my skin, leaving it cold, and I opened my eyes again. I watched her lean over and adjust the alarm before she reached back to me and tucked a bit of hair behind my ear. She seemed to focus on the strands as she wove her fingers through them.

"I need a haircut," I said, and I smiled a little.

"I like it this way," she said.

Okay...no haircut then. I was good with that.

Nicole settled back against the pillow, and I did the same. I opened my hand so my palm lay flat against her back. She wrapped her hand around my hair at the back of my head and stilled. She blinked a few times, her eyelids getting heavy.

"Nicole?"

"Hmm?" She didn't open her eyes.

"Thank you."

"You're welcome, Thomas," she said with her eyes still closed, but the corners of her mouth turned up in a smile. "Go to sleep now."

I closed my eyes and watched the day go by, making sure to stop for that precious thirty seconds a few times before my mind settled and dropped into unconsciousness. At some point in the night, I woke up again. Nicole was still lying on her side, facing me, with one of her legs tossed over mine. I felt warm, comfortable, and…

…safe.

Here—in her house, in her bed, with her—I felt as if nothing could touch me. It felt as if *he* couldn't touch me as long as I was within her arms. I tried to remember the last time I felt this way, and all I could recall were quick flashes of times with my mother. Those times when we sat at the piano and she would sing while I poked at the keys she pointed to on the keyboard…those were like this.

I drifted back off again.

Nicole's alarm awakened me early enough to get home and complete my daily run before Dad even woke up. As far as I could tell, he had no idea I had left the house at all. I showered and shaved quickly before jumping in my car and driving back over to Nicole's house.

I had actually gotten a decent night's sleep, which didn't happen often. I usually needed a good-sized cup of black coffee before I was really awake in the morning but not this day.

I felt *good*.

Nicole rolled her eyes at the gesture but still waited for me to go around the car and open the door for her once we got to school.

I kept my arm around her shoulders as we walked in, only letting go of her briefly when we stopped at each of our lockers.

Hers still made me cringe. I hadn't done anything about it yet.

Nicole was a little nervous as we walked through the halls, but no one said anything, and the sheer number of people outright staring at us dwindled. I left her at her first class just as the bell was ringing but not before I leaned in and gave her a very quick kiss on the side of her mouth.

"See you soon."

I glanced over my shoulder at her as I walked off, unable to stop myself from smiling as I saw her look back at me before she went inside the classroom. I saw Ben on my way to my first class, and we got lunch all worked out between one hallway and the next. By the time I led Nicole into the lunchroom, Ben and Maria were already sitting at one of the round tables, waiting for us.

"What's this?" Nicole asked under her breath as I took her to the already occupied table.

"Ben's on the team," I said with a shrug. "Maria's his girl, and she's usually at practices. I thought you guys could sit together or something."

"So, what? You're choosing my friends for me?" Nicole snapped at me. When I looked at her, her eyes were narrowed.

"No," I said. I paused in the middle of the lunchroom to try to figure out what the fuck she was talking about. "I just figured you'd like her, and she's usually there…"

"And that's *not* choosing my friends in what way?"

"What the fuck, Rumple?"

Nicole closed her eyes and breathed forcefully out of her nose.

"We really need to talk about this," she finally said. "Let's just…get it over with, but after practice, we really, really need to talk."

"Okay," I said, still not having a fucking clue as to what was going on, "whatever you want."

She glanced at me and seemed to share my confusion for a moment. Then she turned toward the table and went to sit down.

I had been right; Rumple and Maria did hit it off. They both liked the same books, and though they didn't have any classes together, they seemed to have the same subjects at different periods and were already making plans to work on their homework together while Ben and I practiced. I still didn't know what she wanted to talk about after practice, but I figured it couldn't be that bad.

Of course, she didn't give me the chance to find out.

As soon as the team started walking off the field, Nicole was motioning me over.

"Sorry, Thomas," she said, "but I have to run. A friend of mine is picking me up. I'll see you in the morning."

"I thought you wanted to talk," I reminded her.

"Um…yeah," she said. She ran her hand through her hair as she stared over at the parking lot. "I know, and we do, but really—I just overreacted a bit. I'm sorry about that. We'll talk about it later, ok? I really gotta go."

"What friend?" I asked as she started heading away from me. I don't think I could have hidden my disappointment if I tried.

"Just a friend," she repeated, "but I do need to go."

And with that, she was gone.

I went to the lockers for a shower, talked to the guys for a few minutes but never really heard much of what they said. I'd listen to it all in my head later just in case there was something important. I didn't understand Nicole's need to see a friend so urgently. I couldn't help myself, so I drove past Nicole's house on the way home. Her car was there, so I stopped.

No one answered the door, which I guess shouldn't have surprised me. She said someone was picking her up. As I turned to leave, Sheriff Skye's patrol car pulled up.

Shit.

I started back toward my car and then stopped as he got out of his. Then I took a few more steps toward my car and then I stopped again, having no fucking idea if I should stay or go.

"Thomas," Sheriff Skye said with a nod. "Nicole won't be

home for a while, I think. She told me I was on my own for dinner."

"Oh, um…sorry," I said. "I didn't know…I mean…I wasn't sure where she was, so I didn't know when she'd be back…so…um…yeah."

Damn, I sounded like a fucking moron.

"She's in town for the evening," he said.

"Oh," I replied. Yep…failed on the old loquaciousness again.

Sheriff Skye stood there with his arms crossed in front of him and a smirk on his face.

"Your father working late at the hospital tonight?" he asked suddenly.

"Yeah," I said with a nod.

"Well, considering we're both on our own for dinner, how about I order us a pizza?"

"Oh…um…well…" More stammering. I sounded just like I felt—like an idiot. "That's okay, really. I should be going…"

"Thomas," Sheriff Skye said as he dropped his arms and motioned toward the porch, "I'd kinda like to talk to you."

Oh shit.

This couldn't be good, could it?

Shakespeare's *Julius Caesar* ran through my head: "He thinks too much: such men are dangerous." Somehow, even though he never had affected me in such a way before Nicole arrived, Sheriff Skye was scaring the shit out of me.

Now, what did he want?

CHAPTER THIRTEEN
equalizer

I tried not to look as scared as I felt as I walked into Nicole's house with her father. The place did *not* feel the same as it did when I was with her alone in her room. Sheriff Skye walked into the kitchen, opened the refrigerator, and pulled out a can of beer.

"Have a seat, Thomas." Sheriff Skye dropped into a recliner, and I perched on the edge of the couch cushion, wondering if it was possible for my balls to rise back up into my body post-puberty. They sure as hell felt like they were trying to. Sheriff Skye continued eyeing me for a little while as he tipped his beer back a few times. He finally put it down on the TV tray next to the chair and leaned forward a little with his arms across his thighs.

"You were in my daughter's bed last night, Thomas."

Oh fuckity fuck, fuck, fuckity fuck, fuck, fuck.

I couldn't exactly lie at that point—he obviously knew—but what the hell could I possibly say that wouldn't get me into a shitload more trouble than I was already probably in?

"I didn't...I mean...I was, but I didn't do anything. I...I..."

He still has his gun on.

A cold chill ran up my back and down my arms. I was having a hard time drawing air into my lungs as if my throat was closing up on me.

He stood up.

Oh fuck…

"Thomas…son?" I heard his voice and saw him take a couple steps closer to me.

"I wouldn't….do anything to her…" I still couldn't breathe. "I didn't! I swear I didn't!"

"I know you didn't," he said. "Nicole told me all about it."

A whole other chill took over at that point as I wondered just what Rumple told him.

"All about what?" I whispered.

"She told me you were upset about something and came here last night. I didn't get any of the details as to why, but I got the idea you weren't in the best of places at the time."

My throat relaxed, and I could breathe again, so I took a really deep breath all at once, nearly choking myself.

"Hey, Thomas?"

"Yeah?"

"Can you keep a secret?"

"Um…yeah," I said.

Sheriff Skye went over to a small table by the door leading to the back yard and opened up the center drawer. He stuck his hand way in the back and pulled out a pack of Marlboros and a box of matches.

"Don't say anything to Nicole, okay? She'd string me up."

I laughed from relief more than humor.

"Want to step outside with me a minute?"

"Okay."

He opened up the back door and ushered me out. A small set of steps led down to a cement patio in the back of the house. A couple of potted plants flanked the door, but there were no chairs or anything, so we sat down just outside the door on the top step. Sheriff Skye leaned back against the side of the house and lit one of the cigarettes from his pack with the flick of a match on his thumb.

It was kind of intimidating.

He stared at me a moment then offered up the pack. I met his eyes, trying to figure out if this was some sort of test. Did he do this with every kid who came over here just to see if they were underage smokers?

Then I remembered I was eighteen.

I still hesitated before taking one, trying to at least keep the shaking to a minimum, then allowed him to hold a second match up for me. I inhaled the smoke and let it burn my lungs as Rumple's father began to speak.

"I was supposed to have quit years ago," he told me. "I don't do it often, but every once in a while, it's good for calming the nerves."

"Yeah," I agreed with a nod. "I don't…um…smoke much, either."

"Wouldn't be good for your running times, would it?"

"Ah…no, it wouldn't." I wondered how he knew about my running times but didn't get the chance to ask.

"We need to set some ground rules here, Thomas," he said. "I know this is all supposed to be some kind of elaborate ruse, and maybe it is…"

He looked at me out of the corner of his eye as he took a deep drag before continuing.

"But I kind of doubt it."

Somehow, he knew I was more interested in her than I had let on. He was also asking me to keep his secret, but did that mean he would keep my secret, too, or was he going to tell her what he suspected?

"How much did Nicole tell you about why she left Minneapolis?"

"Enough," I replied.

He nodded.

"I realize you don't know what it's like to be a father," Sheriff Skye said, "but the hardest thing I ever did was not to jump on a plane and commit murder after I got that phone call. The second hardest thing I ever had to do was respect Nicole's wishes not to press charges and see those two hung. Well…at least in juvie for a few years."

"She didn't want to do anything about it?"

"Nope," he replied. He looked out across the back yard and into the darkening trees of the forest beyond. "She was too embarrassed, for starters. She was also doing something illegal at the time and could have been prosecuted as well. She wanted it all behind her, not dredged up over and over again."

I hadn't really thought about her reasons, but from what I knew of her, it all fit. She didn't want people in her business, and having something like that all over the media would kill her.

"I realize you haven't known Nicole very long, but I want to tell you a little about my daughter," the sheriff said. I nodded and tried to make myself look busy with my smoke. "She was always an independent thing, even when she was little. She would get her mind set on something, and it damn well better work that way, or there was going to be hell to pay. That girl has a temper."

"Heh!" I snorted. Yeah, I was aware of the kitten's claws, no doubt. Sheriff Skye chuckled, too.

"You've seen that side of her more than once, huh?"

"Yeah," I replied, and I could have sworn I heard him say "good" before he went on.

"When I went to Minnesota after that…'incident'," he continued, "the girl I found there wasn't my daughter, or at least not the one I knew. She was timid and scared, and she always waited for someone else to tell her what to do. She never took any initiative. As if there were any way I could have been angrier over everything…"

He paused and shook his head before he continued.

"Seeing her act like that…It just wasn't my girl."

He shoved the butt of his cigarette into the dirt beside him and pulled out another one. I still had half of mine left since I hadn't really been actively smoking it. All I could do was listen to him and try to picture my Rumple that way.

"Then I found out something else from her mother," Sheriff Skye said, "and I was almost as pissed off at my ex-wife as I had been at the two who did that to her."

"What?" I asked when he didn't continue right away. "What did she say?"

"She told me Nicole wasn't like that from the…from what had happened to her. She said Nicole had been acting like that for months—ever since she started dating that schmuck."

I stood up and took a few steps onto the patio. I stared at the bright spot at the end of the cigarette as I inhaled. The sheriff looked off into the woods again while I thought about what he said. I tried to picture Rumple all quiet and waiting for someone to tell her what to do, and I just couldn't see it. Why would she act that way?

"I still don't know exactly what he said or did to her to change her behavior like that," Sheriff Skye said, his words echoing my thoughts. "She doesn't talk about it, and I just hoped bringing her here and away from all of it would help her get *herself* back. I hadn't really seen any signs of her… signs of that girl I knew the last summer she was here… signs of the daughter I used to have... not until the other day."

"What other day?" I asked.

"When she came back from town, found you sitting on the front porch, and started tearing you a new one."

The scene ran through my head again. She sure had been pissed off to find me there. I smiled a little.

"Yeah, I thought so," the sheriff remarked.

"Thought what?" I asked. I looked at his face to find him smirking.

"Kinda cute that way, isn't she?"

My face felt a little warm even in the cool fall breeze near the woods. I smiled at the thought of Rumple all ticked off and coming at me, kitten-claws extended and teeth bared. Yeah, she definitely was kind of cute that way. More than cute.

"Seeing that," he went on, "was when I knew bringing her here had been the right choice. I gotta thank you for that, son."

"You're glad I piss her off?" Was I hearing him right?

"I'm going to guess just by the way you said that, you piss her off a lot, don't cha?"

I nodded.

The sheriff laughed.

"Then I think you just might be good for her," he finally said after he stopped laughing. "Tell me something else, Thomas."

"Okay," I said.

"Do you care about my daughter?"

All hints of a smile left my face as I looked into his eyes. I noticed how similar they were to Nicole's—not just in color but in their expressiveness and the feeling that you could see right into their owner's soul if you looked long enough.

"Yes, sir," I replied. "I do."

He nodded.

"Let me ask you something else," he said as he sat up a little straighter and looked at me dead-on. "Was the last woman you ever cared about your mother?"

I swallowed past the hardening lump in my throat, but it only landed in my chest and started hanging out there. I reached up and rubbed deep into my eyes with my fingers then dropped my hand down and ran it over my thigh instead. I looked back at him, back into his eyes.

"Yes," I said.

"Then maybe Nicole is good for you, too."

We stared at each other for a moment, and I suddenly wasn't as concerned about his potential ground rules as I had been a little while ago. I had no idea what he was going to demand, but at least it didn't sound like it was going to include the words "Get the fuck away from my daughter before I blow your brains out."

A few minutes of silence went by while I thought about what Sheriff Skye had said. I admitted that I cared about her, and he was quite right—I'd never given a shit about any of the other girls I had been with in the past. I honestly didn't care if I ever saw any of them again. I didn't want them dead or anything; I just didn't even think about them at all.

Nicole was different; I thought about her all the fucking time. It was downright annoying, really. If I thought back to the day I first walked her around the entire school, I probably couldn't come up with too many hours that had gone by when I didn't think about her at least once.

My Rumple.

"All right, Thomas," Sheriff Skye finally said as he ended our silence, "it's time to go over the rules."

He straightened his back up against the wall and looked me over.

"Okay," I replied. I mean, what else could I really say? I tried to buckle down and mentally prepare myself. I even attempted to avoid thinking about what I was going to do if he out-and-out forbade me from being in her room or something, but that was even more difficult to imagine.

"When Nicole first told me about you coming over last night and ending up in her bed, my first reaction was you belonged on the damn couch. If you need a place to stay…well, I wouldn't ever turn you out, but that place doesn't mean my daughter's bed."

My eyes dropped to my feet, and I took a deep breath as I tried to imagine sleeping on their couch downstairs while Nicole was up in her room. I didn't like it much, but he didn't leave me hanging for too long, either.

"But I got the idea from her that wouldn't work so well," he continued. "So, you can stay in there with her, but the door stays open."

My eyes went wide as I realized what he was saying. He was giving me permission to sleep with his daughter. Well, not *sleep* with her…but…damn. Just…*damn*. Okay, so having the door open wasn't all that great, and it might be kind of weird, knowing her dad could look in and see me in there with her, but it was better than the alternative.

I looked up at him and nodded.

"I'm pretty good with that," I said honestly.

"And no throwing rocks at the window, for Christ's sake," he said. "I don't need you breaking glass or sneaking around. If it's too late to knock, there's a key outside. Nicole can either show you where it is, or you can call her to come let you in—I'll leave that up to her."

"Okay," I said with a bit of a grin.

"And don't you dare eat all of her cooking and leave none for me," he added.

I laughed.

"Deal," I replied.

"There's one more thing," the sheriff said, his expression turning serious. "And as far as I'm concerned, it's the most important one."

"What's that?" I asked. My palms started to sweat a little, and I wiped my hands down my pants.

His eyes darkened as he looked at me over the smoke trails.

"Don't you hurt her, son," he said, his voice approaching deadly. "She's been hurt enough."

I nodded solemnly.

"I'm not saying I expect you to make sure she lives happily ever after. From personal experience, I know how relationships at your age can come and go. If you two go your separate ways, I know she'll be upset for a while even if she's the one to break it off. I wouldn't hold that against you, but don't you hurt her like that other kid did. Don't you betray her trust. Don't you use her for your own self-gain. You do something like that, and I don't care who your father is, I won't stand by and take it."

"I won't," I promised.

I meant it.

"And for God's sake, Thomas," he added, "if you guys become more than whatever the hell you are now, don't have sex with her when I'm in the house. That would just be…really, really awkward."

I'm sure my eyes about bulged out of my head, and I might have eventually come up with some kind of response, but the sound of wheels on the gravel driveway out front caught our attention first.

"Sounds like the pizza is here," Sheriff Skye said. He stood up and took a last drag off his cigarette just as the front door opened up.

"Dad? Is Thomas here?"

"Aw, shit!" Sheriff Skye jumped high enough to tap a ball over the top of a goal, smashed out the cigarette butt, grabbed all of the butts together, and shoved them underneath an upside down flowerpot off the side of the porch. I had the idea if Nicole found those cigarette butts, I'd be seeing *that side* of her again.

Was she going to notice? I looked him over quickly.

"The pack's sticking out of your pocket," I told Sheriff Skye.

He reached up and placed his hand over the left pocket of his shirt and covered the pack and his heart at the same time. He grabbed the pack out of his pocket, looked around frantically, and then threw the pack into the shrubs at the side of the house.

"Here's goes nothin'," he said as he opened the door with a plastered smile on his face. "Hey, Nicole!"

He waved frantically while still standing in the middle of the doorway. I just kind of hid behind him, not really understanding the dynamic between the two of them and not entirely sure I wanted to be there right at that moment.

"Hi, Dad," she responded. She tilted her head to peer at me and then looked back to the sheriff.

"Hey there!" he called out. He actually waved while still standing in the middle of the doorway. "How's Ron and Timmy?" He danced back and forth between one foot and the other, which made me realize I was doing the same thing. I stopped, and then his words hit me.

Ron and Timmy? Who the hell were they?

"Dad!" she snapped at him with narrowed eyes. He just kind of shrugged at her but stayed in the doorway. I wondered if she could already smell smoke on him.

Nicole took a few steps forward, and Sheriff Skye nearly backed up into me.

"What are you two up to?" Nicole asked.

"Nothing," Sheriff Skye said. He finally walked through the door and skirted around her to sit back in the recliner. "Just some guy talk, ya know?"

"No, I do not know," she replied. "What *is* that smell?"

"Um…smell?"

"Dad!" Nicole yelled. She shook a finger at him. "You said you quit!"

Well, that didn't take long.

"You know how much I hate that," she went on, "and as soon as I'm away from the house? Seriously?"

"It was me," I piped up, "not Sheriff Skye."

They both looked at me, Nicole looking confused and Sheriff Skye just looking like he was trying to catch flies. I nodded my head frantically and even went as far as pointing to myself.

"You—" she started, but the Sheriff interrupted before she could continue.

"Oh no, son," the Sheriff said as he shook his head quickly back and forth, "I can't let you do that."

He looked back to Nicole.

"I know, I was supposed to have quit, but…"

"It was me!" I insisted. "I was a little stressed out, you know? I didn't know why you ran off so quick. I thought I might find you here, but you weren't and…"

I trailed off and shrugged, hoping that was as much of an explanation as she would require.

"I…had something I needed to do," she stammered a bit. "But —"

"He's just covering for me." Sheriff Skye jumped in again. "Really."

"Am not," I insisted. "It was me, Nicole—really."

"Thomas, you don't have to—"

"I'm not!" I said.

"You are—"

Sheriff Skye and I looked at each other, and the absolutely flabbergasted expression on his face was just too much. I busted out laughing, and that set him off as well. Then I couldn't stop, and it was actually starting to hurt my side. I wrapped my arm around myself and bent over a little but still couldn't stop even though I kept saying "ow, ow, ow."

Sheriff Skye put his hand over his mouth to stifle himself and ended up just spitting through his fingers.

"Oh my God, I cannot believe the two of you!" Nicole yelled. She looked at each of us in turn with her hands on her hips and a pretty evil-looking glare in her eyes.

We kept laughing.

"You know," Nicole said, looking back to her father, "I came back, figuring I would make dinner for you, but you know what? You can just forget it now! Order a damn pizza or something!"

Nicole stomped up the stairs and slammed her bedroom door, leaving us staring at the stairs, our mouths open in awe.

"You gonna tell her we already ordered one?" I asked.

"Oh, *hell* no," he replied. "I might cry when I eat it, just to make a point."

"What point?" I asked.

"Not really sure," he replied, "but it will probably make her feel vindicated."

Shakespeare probably would have mentioned at this point that "the commons here in Kent are up in arms." Somehow, I thought Sheriff Skye would have preferred a horde of angry villagers to the wrath of his daughter.

Now, would she also notice how quickly the pizza got delivered?

CHAPTER FOURTEEN
own goal

"So then she comes out of the kitchen," Sheriff Skye was saying through his chuckles, "and she has the gigantic hunk of Swiss cheese in her hands. I mean, it's about as big as her head— and there are these little teeth marks all over it and a trail of cheese bits all over the floor…"

I laughed again, trying to keep from choking on my last bite of pizza. I took a big swig of Coke to wash it down and ended up with bubbles in my nose. The sheriff thought that was particularly funny, and we both started laughing hard again.

Nicole walked in the kitchen and glared at both of us, then glared at the almost empty box of pizza, and followed up with a good nasty look at the empty beer and Coke cans, stacked in an elaborate pyramid on the kitchen table. Without a word, she walked over to the refrigerator and started pulling things out. There was a green lumpy-looking thing and a yellowish-orange thing that might have been a fruit of some kind. She got busy chopping things up on a cutting board and basically ignoring the two of us.

"Hey, Rumple," I said softly, hoping maybe a little Malone charm just might do the trick. I was rewarded with the daggers of hell out of her eyes instead. I tried smiling, but she wasn't buying it. She slammed her hand down on the counter instead.

"Don't call me that!"

"What are you so mad about?"

"What, the sneaking out for cigarettes and lying for each other isn't good enough?"

"Well…it could be worse," I offered.

"You better shut your mouth, son," Sheriff Skye said under his breath, "or she's going to remove something important to you."

"You're right," Nicole said softly as she nodded to me. She smiled sweetly, and I glanced at the sheriff and gave him a little wink. It didn't make me feel too secure, though, when he shook his head slowly and planted his face in the palm of his hand.

"Well, considering the budding 'bromance' you two seem to have going on," Nicole sneered, "I guess I'm lucky I didn't walk in on anything else!"

Sheriff Skye spit beer onto the pizza box, grabbed for it, and knocked the entire can pyramid onto the floor. Nicole turned on her heel and started gathering up whatever the hell she was making. Sheriff Skye looked at me and raised his eyebrows before nonchalantly taking another bite of pizza and another swig of beer. I had to bite down on my lip to keep from laughing again. I glanced over at my Rumple-kitten, but she obviously wasn't going to look at us. I went back to my pizza, but things were pretty quiet except for the noise from a couple of cans that were still rolling around. Nicole finished making herself some elaborate salad or salsa or something like that, warmed up what looked to be fresh bread, put it all on a plate, and huffed at us on the way out of the kitchen.

We busted out laughing as soon as she was out of earshot.

"I have never heard that word before," Sheriff Skye said, "but I don't think I approve."

I snickered.

"I should probably go talk to her or something, shouldn't I?"

"At your own risk," he replied. "Though I think it's really me she's pissed at."

I took a deep breath to prepare myself, got up from the table, and made my way upstairs. Her door was closed, so I did a little more deep breathing preparation before I knocked.

"What?"

"Can I come in?"

"No."

"Aw, come on, Rumple," I said. She didn't respond, so I started knocking again. She ignored me, so I started knocking to a beat, playing a little hip-hop rhythm on her bedroom door until she finally flung it open and glared at me again.

"You are so annoying," she stated, but she left the door open as she went back inside and sat down at her computer desk.

"What are you doing?" I asked.

"Emailing my mom."

"Oh." I didn't really have much else to add, so I fidgeted until she finished typing, sighed, and looked back at me. I tried to give her the most sincerely apologetic look I could conjure up. "I wasn't trying to piss you off."

Nicole's eyes dropped down to her plate, and she pushed some of the fruity-looking bits around for a minute.

"I'm not mad at you," she finally said.

"You aren't?"

"Not really," she said. She poked around at some of the green morsels on her plate. "It's just been a rough day."

"So why did you have to leave before practice was over?"

"I really don't want to talk about that."

"Oh." I scratched at the back of my head. "Um…well, who are Ron and Timmy?"

"Really, Thomas," she said as she looked back to me, "I don't want to talk about it, okay?"

"Okay," I replied though I didn't mean it. It wasn't okay at all. If anything, I wanted to know even more now. I guessed I would have to do my own digging. I continued to scratch my head a bit more and then looked back to see her wiping her cheek. "Hey…"

She shook her head and waved at me dismissively as I took a

step toward her.

"Really, Nicole…I'm sorry…" I didn't know what else to say. I hadn't meant to piss her off or make her sad. What had I done? What was I supposed to do now? "I feel like I just tipped the ball into my own net. What did I do?"

"It's not you," she said as she wiped away more tears. She stood up and seemed to be getting ready to clear her tray away when she suddenly turned to me, wrapped her arms around my shoulders, and started crying.

I had no fucking idea what the game plan was. Was I supposed to make a move here, comfort her, like she had me? I didn't even know what the hell was wrong.

My mind replayed everything that had happened since she got home—the smoking, the goofing off, the pizza—everything. I couldn't come up with a particular thing that would actually make her cry. I thought back to school—she had been pissed that I had kind of arranged lunch, and given what Sheriff Skye had said, I guessed it made sense—she just wanted to make her own decisions. I was okay with that.

Would that make her cry?

I didn't think so, but I really didn't know.

After scouring my brain for any little tidbit to clue me in, I gave up and just put my arms around her. Her face was buried in my chest, and I just held her while she cried, wondering what the fuck I did. After a few minutes, she wiped her face with the back of her hand and seemed to quiet down. I didn't know what else to do, and she didn't seem to be moving away, so I just kept my arms around her and waited. Eventually, she spoke again.

"Sometimes it just all gets to me, you know?" she said.

I had no idea what she meant, but I nodded anyway.

"I didn't mean to take it out on you," she whispered.

"It's okay," I replied.

"It's not," she disagreed. "I shouldn't do that to you. I am still pissed at Dad, but you were just covering for him. I have no idea why you were, but—"

"I wasn't, really," I admitted. "I did smoke one, too."

Upon hearing that, she took a step back from me and looked up into my eyes.

"You were smoking?"

"Um…yeah?"

"Thomas, you're an athlete…"

"Yeah, I know," I said with a shrug. "I really don't do it very much. I mean, almost never."

The look in her eyes was…confusing…and heartbreaking. She looked like she was about to start crying again. There had to be more to this.

"Nicole, why does that piss you off so bad?"

She dropped her forehead against my chest again before she answered.

"The guy I dated in Minnesota smoked," she said quietly. "It just…makes me think of him."

Shit.

That was, in fact, about the last fucking thing in the world I wanted her to be thinking about. Ever. I definitely didn't want her thinking about him when it came to me.

"Nicole?"

She sniffled again and didn't look back at me. I took a step closer to her and wrapped one arm around her waist, bringing her close to me.

"Rumple?"

She finally looked up, and there was fire in her eyes again, but only for a second.

"I won't do it anymore," I told her. "Really, I never did it very much anyway. If it reminds you of…of *him*, then I won't do it anymore. I swear."

"You won't?"

"Not a single one. There are a few in my soccer bag. You can throw them out yourself if you want."

She continued to stare up into my eyes, but I wasn't sure exactly what it was she was seeking. I just looked back at her because her eyes were just really, really pretty and I found it hard to look away from them.

"Would you really do that?" she asked. "No more?"

"No more."

"For…for me?"

"In a heartbeat," I replied.

"Why?"

"Why what?"

"Why does it matter to *you*?" she asked. She seemed somewhat irritated…or maybe just confused.

"That's a very good question," I replied. I gave her a half smile. "I guess it just does."

"You hardly know me," she informed me, refusing to just let it go. "Why would you agree to do something like that for me? It doesn't make any sense."

As I thought about my response, I reached up and laid my hand on her cheek. I leaned forward and looked deeper into her eyes.

"I do desire we may be better strangers," I whispered to her. Her eyes widened a bit.

"More Shakespeare?" she said in a breathless whisper.

"*As You Like It*," I replied, "Act three."

Nicole's lips pushed together as the corners turned up.

"I guess we'll just have to work on that," she replied.

"I guess we will."

She looked at me again for along moment then took a deep breath and sighed.

"Sorry I was such a bitch," she said sheepishly. "It really didn't have anything to do with either of you, just my foul mood. Maybe I can make you both dinner this weekend. Kind of…make up for it?"

"Well, I don't know about the sheriff," I said, "but that would definitely work for me."

Nicole smiled brightly up at me, and my heart began to beat faster. Unfortunately, it was getting a little late, so after Nicole made nice with her dad and said goodbye to me, I headed home.

Sheriff Skye shook my hand as I left.

"Thanks for the entertainment," he said with a goofy smile, which was made even goofier by the way his moustache jumped around.

"Thanks for the pizza, Sheriff Skye," I replied as I headed off the porch and toward my car.

"Hey, Thomas!" he called after me.

"Yeah?"

"Call me Greg."

I think I was smiling all the way home.

Dad's car was there when I pulled in the driveway, but when I got inside, he was in the living room and on the phone. His eyes met mine for a moment, and I gave him a slight wave. He just looked back to some notepad he had on his lap and kept talking.

I went up to my room, closed the door, and locked it. I looked around quickly, but everything was in place, so I could breathe again. I pulled my T-shirt up over my head, dropped my jeans to the floor, and pulled a pair of soft flannel pants out of the drawer. I picked up the dirty clothes, folded them, and placed them inside the hamper. It was getting full; I needed to do some laundry.

"Thomas!"

"Yeah, Dad?" I opened up my door and peered down the stairs.

"Where's the garment bag and the bigger suitcase?"

"Down in the basement," I said. "Do you want me to find them?"

"Yeah."

I went all the way down and poked around the closets in the lower level until I came up with the two pieces of luggage he wanted. I hauled them back up the stairs and into his room. He was pulling clothes out of drawers and laying them out on top of his bedspread.

"Are you going somewhere?" I asked.

"Chicago," he replied. He got down on his hands and knees

and peered underneath his bed. "I'll be leaving right after the game tomorrow."

"Conference?"

"Hospital administration consortium," he replied.

I wasn't really sure how that was different, but I didn't press for an answer, either.

"When will you be back?"

"Saturday," he said. He stuck his hand far back underneath the bed and started feeling around.

"Just an overnight trip? To Chicago?"

"No—a week from this Saturday," he corrected me. "Why would I fly all the way to fucking Chicago for a day, and who would hold a fucking consortium meeting on a weekend?"

I shrugged.

"So…you're gone a week?"

"Didn't I just fucking tell you that?" he snapped. He dragged a pair of dress shoes out from under the bed and smacked my foot with the heel of one of them. I jumped back as he stood up with it and shook it at me. "Don't be so fucking stupid."

"Sorry," I mumbled and quickly got myself out of there. I sat down on my bed once the door was locked again and rubbed at my toe. It was all right. I looked at the clock, seeing that it was still about an hour before I usually went to bed, and I looked at my nightstand out of habit. I took a big breath—maybe I could replace my sketchbook while he was gone and find a better place to hide it.

A week with Dad out of town actually sounded pretty good.

"Thomas, get back in here!" I heard him yell from his room. I got back up and made my way over there.

"Is this the red garment bag?" He stood there, glaring at me.

Well, considering the luggage in his hand was blue, I kind of doubted I was supposed to answer the question. I just shook my head a little.

"I wanted the red bag, Thomas—the *red* one. This one is too small! Now find me the one I want!"

"I'll find it," I said quietly and ran back down to the basement.

I knew my dad was only trying to do what was best and only wanted to make sure I was always on top of my game no matter what I was doing. I wasn't just making excuses for him in my head. There was a lot more to it than what was outwardly visible. He couldn't do everything he did and not be the very best at it without focus, and I'd dropped my focus. He said red the first time —anyway, that's what I told myself.

The question was—did we even own any red luggage?

Friday morning.

I fucking love Fridays.

Fridays with Rumple walking into school at my side were ten fucking times better than any other Friday that had ever occurred before.

I tossed my arm around her shoulders after she got out of my car and smirked at her sideways as I led her into the building. A bunch of people came up to me and wished me luck in the game tonight, and it felt as if the giant number one on my chest was shining like a freaking lighthouse beam. You would think it was, the way it drew people over to me. It made my skin tingle with warmth, and something about having Rumple there sharing it with me just made it that much more fucking awesome.

People crowded around my locker as we stopped there, and I pulled Nicole close to me as they chattered about the last time we played Preston High, squashing them two-to-zero. Nicole just kind of pushed her body against mine and didn't really say anything. Well, to be honest, no one really said anything to her either.

Finally, people walked off, and we were able to move on to her post-apocalyptic locker and then to her first class. I stopped outside the door and leaned back against the hallway wall. I placed my hands on her hips and brought her close to me. She glanced up and caught her lip in her teeth.

"You still gonna make me dinner tomorrow, baby?" I asked her.

"Yeah…I thought I would," she responded. "I was thinking

about making something Italian since it's Dad's favorite. Do you like Italian?"

"Love it," I told her. I let my hands slide up her sides, then over her shoulders, and then all the way down her arms. Once I reached her hands, I wrapped my fingers around them and held them both next to her sides. Behind her, I saw Jeremy's sly look as he walked by and wiggled his eyebrows at me.

I leaned forward and placed my lips against her forehead. I'd done that a couple of times at school, but it was honestly starting to feel like it wasn't enough—like it wasn't something a real boyfriend would find satisfying enough. I still hadn't really kissed her in public…

…and I wanted to.

I tilted my head to the side and slowly inhaled the scent of her hair.

"What are you doing?" she asked quietly.

I held my arms out and behind me a little, but kept my hold on her hands at the same time, which brought her body up against mine. I rubbed the back of her knuckles with my thumbs.

"I'm just playing a pilgrim," I said softly as I leaned in closer to her. My lips touched the side of her chin lightly, and then I nipped at her jaw with my lips as I moved up closer to her ear.

"Playing pilgrim?" she questioned. I felt her shiver.

"Mmhmm," I hummed against her ear. "My lips, two blushing pilgrims, ready stand to smooth that rough touch with a tender kiss."

I gripped her hands a little tighter and then brought them up against my chest before I moved my arms back around her.

"Dear saint, let lips do what hands do," I whispered as I brought my lips to hers.

Warm again…

Soft again…

Mmmm…

I could have lost all semblance of consciousness when my mouth made contact with hers. Her fingers crawled up my chest and landed on top of my shoulders as she kissed me back, matching my light pressure and tilting her head to receive me. I moved one arm around her waist so I could hold her tight against me, and the other moved back up her arm and rested against the side of her face.

"Ahem! Mister Malone..."

I opened my eyes and glanced sideways. I recognized the short, squat man with the short, squat tie standing near us, but I couldn't remember the douche bag's name. Malcom, maybe?

"I'm busy," I growled at him,

"Thomas..." Nicole murmured. She pulled back a little, but I kept her held tight. "We're going to get in trouble."

"No, we aren't," I replied as I kissed her again. My hand moved to the back of her neck and I pulled her closer as I tilted my head in the other direction. Her mouth was so warm and felt so good against mine. I completed the kiss, blinked my eyes, and saw that Malcom guy was still gawking at us. I spoke a little louder. "Because if he says a damn word, I'll have his balls wrapped in a pink slip before the end of the day."

He coughed into his hand a few times but then moved away without saying anything else. I wrapped both of my lips around Nicole's lower one and sucked it into my mouth a little. At first, Nicole's head tilted and her mouth pressed harder against mine as a soft little moan escaped from her. But then I felt Nicole's hands pushing against my chest. She wasn't pushing hard, but I got the idea and backed off a bit though not very much because I really didn't want to stop. She tasted too good...and she was soft.

"You can't just threaten some poor guy's job just because you got caught in a PDA violation!" Her words and tone were harsh, but her eyes were wide, and she was still breathing a little harder than normal. I smiled.

"Yeah," I corrected her, "I can. Just did, actually."

The bell rang, and Nicole growled again. I couldn't help but smile because she was so fucking cute that way. I touched her lips softly with mine again.

"We are not done talking about this," she said as she turned away from me and went into the classroom.

I chuckled under my breath, arrived late to my Shakespeare class, answered the teacher's questions without opening my book, and finally went back to pick up Nicole again. She already seemed to have calmed down a bit or was at least most interested in the homework assignment she had forgotten in her locker. I steered her over that way and tried not to get physically ill at the sight when she opened up the door.

"Couldn't you at least throw out the papers you don't need?" I asked her.

"I need them all," she replied as she knelt in front of her locker.

"How can you even tell what you fucking need in that mess?"

She looked up at me from the floor and scowled.

"I've got my own ways," she insisted, but that was obviously bullshit, and I told her so. I walked her to her next class and decided I wasn't going to the practice field. I had something else to do.

I went to the office and conned the master key out of Mrs. Hope by telling her I couldn't get my locker open. The woman was way beyond cougar-ish with her batting eyelashes and near-retiree status. I smiled warmly, winked at her, and then rolled my eyes as I turned away and headed back to Nicole's locker.

I opened up her locker door and started going through all the stuff in there. Most of it was pretty current, at least, but it was only the beginning of October. If I didn't do something, what would it look like next semester? I shuddered at the thought. I sorted through the papers, lined up the books, and then went back to Mrs. Hope to convince her to loan me a few school supplies.

Once the period was about over, and I was about done, Nicole's locker looked almost as good as mine.

"Only one thing missing," I said to myself and then ran back to my own locker to get one of my soccer pictures from the top shelf. I taped it to the back of her locker and sat back on my heels with a smile. "Fucking perfect."

I was definitely going to have to get a picture of her for the inside of my locker and one for my wallet, too...or maybe for my car. I was also going to have to have someone take a picture of Nicole and me together to add to both of our lockers—I hated selfies. Maybe someone could get a good one of us at the game tonight.

I got a few looks from people as I headed down the hall to the front office. I figured it was because I couldn't stop smiling, but I really didn't give a shit. Hell, any of the guys who had seen my Rumple had to know why I was smiling—she was just too fucking fine, and she was mine. Nothing they could do about it.

Ha!

Fuckers.

I knew she would really appreciate the organization I had imparted and would be glad I spent the time to make it that way. I quickly took the key back to the office and headed back to Nicole's classroom. I poked my head around the doorway and smiled at her. She gathered up her stuff and walked out to meet me, and I grabbed her hand as she approached. I reached over and kissed her cheek lightly.

"How was trig?"

"Awful," she replied. "I hate it. How is anyone supposed to remember all those formulas? And if you get one of them just a little bit wrong, all your answers are wrong."

"That sucks," I said, trying to sound sympathetic. It was hard to do because I was just about as excited as I could be about Nicole seeing her locker. I swung her hand between us and started heading in that direction so she could put her stuff inside before we went to lunch.

We rounded the corner, and I put my hands on Nicole's waist as I stood behind her and watched her fiddle with the combination lock. I still couldn't stop smiling. She lifted the latch and opened the door, and I felt her stiffen under my hands. She looked up to the locker next to her—probably checking the number to see if she was at the right one.

"What do you think?" I asked, unable to contain myself any longer.

"Do you do this?" she asked. Her voice was just barely loud enough to hear over the other students in the hallway.

"Uh huh," I replied. I leaned over and placed my lips against her neck. "You like it?"

"Holy shit, Thomas!" she yelled. "What the fuck did you do?"

She turned and pushed at my chest, knocking me backwards a little. I ran smack into some kid with glasses, who ran into a girl coming from the other direction, and books scattered all over the place. The girl started screaming at the other kid, but I ignored them both.

"What was that for?" I asked. My heart was starting to beat faster. This was not how I envisioned this going down. "It looks great!"

"Where is all of my stuff?" she screeched at me.

"In the folders," I told her, and I pointed down to the bottom shelf. "Red is trig, green is biology—of course—and the blue one is for homework before it's graded. The left side has the ones that aren't done yet, and the right side has the ones ready to turn in. The purple one is…"

"Thomas! How could you do that?" Her eyes were intense, and her hands were balled up into fists. My kitten had turned lioness-mad.

My phone went off with a new text message, meowing loudly and echoing down the hallway.

"Are you seriously keeping that as your ringtone?" Nicole snapped.

"I like it," I said with a shrug.

She glared at me, forgetting the noise from my pocket.

"What the fuck did you do?" she said again as she gestured toward the locker.

"What do you mean?" I was still completely astonished by her reaction. She had to see how much better organized it was. I didn't know how she could have even found today's biology homework at all before I put it in the homework folder. It was at the bottom of a stack of literature notes.

"How the hell did you even get into my locker?"

"I...um...borrowed the key," I stammered. Okay, I didn't really think about her going in that direction, but really, what was the big deal?

"Borrowed the *key*?" she yelled. Damn, she could yell when she wanted to. "Borrowed *what* key?"

"There's a master key..." I said. "I got it from the office so I could...um...fix your locker up..."

Suddenly, the whole thing didn't sound like the great idea it did initially.

"Oh my GOD!" Nicole's hands went up into her hair. "I cannot believe you did that. How could you, Thomas? How could you go through all my stuff like that? Without even asking? Seriously?"

My body went cold, and I started getting that creepy, tingling feeling I sometimes got when Dad was in one of his moods. A shiver ran through me. I feared whatever I said now wouldn't make any difference.

I couldn't seem to pull in a breath. I could still see Nicole, and I knew she was yelling, but her words were lost to me. She threw her hands up in the air and then backed up against the locker next to hers. With her hands over her face, she slowly sank to the floor where she sat with her knees bent.

Shakespeare's words from *A Midsummer Night's Dream* came to me—"So quick bright things come to confusion." Somehow, I'd really, really screwed this up.

Now would she let me fix it?

CHAPTER FIFTEEN
shutout

Most of the hallway had cleared out as students headed to the lunchroom. I stood there like a complete moron while Nicole sat on the floor with her head in her hands. I was afraid to say or do anything because I wasn't sure if she was so angry she couldn't look at me or if it was because she was crying.

I wasn't even sure which one would be worse.

Since no little voices whispered words of guidance in my head, I just sat down in the hallway in front of her and tried to figure out what the fuck had happened. I only wanted to help her, and I thought she would have liked it, but obviously, she didn't feel that way.

"Rumple?" I finally said when the silence was just too much to take anymore.

She tipped her head back up, unshielding it from her hands and her hair at the same time. She didn't really look mad exactly, but her eyes still glared at me. I realized what I had called her and quickly corrected myself.

"Um…Nicole?" I tried again. "I just wanted…I mean, I didn't mean to…"

"I know," she said in a voice that was completely dead. Her

eyes dropped to the ground, and she looked so…so…*unNicole*. I didn't know what to make of it. "It's okay."

Greg's voice echoed in my mind.

"*She was timid and scared, and she always waited for someone else to tell her what to do…*"

Oh fuck.

Oh fuckity fuck, fuck, fuckity fuck, fuck, fuck.

I got up on my knees to kind of crawl the couple of feet between us until I reached her, and when I went to touch her, she flinched.

"Oh no…no…Nicole…"

I pulled my hand back and watched her wrap her arms around her legs.

"I didn't mean it…not like that…shit."

I had to get out of here. I had to get *her* out of here.

I stood up and crouched beside her, slid my arms behind her back and legs and lifted her up into my arms. I rather expected her to take a swing at me, but she didn't. She didn't protest at all.

Fuck.

Without making eye contact with anyone we passed, I carried her swiftly down the hall, out the door, and to my car. I didn't know what I had in mind and just went purely on instinct—instinct I didn't know I had. I opened up the back door, placed her in the seat, and then went around to the other side. Once I was in, I reached over and pulled her against my chest, wrapping her up in my arms and just whispering into her hair.

"I didn't mean it," I told her. "I'm sorry. I wasn't thinking. Please, please…Nicole. Don't be like this."

At least I figured out where I went wrong. Somehow, I was going to have to convince her I wasn't like that guy in Minneapolis —the one that hurt her. I wasn't like him at all.

Was I?

I kept my arms wrapped around her for the longest time, just holding her against my chest and telling over and over again her how sorry I was. At first, she just slouched against me, not moving, but after a few minutes, I felt her arms snake around my waist.

"I'm sorry," I whispered again. My arms tensed and I brought her closer to me. "I wasn't trying to…to…I mean, I only wanted to…help…"

I didn't know what else to say.

"I know," she answered.

I pressed my lips to the top of her head.

"I didn't mean to upset you."

"I know you didn't," she said.

We were silent a while longer until she spoke again.

"He was always telling me what a slob I was," she said softly, and I could hear her breath hitch. "He said if I wasn't so stupid, I would be able to organize myself. I tried to tell him I always knew where everything was…but he didn't listen very often to what I said."

I clenched my teeth and tried to stop myself from putting my fist through the window. I closed my eyes and counted to seventy-six. Finally, I could speak without snarling.

"Did he hit you?" I asked softly. I didn't *want* to know, but I still *had* to know. She was silent way too long, and I tightened my arms around her.

"Only once," she finally said.

I closed my eyes tightly, trying to rein in the anger that was threatening to boil up to the surface of my skin, probably creating blisters, or at least scaring the shit out of her. It was that possibility that kept me in check.

"If you tell me his full name, I will destroy that motherfucker."

I felt her shake her head.

"No," she whispered against my chest, "I don't want you to do anything."

I held myself still and tried to take a few deep breaths.

"If that's what you want," I told her.

"That's what I want."

"I don't like it," I said, just to make sure that part was clear.

"I know," she replied. "Just…don't."

"I won't," I promised, thought about it for a second, and then added, "but if I ever see him on a soccer field, all bets are off."

I felt, more than heard, her chuckle.

"You have to tell me when I do something you don't like," I said. "I want you to tell me. I don't want to be a shitty boyfriend like that."

"It's just pretend, Thomas," she scoffed. "It's just for show."

I stiffened and looked into her eyes.

Now or never…

"What if…" The words caught in my throat. I swallowed and tried again. "What if I don't want to pretend?"

Nicole's eyes narrowed slightly. Her brows squished together, and she looked up at me.

"Thomas…" she said softly, "it's not…not real."

"What if I want it to be real?" I whispered. I shifted a little closer to her, as if that were possible. I moved my hand slowly up her arm until it lay across her cheek. I leaned forward, looked into her eyes, and placed my lips against hers.

I heard her sharp intake of breath and then a soft moan as her grip on me tightened, and her lips molded against mine. My head tilted to the side, wanting more. I kissed her again and again. I turned my head the other way and felt her hand grasp the back of my head and pull me closer. I opened my mouth a little—just enough for my tongue to reach out and touch her lips.

Her mouth opened to me without hesitation, and it was my turn to moan.

She tasted so fucking good. She reached out with her tongue and touched mine, and I didn't hesitate to lick across her lips before I delved into her mouth. My tongue explored, and her little soft moans started driving me over the edge.

"I don't want to pretend," I said again. My mouth never left hers as I spoke. "I want it to be real. I want you…"

I felt her nod though she never spoke or broke away from me. Her tongue entered my mouth again and ran along mine. I couldn't get enough of it, and I sucked on it with my lips as my own tongue traveled along hers. Nicole pressed harder against me, and my head hit the back of the seat as she crawled into my lap and started kissing me in earnest.

So fucking good...

She moved her hands to my shoulders and then back down to my chest. She grazed me slightly with her fingernails through the fabric of my jersey. I groaned against her mouth, and I slid my hands down to her back, and I pulled her against me as we kept kissing and kissing and kissing.

At some point right before we would have needed ChapStick, Nicole pulled back, and her eyes met mine again. She was flushed and breathing hard, but most importantly, the fire was back in her eyes. I tilted my head down and kissed her once more but only lightly.

"If this is going to be real," she said, "there's something we have to make perfectly clear."

Nicole straightened up in the seat, raising herself enough that we were more on eye level. She took my face between her palms and held me still.

"What?" I asked, feeling a little nervous.

"Thomas Malone, don't you ever fuck with my shit again, you hear me?"

A smile crept across my face that I just couldn't stop.

"You think this is funny, Malone?"

I shook my head.

"I think you're beautiful," I told her. "And I like it when you call me that, Rumple."

"What? *Malone?*" she asked as she shook her head. "That is your name."

"And for that name which is no part of thee, take all myself."

She scowled at me, but I saw the corner of her mouth twitch. Leaning forward again, I wrapped my lips around her lower one, sucking on it and running my tongue over it. Her hands tangled back into my hair, and she held me against her. I slowly backed off, reveling in the feeling of her fingers tugging at my hair.

"Shouldn't you be practicing for a game tonight or something?" she asked with a raised brow.

I tucked my head down against her shoulder and tightened my grip.

"Yeah, probably," I said with a shrug.

"Maybe you should get out there, then."

"I probably should."

"You better play damn well tonight, too," she added. "I expect a shut out game."

She pushed her hand under my jaw and tilted my head up to align with hers. She placed her lips against mine and punctuated each word with a kiss.

"*Just. For. Me.*"

My heart began to beat faster at her words, and I looked into her glorious eyes.

"You got it."

I couldn't think of anything I would rather do. It was an exhilarating sensation, and I felt more like *me* than I had in a really long time.

I was going to win this game.

I was going to win it for *my* Rumple.

I walked into the locker room about as pumped up as I could be.

"You fuckers ready to kick some ass?" I screamed as I jumped up on the bench next to the lockers.

"Fuck yeah!" Jeremy responded. Several other guys responded in kind.

"Shutout! No fucking scores for these assholes!" I yelled. I pointed over to my defenders. "European defense tonight. You fuckers push them to the sides and then right through to the middle —no crossovers. I'll take it from there."

"You got it," Paul piped up.

"Klosav, Clint—you guys do your shit, and we'll be set."

"Fucking A!" they both yelled at once.

"Frankie, if you get one more offside call against you, I will personally kick your ass after the game. Don't give away the motherfucking ball, you hear me? Stay onside the defenders."

"Whatever you say, captain." He gave me a strange little smile, but I ignored him.

"Tony." I looked down at the freshman who was on the floor near the door to the showers, lacing up his cleats.

"Yeah?" he said. He looked a little concerned.

"You're starting tonight. Center. Get me a fucking goal."

His eyes widened, and he smiled.

"Fucking A," he replied.

I dropped down on the bench and started pulling my stuff out of my bag with one hand while I opened my locker with the other. I lined everything up on the bench—shin guards first, then socks, then my cleats. I put them on, right side first, then the left, laced up the cleats, tucked down the laces, and stood up to stretch.

Shut out game.

For my Rumple.

Mine.

I couldn't stop smiling.

"You're in a good mood," Jeremy said as he plopped down beside me with his cleats still untied.

"We're gonna kick ass tonight," I said with a maniacal grin.

"I'm a little surprised," he said in a softer voice. Some of the other guys started walking toward the locker room doors, ready to head to the field. I could hear the band start to play outside. "I didn't think things were going so well there a while ago."

"What do you mean?"

"Well…you and Nicole…in the hall."

"Oh, you saw that?"

"Yeah, but even if I hadn't, it's all anyone was talking about at lunch."

"Shit, she won't like that," I mumbled.

"Since when do you care?" he said, his voice even quieter.

I looked at him, thought about making a smart-ass remark in return but just couldn't bring myself to do so.

"Since she's my girl," I replied with a shrug.

He laughed and clapped his hand on my back.

"I never would have thought it," he said with a grin. He bent over to tie his laces as he continued to chuckle. "Malone thinking about someone other than himself."

"Fuck you," I said, but I was still smiling.

"Let's go kick some ass." Jeremy jumped up and offered me a hand. I took it, and he nearly pulled my arm out of my socket.

"Ow!"

"Pussy."

"Suck my cock."

"I've seen bigger fingers!"

I took a swing at him, but he ducked, laughed, and ran. I chased after him, and the rest of the team followed.

It was going to be a fucking awesome game.

Shakespeare might have told me that playing soccer was "meat and drinke to me." Somehow, it was days like this that made me completely agree.

Now to kick some motherfucking ass.

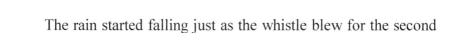

The rain started falling just as the whistle blew for the second half.

So far, so good. No score on either side.

I wasn't sure if Tony was nervous because he started or not, but I was regretting telling the coach to put him in. He's fucked up about six times, two of which should have been goals. I never looked over to the stands if I could avoid it, but I knew Nicole was up there watching me. It made my heart beat a little faster and my skin tingle.

I wiped rain or sweat or whatever it was off my forehead with my sleeve and crouched down as the other team's striker made it past the midline. He weaved left and then right, making it past Paul and heading off to the side. Out of the corner of my eye, I could see their left wing crossing over to the right side.

"Jeremy! Right!" I screamed. I wasn't sure if he couldn't hear me as the rain picked up or if he just wasn't sure which way right was, but he ended up going the wrong way and leaving the wing wide open.

The striker neatly tipped the ball to the wing just behind Paul and well onside. Jeremy moved into center as the striker made it to the top of the box. Paul wasn't moving as fast as their wingman, and I could see he was going to position near the corner. I jumped sideways and watched the center striker as the ball crossed over the box at perfect head height.

The striker nailed the ball perfectly, and I watched it as it angled toward the net, jumped, and tipped it with my fingers just over the top bar of the goal. I could hear the crowd screaming as it soared out of bounds behind me. Corner kick for the other team, but not a goal.

"Left, Martin!" I yelled at Jeremy. I waved my hand and he moved into position. Paul set himself up right at the post as their center striker moved to the corner of the field. The crowd screamed at him while I yelled at the players on my team to get into position.

The striker's kick was good—sailing right into the box. I looked left and right, taking in the scene around me and calculating the greatest risk as the ball soared into the area above my head. Jeremy got a head on it, but it wasn't enough, and the ball dropped right at the top of the box where one of the midfielders was in perfect position for a goal.

It was low and to my right. I dived as the rain poured down, snatched the ball before it hit a puddle, and pulled it close to my chest. As I lay covered in mud with the ball tightly held to my body, I could hear the crowd screaming my name.

I lived for this shit.

Four minutes left in the game.

I brought the ball to the top of the box and punted it nearly to the other goalie. Tony didn't make it in time to get foot to ball, but as the defender on the other team knocked it away, Jeremy was there to put it back on their side.

Clint trapped the ball and ran it up the right side then crossed it over to Klosav. Klosav managed to knock it right at the top of the box, where Tony was waiting. He dodged left then right, and the defender lost his footing. Tony straightened his leg and nailed the ball in the upper right corner, and the crowd went insane.

Two minutes later, as I picked up the ball after a lame kick from our opponent's offense, the whistle blew, and the game was over.

One-nothing.

Shutout.

Just for my Rumple.

For the first time since the game started, I dared to look over to where I knew she was sitting with Maria and Rachel. As I high-fived the other players, I walked toward the tunnel and saw her smiling down at me.

I leapt over the fence near the edge of the field, pulled Nicole into my arms, and planted a big-ass kiss on her. Somehow, I just didn't care who might have seen us—I wanted everyone to know she was my girl. What could possibly be wrong with that?

"Shutout game," I said. I reached out and tried to tap her nose with a mud-covered, gloved finger. She turned at the last second and the mud ended up on her cheek instead. "Just for you, baby."

"Ugh! Thomas!" Nicole squealed with a laugh. She pushed at my chest, which only served to get more mud on her hands. "You are a mess!"

After pulling off my gloves and dropping them on the ground, I held her up with one arm. I reached over to brush a bit of mud off her face with the opposite hand but only managed to smear it around. I still told her it was better.

"Nice save there at the end," she said. "I thought the last one was going to go over your head."

"No way," I said. "I just wouldn't allow that."

Nicole snorted and shook her head as I dropped her back to her feet.

"Nice game, son," I heard from behind me. I dropped my

hands from Nicole's waist and turned to see Dad in the business suit he usually wore when he was traveling. He walked up to us and reached over to pat me on the back.

"Thanks, Dad," I replied as my heart started to beat a little faster, and my throat tightened. "You remember Nicole, right?"

"Yes, I do," he said as he turned his smile to her. "It's a pleasure to see you again, Miss Skye."

"Thank you," Nicole said. She glanced at me and bit down on her lip. Nicole's eyes stayed on mine as she leaned against me slightly. I put my arm around her, and as I glanced over her head at my dad, our eyes met, and his narrowed just a little.

Shit.

He didn't like something.

He knew I was seeing Nicole—we'd talked about her doing my homework and shit for me. This display shouldn't have shocked him too much, so why the look?

I felt Nicole's fingers trail up my side.

"How is your side today?" she asked, just a little too loudly.

Oh fuck, no! Rumple—you aren't going there.

I tightened my arm around her and I held her close to me.

"Nothing wrong with me, baby," I said. I kept my eyes on Dad, who was looking at Nicole with a small smile. "It's all good."

"Thomas," Dad said, "I've got a flight to catch early in the morning, so I'm heading to Seattle now. Walk to the car with me."

"Sure," I said as I tried to hold a smile. "I'll be back in a bit, okay, Nicole?"

She glanced from me to my father and then nodded before releasing my arm.

"You want to explain that?" Dad said softly as we started across the parking lot. The sun had mostly gone down, and the tall security lights cast weird shadows all over the place.

"Explain what?" I asked. I had a pretty good idea but didn't want to make it that obvious.

"I thought you were just holding out for homework," Dad said. "You act like you are fucking dating her or something."

"She's pretty bright, Dad," I told him. This was a conversation I figured was going to happen, so I had already worked out most of it in my head. "She wouldn't fall for the usual shit. It actually works out great because the other girls aren't bugging me; Nicole's doing the extra work I have for school, and I still have someone to suck me off. It's perfect, really. Kind of like one-stop-shopping."

I laughed and then held my breath, hoping he was going to buy it. He glanced at me sideways for a second, and the long shadow he cast under the bright lamps covered me.

"She looks clingy," he said. "Fuck her and get rid of her. I want to be able to throw that shit in her father's face."

"It's working out well, though," I said again, hoping he'd drop it even though I knew he wouldn't.

"Fuck her and dump her," he repeated. "Or just dump her if she won't spread her legs. I don't want you distracted. The Messini will be here for the next home game. Get her out of the way before then."

"Okay," I said with a nod, "but it's going to be hard finding someone else who can do all the homework."

"Drop those fucking AP classes, then," he replied.

"I'll figure something out," I said quietly.

I watched him drive off and then turned around and headed back to the field, trying to figure out what the hell I was going to say to Nicole. I probably could have told her the truth—she already knew a little—but I didn't want to. I didn't want her to know what Dad had said about her.

I shook my head, sending droplets of rain from my hair to the ground.

One thing was for sure, I wasn't going to dump her tonight. I had an entire week before Dad returned home. If I had to end things with Rumple before then, I was going to make the most of the next seven days.

My phone meowed, and a message from Jeremy asked where I had gone. I quickly typed a response and jogged the rest of the way back to the stands.

When I got back to Nicole, I wasn't in the mood for heading out with the rest of the team. She definitely noticed my change in demeanor even though I tried to cover it up as much as I could. Every time I looked at her, my Dad's words were in my head: *Fuck her and dump her.*

I couldn't do that—not to Rumple.

"Is everything all right?" she asked quietly as kids started climbing into cars and heading for a little late night party on the beach.

"I'm okay," I told her. "It's just too fucking cold for a beach party tonight."

She eyed me, obviously not falling for my line of bullshit.

"What do you want to do?"

"I might just head home—I have to train in the morning."

"You train every morning," Nicole said.

"Saturdays are more intense," I said with a shrug. "I train the most on Saturdays and Tuesdays."

She looked me over again but finally nodded.

"Do you want to come over for lunch when you're done? Dad's heading on a fishing trip in the morning, but he'll be back later in the afternoon."

"That would be awesome," I said, and I meant it.

⟶ ••••◗◍◖•••• ⟵

Saturday morning I was up early for my run. I pushed myself harder as thoughts of the Messini brothers coming to watch me crept through my mind. I did my first mile in slightly under five minutes and then did the next two in six.

Too bad Dad wasn't here to check my times.

After the run, I headed to the basement and hit the free weights. By the time I was done, I was completely wiped out and ready to pass out in bed before I even managed to shower. I couldn't do that, though, because Nicole was expecting me for lunch, and I wasn't about to disappoint her.

Not yet, anyway.

As I washed the sweat from my body, I tried to think about what I was going to tell her. Dad's instructions had been about as clear as they could be—I had two weeks to get rid of my Rumple. If I didn't...well, I didn't even want to think about what he might do. Dad was really good at finding shit on people, and I definitely didn't want to chance his looking into Nicole's life in Minnesota.

Fuck her and dump her.

As I considered Dad's "plan," the first part of it bounced around in my head, and I realized I hadn't gotten off—not once— since I had Lisa on her knees in the locker room the same day I bumped into Rumple for the first time. I hadn't done anything with anyone other than Nicole except for a quick make-out session that I hadn't even been into with Crystal Lloyd on the bus. I'd been in a bed with Nicole, but we hadn't done anything other than kiss.

She's been my girlfriend for about twenty-four hours.

Should we have fucked by now?

Shit —I had no clue. I'd always skipped the girlfriend part and gone straight to fucking, or at least a blowjob. I had no idea what was normal or not. I knew with Jeremy and Rachel it wasn't like that, since he had told me a little bit. They were going out for a while before he started sticking his dick in her. I didn't know how long, though.

How long they had been dating—not how long his dick was.

Perverts.

The combination of thinking about whether or not I should have fucked Nicole by now, how long it had been since I had gotten off at all, and my hands full of suds, well...sometimes things just start happening before you even realize it.

Dad always said jerking off was for losers who couldn't get a girl to do it for them. I hadn't jacked off in...damn...a long time. Maybe since I was fifteen. If I thought about it, I would have been able to come up with an exact date, but I was more interested in my growing erection and thoughts of my Rumple.

Maybe making a few "drain babies" wasn't a bad idea.

I closed my eyes and wrapped my hand around my dick.

In my mind, she sneaks into the bathroom and opens up the shower door. Her hand reaches around my waist, and her fingers wrap around my cock. She strokes me slowly at first—running the soap from my body around my shaft and getting it nice and slick. Her fingers grip me a little harder, slide down my cock, and then back up. Her other hand runs over my balls, playing with them gently as she presses her body against my back. I can feel her tits against my skin.

I placed my open palm against the shower wall and leaned against it, pressing my weight against the cool tiles with one hand as the other began to work a little faster. My thoughts raced.

Nicole moves in front of me so I can see her naked breasts and pussy. She backs up against the shower wall and wraps one of her muscular legs around my waist. I slide into her easily with my cock covered in soap, and she feels so, so good…

I heard my breath start coming in gasps as I worked my hand up and down my shaft, sliding my thumb over the moistened tip on the down stroke. Images of Rumple with her head thrown back against the wall as I impale her repeatedly cascaded around in my mind as I thrust into my hand.

"Oh, fuck…fuck…Rumple…"

My balls tightened and my knees buckled a little as I shot come onto the shower floor. I moaned out my nickname for her along with another string of curse words as my orgasm subsided.

Fuck, that felt good.

Stepping carefully onto the bathmat, I dried off and started going through my normal bathroom routine. Shave first, then brush teeth, then deodorant, and then fuck around with my hair for twenty minutes even though it doesn't look any different than it would have after two minutes of just running my fingers through it. I pulled my jeans up over slightly damp legs, tossed on a plain white T-shirt, and pulled a green polo on over it.

I was pretty sure jacking off hadn't felt quite that good before. If just thinking about getting in Nicole felt like that…*holy shit.* Fucking her was going to be good.

I wondered if we would do it today.

Strangely enough, I was looking forward to her cooking more than anything. I didn't mind waiting for the other stuff if she wanted to wait.

Getting into my car hadn't been too painful, but once I got to the Skye residence, I had apparently overdone the workout a bit, and sitting still for a few minutes was just enough for my muscles to stiffen up. I groaned as I pulled my legs out from under the steering wheel and placed them on the ground next to the Jeep. Then I had to use both aching arms to pull myself out of the car. I shuffled across the driveway and up to the front porch and managed to smile when Nicole opened the door.

She was too damn beautiful not to smile.

And she was mine.

My Rumple.

For now, at least.

Rumple had opted for a picnic and had apparently decided to go all out with lunch. She had a bunch of different fruits—I didn't even know what half of them were—and cheeses, and crackers, and breads. She had hoped we could eat on a blanket in the back yard picnic-style, but the rain started right after I got there, so we picnicked in the living room instead.

With my post-workout appetite, I devoured everything she put in front of me as she told me the names of the different fruits and cheeses. Apparently, her mother had a few wine and cheese parties, and she had learned a lot about cheese. It was awesome.

Well, except the brie. That shit was nasty. It kind of reminded me of feet.

We ate and I asked her a thousand questions about her mom and about living in Minneapolis. She missed her former home, and I was torn about how to feel about it. I still wanted to rip the dicks off the two guys who had done that shit to her, but I was also glad she was here with me now.

Now.

For now.

Shit.

I knew I needed to tell her about what Dad had said the night before, but my muscles were still really sore, and I felt like shit. I didn't want to make it worse by talking about that crap on top of everything else, so I didn't say anything about it.

We finished up the last of the picnic, and I helped her carry everything back to the kitchen to clean up and put everything away. I was covering up pretty well until she had me put a server tray away on a top shelf, and she heard me hiss as I reached up high.

"Are you okay?" Nicole asked.

"Um…sure!" I said. I gave her a half-smile and hoped she was going to buy it.

No such luck.

"Bullshit." She put her hands on her hips." What's wrong with you?"

"Sore muscles," I admitted. "No biggie."

Nicole's eyes darkened and her voice lowered.

"Did your dad…?"

"No, no," I said, shaking my head. "Dad's out of town for the next week. Really, I'm just a little sore from my workout."

"A little sore?"

"Well, quite a bit, really."

"Thomas," Nicole sighed, exasperated. "Why didn't you just call? We didn't have to hang out today."

"I didn't want to skip it," I said. I narrowed my eyes and looked toward the window. "I…I wanted to see you."

She took a step closer, and I looked back at her as we both reached for each other's hips. I leaned down and kissed her, totally not caring that she kind of tasted like brie and figs. I placed my forehead against hers and kept my eyes closed. My knees wobbled a little.

"You are falling asleep on your feet," Nicole said. I couldn't really argue, so I let her lead me over to the couch in the living room. "Lie down before you fall over."

I couldn't disagree with her as I dropped down onto the couch and dropped my head to the little pillow sitting up on the corner by the arm. I groaned. Something about lying down made the aches in my muscles more apparent. The backs of my legs were burning, and the pressure of the couch cushions under my shoulder was enough to make me cringe. I squeezed my eyes shut for a second and tried to force my muscles to do what I wanted them to do.

"I think you might have overdone it," Nicole said as she watched me shift around and try to get into a comfortable position. "Do you need anything?"

"Just you," I said. I stopped wiggling around and patted the cushion next to me. Nicole smiled and sat down on the edge of the couch. I put my arm around her waist, and she placed her hand on my shoulder.

"World Cup semifinals start soon," she said as she pulled the remote off the coffee table in front of her and flipped on the television. "US Women's team is playing today if you want to watch."

"Okay," I said with a yawn, "but you have to lie down with me."

Nicole raised her eyebrows at me, but lay down with her back against my chest so I could slide my fingers over her belly and pull her close to me.

"So, do you have a thing for Heather Mitts like every other soccer guy does?" she asked.

"Nope," I replied. "Hope Solo."

She smacked my arm, but I just smirked, not really giving a fuck because I had Rumple's warm little body spooned up against mine on a little bitty couch, so she had to be extra close. My arm was wrapped around her middle as I closed my eyes.

"Figures," she mumbled. "Mitts is on the bench anyway."

"Mmm…" I only barely heard her. "US and Brazil, right?"

"Yep." Nicole said something else, but I missed it.

My head felt warm and fuzzy, and when she asked me something about the first goal of the game, I just grunted and nuzzled her hair. She smelled so fucking good.

I could hear the sounds from the television, but they weren't really penetrating my conscious mind. At one point, Nicole was griping about the referee being insane and possibly smoking crack, but I didn't hear or see the call. The only thing in my head was the feeling of her warm body pressed against mine. Despite the ache in my muscles, I was comfortable here with her.

I dozed.

My mind conjured up a new view of our picnic with the rain holding off until we were already set up in the back yard. We were munching on the bread and the cheese when the rain started pouring down on us, and we had to grab everything quickly to get it back inside. Nicole got soaked, and we both laughed as the rain covered us, and I covered her in kisses.

I heard her father's voice, but my head was still full of fog.

"Did you wear him out?"

I felt Nicole's body shake a little as she giggled softly. In my head, the three of us were sitting on the picnic blanket in the rain. I kissed the side of Nicole's neck while she and her father conversed.

"No, he came this way. I think he did a bit too much during his workout this morning."

"So, no more pretending?"

"You think you're pretty smart, don't you?" Nicole snickered.

"I thought it was obvious from the first time I saw him over here, and you were yelling at him." Greg laughed quietly through his nose.

"Whatever."

"You kids are pretty oblivious sometimes," he said. "I guess I could let you borrow one of the police detective handbooks to help you figure it out."

"Very funny!"

"How was the game last night?"

"It was good," Nicole said softly. "Thomas played really well —shutout."

"Do you miss it?"

"I was there," she said. "How could I miss it?"

"You know that's not what I mean." Greg's voice darkened a little.

"Sometimes," I heard Nicole mumble. "Not enough to play right now. It's okay just having someone to cheer for, you know?"

"I guess so," he said.

"He needs someone on his side," she said so quietly, I thought I had probably dropped back into my dream. She shifted in my arms, and I felt her nose against my jaw.

"I have to admit," Greg said, "he seems pretty different when he's here compared to what I've seen of him in the past."

"I wish I knew which one to believe," Nicole said.

The warmth of her breath against my neck kept me comfortable and soothed as I continued to drift in this strange dream about Nicole and her Dad's conversation—so different from the way my father and I talked. I suppose that's what made it the most dream-like, since it didn't really make any sense to me at all.

Maybe Shakespeare would have said I only wanted "to sleep: perchance to dream." Somehow, their conversation was completely surreal to me.

Now how long could I just sleep here with her?

CHAPTER SIXTEEN
half-time

Lying on the Skyes' couch, wrapped up in warmth, my dream continued.

"What do you mean *which one to believe*?" Greg asked.

"Well," Nicole started and then paused. I could feel her body twisting in my arms and felt her fingers pushing the hair off my forehead. "It's like he's a different person depending on what he's wearing. He even said something about it once, when he was dressed up for that banquet thing you dragged me to. He was so... *suave*, I guess, because he was wearing a tux. Then when he puts on his jersey, he acts like someone completely different. That first day he was here—when I found him at the cemetery—that was the first time I thought this is the real Thomas, you know? Not an act."

"That's got to be a little confusing for you, hon," Greg said.

"It's giving me whiplash."

I felt her hand on my cheek and pushed against it instinctively even in sleep.

"His Mom's death...that really messed him up, you know?" she said softly.

"It messed them both up," Greg replied.

"Did you know her? Did you know Thomas's mom?"

"Yeah," he replied, "I did."

My dream deepened as I felt Nicole's fingers twisting bits of my hair around my ear. I lay back on the picnic blanket in the yard, and the rain misted over us though we never got wet. Fucked up dreams.

"They dated in high school…"

"She left town and moved to Chicago, following some artist type…"

"Lou brought her back here…"

The words in my dream didn't really make sense to me still, and the sensations of Nicole's touch were more than enough to capture and hold my attention. I sighed and nuzzled against her, feeling her hair tickle my nose as I basked in her scent.

Warm…delicious…my Rumple.

"They got married…"

"Thomas came shortly after…"

The voices in my dreams faded with the scene, casting me in deeper sleep. As I felt consciousness grip me again, I groaned at my stiffened muscles as I shifted on the couch. I rolled off and on to the floor with a thump and a gasp.

I heard giggling.

"Oh fuck, that hurt," I moaned. I flopped over onto my back and rubbed at my shoulder, grimacing.

"You're funny," Nicole said as she crouched down next to me. "Hungry?"

"Very."

"Get up, then."

She giggled again as she headed into the kitchen and left me on my back. I tilted my neck backwards painfully as I watched her saunter out of the room, her long legs teasing me with the tightening muscles as she walked. I moaned again as I rolled over and pushed myself up on my hands and knees.

"I thought you soccer players were supposed to be in good shape." Greg's voice jumped out at me from his chair. I startled, having no idea he was sitting that close, and just about fell off and on to my face.

He laughed at me, too.

"Anytime you want to come lift weights with me," I suggested as I looked up at him, "you let me know. We'll see how you're doing a couple hours later, old man."

He laughed again as he stood and offered me a hand. I took it, and he hauled me from the floor.

"I think I'll give it a pass," Greg said. "Fishing is more of a sport for my tastes."

"Fishing? A sport? Seriously?"

"Of course it's a sport!"

"Oh good lord," Nicole groaned. She rolled her eyes as we walked in and sat at the table. "We'll never hear the end of this one now."

"Fishing is the greatest sport there is, right after baseball…"

She was right. He didn't shut up through all of dinner.

Despite my gagging noises and complaints about how freaking boring both of those so-called sports were, before the meal was through, my stomach was cramping up due from laughing. Greg shook his finger at me, and as soon as the dishes were cleared, he dragged me around the house to show me all his sportsman spoils, including a deep freezer filled with enough dead fish to…um… well, to fill a deep freezer.

Nicole joined sides with me as we argued about how much better soccer was over baseball, and eventually, Greg gave up and went upstairs. He yelled down to Nicole and me not to be too loud before he shut his bedroom door for the night. Nicole sat down on the couch next to me and glanced at me sideways with her teeth embedded in her lip.

"You still look tired," she said softly.

I shrugged.

"Do you want to go home and get to bed?"

I didn't have to think about that one for too long before I was shaking my head vigorously. I reached over and grabbed her hand and pulled it over into my lap, suddenly feeling weird about it all, and thinking maybe I shouldn't have touched her. I let go, but her hand was already in my lap, so that seemed stupid, too. I picked her hand back up again and just stared at our fingers laced together.

"You said your dad is out of town?" Nicole asked softly.

"Yeah," I confirmed. "He'll be back next Saturday."

"Do you…um…want to stay here tonight?" Nicole's cheeks turned pink when I looked up at her.

"Could I?"

"Well, then you wouldn't have to be alone all night, right?"

"Yeah," I agreed with a nod. I looked up at the clock and saw it was a quarter past ten. "Um…I could run home and get some shit…you know, clothes for tomorrow or whatever."

"Okay."

"Be back soon?"

"I'll be watching for you," Nicole said with a smile and another lip bite.

"I'll hurry," I said. I stood up, and she stood with me. I grabbed both of her hands, stared down at them in mine for a minute, and then looked back to her eyes. She was looking up at me through her lashes and just looked so damn beautiful—I couldn't help but lean in to kiss her.

Her lips were soft, smooth, and warm against mine. I tasted her gently, just running the tip of my tongue across her bottom lip before I pulled back from her warmth.

"Sometime too hot the eye of heaven shines," I whispered against her mouth. I took a step back and saw how her chest was rising and falling with her breaths.

"Do you always quote Shakespeare to girls?" she asked.

"Never have before," I replied with a shrug. "I'll be back soon."

"You'd better be," she replied.

I practically ran to my car and took the evil curves between our houses far quicker than I should have. I scampered up the front steps and left the door wide open as I leapt up the stairs, two at a time. I threw some stuff in a backpack and raced back the same way, barely remembering to close the door to the car before I ran back inside Nicole's house.

Even though I had slept with her in her bed twice before, I felt weird standing on the porch with my backpack full of shit to spend the night at Nicole's house. The other times had been pretty spontaneous, and this felt a lot more planned. Was I supposed to ring the bell or knock? I had been there just twenty minutes before, so maybe I should just go in. She said she'd be watching for me—did that mean she already knew I was here, and she'd just open the door without me doing anything?

All of this shit was just too unfamiliar to me. I didn't know what to do.

Thankfully, Nicole *was* apparently watching, because she opened the door before I managed to make a decision or chicken out and just go back to the car.

"You're soaked."

I glanced down, and she was right. I hadn't really noticed the rain soaking through my shirt. I dripped into the foyer, and Nicole made me stand there while she got a towel from the bathroom.

"You want a shower or anything?" she asked.

"You want to join me?" I replied with raised eyebrows. The comment just kind of jumped out of my mouth without discussing itself with me first.

"Do you have to act like an adolescent boy?" she asked.

"I am an adolescent boy," I reminded her. She dried my hair with the towel and then pushed me up the stairs to her room. Nicole took a handful of clothes into the bathroom to change, and I just kind of stood in the middle of the room and looked around, noting the few changes from the last time I had been here.

When she came back, I took my backpack into the bathroom, changed into some lounge pants, and brushed my teeth. I debated putting on the Donovan T-Shirt I brought with me, wondering if it would be better to leave it off.

It was kind of hot tonight.

All right, that was bullshit; it was actually pretty damn chilly.

I put the shirt on.

I returned to the room to find that Nicole had already climbed into bed, so I climbed in after her. I was on my left side, which really didn't hurt anymore, but it still felt all wrong immediately.

"Nicole?"

"Yeah?"

"Can we...um...switch sides?"

"Switch sides?" Her eyes narrowed in confusion.

"Yeah," I said. I ran my hand through my hair. "I was...I was on the other side of you before."

Her mouth turned up into a half-smile, but her eyes remained curious.

"O...kay..."

We fumbled around a bit before we ended up with her going over the top of me while I shuffled to the other side of the bed. She landed beside me with a soft thump, and I rolled to my side and placed my hand on her hip. I sighed, feeling much better.

"Did that really bother you?" she asked softly.

I glanced up at her and then looked away immediately. I pushed my head against the pillow a bit more and shrugged. I didn't know what to say. I knew it was weird to be so fixated on that kind of shit, but I couldn't seem to turn it off.

Finally, I spoke up.

"Sometimes my head just kind of...decides things should be a certain way," I told her. "Once it's decided, it just feels weird if things aren't where they are supposed to be."

"Like in my locker?" she said. She raised an eyebrow at me. I licked at my lips nervously.

"Yeah, sort of," I said and then decided that really wasn't right. "Well, I mean...it *was* a mess..."

Nicole cleared her throat and glared at me. I cringed.

"But usually other people's stuff doesn't bother me that much because I don't usually come into contact with it. I just...like things to be organized."

I lowered by eyes and turned my head into the pillow for a minute before I looked back at her through my eyelashes.

"I thought you'd like it."

"I didn't."

"I know that now."

"Good." Nicole reached out and ran her hand through my hair and seemed to be watching her fingers as they moved over my head. After a minute, she looked around her own room. "This place doesn't bother you?"

"Not really," I said. I smiled a little. "It was like this the first time I saw it."

"So, since the mess is all in the same place, it's okay?"

"It's not in exactly the same place, but essentially—yes."

"Not exactly?"

"Well, you had three Clare books on the nightstand when I was here before," I told her. "Now there are only two and a Bracken book has been added. You had a blue shirt over the rocker arm before, and now your jeans are there. The hamper lid was open before, and there were hoop earrings on the dresser, not a necklace. There was English homework next to your computer, not biology, and two pencils were with it, not a pen, and a pair of socks was sticking out from under your bed before. Those are gone."

Nicole's eyes went wide, and her mouth dropped open.

My chest tightened when I realized everything I had just revealed. I wanted to take it back.

I couldn't.

My heart started to pound faster, and my hands went cold and numb.

"Holy shit," Nicole finally breathed out.

"I don't…I mean…I was just…um…kidding."

"No." Nicole shook her head slightly. "You weren't."

I squeezed my eyes shut.

"Thomas?"

I didn't answer even when I felt her hand against the side of my face.

"Thomas. Look at me."

I opened my eyes slowly, waiting for the expression that would tell me she knew I was a complete freak, and she would probably toss me right out the window.

"Do you really remember all of that?"

"Maybe," I whispered.

"Thomas…that is incredible."

I tucked my head against her shoulder, and it felt like my skin was trying to implode into my body or something. It was all tight and making everything inside of me hurt.

"Oh my God," Nicole suddenly said. I heard her slight gasp. "You said something about this before—that you would never forget anything again after…after your mom…"

Both her hands captured my face, and she turned my head up. I looked into her soft blue eyes, waiting for the loathing that was sure to appear when she put it all together.

Not only did I kill my mom, but my dad hated me, *and* I was a total freak of nature as well. As I stared, her look did change, but I didn't see the loathing I expected.

It just wasn't there.

Shock, yes, and maybe even a bit of awe but not the hatred I had anticipated. Not the disgust. There was no hint that she considered me Shakespeare's "lump of foul deformity."

"I remember everything," I said quietly.

I couldn't look at her. I could still feel her eyes on me, but I kept mine on the open door across the room. I wondered if Greg was asleep by now or if he could have been out in the hallway or maybe even able to hear us talking from his own room. Strangely, the idea didn't really freak me out as much as I thought it would.

"That's why you don't bring anything to class, isn't it?" Nicole surmised. "You aren't being shitty; you really don't need it."

"Not if I've already read the chapter," I told her. I clenched my hand into a fist behind her back. "I don't really need to take notes or anything."

"And here I thought you were just being a prick." Nicole let out a short, soft laugh.

For the longest time, she said nothing. I didn't really have anything to add, so I stayed silent as well, letting my mind conjure up all the possible things she might be thinking. The one I kept coming back to was her wanting me to leave. Finally, I couldn't stand it anymore, and I had to know.

"Should I leave?" I asked quietly.

"Leave?" Nicole repeated. "Why would I want you to leave?"

I just shrugged. It was too obvious to voice.

"Thomas?" I felt her fingers on my jaw again as she tilted my head to look at her. "I don't want you to leave."

"Even though I'm a freak?" I asked.

"Thomas…" She shook her head slowly. Her expression was confused and a little sad. "It doesn't make you a freak."

With that, she moved closer and pressed her lips against mine. She wrapped her fingers into my hair as she rose and kissed me harder. She pushed me back into the pillow, and I groaned quietly. The pressure of her tongue on my lips was too brief, and she soon backed off and just looked at me. She left her fingers still tightly twined in the hair at the back of my head.

"Why are you so worried?" she asked.

"I didn't think…I thought you would think I was…weird."

She laughed softly again.

"Thomas," she said, "you are a little weird. Not in a bad way at all, but you certainly do have a few…idiosyncrasies."

She kissed me again, and again it was too brief.

"And I kind of like them."

"You do?" I was a little astonished.

"Yeah, I do." She propped herself up on her elbow a little, and my hand finally managed to open up to press against her back. She reached over and ran her fingers lightly over my temple and down my jaw. She kept going down my neck, across my shoulder, and finally rested her hand on my bicep, right where the T-shirt ended. "There are some things you do though…"

Her voice trailed off, and I felt panic welling up in the pit of my stomach.

"What?" I wondered if I really wanted to know. Her hand ran over my arm again.

"You have beautiful arms," she said quietly. Her finger traced the outline of the muscle there. "But sometimes…how you use them…well, that bothers me."

My eyes narrowed.

"What do you mean?"

"Every time you get pissed off about something, you start hitting people," she said. "We were supposed to talk about that, you know."

"I remember."

"I bet you do." She turned her gaze from my arm and met my eyes again. "I don't like it, Thomas. You can't just lash out and threaten people when you get mad."

"I don't," I said. Even as the words left my mouth, I knew it wasn't really true. "I mean…not every time."

"Most of the time," she amended. I could tell by the tone in her voice she wasn't going to back down any more than that.

"Sometimes I have to," I said.

"Why?"

"I'm not going to let anyone talk shit about you," I told her. "I said I'd protect you, and I will."

"That doesn't mean beating people up and shoving them into lockers."

"He learned to keep his mouth shut, didn't he?"

"That is not the point."

"Yeah," I corrected, "it is. That was the goal—to shut Clint's ass up, and it did. He knows better now, and so does everyone else. What did you expect me to do, tell him to 'please stop' and expect that to work?"

"That doesn't mean you have to get violent!"

"What else am I supposed to do?"

"Well, what did you do to Crystal? You didn't hit her, did you?"

"Um...no." I looked away again. I really didn't want to go there. After I didn't say anything else, Nicole prompted me to elaborate. "I just...took care of it another way."

"Did you threaten her?"

I shrugged again since I was getting so good at it.

"How?" she pushed.

"You really don't want to know," I informed her.

"You are only making my point, you know."

"What *is* your point?" I asked.

"I don't want you to hit people anymore," she said, "or threaten them."

She took another deep breath and dropped her eyes back to her fingers where the fiddled with my shirt sleeve.

"It reminds me of...of..." She didn't finish the sentence.

"Him?" I whispered.

Nicole nodded.

I looked at her eyes and tried to figure out just exactly what I was supposed to do. I told her I would protect her, and I wasn't going to back down—not from that. I wasn't going to put up with anyone giving her any kind of grief for anything. Not Clint, not Crystal, not anyone.

But I didn't want to remind her of that guy in Minneapolis, either. I definitely did not want that, but what else could I do to make sure she was safe? What could I do to keep her happy here?

"I said I'd make everything okay for you," I reminded her. "How else am I supposed to do that?"

"You already do," she said softly.

Now I was really confused.

"But you're telling me not to do that anymore!"

"You don't have to go after other people to make everything feel all right," she said. "You do that just by...by being here."

I had said it before, and I would continue to say it: girls made no sense whatsoever.

"I don't understand," I admitted.

"Remember when we were here, and I was upset the other

night?" she asked. "Remember when you just hugged me?"

I raised an eyebrow at her.

"Okay…you do remember." She took a deep breath and let it out through her nose in a huff. "Just doing that made it better, and when I was…upset with what you had done with my locker and… and you took me outside and held on to me—that made me feel better, too. You didn't have to beat someone up to make me feel better. You fixed it just be being there for me."

I wanted to argue with her and tell her the only reason I could do that was because I had already taken care of the kids at school so they wouldn't bother her again, but I was captivated by her eyes instead. The way she was looking at me…so intensely…it made my heart start pounding in my chest again.

That look was what did it. As soon as my eyes met hers, I knew immediately that I was done for. I would do absolutely anything she asked if she would just keep looking at me like that. Was that all it took? Just *being there* for her? I didn't even know what that really meant, but I did know at that instant that she had me—heart and soul. I could feel it in my mind and every aching muscle in my body.

"Anything," I whispered. I slipped my other hand around the back of her head and pulled her to me. I pressed my lips to her warm mouth, and I kissed her over and over again. I felt her fingers grip on to my arm, and the nails biting slightly into my skin felt wonderful. I broke away for a moment, murmuring against her lips. "I'd do anything for you…anything you want. Just tell me what you need because I don't know what to do."

She smiled down at me for a long moment before speaking again.

"Are you tired?"

I shrugged and shook my head against the pillow.

"I had a pretty decent nap today," I reminded her. "Are you tired?"

"Not so much," she said, and she kissed me again.

I had no idea how long we had been lying there in Nicole's

bed, facing each other and making out. I hadn't looked at the clock for a while, and my brain was far more interested in keeping track of the feel of Rumple's lips on mine than it was on how long we'd been at it. If I really wanted to know, I could always figure it out later.

I found a nice, soft, warm spot of skin at the place where Nicole's neck and shoulder came together and sucked lightly on it. I didn't do it hard enough to leave a mark—her skin was too perfect to be marred like that. Nicole's fingers made little trails down my arm all the way to my wrist and then back up again. I traced my fingers against her side, pushing the hem of her T-shirt up a little.

I danced the tips of my fingers along the skin on her side. I drew little circles and then a few other shapes as I tasted the skin of her neck and shoulder. Nicole jumped a little as I hit a ticklish spot, and I smiled into her skin.

Her hand pushed against my shoulder, and she rolled me away from her and onto my back. Before I could protest, she tossed one leg over me and straddled my stomach.

"You should take your shirt off," she said. Her teeth bit into her bottom lip.

"Oh, really?" I replied with raised eyebrows. She nodded, and I could see her cheeks tinge with pink in the glow of her bedside lamp. I flexed my back and brought myself up just enough to pull my shirt over my head.

I watched my Rumple's mouth turn up in a sly smile as she glanced from my face to my chest. She reached out and started with her fingers at my shoulders before they slowly traced down— over my pecs, brushing against my nipples, and then to my stomach. Her touch was light and brought goose bumps out on my arms. When she circled my navel with her finger and then followed the thin line of hair below it, I had to pull up my knees to keep her from sliding any farther back. If she did, she was definitely going to notice the effect she was having on my body.

She glanced from where her hand was resting on my stomach

to my eyes. She was breathing a little heavier, and my heart was practically making my chest jump up and down. I was torn between wanting to flip her over and bury myself in her as quickly as possible and wanting to make sure I didn't push her into anything she wasn't ready to do. I was pretty sure if I did that, this relationship would be over.

I was going to let her lead.

I licked my lips quickly and gripped her hips with my hands, hoping to keep them steady. With my fingers, I found that spot where the hem of her shirt met her sweatpants. I touched the soft skin of her sides, spreading my fingers out to reach more of her.

Nicole leaned down and touched my lips with hers, kissing me hard as her tongue tangled with mine. Her hands roamed over my chest again, and I used my fingers to creep up her sides a bit more. I stopped before I got to the bottom curve of her tits because I was feeling far too good to press my luck.

I was ready for anything she wanted—she could have all of me or just some of me—whatever made her happy.

That was when, without breaking our kiss, Nicole's fingers left my chest and ran all the way down my arms. When she reached my hands, I was expecting her to push them back down and away from the tender, soft flesh they wanted to touch so badly. I even started to slide them back down myself, but she gripped my fingers and pushed them up until I was cupping both of her glorious, soft breasts.

I thought Shakespeare would have agreed that "We are such stuff as dreams are made on." Somehow, I was going to have to keep myself from going too far.

Now, was she going to let me get my mouth on the girls as well?

CHAPTER SEVENTEEN
intercept

In case there was any doubt, Nicole's tits were absolutely perfect. They fit perfectly into my hands. Her nipples hardened perfectly against my palms. They were perfectly soft and round and just...just perfect.

Nicole moaned into my mouth as my thumbs and forefingers rolled her nipples between them. The sound alone made me want to buck my hips up against her, but I restrained myself even though I could feel her pushing her heat against my stomach.

I sat up a little and rolled us back to our sides. I kept one of my hands on her breast under her shirt, and I kissed her a couple more times before I pulled both my mouth and my hand away.

"We should stop," I said quietly as I tried to regain my breath.

"Why?" Nicole pouted.

"Well, the door is still open," I pointed out. "I really don't want to see Greg's head peek in while I've got my hand up your shirt. Besides...I don't want to...to push."

"You aren't," she told me.

"I will if we keep this up," I said. I propped myself up on my elbow and looked down at her. "I want you. I really, really do. I don't know how to do this boyfriend thing, though. I don't want to…fuck it up."

Nicole smiled and reached up to stroke her fingers over my jaw.

"All right," she said.

We both settled back down on the bed, and I wrapped my arm around her waist. She started pushing the hair off my face and around my ear again.

"I love the way that feels," I told her.

"What?" Nicole asked. She tugged a bit at my hair before she tucked it behind my ear. "This?"

"Yeah. It feels good."

She giggled into my shoulder and kept up the motion as I felt myself starting to drift off. My mind cycled through the day—my run, workout, the picnic lunch with Nicole. I listened to the highlights of the game in my brain and shook my head a little at the weird dream I had. It was strange that I remembered it at all—dreams were the one thing I didn't usually recall. I relived the spicy taste of Nicole's taco salad and the laughter over Greg's fishing exploits.

It was a good day.

I drifted off.

I woke to Greg's voice.

"Nicole? I gotta go into the station this morning," he was saying. "A bunch of kids got picked up at the beach last night, and I need to go calm some parents."

"Okay, Dad," Nicole's sleepy voice said.

"I should be back this afternoon."

"'Kay."

I listened to the thump of his feet on the stairs and the opening and closing of the front door. The house went silent, save for Nicole's yawns. I looked over at the clock, and saw it was still pretty early—just past seven thirty, and I was glad Sundays were my off-days for workouts.

I pulled Nicole's body close to mine and tucked my face into her hair. She squirmed and giggled a little then tried to push my hand away from her stomach. I held tight, grumbling, and wrapped my other arm around her as well.

"Thomas!" Nicole cried. "Let me go!"

"No way," I told her. "You're warm."

She laughed again.

"I have to pee!"

With a big, overly dramatic sigh, I released her, and she ran off to the bathroom. When she was done, I took my turn and then pulled her back into bed with me. We lay in bed while half asleep before hunger finally drove us from the blankets.

We ate and then decided we really ought to get some work done on our biology project. After a lot of debate and orgasm jokes, we decided to do our research on the creosote bush. I made about a dozen "bush" jokes, but Nicole said the plant reminded her of visiting her grandparents in Arizona, so that's what we were going to study. At first, we tried pulling up information on her computer, but the damn thing was ancient, took forever to load, and the dial-up connection was driving me fucking bonkers.

"We should just do this at my place," I mumbled.

"Okay," Nicole said to my surprise. "I've never seen your house."

I tensed up a bit. I'd never taken anyone to my house. Even the guys on my team had only been on the outside of it. Just the thought of it put me on edge immediately though I wasn't sure why. I didn't have a valid reason to say no, so the next thing I knew, we were in my car and heading to my house.

Even the front door seemed ominous to me as we walked up the steps.

"This house is incredible," Nicole exclaimed as I fished out my key.

"It's okay," I replied. I opened the door, and we walked in.

"Do I get a tour?" Nicole asked.

Was I supposed to give tours?

"Um…okay," I said. I ran my hand through my hair. "This is the kitchen—you know, where we eat and shit."

"You shit in the kitchen? That's not very hygienic!"

"That's not what I meant!" I laughed along with her. "This is the, um…living room, I guess. Or great room—whatever you are supposed to call it."

"Who plays?" she asked, and I froze.

She was gesturing at the piano.

"Um…no one," I replied, and I tried to steer her off toward the stairs.

"You have a grand piano that no one plays?" she asked. She held on to my hand but kept her feet planted. Her voice lowered. "Did your mom play?"

"Yeah," I said. "Um…she taught piano."

"Did you learn?"

"Yeah."

"But you don't play anymore?"

"No." I could feel a tiny droplet of sweat at the back of my neck.

"Why not?" she asked quietly.

I looked at her eyes, and she reached up to touch my face.

"Too many memories?"

I just nodded.

"I'm sorry," she said.

I gave her a tight-lipped smile and then led her down the hall and up the stairs, pointing out the various guest rooms that no one used, the bathroom, and Dad's study.

"Is that where the computer is?" she asked as she looked at the closed door.

"No," I replied. "I never go in there. I have a laptop in my room. Last door down the hall."

I took her into my room and tried not to dance from foot to foot as she looked over everything in it. She ran her fingers along the edges of the CDs, pulled one out, and then carefully pushed it back to where it was before as I let out a sigh of relief.

"I won't mess anything up," she said with a wry smile.

I tried to laugh.

"Sorry," I said. "I just…I've never had anyone in here before."

"No one?"

"Not outside my family, no."

She gave me a strange look and then went back to her surveillance.

"You have a lot of trophies," she said. The tip of her finger traced my name on an MVP award from freshman year. She looked around for another minute and then sat down on the edge of my couch. "So where's the computer?"

I grabbed the laptop from its shelf in the closet and pulled out a small, folding table from beside the couch. I set the laptop on it, and we started our research again at top internet speed. After a couple hours, Nicole said she was hungry.

"Should we go back to your place?" I asked.

"Don't you have food?" she teased.

"Um…some," I said. "Considering what you tend to make, I don't know if you would really consider it food or not."

I was right. She was pretty appalled at what we had in the fridge.

"Thomas, this is…disgusting," she said as she eyed some of the green items on the bottom shelf.

No, they hadn't been green when they went in there.

"Um…yeah," I agreed. I couldn't really argue with her. "I usually eat something from the freezer or the pantry."

"I can see why." She looked up at me from her crouched position on the kitchen floor and raised her eyebrows. "Bring me a trashcan."

I hauled the kitchen trashcan out from under the sink and over to the fridge.

"I can't believe you keep your locker looking like something out of *Better Homes and Gardens*, but your fridge looks like it's out of an episode of *Clean House*."

"I hardly ever look in the fridge," I said with a shrug. I took another handful of something from Nicole and tossed it in the bin. It may or may not have once been a mesh bag of peaches. "I usually eat stuff out of a box from the freezer. I don't really know how to cook."

"I get the idea you never look past the top shelf," she said as she pointed to the neatly lined bottles of Gatorade. There were six different flavors, arranged in rainbow order.

Yeah, rainbow order.

"Pretty much," I replied.

"Okay," Nicole said, "I'm going to need bleach for the rest of this."

While Nicole washed down the shelves of the now nearly empty refrigerator, I hauled the trash to the cans outside. She ended up finding something she called "reasonably edible" in the pantry and cooked it up for lunch while I put plates and forks on the table. We spent the rest of the afternoon on our project and didn't even realize how late it was until Nicole's phone rang.

"Um…hi," she said as glanced over to me. I figured it was Greg and hoped she wasn't in trouble or anything for being over at my place. She turned around and talked kind of quietly. "Yeah, I can…but you have to give me about an hour…okay, a half hour… I'm not even home right now…It doesn't matter…"

I tried not to listen, but it was kind of hard. I figured out pretty quickly it wasn't her dad, but I had no idea who it might have been. She gathered up some of the papers we had on the table as she said "uh-huh" into the phone a few more times. Finally, she bit down on her lip and looked up and me.

"I'll be there soon, okay?" She ended the call and shoved the phone into the pocket of her jeans. "I gotta go."

"Everything okay?"

"Yeah," she said. She reached up and pulled her hair out of the hair band that had been keeping it out of her face. She shook her head, and her hair fell around her back and shoulders. "But I need to get home."

I didn't like it.

Everything had been just fine before she got that weird phone call, and now she was running off? I remembered the other time she had just taken off without telling me why, and I remembered what Greg said when she finally came back home.

How are Ron and Timmy?

I looked back at her, and her demeanor was completely different. She had been annoyed with the state of our fridge, but she had been smiling and relaxed. Now, she was agitated and nervous. She wiped her hands on her jeans and gathered up the rest of the project stuff to shove it into her backpack.

"Why?" I asked, because I'm a total idiot who doesn't know when to fucking shut up.

"I just…um…" she stammered. "I need to help out a friend."

"What friend?" I pushed.

"Thomas," Nicole sighed, exasperated. She looked over at me and took another deep breath. "Please don't ask. I'm not going to say, and it's just going to piss you off, okay?"

"No," I said, "it's not *okay*. Why won't you tell me why you have to leave?"

"I just can't."

"Why not?"

"I can't tell you."

"Why can't you tell me?"

"Thomas, for the love of God, stop it!"

"Stop what?"

"I need to go now," she said as she shook her head at me. She walked up to the front door, opened it, tossed her backpack over her shoulder, and looked pointedly at me. I stood in the doorway to the kitchen and just looked right back at her, not moving.

"Come on," she said. Her expression softened. "You could maybe have dinner with Greg, and we could do something when I get back."

Dinner with her dad while she went off to who-knows-where with who-knows-who?

Yeah, I don't think so.

I walked over to the coatrack next to where she was standing, grabbed my keys out of my jacket, and shoved them at her.

"Take yourself home," I growled. I stomped back into the kitchen and yanked open the now clean refrigerator. Her evasiveness pissed me off. I grabbed a bottle of Gatorade and slammed the door shut again.

"Thomas…please don't do this."

"Don't do what?" I snapped. "Don't run off without telling you why or with whom? Oh, wait…no…that's you!"

"I'll explain what I can later," she said, "but I really have to get going."

"Who are Ron and Timmy?" I asked as I glared at her. Her eyes went wide for a minute, and her voice dropped.

"Ron is Greg's friend from town," she said. Then she went all quiet.

"Who is Timmy?"

"Thomas, please don't go there. Really, I have to leave and…"

"Then fucking drive yourself!" I yelled back at her. "Just fucking go!"

She stood silently in the doorway with her quivering lip being attacked by her upper teeth. She looked down at the car keys in her hand and then looked back to me. I dropped my eyes to the bottle of blue Gatorade and started pulling at the loose corner of the label.

"I'm sorry. I just can't…"

"Whatever," I said without looking back at her again.

"I'll be back," she replied.

"Don't bother."

"I have to at least bring the car back," she said softly.

"I'll get it myself."

"Thomas, that's—"

"If you're going to leave, then just get out already!" I screamed at her.

Nicole's words halted in her throat as she turned and ran out of the house. I heard the door open and close as my chest started to feel as if it were compressing inward. As soon as I heard the car start down the drive, I wanted to run out and stop her, but I didn't move.

Instead, I yelled, banged my fist on the table, and knocked over my Gatorade. The amount of destruction just wasn't good enough at all, so I picked the bottle up and threw it against the wall. As a big blue puddle formed on the kitchen floor, I dropped my head into my hands and wondered how I could have fucked it up so badly in the first forty-eight hours.

I just wanted to know where she was going and why. What was so wrong with that? I wanted to know who called and who she was going to go see. That was all.

I didn't want her to go.

But I practically threw her out.

And I told her not to come back.

Shakespeare came to mind, of course, and I thought "I will speak daggers to her, but use none." I wondered if it really made any difference in the long run. She was still gone.

I leaned my head on my forearms and just listened to my own breathing until the mess on the floor got to me. I grabbed some paper towels, wiped up the spill, and then used some of the bleach Nicole had out for the shelves of the refrigerator.

Once the floor was wiped up, I paced around the house. I was about as agitated as I could possibly be as I ran through the last six minutes and twelve seconds Nicole was in my house.

I knew I shouldn't have brought her here.

I didn't know exactly why being here made all the difference, but I was sure it did. I didn't really want to bring her here at all. I didn't want my Rumple to be...*tainted* by this place. Her house was warm and friendly and full of laughter and good food smells. My house was cold and full of pain.

My head jerked up as my mind spun around and found its focal point—its single need.

I headed up to my room to find some relief from the tumult.

I drew.

Without my sketchbook, I was stuck with lined notebook paper, but I cared less about that than I did about the sudden need to get pencil to paper. Even if it was notebook paper and a number two instead of linen paper and charcoal, I had to draw. I just had to.

Nicole was the most vivid thing in my mind. More so than favorite soccer games, high-class meals in Portland, or birthday blow jobs. My mind grabbed on to everything about her—the way her hair moved when she turned her head, the slight clenching of her jaw when I was being a smart-ass, the look in her eyes as she lay down beside me and ran her fingers over my hair…

…and that's what I drew.

The curve of her cheek against the pillow and the strands of her hair cascading all around her came first. The pencil flowed over the rough paper to create the edge of her T-shirt near her shoulder then the line of her neck.

My hand worked nearly as fast as my mind as I captured what beauty I could, eventually slowing down to make sure the detail was spot-on, especially the look in her eye. I didn't know what the look meant. I wasn't even sure if I had ever seen a look like that before—not directed at me, certainly. I just knew I liked it.

The sun began to set outside my window, and my stomach growled a little. I ignored it and kept drawing. Eventually, my eyes started to blur, so I made myself take a break. I lay down across my bed and looked at the picture in my hand. I tried to position myself just as I had been last night and put the picture down where she should have been.

I dozed.

Through the clouds of sleep, I felt the soft tips of her fingers on my cheek, over my jaw, and into my hair. I was pretty sure I moaned as I rolled to one side and opened my eyes.

I hadn't been dreaming.

"Hey," Nicole said. She sucked her lip into her mouth and glanced around nervously. "I knocked, but you didn't answer. I, um…I still had your keys and everything, so I came in to make sure you were all right."

"I'm fine," I lied.

She raised her eyebrows.

"Well, I'm not," she replied.

Fuck.

Now that she was here again, and the memory of her lying next to me was the most important thing in my head, what had happened a few hours ago didn't matter so much anymore. She was here. She came back. Even though I had been an ass and told her not to, she still came back.

"I'm sorry," I said. "I didn't mean to...to freak out on you."

Nicole's mouth turned up into a slight smile, but her eyes stayed melancholy.

"I'm sorry, too," she said. Her fingers stroked my cheek. "I know just taking off like that was...well, it was rude. I didn't know..."

She sighed and shook her head.

"Why did you have to leave so quickly?" I asked.

Nicole placed her hand on my shoulder and rubbed against the muscles there. It felt good.

"Some stories aren't mine to tell," she said softly. "I asked if... well, if I could tell just you, but..."

She let out a big sigh.

"Well, Thomas, you have a bit of a reputation."

"I guess I can't argue with that." I tried to smile a little, but I still didn't like what she was saying. I guess being king of the hill wasn't always a good thing. I looked up at her hopefully. "You can't even tell me who this Timmy is, though?"

Nicole shook her head.

Since my focus was always on soccer, my first thought was of the goalie, Tim Howard. Images of his pictures from ESPN's *The Body Issue* flashed in my head. He was tall, ripped, and one of the best goalies in the world. I thought about my Rumple running away from me to be with him, and it felt like there was a fist squeezing my heart. A question I didn't want answered popped out of my mouth without warning.

"Are you...are you seeing him, too?"

Nicole laughed. Her hand covered her mouth, and she laughed even harder. I narrowed my eyes at her because I didn't think there was anything funny about any of this shit, but she just kept laughing until she had to wipe tears from her eyes.

"Um…no, Thomas, I am definitely *not* seeing Timmy." She giggled again. She looked at my face and must have seen how humorless this was to me.

I rolled over to my stomach and propped myself up on both elbows. I stared at the gold duvet on my bed.

"Don't look like that," Nicole said. Her hand ran over my jaw again. "I promise you have nothing to worry about."

Well, that wasn't going to stop me from worrying anyway.

"What's this?" Nicole said, and she reached over me to grab the paper that had been hidden behind my body.

"Nothing!" I said, and I grabbed it away from her, but it was too late. She had already seen it.

"Did you draw that?" Nicole asked.

I held the paper against my chest so she couldn't see any more of it, but apparently she already had seen enough to understand. I felt as if I wanted to retch.

"Is that a picture of me?" she asked. Her eyes were soft as she looked at me, and I could feel any resolve I might have had, along with my better judgment, crumbling. "Let me see it."

I handed her the paper.

"It's not done yet," I said quietly.

She looked from the paper to me, back to the paper, and then back to me again.

"Thomas…this is…" She stopped and looked at the picture again. "This is incredible."

"It's only on notebook paper," I pointed out, "and I didn't have the right kind of pencil, and the shading isn't right yet, and—"

"It's beautiful," she said. She leaned closer to me and tilted her head to the side at an awkward angle to get to where I was. She looked into my eyes before she slowly moved in and touched my mouth with hers. It was much too quick, as far as I was concerned, but even with its brevity, all the anger I had felt toward her evaporated.

I moved my hand up and cupped her face, bringing her back to me. I kissed her lips again and then kissed along her jaw.

"I am glad 'tis night, you do not look on me," I quoted, "for I am much ashamed of my exchange."

I felt her mouth turn up in a smile, and I pulled back to look at her again, glad to see she was more relaxed. As I looked at her, I couldn't even understand why I had been so mad. Maybe it was just because she was leaving, and I didn't want her to go.

"You're beautiful," I told her.

Her smile became more genuine and less sad.

"Did you eat anything for dinner?" she asked, and I was grateful for the topic change.

"Nah, I kind of fell asleep instead. It's getting late though."

"I brought your car back," she said.

"I kind of figured."

"I'm sorry I ran off on you," she said. So much for topic changes. She fiddled with the edge of my shirt, and apparently she figured out she had switched the subject back as well, so she changed it again. "Want me to make you something?"

And she said I was going to make *her* head explode.

"There isn't anything here to make," I reminded her.

"Maybe I'll take you grocery shopping." She smiled at me, and I rolled myself up to a sitting position. I thought about what my dad would think if he saw in the refrigerator a bunch of fresh vegetables neither of us could even name.

"I think that would spawn a few too many questions," I said.

"I guess so," she admitted, and she sounded defeated. She also looked really tired all of a sudden.

"It's getting late," I said. "We have school tomorrow, too. I'll take you home."

"You still need to eat."

"I'll find something when I get back."

"I'm not leaving you here by yourself without anything decent to eat for dinner," Nicole said. "So just get your overnight bag repacked. It will make it easier for you to take me to school tomorrow."

Who was I to argue?

Long before Sherlock Holmes, Shakespeare's Henry V said, "The game is afoot." Somehow, when it came to having a real relationship with Nicole, I had the feeling I was playing with chess pieces on a monopoly board.

Now, hopefully Nicole at least understood the rules of the game.

CHAPTER EIGHTEEN
booking

The combination of waking up beside Nicole and walking out of her house to take her to school in the morning had me smiling. She made a real breakfast while I was in the shower—bacon and eggs, toast, hash browns—the works. I was stuffed and loving it. Without any valid reason to change it, we did the same that night, and the night after.

In the evenings, we worked on our project and watched TV with Greg. The project was nearly done though it wasn't due for another week. Nicole seemed to really appreciate that we didn't have to go and look things up a second time—once we found the information, I remembered it. I was learning a lot about the Arizona landscape and why Nicole loved it so much as well as the weird little bush that grew there. It was obvious how much she missed her grandparents, who had both died when she was young.

Nights were the best. We still didn't go past making out and a little boob groping, but I wasn't complaining.

Wednesday was another rainy day, and I held an umbrella for Nicole as we ran across her driveway to my car. Once she was settled, I got in the driver's seat and started toward school. Nicole's phone rang right as I pulled into the street.

"Yeah, I should be able to do that," Nicole said with a sigh. "Can you pick me up? Okay…see you then."

She glanced over to me as she hung up, bit down on her lip, and shoved her phone back into her backpack. I tried to be patient, hoping she would tell me what the fuck that was all about before I had to ask. I started drumming my fingers on the steering wheel and looking at her sideways.

"I'm not going to be able to be at your practice after school," she said as we reached the school parking lot. "I need to go help a friend."

"Timmy?" I asked. I tried to keep the bitterness out of my voice, but I wasn't very successful. I shoved the gearshift into neutral and yanked up on the parking brake.

"Please don't," she said quietly. Her fingers played with the strap of her book bag.

"Why can't you tell me?" I pushed even though I knew it wouldn't matter.

"The same reason I can't tell my dad about what your dad is doing," she snapped back. "I promised I wouldn't."

Touché.

"Fine," I said with a sigh. I took a deep breath before opening the car door and the umbrella, trying to do both at the same time and still ending up with water all over the damn window controls. I tried to wipe them off and just ended up getting the seat wet.

I growled, cursed, and then finally gave up. If there was a break in the rain, I'd come clean it up then. Nicole had her lips smashed together to hold in her giggles.

Not appreciated.

I held the umbrella over her and walked her into school, feeling my ire drop significantly as her fingers wrapped around the top of mine, holding the umbrella. I dropped her off at her first class with a quick kiss and headed back toward the lockers.

Paul was there, which meant I didn't have to go looking for him.

"Hey, Paul!" I called out. "I have a question for ya!"

He turned and walked over to me, and we started down the hallway.

Paul grew up in the nearby borough and only started coming to school in town his freshman year when his parents moved into town after some fallout with the municipal council leaders or whatever. I didn't know the details, nor did I give a shit. Their little township tried to run things separately from the rest of town even though they were still bound by the same town charter. They didn't like the rules. My dad didn't like their resistance, and they didn't like him.

Or me.

"You know most everyone from your old town, don't you?"

"Pretty much," he said with a nod.

"How about a guy named Timmy or one named Ron?" I asked.

"There's Ron Jones," Paul said. "He's one of the municipal council guys."

"What about Timmy?"

"Doesn't sound familiar," Paul said. "Why?"

I ignored his question.

"Does Ron have a family?"

"He's got a couple of kids," he told me. "I was in the same classes as his daughter, Rachel."

"Any more?"

"I think she had a sister or something. I didn't really know them too well since my parents never got along with them."

"Oh, yeah. Okay, cool."

"Why do you want to know?" he pressed.

"Just curious," I shrugged.

I turned and walked off then immediately ducked into the bathroom. Thankfully, there was no one else in there. I pulled out my phone and browsed my contact list.

"Hey, Malone."

"Hey. I need some info."

"Sure."

"Whatever you got on Ron Jones, and a guy named Timmy

from the next township over."

"Last name?"

"I dunno. Maybe the same," I said.

"I know the other name—he's on the council, I think."

"That's the one."

"Okay, I'll get back to you."

Iago's warning came to mind: "O, beware, my lord, of jealousy." In the back of my head, I knew Rumple was going to be pissed about me digging into her relationships. I didn't care. I just needed to know who the fuck Timmy was.

It didn't take long. Right before lunch, my phone started meowing furiously as I got a call back, but he had nothing on Timmy Jones.

What the fuck?

Nothing interesting came up for Ron Jones, either. Just that he was a council member with two daughters, both over eighteen. I got an address at least, though I didn't know my way around town except how to get to the mall. Like I said, the residents didn't care much for the Malones, so I pretty much stayed away from town if I could. Dad always thought it was best to let him deal with the politicians and keep me away from all of it. There were times he'd bring me along to rub the soccer stuff in their faces, but that was about it. The couple of times I had been to social events with him, it had been pretty obvious we weren't welcome.

Of course, it might have been because I had fucked one of the alderman's daughters, and her dad walked in on us.

Whatever.

It was pretty quiet in the lunchroom, and Nicole kept asking if I was pissed at her because she was going to miss my practice. I just shrugged, not really knowing what to say. It wasn't like she was going to tell me anything. She leaned over and kissed the side of my mouth when biology was over, and I felt like a total shit for being such a total shit.

"I just don't want you to go," I whispered into her ear.

"I know," she whispered back. She gave me a small smile

before she walked out.

I was already on the field practicing when school let out, so I had a good view of the parking lot as kids starting getting in their cars to head home. I was doing a little ball juggling when I saw a posh Jaguar pull into the lot and drive up next to the main doors. Nicole walked out and got in the passenger side. All I could see of the driver were dark glasses and black hair.

I don't know why that set me off exactly, but it did. I slammed the ball into the goal with my right foot and took off toward the parking lot.

It wasn't difficult to follow them, and I would have stayed right behind them if some asshole hadn't cut me off and then stopped at the fucking red light as the car Nicole was in kept going. I pounded on the steering wheel and screamed, but there wasn't enough room for me to get around. By the time the light changed, the Jag was out if sight.

Now the township isn't all that big—not even big enough to *be* a township—so I just drove up to the corporation limits, pulled over for a minute, and added the address for Ron Jones into my GPS. Of course, the maps for the area seriously sucked because the subdivision was so new, and I ended up turning around a half dozen times before I finally noticed the huge, mosaic tiled drive that led to a large ranch house. I wasn't sure if I had the right place or not. There weren't any other cars, not even in the driveway.

Fuck it.

I parked, went up the porch steps, and banged on the door.

Nicole opened it.

"Thomas?" Her expression quickly moved from shock to seriously ticked off. "What the...?"

Of course, now that I was there, I had no clue what to say or do. Before I came up with anything brilliant, the dark-haired guy walked up and stood behind her, glaring.

"I thought Sophie said you weren't going to say anything to him," he said, his voice as dark as his hair.

"I didn't," Nicole responded. She glared at me. "What are you doing here? How did you even *get* here?"

"In my car," I replied.

"Don't be a shit!" Nicole yelled back at me.

The guy laughed.

"I saw you leave school..." I started to say, but I trailed off.

"You followed me?" she gasped.

"Not...exactly..." I stammered. "I lost you in town."

"Then how did you get here?"

"Um..."

Shit.

"Dammit, Thomas!" Nicole yelled. She turned sideways to look at the man and ran her hands through her hair.

"I just want to know what the fuck is going on!" I finally yelled. I wasn't really mad, just fucking frustrated with all of this shit.

"You don't belong here," the dude said, and I was pretty sure he must be Ron Jones. He looked a little familiar, like I might have seen him at a council function. "You aren't welcome. Get back in your car and go."

"Ron," Nicole said softly. "Please—he's already here...Once he sees..."

Nicole's voice trailed off as a loud, unearthly wailing sound came from inside the house. It was like nothing I had ever heard before, and I immediately took a step away from the door.

Ron snickered.

"He won't tell anyone," Nicole said confidently as she walked back into the house.

"What, out of the goodness of his heart?" Ron didn't even bother trying to hide is contempt.

"Don't fucking yell at her!" I really, really didn't like him talking like that to her. I took a step forward again but then realized I was making a move on a local bigwig. I faltered then heard that insane sound again and cringed.

Nicole disappeared behind the door, and I fought the urge to go in after her. I mean, it's not like this guy was going to punch me or something to stop me. As a public figure, he knew better than to do something so stupid. Nicole was only gone for a second, and when she came back, she was holding…

…a little kid.

A baby, really.

"Thomas," she said with her eyes shooting those beautiful blue daggers and her kitten claws set to castrate, "this is Timmy."

"That's Timmy?" I said, unable to hide my astonishment.

Then my entire body went cold, and my stomach lurched.

The kid wasn't like a newborn, not that I had much experience with babies at all, but he was sitting up in Nicole's arms and looking at me, and I knew that little babies couldn't hold their heads up. He was looking around from face to face like he was trying to figure out what was going on, too.

Timelines started flashing through my head.

Nicole had been partying after her division championship.

Division championships were typically the end of the fall season.

If she…if she got…

Fuck.

"Is he…is he yours?" I looked at her eyes and was in full-blown panic mode. What if this kid was hers? What if she had a baby from one of those fuckheads? What if…what if she was planning to raise a kid when she got out of high school?

What the fuck would I do about that?

I'd fucking help her. That's what I'd do.

Images flashed through my head in rapid succession: Nicole and I with little Timmy on walks in the park with her pushing a stroller; taking picnics on her living room floor with him crawling around us; seeing him get a little older and taking him to the beach; teaching him to kick a ball into a goal.

"Oh, for goodness' sake!" Nicole shrieked at me. "Of course not! I'm just helping Sophie!"

For a second, I was disappointed.

Then my higher cognitive functioning kicked in, and I was

seriously fucking relieved.

"Nicole, you need to stop talking," Ron said with his deep, ominous voice.

"Ron, please!" She turned to him, and her eyes begged. "He won't tell anyone. I swear he won't. Will you?"

She turned back to me, and I could only nod as I tried to wrap my head around whatever the fuck was going on. Ron glared at her.

"That's between you and Sophie," Ron finally said. "But you keep your mouth shut until she gets home."

Nicole sighed and looked back at me again.

"Go home, Thomas," she said after a moment. "I am seriously fucking pissed at you, and when I'm done here, I'll be at your house to set some fucking limits. You got it?"

Ron snickered again.

I already hated the fucker.

But I couldn't be too pissed because even though she was obviously really mad at me, she said she was going to come and talk about it. Hopefully, that meant I was at least going to be offered my three shakes.

Or was it time to castle?

Fuck.

How do you play these games when the rules don't make any fucking sense?

At least she wasn't showing me a red card. Not yet, anyway. I could handle a booking as long as it was just the cautionary yellow.

"Okay," I said quietly.

Nicole handed the baby back to Ron then placed her hand gently on my chest and pushed me from the doorway onto the porch. She closed the door softly behind her and looked up at me.

Claws still out.

"I'm going to try to work this out," she seethed, "but you have really, really made this difficult! Why couldn't you just trust me, huh?"

"I trust you," I replied.

"The hell you do!"

"I do!" I said more adamantly.

"Then start acting like it! When Sophie gets back from work, I'll talk to you. For now—go!"

She turned around and went back into the house, shutting me out as I stood there on the porch with my mouth hanging open.

I closed it, turned around, and walked slowly back to my car.

For some reason, Shakespeare whispered in my ear the phrase "not so much brain as ear wax." Somehow, I thought I might have run out of "Get Out of Jail Free" cards in this Monopoly game.

Now, was she going to take my queen?

CHAPTER NINETEEN
the twelfth man

My phone meowed just as I was pulling out of the driveway.

I had left it on the passenger seat when I went to find Nicole.

Two missed calls.

I checked the number.

Shit, shit, shit.

Before my shaking hand could hit the recall button, the phone was meowing again.

"Hey, Dad."

"Don't you 'Hey Dad' me! Why the *fuck* weren't you at practice?"

"I...um..."

Shit. I was not ready for this.

"Fucking answer me!" he screamed through the phone. "Were you out boning that bitch, because I told you *no fucking distractions*! Ten days, asshole! Ten days before the Messini brothers come to see you. *Ten fucking days*!"

"I know, Dad...I was just..."

"Just what?"

I didn't want to do it, but I only had one card to play that didn't lead to total disaster.

"Just…not feeling well."

"Not feeling well?" he repeated. His voice dropped significantly in volume. "You sick?"

"No...um…" Damn! Now I was stammering. "I don't think so. It's just…it's nothing."

"Tell me what the fuck is wrong with you!" he yelled.

I took a long, audible breath.

"My ribs are really hurting today," I lied. "I took Motrin, but it just wasn't taking the edge off. I think I overdid it when I was working out yesterday and maybe pulled it or something."

He went completely quiet for a minute.

"The prescription is in my bathroom," he said softly. "Take one, and one only."

"Okay," I said. "Thanks, Dad."

"No problem. Just get some rest tonight, okay?"

"Yeah, sure."

"You have to be in top shape next week, son. You can't fuck it up."

"I won't, Dad. I swear."

"That's my boy."

He hung up.

I wanted a cigarette.

"Fuck."

I stopped at the end of the street, rubbed the heels of my hands into my eyes for a minute, tried to take some deep cleansing breaths or some such shit, and drove home. The house was dark when I got there since the clouds had thickened and there was even some thunder in the distance. I turned on the lights in the kitchen and the living room just to make it a little brighter. Then I went upstairs and into Dad's bathroom, dumped one of the pain pills into my hand and then into the toilet.

I knew he counted them.

I went into my room, stood there staring into space for a minute, and tried to figure out what the fuck was happening.

I wasn't stupid. I'd seen after-school specials. I knew a lot of shit about my life was fucked up: my Mom was gone, my Dad had to deal with being a single parent, and I had no real understanding about what a relationship between a man and a woman was supposed to be beyond tab A into slot B. I knew, when it came right down to it, my Dad shouldn't fucking hit me.

And I knew that he knew it, too.

I had only ever used his guilt on him once before, when I was fifteen and wanted to go to an all-night party at the beach. He said no way because I had to train the next day, and I sulked around until he finally blew up. Then I told him I was supposed to go the prior weekend, but I hadn't been able to.

I was too bruised to be seen in public.

He let me go.

I felt like shit then, too.

I knew why he acted that way because ultimately, whether he should be doing it or not, whatever pain he inflicted on me was nothing like the mental anguish I had inflicted on him when I killed his wife—the only person he had ever loved. I thought I knew what that was like for him before, since I lost her too, but now that Nicole was around…well, the very idea of anything happening to her was just…unthinkable.

I'd freak out.

I'd go insane.

I'd implode.

I'd probably punch and kick and destroy anyone who came into contact with me, and if I got a hold of the person responsible for hurting her…well, whatever happened wouldn't be pretty, that was for sure.

I went into the kitchen, thought about eating something, but just grabbed a Gatorade instead. I needed to go to the store; I was almost out of the blue ones. I tilted my head a little so I could see the bottom of the fridge, and it did look a lot better. It reminded me that Nicole was going to come over at some point, and she was going to string me up by my balls.

I lost my train of thought as I imagined Nicole's hands on my balls.

I shook my head, went into the living room, and played a little FIFA on the Wii. I was Germany and creamed the Spanish team, the way the last World Cup should have been. When I was done, I tossed the controller back in its drawer and looked at the pouring rain out the window. It was getting dark, and I hadn't heard from Nicole.

Was she still coming?

Did she have to stay later than she thought?

Was she making Greg dinner? Had she forgotten about me?

Did she get in a…in a…

Shit.

Fuck.

My chest tightened up again, and I had to fight the bile trying to rise up my throat. I swallowed hard and washed it down with a big gulp of blue Gatorade.

It had started to rain harder. What if she was hurt? What if Ron had shitty eyesight, and he hit something trying to drive in the dark? What if a lamppost or something got hit by lightning right in front of them?

I felt like the twelfth man on a team, just waiting on the sidelines but unable to actually do anything about the play. All I could do was try to come up with some chant to spur on the team.

My stomach clenched again, and I tried telling myself I was just hungry, but the idea of food made me want to vomit. I looked down at my shaking hands and realized I was starting to hyperventilate.

I couldn't stand it. I had to go find her.

I grabbed my keys and headed for the door. Just as I got there, I saw headlights coming up the drive.

Thank fuck.

I didn't care if she yelled at me, slapped me in the face, or told me she never wanted to see me again. She was okay, and at the moment, that was all that mattered. As soon as she started running from the car to the front door, I was out on the porch, grabbing her into my arms and holding her against my chest.

She was real.

She was okay.

My hand went up her back and came to rest on the back of her head, tangled in her wet hair. I tucked my head against her shoulder and inhaled the scent of her.

"Thomas, I'm getting drenched!"

Oops.

I pulled her inside, kissed her forehead, and told her to wait while I ran upstairs for towels. I gently dried her arms then her face and her hair. I ran back upstairs and grabbed a clean jersey, some sweats that were too small for me, and a pair of dry socks. I ran them all back down to her and then ran the wet towels into the laundry room to get them washed. Once they were going, I raced back to Nicole, realized I had left her hair sticking out all over the place after the rubdown, and ran back up to my bathroom to find a comb.

When I got back, she was holding in giggles.

"What?" I asked.

"You!" she said as she finally lost her hold on her mouth and started chuckling. "You just made fifteen laps around the house."

I smiled a little sheepishly.

She reached out and put her hand on my cheek.

"Are you okay?"

"Yeah," I said. "I just…was starting to…worry, I guess."

"Did you think I wasn't coming?"

"Maybe." I didn't want to admit I was practically having a panic attack worrying about her. I reached out, lay my hands on her sides, and pulled her close again. It was good to feel her against me.

"I'm still mad," she informed me.

"I know," I mumbled. I tried to look properly chastised, but I wasn't sure it was working. Well, she hadn't really started yelling at me yet, so the look was probably a little premature. I straightened up, un-pouted my lip, and waited for the shit-storm.

"How did you find me?" she asked. "Did you follow me or not?"

"Well, I—"

She suddenly leaned forward and grabbed hold of my chin.

"And don't you dare lie to me, Malone!" she snapped.

Meow.

"I tried to follow you," I admitted, "but I lost you."

"You said that," she reminded me. "How did you get to Ron's house?"

"My GPS…and a little luck."

"Thomas!" she yelled, obviously exasperated.

I sighed and gave up. I reached out for her hand, and she let me lead her to the couch.

"I've got a…friend," I told her. "He's a skip-tracer. He can find out almost anything about anybody. I called him, and he got me the address."

Nicole looked into my eyes for a long, long time. Her expression remained guarded and thoughtful all at the same time. When she finally spoke, I jumped a little.

"Spill it," she said simply.

"Huh?"

"Everything you had this guy find out about me. Everything."

"Um…well…"

Okay, this was not going swimmingly right at the moment.

"Out with it!"

"Okay!" I ran a hand through my hair. "He did a little background search on you but nothing too detailed, okay? All I wanted then was your phone number, really."

"You could have asked for it."

"Not right at that time," I said. I tried to give her a smile, but it faltered. "You weren't speaking to me."

"Humph."

"He gave me your IM account info, too."

"So, you got all this info—my IM and my phone number—but you never called or tried to friend me?"

"I didn't need to friend you," I said—like a total idiot.

"What do you mean?"

"I…um…hacked your IM account."

"Oh my God," Nicole said as she put her elbows on her knees and her hands on her head. "You really have no boundaries, do you?"

"I just…wanted to talk to you," I admitted. I felt like a total tool.

"You are such a fucking stalker," she said. She obviously wasn't overly happy, but she didn't seem nearly as mad as I had expected, either.

"You don't have Facebook or Twitter," I said with a shrug.

"No more of that shit," she said as she shook a claw at me.

"I won't," I promised. I waited a minute, and when she didn't say anything else, I made my move. "Are you going to tell me what the big deal is? I mean, it's just a kid. Why all the secrecy?"

Nicole huffed through her nose and rubbed her temples with her fingertips.

"I talked to Sophie, and she is seriously mad at me," she said. "You know, you and your dad are not exactly popular around there."

"I know."

"Why is that?"

"Um…my dad managed to get a section of land annexed to make the parking garage at the hospital bigger. They claimed it was like…I dunno…supposed to be for a park or something. It was a lot of bullshit."

I waved my hand dismissively.

"I am *not* having that conversation with you tonight," Nicole replied. "Eventually, I convinced Sophie that you would never, ever tell anyone about Timmy, and if you make a liar out of me, I'm going to put your balls up on a pike in front of the school. Got it?"

"Um…yeah," I said, and I was again torn between feeling threatened by the act she suggested or once again turned on by the idea of her touching my balls. "I won't say anything. Who would I tell?"

"Your dad?" she suggested.

"No fucking way," I said. It was apparently a good enough promise.

Nicole nodded and went on.

"I'm going to make a long story short," she said. "Sophie was seeing a man in Portland…an older man. He was campaigning to be mayor. Their involvement was obviously very hush-hush because she was only barely eighteen, and he's married. She ended up pregnant."

"Okay, so he doesn't want anyone to know." I figured. "What's the big deal?"

"It's a little more complicated than that," Nicole said. "You were there—Ron's a politician, too. He needs votes and has two daughters and now a baby as well. They are in a ton of debt because he uses all the money for campaigns and trying to keep up appearances. Sophie is working all the hours she can, but if anyone finds out about Timmy, she's screwed."

"She's already been screwed," I piped up. "He should have had the sense to wear a glove."

Nicole dropped her head to the side and glared at me.

"Sorry," I said with a shrug. It was still true, though. I never fucked a girl without using a condom. "I still don't get why the baby has to be a secret."

"I'm getting to that bit."

"Okay."

"When Sophie told the guy in Portland, he wanted her to… well, to get rid of it, but she couldn't. He was really mad, saying she was going to ruin his life and whatever. He said if she ruined him, he'd ruin her, too."

"He knows she needs money," Nicole went on. "He's promised to support the baby but only if she keeps it a secret until after the first of next year. That's when he'll be elected mayor, and he wants to make sure he gets what he wants. If anyone hears about Timmy, he won't. So, he said he'll support Sophie and the baby if she keeps the affair quiet long enough. If not, he says he'll fight her on it, drag her through courts and whatever. He's got money, and there's no way she could afford a lawyer or anything. He knows it."

"So, if she keeps it all quiet," I recapped, "then he'll pay her off? Sounds to me like he's stringing her along."

"I think so, too," Nicole said with a nod, "but Sophie refuses to see it that way."

"He'll never pay her shit."

"I know," Nicole said softly, "but she still thinks she loves him. I know she loves the baby, and since Greg and I are the only people who know about him, they're kind of short-handed when it comes to help. I babysit when she has to work because Ron has all these council commitments he can't miss. It's not like he could take Timmy to a meeting or anything."

"So why the disappearing act?" I asked.

"Sophie works at the diner," she told me. "Sometimes when the loggers come through or a bus stops or something, they get slammed and call her in. She can't tell them she can't make it because of the baby, or everyone would know."

"So Rumple to the rescue."

"Something like that." Nicole gave me a wry smile.

I relaxed against the couch, my fears abated. I still felt like a shit for being so paranoid, but was so glad it wasn't what it appeared to be. I couldn't help but feel good overall.

"All right, Malone," Nicole said as she sat up straight. "Greg said he gave you some of his own ground rules, and now it's time to talk about mine.

I took a big breath and tried to calm the sudden attack of nerves. I looked up at Nicole where she was sitting on the couch, a whole cushion away from me, and gave her a nod to go ahead.

"No more spying," she said definitively. "If you want to know something, you ask me. Chances are I'm going to tell you. And I don't just mean spying on me. Don't go looking up anyone else just because I'm not telling you something."

I nodded more vigorously. I could deal with this.

"Tell me what you're thinking if it's important to us," she said.

My hands were getting all sweaty for some reason. I rubbed them on my thighs and tilted my head to the side.

"What do you mean?"

"I mean if something is bothering you, tell me it's bothering you. Tell me why some things upset you so much. I want to understand."

She was making a pretty big assumption that I had any idea what was going on in my own head.

"What if I don't understand, either?" I asked.

"Then tell me anyway," she said, "and I'll help you figure it out."

I felt my mouth turn up in a bit of a smile. I liked the idea of figuring shit out with her.

"I'm going to tell you if something is bugging me as well," she promised, "and I'll try to do it before it becomes too much of a big deal."

"Okay."

"We both kind of have a temper," Nicole said a little sheepishly. "That isn't going to help. I'll try to keep mine in check, okay?"

"Yeah," I nodded. "I'll try, too."

"Good." Nicole gave me a real smile then and reached over to give me a quick hug. She backed off again and leaned against the back of the couch.

I tried to process everything she had said, not sure if I was completely successful or not. What she was saying wasn't that complicated, but I still didn't know how this was going to change anything. Nicole interrupted my internal ramblings.

"You have to trust me, Thomas," she said. Her voice softened and she leaned toward me a little. "I don't know that much about relationships either, but I know we have to be able to trust each other. If we don't, it's not going to work. At least, that's what Greg keeps telling me."

"I do trust you," I said, but even as I said it, I wasn't sure exactly what it meant.

"Then act like it."

"How?"

"If there is something I'm not telling you, there is a good reason for it. If it's something important that you need to know, you have to trust that I'm not going to hold back."

"Okay," I replied. I didn't really know what else to say. The whole subject had me on edge, and I didn't know what I was supposed to do.

"You thought I was going to visit some guy, didn't you?" she said.

"You were."

"He's an infant."

"I didn't know that."

"And you didn't trust me to be with another guy our own age."

I thought about that one for a minute. Was that it? It didn't seem right.

"I didn't know if *he* was trustworthy," I told her, "not you."

"It's kind of the same thing there, Thomas," she said. "You have to trust me to make the right decisions for myself, too."

I had no fucking idea what that meant.

"I'll try, I guess," I said.

"Thomas?"

"Yeah?" I looked up at her.

"Do you want this to…um…work?"

"What do you mean?"

"I mean you and me—us. Do you want us to work?"

I looked at her, froze, and I tried to think about what it would be like if it *didn't* work. What school would be like—seeing her, but not *being* with her? Would I want to go back to playing soccer without her watching me?

Fuck no.

"I want it to work," I told her. "I do. I don't know what *it* really means, but I want it to work."

"So do I," she replied. "As far as what that means exactly, we'll figure it out together, okay?"

I nodded. Together sounded good.

Nicole sighed and ran her hands through her hair at the same time I did. She giggled a little, recognizing the gesture, and I wondered if she had always done that or if she picked it up from me.

"I'm going to go home," Nicole said. "I need…a little space right now, okay?"

I knew my expression gave away my thoughts at the whole idea, but I also knew I wasn't going to be able to sleep at her house all the time. Dad would be back in a couple of days, and who knew how that was going to complicate everything? I hadn't even thought about how I was going to deal with that.

He's going to make me dump her.

"Okay," I said softly. I looked down at my hands on my thighs.

Nicole reached out and put her hands on top of mine.

"Come pick me up for school still?"

"Sure." I tried to smile, but I didn't pull it off too well.

Nicole reached out and touched the side of my face.

"Have you eaten anything?"

"Not really."

"I'll call my dad to come get me and then fix you something." She stood up and started heading for the kitchen.

"You don't have to do that." I jumped off the couch and followed her. "I can fend for myself. I can drive you home, too."

"I know you can," she replied. "I want to make you dinner, and I want Dad to pick me up."

I couldn't really argue with her, especially since the whole conversation was making my stomach growl. She dug around in our pantry, mumbling about the shit within, and ended up finding spaghetti and sauce to make. Once the pasta was drained, she made up a plate for me, and a few minutes later Greg's cruiser appeared in the driveway.

"I'll see you tomorrow," she said.

I reached out for her, and she didn't pull back when I wrapped my arms around her.

"Thanks for dinner," I said. I kissed her softly but didn't try to press for anything else. If she needed space, I would give it to her —even if it did drive me bonkers.

She left me to go back home, but I didn't feel that bad about it. I was going to miss sleeping next to her tonight, but we were going to work everything out together, and that was the thing that really mattered. At least, I thought it did.

Shakespeare said, "…out of this nettle, danger, we pluck this flower, safety." Somehow, Nicole had become my safe flower.

Now, how could I ever manage to give that up?

CHAPTER TWENTY
set piece

I lay on my bed and stared at the ceiling. I had seen the day pass through my mind so many times, it was starting to blur my mental vision. Even as Nicole's rules slid around in my brain, all I could really think about was what to do when Dad got back home.

It wasn't just a matter of not being able to sleep in her house or in her bed anymore. He said I had to dump her, and if I didn't, he was going to find out. There was just no way of keeping anything like that from him long-term. Even if I dared try to hide if from him for a while, eventually he'd catch on. Once he did, he wouldn't stop at just punishing me.

What the fuck am I going to do?

I had no idea.

So, I did what any normal teenage boy would have done.

I refused to think about it.

I was up early the next morning, took my run, had a shower, and snarfed down some cereal before I went to pick up Nicole. I was really early, but she was ready anyway. We headed to school, and I parked near the soccer field.

"Got your soccer bag?"

"Seriously?" I asked her with a raised eyebrow.

She chuckled and shook her head.

"Don't leave home without it?"

"Not much, no," I replied.

"Let's play." Nicole opened up her door and headed out toward the field. I grabbed the ball out of my bag and jogged through the fog to catch up with her.

"You really want to play?" I asked.

"Why not?"

I shrugged. Why not, indeed?

We couldn't actually play a game with just the two of us, so I started juggling and then kicked the ball toward Nicole. She took a quick step back and tapped the ball with the inside of her foot, then her knee, then the outside of her foot before sending it back to me. We went back and forth for a while, and I was seriously impressed with her ball-handling skills.

That thought distracted me enough that I missed the damn ball.

I let it roll off behind me, took the couple of steps I needed to reach her, and wrapped my arms around her waist. I pulled her close to me and planted a big kiss on her lips. Her hands went up around my shoulders, and I started kissing across her jaw until I reached her ear.

"You are fucking phenomenal," I told her.

"Hmm…" she hummed against my cheek. "You ready for your game tomorrow?"

"Yeah, I think so."

"What are you going to do after the game?"

"I dunno," I said. My lips started making their way down her neck. I pushed the collar of her sweater out of the way a bit so I could reach more skin. "Probably some party or something."

"Is there one the team has to go to?" she asked.

I pulled back.

"What are you getting at?" This seemed like more than just normal questioning.

Nicole looked off to one side, shrugged one shoulder, than

raised one eyebrow.

"Greg's working a double starting Friday evening," she said. "You want to come back to my place after the game?"

"Sure," I said. Being at her place was better than any lame-ass party anyway. "But what difference does it make if Greg's there?"

Nicole rolled her eyes at me.

"You do know he gave me the same rule, right?" she said.

The same rule? He told her not to hurt me like she had been hurt? No, that didn't make much sense...

Oh.

Oh, wait!

Sex!

He said not while he was in the house.

Was Nicole suggesting what it sounded like she was suggesting? My heart began to pound in my chest, relocating all the blood in my body to my cock.

"Do you mean...um...you want to...?" I couldn't complete the sentence. My palms were starting to sweat again. When the fuck did that start happening?

Nicole cuddled up against my chest, tucking her head in.

"I don't know," she said quietly. "At least he wouldn't be in the next room or possibly walking down the hall to peek in at us. Maybe just...see what happens?"

"Yeah," I said and then cleared my throat so I could say it again, only audibly. "Yeah, I'd like that."

"Cool."

Tilting my head to get a better angle, I looked down at her. Her cheeks were kind of tinged with pink in the soft morning light as the sun rose up over the trees. I ran my finger over one of her cheeks and smiled to myself. I took a couple of deep breaths to gain some control over various self-minded parts of my body and sighed out the last one.

"I suppose I should do the right thing and get you to class on time?"

"It would probably be a good idea," Nicole agreed.

I picked the ball up and tucked it under my arm. I reached out, took Nicole's hand in mine, and we walked to the building with our arms swinging between us. There were other kids arriving in the parking lot, and lots of them already inside the school. I barely saw them because my eyes were on my Rumple.

I looked down at our clasped hands as Shakespeare rattled through my brain—"now join your hands, and with your hands your hearts."

I wished I would never have to let go.

<hr />

The game was great.

Well, as far as I know. I really hadn't paid much attention.

My attention was otherwise focused on the beautiful, blue-eyed girl in the stands, watching me.

Waiting for me.

The final whistle blew, and I did the usual shaking hands with the other team before walking off to the locker rooms. I looked up at Nicole in the stands, smiling and waving at me, and felt my pulse rate increase.

"Going out to the beach?" Jeremy asked.

"Nah," I said. "Got other plans."

"Oh, really?" He elbowed me in the gut, and I smacked his dark, curly head. "I think Rachel and I are going out there for a bit, but then we're heading off for a little more privacy."

Jeremy waggled his eyebrows, and they looked like two fuzzy caterpillars trying to make cocoons on his forehead. I shook my head at him but couldn't stop my own smile.

"Yeah," he snickered, "I thought so."

"Fuck you!"

"Pussy!"

"Pussies can take a pounding!" I shot back.

We laughed, stripped, and showered before heading out to where our girls were waiting for us. Nicole said goodbye to Rachel and took my hand. The car ride was quiet, and Nicole was chewing on her lip as she stared out the window. I reached over and placed my hand on top of her thigh.

"We don't have to do shit," I told her. "If you changed your mind or something…it's okay. We could order pizza or something and watch TV."

Nicole looked over at me sideways, and her mouth turned up in a smile.

"Thanks," she said softly. "I think I'm just…a little nervous. The last time…"

I shushed her.

"Don't think about it," I said. "Just play it by ear, right? Whatever happens, happens."

"I don't want you to be disappointed," she said. "I could tell how distracted you were on the field. I thought a couple of shots were going to get past you."

Ditch her before she becomes a distraction.

"I wasn't," I lied, "and I didn't let anything by."

"That one at the end was close," she said. "You should have had it solid, but it ended up with them getting a corner."

"I punched it over—no problem," I argued.

"You should have had it in your hand," she retorted.

She was probably right.

"Whatever," I said instead. I pulled into her driveway and shut off the engine before I turned to her. "Rumple, I mean it—we don't have to do anything. Let's just order some food and hang out, okay?"

"Okay," she said with a smile, "but no pizza—I already have dinner planned."

"Fucking-A!"

She really did have dinner all planned—including candles and linen napkins on the kitchen table. I had no freaking clue what we were eating—she said it was Indian. I wasn't sure if that was Native American or actually India-Indian, but it was really good. The food was a little bit spicy and had this thick bread to eat with it and a bunch of little sauces in a dish for dipping. By the time we were done, I was ready to roll right out of the kitchen, I had eaten so much.

"You are a glutton," Nicole said. She reached over and put a dollop of some green minty sauce on my nose then leaned in and licked it off.

"You cook like a fucking rock star," I told her.

"Do rock stars cook?" She giggled.

"Um…I dunno, but if they did, it would be like this!" I hoped she bought it.

Maybe she did, maybe she didn't, but we ended up ignoring the dishes and moving to the couch to make out instead.

I leaned back against the arm of the couch, and Nicole crawled over the top of me, her lips nipping at my jawline while I just put my head back and basked in the feeling. Her fingers ran up my arm and traced over my biceps. It tickled, but I still liked it. I snaked my arms around her back and pulled her against me. I could feel her tits against my chest, and I had to close my eyes and smile.

I raised my head again and brought my hands up over her shoulders and cupped the sides of her face. She looked up at me, and I could see the slight blush in her cheeks again as I moved forward and took her mouth with mine.

My Rumple.

Fingers, hands, lips—I wanted to touch her with every part of me.

She *was* nervous. It was obvious. I had a pretty good idea why, and I didn't want her upset, so I just let her do what she wanted and followed her lead. Where she touched me, I touched her. I skimmed her sides, slowly moving up and down and sometimes gripping her a little harder when she used her tongue to reach into my mouth, and I couldn't help but moan. She was straddling my stomach at first but then moved herself down a little and ripped my shirt off over my head.

"I love your chest," she said as she tossed my shirt behind her. She glanced away and bit down on her lip again. Her fingers started at my shoulders and worked their way down to my stomach. She outlined each muscle with her fingertip, making my skin quiver a little. I watched her looking at me, and it made me feel all warm inside even though the air in the room was a little chilled, and I could hear the rain starting to come down again outside.

I tugged at the ends of her shirt, where my fingers had been playing with the hem. She looked back to me and grasped the end of her shirt and pulled it up over her head.

Fuck me hard.

Deep blue lace.

My boner rivaled the Washington Monument.

I'd had my hands on her tits before while we were lying in her bed, but it was always a bit dark in there, and there was always the possibility of Greg peeking in. I'd never really seen her tits. I'd felt them up as much as she'd let me at night and sometimes woke up holding on to one of them like a teddy bear, but I'd never seen them. I definitely hadn't seen them held up in a bra as if they were on fucking display just for me.

Sitting up, I moved my hands until they were right over them, hovering a little and trying to figure out just where I wanted to latch onto first. My fingertips won the mental debate, and I touched her over the top of the lace. Her skin was so soft and prefect that I had to lean over and taste it.

I kissed the tops of her breasts and then looked quickly up to her eyes to make sure it was all still okay. She still looked nervous, but she nodded at me to continue, and I wasn't going to argue about that. She placed her hands on my shoulders and seemed to balance herself there as I peppered the line with tiny kisses from left to right where the lace met her skin. Then I ran my tongue along the ridge from right to left.

She tasted better than her own cooking, which was like a fucking rock star. I'd never tasted a rock star's tits, but I was pretty sure they couldn't be anywhere near as good as my Rumple's.

She reached behind her back to the clasp, the dark blue fabric falling forward, and I got my first really good look at perfection. I

was in awe. The Washington Monument became even more…
monumental…and I was pretty sure I was starting to drool. I slid
her bra off her arms and cupped both breasts in my hands, glancing
only briefly to Nicole's face to see her smile before I rolled them
around and brought my mouth down to say hello.

She groaned, and her hands wrapped around my head as I
sucked the first nipple into my mouth. That wasn't enough, so I
switched to the other one. I went back and forth, and even tried
bringing them close enough together to suck both at once. I was
nearly successful, and rolled my tongue around each in turn before
tilting my head back up and kissing her deeply.

"You are so fucking beautiful," I told her between kisses, "it
fucking hurts to look at you."

"Hurts?" she mumbled back. She tugged at my hair, pulling
my head backwards as she started kissing down my neck.

"Yes, it hurts," I replied. "In a good way."

"Good."

We stayed on the couch with just our top halves bare,
touching, kissing, and talking very little until the rain slowly
tapered off, and the clock on the wall said it was close to midnight.

"Are you ready to go to bed?" Nicole asked, blushing for the
tenth time that evening.

"If you want," I said.

"Okay."

After watching Nicole gather up her shirt and bra, I followed
her up the stairs to her room. We still took turns in the bathroom,
which was both good and funny, considering what we both kind of
thought we might maybe sort of be in here to do…if we decide to
do it.

I sat on the edge of her bed in some soft lounge pants with
images of soccer balls all over them. Nicole glanced at them and
stifled a laugh.

"What?"

"I can't believe those come in your size," she snickered. "They
look like something an eight-year-old would wear."

"Eight…eighteen—what difference does it make what's on your pants?"

"What's in your pants makes a difference," Nicole blurted out. Her eyes went wide and she slapped her hands over her face.

I laughed.

"Come here," I said, and I reached out to take her hands. I pulled her toward me, and she ended up straddling my lap and weaving her hands through my hair. I slid my hands up her back and played with the thin straps of the sheer camisole she wore. From this position, I had to look up at her, and she was a glorious sight to behold. "Beautiful."

Her fingers grazed over my cheek and pushed my hair away from my face. I looked into her eyes and tried to understand her wordless statement as she stared down at me for a long moment then brought her lips back to mine.

Go slow, I reminded myself.

I wanted to lay her down on the bed, cover her with my body, and fuck the shit out of her.

Well…in some ways I did.

I also wanted to keep it slow and soft and gentle, and maybe just kiss her all night. Even though she was continuing to be the aggressor as far as what would happen next, she still seemed hesitant every time she did something new or different.

I didn't know if it really made me a better person, and it probably didn't, but I was always at least upfront with a chick about my intent. I never did the "I'll be your boyfriend" or "Gimme a little, and I'll take you to the dance" or any shit like that. I told them what I wanted, and they were either interested, or they weren't. Most of them were using me just to say they had fucked me anyway, and I was just using them to get off. I wasn't a fucking saint with the girls, but at least I had been straightforward. The guy Nicole had been with had tricked her, lied to her, and used her in a totally different way.

And it showed.

I'd been with shy girls and hesitant girls, especially virgins who weren't sure what to expect, but none of them acted quite like Nicole did. She shivered sometimes or would take a deep breath like she was trying to center herself. I looked into her eyes, and there was more there than just shy hesitation.

She almost looked like she was going to cry.

"Are you okay?" I asked. I reached behind my neck, took her hands, and brought them back around me. I held them against my chest for a minute and then brought them up so I could kiss her knuckles. I let go, and she gripped my arms hesitantly; then she nodded.

"You sure?" I brushed my fingers over her cheekbone and kissed her softly. "Remember, we're just gonna see what happens, right? I'm not...I mean, you know I'm not expecting anything, don't you?"

"But you've..." She stopped and looked over her own left shoulder.

When I reached up and tilted her head back so she was looking at me, I could see tears in her eyes.

"What is it?" I asked, starting to freak out a little. Did she think I was pushing her into this? Did she really not want to? Had I hurt her somehow? "What did I do?"

"You have...experience," she said softly as she looked away again. "I mean, it sounds like you've slept with most of the females in the senior class and half the juniors...and a lot of them knew what they were doing when they were with you..."

"So what?"

"So what?" she looked back at me, and one of the tears escaped. "So I don't think I can live up to those expectations. I'm not...that good at it. I mean, I've only been with...well, with..."

"I know," I interrupted. I didn't need the reminder.

"I don't really know what I'm doing," she said. "I'm not going to be as good as they were, and you're going to be disappointed."

"What the fuck!" I sat straight up and grabbed her wrists. "Who the fuck said I'd be disappointed?"

She kept looking away from me and just shrugged instead.

"Just me, I guess." The tears started rolling down her cheeks.

Shit.

I probably shouldn't have yelled.

What do I do now?

Oh wait…I'd done this one.

Just hold her.

So I did, and she cried, and I felt like shit. Eventually, my thighs started to fall asleep under her, so I pushed and pulled at both of us until we were positioned on the right sides of the bed, and I could wrap my arms around her. I held her against my chest and kissed the top of her head until she quieted down and seemed to relax.

"I wanted everything to be perfect tonight," Nicole whispered against my collarbone. "I screwed it all up, going emo."

"Hey," I said as I placed my finger under her chin and tilted her head up to look at me. "I spent my whole day with you, starting with opening my eyes and seeing that picture I drew of you. I got to take you to your classes, eat lunch with you, and I knew you were watching me during my game. You made me dinner, and even though I don't know what the fuck I ate, it was awesome. I got to play with your tits, and now I'm in bed with you in my arms. If that isn't perfection, I don't know what is."

Nicole snickered and then laughed. I placed a kiss right on her lips.

"There is no way I could possibly be disappointed," I told her. "There's nothing I've ever wanted more than to be with you—whatever that means. Just knowing I'm with you makes it far better than being with anyone else, and I'm only talking about lying here with you. Whatever else happens is bonus."

With her face between my hands, I brought her over the top of me and raised my head off the pillow to kiss her deeply. She placed her hands beside my head to hold herself up as she kissed me back.

With my head resting against the pillow and Nicole's fingers twisting my hair back around my ear, I was fairly certain I couldn't have been much happier. Every few minutes, I'd kiss her, or she'd kiss me, and we'd just look at each other. Well, sometimes I looked at her tits because the camisole she wore was nearly see-through, and I was quite grateful for that.

"When does your dad get home?" Nicole asked.

"Tomorrow evening," I replied. "I think his flight gets in about five, so he'll be home around seven or eight, I guess."

"That means you probably won't be here tomorrow night, then," she said, surmising.

"Probably not," I agreed, "but I don't want to think about that right now."

"Okay," she said. Her fingers let go of my hair, trailed over my cheek, and down my neck. She flipped her hand over and rested her palm on my chest.

"You can fondle my abs, too, if you want." I winked at her sideways.

Nicole snickered but didn't hesitate to drop her hand to my stomach. It made my abs clench a little, and the sensations found their way down to my cock.

Little bastard—just relax, for fuck's sake!

Well, he wasn't going to listen to me, obviously. Then he reminded me that there were some perfectly nice tits right next to me, and I wasn't doing anything about them at all even though the owner of said tits was molesting my chest and stomach. My hand listened to my cock and moved up from her waist to get a better angle.

I traced one nipple through the thin fabric and felt her skin tighten up the same way mine did when she touched me. Her nipple puckered up as well and then started screaming for some mouth-action, and who was I to say no?

Oh, fine. It didn't scream, but I pulled the camisole down a bit to suck on it anyway.

Nicole moaned as my mouth wrapped around her nipple, and her hand suddenly dropped south…

…and grabbed on to my dick.

"Oh, fuck!" I cried out.

She pulled her hand back.

"I'm sorry!"

"Oh, fuck no, Rumple…baby…" I wrapped my arm back around her, and I brought her closer to me. "Don't stop."

"Oh…"

I glanced up at her and gave her a half-smile before latching on to her other nipple and listening to her moan as she reached back down and palmed me through my lounge pants.

"Jesus," she murmured.

"What?" I mumbled against her breast.

"You're…big…"

Well, there wasn't any stopping a smile crossing my face from that comment. I let go of the nipple that had been occupying my attention and slowly kissed and licked my way around her breast and then up to her neck. I nibbled at the hollow at the base of her throat and tried not to completely lose it when her little fingers wrapped around my cock and slowly moved up and down.

"That feels so fucking good," I told her. I moved one hand around to cup and massage her tit while my lips took the rest of the trek up to her mouth. Our tongues touched and moved against each other's as I tried not to buck my hips into her hand too much.

"You like it?" she said quietly with my tongue still in her mouth.

"Mmhmm," I moaned back at her. I kept kissing her, and she moved her deft little fingers up and down my shaft. When she got to the tip, I moaned in protest as I felt her hand move back to the top of my pants. My complaint was short-lived, because a second later, she was sliding her hand under the waistband, and I could feel her warm fingers on my flesh.

I rolled onto my back, bringing her with me so I didn't have to stop kissing her. She was still on her side next to me, bent over my head with her mouth locked to mine and her hand still down my pants.

"Take them off?" she whispered.

I wasn't entirely sure if it was a question or a command, but I wasn't about to ask. I reached down and pushed the lounge pants off my hips and then looked down to see her hand still wrapped around me.

"Oh fuck, Rumple," I mumbled. "That looks so good."

"Show me how you like it," she said.

I reached down and placed my hand over hers, moving along with her, but still letting her drive my stick.

What? She said she could drive a manual!

I moved her hand up and over my head, showing her how to palm the tip before running back down. Her fingers wrapped around a little tighter at the base, holding me perfectly as she slid her hand back up. I arched my back a little and yelled out again.

"Oh fuck, yes!"

"You really like it?" she asked again.

"Baby, it's awesome," I told her. I reached up and put my hand on the back of her head, bringing her back down so I could kiss her some more. She smiled against my lips, and her hand started moving a little faster.

I didn't know if it was just because I hadn't gotten off much lately, or because it was Rumple's hand wrapped around my cock, but the building release came up on me quickly.

"Fuck...baby..." I moaned again. "I'm gonna come if you don't stop."

She didn't stop.

My thighs tensed, followed by my glutes. My hips lifted off the mattress and the sensations ran up from my toes and down from my abs, met in the middle and intensified. I'm pretty sure I screamed as my balls tightened, and the waves of pleasure exploded down and out my cock, covering her hand and my stomach.

Shakespeare definitely would have referred to me as a "mountain of mad flesh" at that point. Somehow, I had never felt such release.

Now it was her turn.

CHAPTER TWENTY-ONE
touch line

I lay on my back and panted for a couple of minutes. I could feel my cock deflating though it was also the only place reminding me I had a pulse. The rest of me felt like I was floating in a sea of Nicole's hair.

She still smelled good.

I tried to get up to find us a towel, but Nicole pushed me back against the bed and did it herself. I could hear her in the bathroom, running the water in the sink, and a few seconds later, she came back with a less-sticky hand and a slightly damp towel, which she gave me. I cleaned up and then pulled her back down to me.

"You are so…fucking…fantastic…" I said between kisses. I felt her mouth turn up in a little smile.

"It was good?"

"*Fucking fantastic*, I told you."

She smiled again, and I snuck my hand back to cup her breast. I started kissing down her neck, shifting slightly so I could reach more of her effectively and guiding her onto her back at the same time. I kissed the top of each of her tits before sucking one into my mouth. I slid my other hand down her front, running over her stomach and playing at the top of her shorts.

Nicole giggled.

"What are you doing?" she asked.

Now I was confused.

"Um…I was going to…" I stopped and brought my eyebrows together. She was looking at me like she was confused, too.

"Oh," she said with sudden understanding in her eyes. "You don't…have to do that."

"I want to," I said, still confused. Why the fuck wouldn't I return the favor and get her off, too? Had I somehow crossed the touch line and was totally out of play? "You don't want me to?"

"It's not that," she said. She moved her gaze away from my face, refusing to meet my eyes.

"What is it, then?"

"It just…wouldn't work," she replied.

"What is that supposed to mean, 'it wouldn't work'?" I demanded. She was being fucking cryptic, and it was starting to piss me off. I was bad enough at this relationship shit. I didn't need anything else hampering me.

"I'm just…not really…very…*orgasmic*," Nicole finally said. She looked away from me again, embarrassed.

"What do you mean?"

"I just…don't have them," she said quietly. "At least, not with someone else. And it takes a really long time for me to warm up even if it's just me, and it's late, and—"

"It's not that late," I interrupted. I knew she was just making excuses.

"It would be if you tried," she said.

"You said we were supposed to say it if something was bothering us," I reminded her. "Say it."

Nicole looked everywhere in the room except at me and then let out a sigh.

"I'm just…not any good at it," she finally said.

I looked at her face, and the same expression she had when we first got to the room came over her—something between anxiety and sadness.

And it hit me.

That motherfucker.

"That's what he told you, isn't it?" I snapped at her. I didn't really mean to be angry with her, but I wanted to kill that bastard. "He told you there was something wrong with you because he was a lazy-ass shithead who didn't know how to get a girl off."

"He did…*try*," she said somewhat sheepishly—like she should be embarrassed by it. "A couple times."

"Not good enough," I said and shook my head definitively. I took her face in my hands and pulled myself up so I was hovering over the top of her and looking down into her big, blue eyes. "There is nothing wrong with you. You are fucking beautiful and smart and all kinds of other shit I just don't have the words to describe, but it's all good. Nothing is wrong with you. He's just an asshole who better never get close enough for me to get my hands on him."

Nicole finally smiled a bit, and the look in her eyes softened.

"Thank you," she said.

I just kept looking at her and then let a huffed breath out my nose.

"You realize what you've done now?"

"What?" she asked with wide eyes.

"You have presented me with *a challenge*," I informed her, and I raised my hands up in a grand, completely overdone gesture. I dropped them down again, then leaned over her and brushed her nose with mine. "And this challenge, I will definitely win."

"You are wasting your time," she said.

I narrowed my eyes at her and then placed my hand on her hip, slowly brought my fingers to her breast, then back down to her hip again. I moved them around to the front and cupped her heat.

"I like this place and could willingly waste my time in it," I quoted.

My Rumple's smile returned, which was all the encouragement I needed.

"You just gotta tell me what you do when you're alone," I said.

"Um…" Nicole mumbled as she tried to chew her bottom lip right off. "Just…um…touch myself..."

"Oh yeah?" I said with a bit of a smirk. "What else?"

"I think about…stuff."

"What do you think about?" I asked her. I nuzzled up against her cheek. Actually, the idea of her touching herself was really getting me hot. "When you're touching yourself?"

"Um…" Pink tinged her cheeks.

"What is it?" I asked again.

"Well," she said quietly, "lately I've thought of…you."

"Have you now?" I said. My cheeks were starting to hurt, I was smiling so much. Well, smirking, really. "What do you think about?"

"Um…just you," she said all nonchalantly.

Not going to put up with that shit.

"What about me?" I pressed.

She shrugged and bit into her lip again.

I leaned over close to her ear as I moved my hand slowly up her side.

"You think about my cock, don't you, Rumple?"

I heard her gasp and felt her body tense against mine. At first, I thought I had upset her, but when I looked more closely, her eyes were dilated as she looked up at me, and her lips were parted.

It was turning her on.

The tip of my nose outlined her ear as I whispered soft words that made her breath come in pants.

"I bet you think about my cock…seeing it…touching it… thinking about how it would feel sliding between your legs…"

She whimpered.

"Oh, you like that, huh?" My smirk returned. "My Rumple likes a little dirty talk, does she?"

I could see the heat rise to her face and neck in her blush. She tried to hide her face against my chest, put I pulled back and looked into her eyes.

"You like thinking about my cock, don't you?" I said, and

watched her blush deepen. I moved my lips back around to her ear. "You lay here at night without me and think about my cock running over your pussy, don't you, Rumple?"

Nicole moaned, and hand job or not, the sound went right to my cock. I slowly traced a line between her breasts and then circled around her navel with my fingertip. Her skin was so soft, and my light touches made her tremble.

"You want to feel it, don't you?" I whispered. "You want it right…here…"

My fingers reached the elastic of her shorts, and I slipped them underneath. I felt soft curls tickle my knuckles as I delved deeper, finding the smooth, wet flesh between her legs.

"Oh, baby," I murmured, "you want me, don't you?"

"Yes," she breathed out. One of her hands grabbed the back of my head while the other grasped my forearm, right above where my hand disappeared into her shorts.

My fingers explored, running along her folds and gathering up the wetness I found there. I touched her lightly, gently, and teasingly. Only when I felt her tilt her hips up did I give her any more pressure. With my thumb, I slowly circled around her clit and then dropped back down to find the fucking promised land of her opening.

God, I could hardly wait to get my cock in there. It was straining as it was, but this was about only her right now.

"You like that, Rumple?" I hummed into her ear. Her grip on my hair tightened. Slowly, I brought the tip of one finger to her opening and slid it in.

Tight and wet…so fucking good.

Another finger. In and out so, so slowly, talking to her the whole time. I'd increase my tempo a little, then slow back down again, just alternating the rhythm and fucking her with my fingers while I talked dirty to her and felt her squirm below me.

"You wish that was my cock, huh?" I asked. "You like to touch yourself and wish it was my cock sliding up in there?"

"Oh…ugh! Yes…that feels…oh my God…"

I smirked. Yeah, she was definitely going to get off.

"Yeah, you like that, don't you, baby?" I hummed softly into her ear. "I bet you're thinking about it being my cock shoved up inside of you—making you scream."

She groaned again—loud and long.

Damn! There was no way I was ever going to be able to have sex with her if her dad was home—they might have been able to hear her at school, she was so loud.

I loved it.

I slid my fingers back and forth, feeling how wet she was getting around me. My thumb rolled around her clit—keeping up the pressure and not relenting.

"There ya go, baby," I told her. "I can feel how hot your pussy is, just wishing my cock was stroking in and out of it…wanting me so fucking bad you can't stand it…You want me like that, don't you? You want my hard cock in that tight, hot pussy of yours? Maybe holding you up against the wall and pounding into you until you can't fucking stand it anymore?"

"Oh! Oh, God! Thomas!" Nicole cried out. I didn't slow down, just kept moving my fingers in and out of her and circling her clit until I felt her start to clamp down on my fingers. I pressed against her clit with my thumb, and felt her thighs shudder as she gasped and went rigid.

Take too long my ass.

I smirked for the umpteenth time.

Nicole just lay on her back, trying to catch her breath as I basked in the glory that was my Rumple, post-orgasm.

She was fucking beautiful.

"Told ya," I snickered.

She punched me in the shoulder, and I pretended it was hard enough to hurt, but I couldn't stop smiling. I rolled onto my side and propped myself up with my elbow so I could look down at her.

"You're very proud of yourself, aren't you?" Nicole said. She squished her lips together in a vain attempt to hide her smile.

"Most definitely," I replied. I ran the tip of one finger over the edge of her shoulder and down her arm. "You were beautiful. You *are* beautiful."

She wound her fingers into my hair and started pushing it behind my ear. I smiled again, closed my eyes, and thoroughly enjoyed the recap of the day.

⟩⟩●⟩●◉●⟨●⟨⟨⟨

I heard the car door slam, and the little bubble that had been around me for the last week burst at the sound.

"Thomas!"

"In here, Dad."

The thump of the suitcases in the foyer echoed around the house. Dad came around the corner and entered the kitchen, carrying a bottle of water and a paper bag from some fast food joint. He dumped the trash in the garbage can and looked me over.

"You run this morning?"

"Yep." I had gone for a run too—with Nicole. She was quick, but I still had to slow it down so she could keep up with me.

"Time?"

"Five-fifty," I lied.

"Good! Game last night?"

"Shut out."

"Yeah!" He raised his hand up in the air, and I high-fived him. "You make sure you keep that up for next weekend, got it?"

"Definitely."

"Wayne Messini's flight doesn't arrive until a little later than I thought. They won't get here until right before the game starts, so you won't be meeting them until afterwards. You make sure you're on your best game, got it?"

"Yep."

He took a step toward me, and I tensed but stood my ground. He brought up a single finger and poked me in the forehead.

"Focus," he said. "No distractions."

I nodded.

He dropped his hand and took a step back, tilting his head to the side.

"Did you get laid?"

He turned and went to the fridge.

"Yeah," I said. It was sort of true.

"Dump her?"

"Um…not yet."

"Don't waste any time," he said as he rummaged around. I hoped he wouldn't notice how clean it was. "You going to fuck her again?"

Though this line of talk had been occurring between us since he found out I had lost my virginity on the school bus, riding back from an away game, this time it felt really uncomfortable. I didn't want to talk about Nicole this way, and I didn't want him thinking about her like that.

"I…don't know," I finally answered.

He straightened up and looked over to me, his eyes narrowed. *Shit.*

"You never fuck a girl twice," he said. It wasn't a question. "Why are you even thinking about it?"

Fuck.

Too close.

I needed something plausible, and fast.

I put my game face back on and shrugged.

"I think I can talk her into anal," I said, and my stomach turned. I could taste bile in the back of my throat. "She said she might."

Dad looked at me, his eyes still narrowed as he stared at me. I didn't move—didn't drop my gaze from his. I just kept looking right in his eyes and tried to breathe as slowly as possible. The corners of his eyes tightened, and right about the time I thought I was going to burst, he threw his head back and laughed.

"I can hear it now!" he said as he laughed again. "Hey, Sheriff, I hear your daughter takes it in the ass!"

He closed the refrigerator without getting anything out of it and clasped me on the shoulder as he walked out of the kitchen and into the living room to turn on the TV. I kept my smile on as long as I could, and then I took off up the stairs and to my bathroom for a few minutes, where I debated getting sick. I didn't, but my stomach still felt queasy.

I sat on the edge of my bed and closed my eyes, trying to relax a little. I wished tomorrow was a school day because I really wasn't sure I could handle being here with Dad right now—not if he was going to keep saying shit like that. I know it was just his way of connecting with me or something, but while it had never bothered me in the past, hearing him say that shit about Rumple just made me want to punch him.

And that would not go over well. Not at all.

I needed to think about something else for the sake of my own sanity.

⇒●●◐●○◑●⇐

Sunday sucked. I didn't see Nicole at all.

Monday was good. I stayed outside Nicole's classroom doors until the last possible second before the bell rang and was late to all my own classes, but I didn't give a shit about that. She stayed for practice, and we got to make out in the car for a bit before I took her home. We even IM'd that night for the first time since Rumple didn't have any text messaging on her phone.

SoccerGod2014: Hi

BeautifulSkye18: Hi…is that you, Thomas?

SoccerGod2014: Yeah. I miss you

BeautifulSkye18: I miss you, too

SoccerGod2014: Can I come live at your house?

BeautifulSkye18: Sure!

SoccerGod2014: Heh. I guess that probably wouldn't work too well, huh?

BeautifulSkye18: I don't know. Is your dad bugging you?

I wondered what she really wanted to say.

SoccerGod2014: A little. It's OK tho

BeautifulSkye18: No it isn't

SoccerGod2014: He just wants me ready for Friday's game. Messini watching has him a little excited

BeautifulSkye18: Yeah—excited. Whatever

SoccerGod2014: Don't

BeautifulSkye18: Sorry

SoccerGod2014: it's ok.

BeautifulSkye18: Greg's calling me. Brb

SoccerGod2014: I gotta get to bed anyway

BeautifulSkye18: Ok—cya tomorrow

SoccerGod2014: I'll be there

BeautifulSkye18: Gnight

SoccerGod2014: Gnight

I felt a little better as I crawled into bed and let the memory of every touch of our fingers and every kiss from the day roll through my mind. I only watched the day twice before I fell asleep.

Tuesday was a whole different story.

Dad was home as soon as I walked through the door, standing in the entryway with his arms crossed over his chest.

"You're not practicing at lunchtime," he said.

I swallowed and slowly lowered my book bag to the floor.

"There was…uh…"

"Don't you bullshit me."

I froze, bracing myself.

"You really have a thing for her, don't you?"

I glanced up at his face and was a little confused by his expression. He didn't seem angry—he was more…introspective. I took another breath and took the chance.

Like an idiot.

"Kind of," I said quietly.

"Do you think your timing could have possibly been worse?" He hissed out the last few words, dropped his hands to his sides, and balled them into fists.

Shit.

"She's not hurting my game," I tried to tell him.

"Not taking the chance," he replied. "You're done with her."

Done with her.

Done with Nicole.

My Rumple.

"I don't want to—"

"I DON'T CARE WHAT YOU WANT!" he screamed. I jumped back as his fist collided with the wall and left a gaping hole in the plaster. "No piece of pussy is going to ruin your chances, you hear me? This ends now! Call her now!"

With my heart pounding in my chest and the heat of rage climbing up my face, I took a single step forward and glared at him.

"No!" I yelled back.

My dad's face went blank, and when he spoke, he was far too calm.

"Come in here," he said. "I want to show you something."

He turned on his heel and went into the kitchen. I followed, reluctantly.

The kitchen table was littered with photographs.

Oh fuck.

I turned my head away immediately. My mind had already conjured up what those images might have entailed, and I didn't need the constant reminder of what had happened to her. Even though I knew it was too late to expunge my brain, I wasn't going to look any more.

"I'll fucking post them all over town," he said, and he handed me the phone. "Call her. Now."

Shakespeare said, "So quick bright things come to confusion." Somehow, I couldn't have agreed more.

Now it was over.

CHAPTER TWENTY-TWO
penalty

I rolled onto my side and wrapped my arms around my stomach. I would rather have taken a ball from a pro striker at ten feet away right to my gut than to have to relive that conversation again.

But I would relive it.

Over and over again.

Ring...

"Hey."

"Hey, Thomas! What's up?"

My Dad crossed his arms and stared at me. I tried to turn away from him a little, giving myself the lame illusion of privacy.

"Nothing. Just needed to talk to ya." I was suddenly glad I was wearing my practice shirt with my number on it. The costume fit, at least. I took a deep breath, stood up straight, and squared my shoulders. "We're done."

"Done with what?"

Shit.

"Us, babe," I told her. "You and me. Not working out. Tried this boyfriend shit, and this just isn't working for me."

Better this way...at least I hadn't fucked her.

He wouldn't hurt her if I did what he said. I glanced up at him, and he was smirking.

"Thomas...what do you mean?" Her voice was so soft, and I felt my gut wrench.

"It should be pretty fucking obvious," I snapped at her.

"Is your dad there?" Again, her voice was so soft. "Is he making you do this?"

No...Rumple...please don't go there.

"No, I'm just tired of playing this game," I told her. "You're red-carded. Thrown out. No longer interested. You get it?"

"But...Thomas...everything was fine—"

"Maybe you thought it was." I forced my voice to stay light-hearted, cool, and callous. Yeah, it was all of those. "You do give a good hand job, but it's just not worth my time anymore."

You have to believe me...you aren't safe around me anymore. You probably never were.

"Thomas, what the hell is wrong with you?" she finally yelled. "You aren't making any sense!"

"It's pretty simple," I told her. "Get your own fucking ride to school, bitch."

I hung up.

"That's my boy." Dad clasped me on the shoulder. "Someday you'll understand why I do these things for you."

I didn't think I would ever really understand.

⸺•••◦◗◖◦•••⸺

She tried to talk to me in the hallway at school Wednesday, but I turned and walked away from her. I didn't go to the lunchroom at all—just went straight to the practice field with Paul and Clint. She came out and tried to interrupt our practice, but I told her to fuck off and headed into the locker room.

I changed the ringtone, shut off my phone, and deleted my IM account.

I managed to totally avoid her the rest of the day.

I pushed all thoughts of her from my mind and thought of nothing but my game. At night it was different because my mind kept replaying every time I saw her eyes meet mine in the hallway. I could see the sadness and the lack of understanding in them. I could see the questions on her face, but I couldn't reply to them.

It was better this way—quick and hard.

She'd heal faster, and she was strong—so fucking strong. I knew she'd be okay. Better off, really. What could I actually offer her long-term?

Nothing, that's what.

On Thursday, Jeremy tried to bring her up to me, and I told him to fuck off, too.

Kick, pass, run, catch, throw, punt.

It was all I allowed myself to think about.

Friday.

Mind in the game—nothing else.

I saw nothing but the ball and the players.

Still scoreless at the end of the second half, but that also meant *I* hadn't fucked anything up. I knew they were out there—Wayne Messini and whoever might have accompanied him from Real Messini. They were watching me, not the strikers. I didn't let it stress me.

Just me and the ball and the net.

Nothing else mattered.

Klosav scored at the end of the second half.

I win.

Ha!

Fuckers.

Coach Wagner yelled for me as I walked out of the shower, explaining that there was someone outside waiting for me with my dad. I acknowledged him and started getting my stuff together.

"Is it true?" Jeremy dropped down on the bench next to me.

"What?"

"That one of the Messini brothers is out there waiting to talk to you?"

"Oh…yeah."

"Oh yeah?" Jeremy repeated. "Dude—that's major!"

I nodded.

"Holy shit."

"I better go," I said as I stood up, buttoned up my jeans, and headed out. Dad was right by the exit.

"That was a damn fine game, son!" Dad beamed as I walked out of the locker room with my hair still wet. He was standing with a tall, pale-faced man and a young blonde woman dressed in a tight red shirt. I recognized him immediately.

"Thanks, Dad."

"Wayne Messini, may I present my son, Thomas Malone— keeper prodigy."

"It's a pleasure, Thomas," the pale, black-haired man said as he reached for my hand. "I've heard a lot about you."

"The pleasure is all mine," I replied. "Hopefully, I did not disappoint."

"Not at all—you have some very impressive moves!"

"Thank you, sir."

"Thomas," Wayne reached down and grabbed the blonde by the hand. She sauntered up beside him and licked her red lips as she looked at me. "This is Tiffany. She works with some of the players for Real Messini."

"Hello," I said. She reached out her hand and I took it briefly. She raised her eyebrows at me and obviously looked me up and down.

"I bet you're hungry after all of that running around," Dad said. "Let's go have some dinner in town and talk a bit."

I ate, but my stomach wasn't too happy about it. Food wasn't sitting well in general, but I wouldn't let myself think about that, either. I hadn't really had much to eat for a few days—worried about the game, I guessed. I ate too much, and my stomach rebelled. I excused myself and went to the men's room.

When I stepped back out, Tiffany was there, waiting for me. I almost ran right into her.

"You really played an excellent game," she hummed at me. She placed her hands on my shoulders and then ran them down my arms. She took a step closer to me and tilted her head to be close to mine. "Wayne's impressed."

"That's good," I said. I wanted to take a step back, but the door was right behind me.

"Very good," she said. Her hands went back to my shoulders, and then she drew her fingers down my chest. "You are definitely going to be fun to play with."

Her nails scratched over my abdomen. I had to swallow hard to form any words.

"What do you do, exactly?" I asked.

"I keep the boys happy," she responded with a smile. "In whatever way they like."

Fuck me hard.

"Oh, really?" I stammered. My teen hormones were perking up and starting to take notice, but a flash of blue eyes in my head fought against them.

"You will make a fine, fine addition to the team." Tiffany hummed into my ear as her hand slid down over the front of my jeans.

I moved my hands to her hips rather instinctively or maybe reflexively. I stroked slowly up her sides and looked down at the tightly wrapped tits in front of me. I could clearly see the outline of her nipples through her shirt.

Her tits were too big and probably fake, too. When I glanced up to her eyes, I saw they were bright green and just…wrong. Tiffany took another step closer, pressing her body to mine and pushing her hand firmly against my crotch.

Down, you little motherfucker.

I was going to have to play this off in some way that wouldn't give rise to any suspicions. I gave her my cockiest smile and a bit of a wink.

"The middle of a restaurant isn't the very best of places to get to know each other," I told her. "It's good to know some of the… uh…*benefits* of the team, though."

She giggled, and the sound made me want to retch.

We walked back to the table with her holding on to my arm.

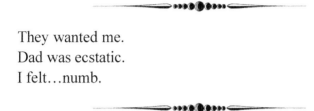

They wanted me.

Dad was ecstatic.

I felt…numb.

Days turned into weeks.

I dropped AP Biology and the Shakespeare class. I had almost all the credits I needed to graduate, anyway.

I trained with the school team.

I flew to Seattle twice a week to train with the Sounders.

Real Messini sent a special trainer to me three times a week.

It was tiring, but at least at night I was usually too wiped out to think.

Nicole stopped trying to contact me, and that bothered me a lot. It was stupid because I was the one who had done all this to her. I watched her sometimes, and whenever I did, I could feel her hand in my hair and the heat of her body close to me as we slept.

I missed her.

Horribly.

National championships.

I was in the zone, not really thinking about much of anything as we walked onto the field to play some team from Minnesota. The temperature was perfect for a game—January in southern California was not too hot or cold. There was a nice breeze, too, which felt good, but I was trying to figure out how to compensate for punting.

The band played the national anthem, and the announcer started introducing all the players. Again, I wasn't really paying any attention until I heard one particular name.

Number seventeen.

Forward striker.

Dennis Johnson.

I zeroed in on the player—maybe five-nine, medium build, with kind of shaggy, eighties hair. I knew it was him. I just knew it.

I clenched my fists in my gloves, narrowed my eyes, and bounced up and down on the balls of my feet. I had complete focus but not necessarily on the ball.

I was going to hurt that motherfucker.

Bad.

Then the whistle blew, and the other team started with the ball. Back to the midfielder, then to the left wing. Klosav was right by my target.

Target.

That's what he was.

I stayed close to the goal as he moved up with Jeremy close by, shielding Dennis from me. I moved to the left to get a better view, and the ball crossed over. The other forward's header was right to my feet, and I tossed the ball back and forth with my toes as the defenders moved up the field, and Dennis continued closer to me—trying to put on some pressure.

I'll give him some fucking pressure.

Instead of picking up the ball when he neared, I kicked it off to Jeremy. Dennis turned his back to me at the same time the ref turned away as well. I stepped up a couple of yards and slammed my palm into his back.

He stumbled a little and glared back at me.

"What the fuck?" Dennis spun around and curled his lip at me.

"So sorry," I snarked back.

He walked off.

The next time he was close, the ball was in the box and my

hands were on it. I let my inertia carry me forward, dropped my shoulder, and nailed him in the chest.

"What's your problem?" he asked with narrowed eyes.

"You're a bastard motherfucker," I said simply as I tossed the ball over to midfield. "And by the time this game is done, you'll be leaving on a stretcher."

"Fuck you."

Play continued.

Second half. We were up one to nothing with fifteen minutes left in regulation time. I needed another fucking goal from my offense and was screaming at them to score. I had slammed into Dennis at least a dozen times, but I was careful to keep my eye on the ref, and none of the fouls were called. Dennis was seriously pissed, and their coach started yelling to the ref to watch me. Tony subbed in for Clint, and a free throw got the ball into the other team's box. Tony slammed it home, but the goalie tipped it off to the side. Paul headed in the resulting corner kick.

Two to nothing.

Four minutes left, and they were getting desperate.

Jeremy stumbled, and Dennis ended up with the breakaway. He dribbled the ball up the side and then toward goal, and it was just the two of us in the box. I ran up, full speed. I didn't even look at the ball as he chipped it over my right shoulder; I just dropped my head and collided with him. Once he was on the ground and under me, I brought my arm up high, and slammed my elbow into his balls.

He started screaming.

I hit him again.

And again.

"That's what you get you stupid motherfucker!" I screamed at him. Jeremy grabbed me by the arms and hauled me off of him, but I wrenched one arm away, which gave me enough room and leverage to kick his shin.

I heard the crack.

More screaming.

Red card in my face.

All worth it.

Shakespeare probably wasn't speaking to me anymore, but if he did, he might have said "that can such sweet use make of what they hate." Somehow, the sweetness of this hatred seemed worth the cost.

Now, I wondered what my suspension would be.

CHAPTER TWENTY-THREE
save

I didn't wait in the locker rooms for anyone else. I didn't even shower, just changed my clothes and left, walking back to the hotel. It was only about a mile from the fields, and I kind of doubted anyone was going to let me back on anytime soon.

Definitely worth it.

I almost wanted to call Nicole and tell her the motherfucker paid for what he did to her, but I didn't. He didn't even know the reason, but I didn't care about that, either. I went to the hotel's little convenience store and bought a pack of Camels before heading up to the room.

I went out on the balcony and lit up. I hadn't had one since that evening sitting on the back porch of the Skyes' house with Greg.

She was so mad at us.

I smiled a little and took a deep drag off the cigarette. It tasted like shit and reminded me of how I had told her I wouldn't smoke anymore. I tossed it over the balcony rail after taking about three puffs and then started tapping my fingers rhythmically on the railing.

Everything in my body felt tense, like a tightly coiled spring being stretched too far apart, just waiting for someone to let go. I looked down over the edge at the traffic some ten stories below. I gripped the handrail, loosened my fingers, and then gripped it again.

I yanked the pack out of my pocket and flung it out over the street as hard as I could.

Think soccer. Only soccer.

I was probably in a shitload of trouble. Red card, suspension —yeah, that shit happens—but I broke his leg, and Dad didn't have as much pull with the authorities here as he did in Oregon. He was going to be pissed.

With that thought, I heard the door to the room open.

"What the fuck was that?"

I didn't turn around or look at him or anything. I didn't see any point. I just stared out over the railing and watched the cars go by.

"You stupid idiot!" I heard Dad walk up behind me. "Do you have any idea how that looks? You're lucky it wasn't being televised! The Messini haven't signed the contract yet, you know! You're lucky I was there to do some triage and the kid's leg wasn't broken!"

"Not broken?" I tried not to sound disappointed. "I heard the crack…"

"You cracked his shin guard, asshole."

"Oh."

"You're out of the rest of the tournament," Dad told me, "but at least you aren't getting arrested."

I tried to find a reason to care but really couldn't. I waited for his fists with the numbness of indifference, but he just kept yelling at me, and I just pretended to listen. He shoved me twice, but I just couldn't bring myself to care. I deserved it all, and I wouldn't take it back if I could. Eventually, he stopped and left, saying he was going out to eat, and I could fucking rot in here as far as he was concerned.

I walked into the bedroom half of the suite and dropped down on the bed, face first. I grabbed ahold of one of the pillows, pulled it under my head, and wrapped my arms around it. I closed my eyes, and memories of her scent floated around in my head.

My fingers itched and still felt tense even when I flexed them. When I opened my eyes, I noticed a little notepad with a pen next to it on the side table. I rolled over, grabbed them both, and started sketching.

It was just her face. She was looking at me with her eyes bright and excited. It was rough, but I only had the pen to work with, so I guessed it was as good as it was going to get. I pulled the little paper off the pad and brought it close as I rolled back onto the pillow.

"I miss you," I said softly. I shook my head at how stupid I was—talking to a fucking piece of paper. After I folded it into a small square, I grabbed the pillow and pulled it under my head again. The paper stayed in my hand underneath, gripped tightly in my palm.

I closed my eyes and tried to ignore the pounding in my chest and the burning behind my eyes.

Dad might not have had as much pull in California, but he had enough friends with pull to get me off pretty easy—suspended for the rest of the tournament, which was only one game—whatever—and Dad had to pay a five thousand dollar fine to the league.

Dennis Johnson was going to be fine, unfortunately.

I apologized…for disrupting the game.

Whatever.

"So why did you do it?"

Freakazoid Amy Cutter plopped down next to me in the library during study hall. I started the period at the field, but the normal rain switched to a thunderstorm, so I had to come back inside. Amy had been taking it on herself to stop by every couple of weeks and offer me some words of sage advice, which just pissed me off.

"Do what?"

"Beat the shit out of some poor soccer fool?"

"Some people just need to have the shit beat out of them," I replied.

The teacher shushed us, and I gave her the finger. She just glared at me and shook her head. It was good to own the school.

Amy leaned over the table and looked at me through darkly lined eyes.

"It has something to do with Nicole Skye, doesn't it?"

"Fuck off," I replied. "Why don't you go lick a rug?"

"Why don't you admit you're pining for her?"

"Fuck you."

"I see the way you look at her." Amy continued to press. "You know, when you think no one else is looking? And that guy *was* from Minnesota, and she—"

"Shut the fuck up!" I yelled at her as I stood up and balled my fists at my sides.

She just looked up at me passively as I tried to control my breathing, and the teacher continued to mouth off to me. I ignored her.

"Feel better?" Amy finally asked.

"No!" I snapped back.

"Maybe that should be a clue to you," she said as she stood up. She took a couple steps backwards then turned and left. I flipped off the teacher again, grabbed my shit, and left.

Lunch hour hadn't technically started yet, but I walked in to the cafeteria and grabbed a Gatorade anyway then dropped my ass down in a chair near the back door. I opened the bottle, didn't drink any of it, and just stared out the window instead.

My stomach hurt.

"Thomas?"

Oh fuck, no.

I stood, leaving the Gatorade and trying to walk around her without making eye contact.

"Thomas, please…" she called out, but I kept walking, trying

316

to stop myself from doubling over from the ache in my gut.

She would have been so much better off if she had never met me. I had tainted her life with the vileness of my very existence. I shouldn't have been here to hurt her or anyone else.

I'm the one that should have died in that car wreck years ago.

The world would be a better place.

I had to agree with Shakespeare, and likened my life to the one led by *The Scottish Play's* title role—"a tale told by an idiot, full of sound and fury, signifying nothing." Somehow, I just didn't see any reason to it anymore.

Now, I no longer cared.

—————————⟫••◉◉◉••⟪—————————

I ran.

Even with my running shoes, the early morning sheet of ice along the roads was making it impossible to run on the cement, so I stuck to the dead, brown grass, which crunched under my feet with every step. Air came out of my mouth in short, hot breaths—the condensation from the cold air leaving vapor trails all around me.

My times were fantastic.

My legs had strengthened, and as I pushed against my thighs, I could feel the ache in the muscles as I propelled myself forward. Down a slight hill then back up again with the evergreens blurring beside me. I ran in quick, steady, monotonous steps.

Toward nothing.

—————————⟫••◉◉◉••⟪—————————

School let out early, and I went to the diner for food with a bunch of guys from the team. I wasn't in the mood, but Jeremy had been giving me shit about not going out anywhere. I didn't want to have another conversation about me needing to get laid, so I went with him.

I parked close to the restaurant. I was a little early, and though there were a few people milling about outside, most were just getting there, parking their cars and trying to make snowballs out of the bits of white fluff they scraped off the curbs.

Jeremy called me over to his car and started going on about

Rachel being pissed at him about…something. I wasn't really listening. My attention was diverted by the all-too-familiar sound of an old Hyundai as it chugged into the parking lot.

I only glanced over as she pulled into a spot about five cars away from us. The car revved once before it went silent. I could see her through the slightly fogged window with her phone up to her ear, and I wondered who she might be talking to since everyone from school was pretty much here.

Probably Sophie, and probably about babysitting.

Okay, so my look was more than a glance. I stared at her as she got out of the car and started making her way across the parking lot. She wasn't looking at me, though, so I kept watching her as my chest tightened up on me.

I wanted to go over to her and hold her arm to help her across the ice.

I wanted to tell her it was all a mistake.

I wanted to just put my arms around her and tell her I was a fucking moron, and I really didn't think I could survive without her.

I just stood there instead, watching her struggle as she held her hands out for balance, and ignoring Jeremy's rumbling voice, barely reaching my ears.

"Have you heard a fucking word I've said?" he asked.

"Rachel is sick of going to all the action flicks, and you never let her pick the movie," I said without looking away from her. I didn't even listen to the words I regurgitated to him.

"Yeah, right. So anyway…"

My eyes moved briefly from Nicole to Clint's Buick as he pulled into the parking lot going way too fast for the slick roads. With that rear-wheel-drive boat of his he drove, there was no way so much inertia could offset the icy conditions, and he overcompensated and started to skid. The car lurched wildly to the left and then to the right.

Right toward Nicole.

I didn't think.

I just moved.

The pressure against my thighs as I pushed off from the ground was actually painful. The screeching sound was blaring through my head, but I couldn't concentrate on that. All I could see was her face, her eyes wide with shock and terror as she stood immobilized and stared at the car skidding sideways toward her.

My strides were true, despite the slick surface. I could see my goal—her beautiful, beautiful face. I leapt forward, arms outstretched, grabbed her right by the head, and pulled her against my chest in the most important save of my life.

We were both flying sideways and then down toward the ground, and I could see the side of the old, red Buick as I brought her body closer to mine, cocooning her in my arms and legs as I braced myself. As the screeching of tires enveloped me from behind, the impact of the steel against my back shoved us both partway underneath another car.

Shakespeare said, "Pain pays the income of each precious thing." Somehow, whatever I felt didn't matter at the moment.

Now why was everything going dark?

CHAPTER TWENTY-FOUR
sidelines

It was an odd feeling.

Crushing…suffocating.

I struggled to pull air into my lungs.

A strange, unnatural ripping sound replaced the screeching in my ears.

Everything was black.

White.

Red.

When I pried my eyes open, I was enveloped in a sea of brilliant blue.

I parted my lips, and they felt dry and cracked. I swallowed and forced out the only words that mattered.

"Rumple?" My throat hurt, and my mouth felt like it was coated with the plaque of morning breath. I ran my tongue over the roof of my mouth and tasted copper. I swallowed.

"Thomas?" Her beautiful, confused voice sang to me. "What…?"

"Are you okay, Rumple?"

"Oh my God…Thomas…Thomas…"

Numbness in my legs.

Queasiness in my stomach.

I fought it down.

"You…okay?" I repeated, gasping. There was something thick and liquid on my chin.

"I'm fine, Thomas," she whispered, and there were tears in her eyes. "Don't move, okay?"

Her fingers were against my cheek—warm and soft. She pushed stray hairs from my forehead as the sound of sirens approached. Her touch felt so good, and I knew I was the dumbest asshole in the world to have given this up for so long.

"I never wanted to hurt you, Rumple," I told her. A little voice in my head told me I had to tell her—it was important she knew. My side ached, and it felt warm and sticky, which didn't make any sense in contrast to the cold cement below. I was vaguely aware of a lot of screaming around us—the voices of other students, patrons —maybe the diner manager.

"Don't try to talk, baby," she said. The movement of her fingers in my hair was faster—frantic even. "Just lie still, okay?"

"You're so beautiful," I said. I wanted to wrap my hand around the back of her head and bring her closer so I could kiss her —if she would let me, but my hand wouldn't move. There was a sharp pain in my back—up high, near my shoulders. Really, I couldn't seem to get much of me to move at all.

"Oh, Thomas…your leg…"

My leg? My legs didn't hurt—just my shoulders and my side.

I coughed.

"Stay still," she whispered again. Her eyes were all wet. Was it raining? It was too cold for rain.

"You're okay?" I asked again.

"I'm okay, baby."

"Good."

"Help is coming," she told me. She was repeating someone else's words, but I couldn't make out whose they were. "Almost here."

My eyes blurred and closed. The soles of my feet were all

tingly.

"Thomas? Thomas, look at me!"

I pried my eyes open again, and pain shot through my head.

"Just keep looking at me, okay?" Nicole said.

I wanted to tell her I would do anything she said, but my tongue felt thick in my mouth. I coughed, and the bright copper taste returned.

"Baby, please," I heard her beg. "Just hang in there, okay? I'm right here. You're going to be fine."

Fine.

I was pretty sure that was not the case.

"Art thou not, fatal vision, sensible," I whispered. My eyes drifted closed again, shielding her face from me.

"No...Thomas...no!" she cried. "You stay with me, you hear? Stay with me!"

I forced my eyes open, just so I could see her a bit longer.

I had to tell her.

"I love you." I tried to move my hand up her back so I could touch her face, but it still wouldn't move. "Since you first touched me...I just didn't know...what it was. You showed me."

"Oh, Thomas...I love you, too," she whispered back. "Never stopped."

She loves me.

My Rumple loves me.

There were sirens in the distance, coming closer.

"I'm sorry I'm an asshole," I choked out.

"You aren't," she said, and her mouth turned up into a smile though there was still panic in her eyes. "You're an idiot, and I really want to smack you silly sometimes, but you're not an asshole."

"In thy orisons be all my sins remembered," I mumbled. There was no way Ophelia could have held a candle to my Rumple, though.

Pain shot through my head again and blurred darkness stole my vision from me. The sounds of emergency vehicles surrounded us. I tried to open my eyes to see what was going on, but I didn't seem to have the strength.

"No! Thomas! Open your eyes! Open your eyes, do you hear me?"

Darkness.

"Thomas!"

Depth.

"God—no! No! THOMAS!"

Cold.

"He's not breathing! HE'S NOT BREATHING!"

I could still feel her arms around me and her hand against my face.

The meaning of Hamlet's words hit me harder than the impact from Clint's Buick: "To sleep, perchance to dream: ay, there's the rub; For in that sleep of death what dreams may come, When we have shuffled off this mortal coil, Must give us pause: There's the respect, That makes calamity of so long life." Somehow, I thought all that really mattered was that Nicole was okay.

Now to see what comes next.

CHAPTER TWENTY-FIVE
injury time

Bright, blinding light filled my eyes, but it didn't hurt. It was just warm, like the perfect spring morning when there's sun on your back as you walk through the trees. Soft, calm, peaceful.

Her hand slipped through mine, her fingers so much bigger, they made me feel safe. I had to look up to see her face. She was so pretty—with creamy skin and deep brown hair.

"Can I stay with you, Mom?"

"No, sweetheart. It's not time yet."

My eyes narrowed as I looked up into her shining face.

"But I want to."

"I know, Thomas." Her hand ran over the top of my head. Her touch made my skin tingle, and I smiled up at her before dropping my eyes again. We walked though there didn't seem to be any path or destination. We just moved alongside each other.

I looked down at my feet and saw the bright red cleats I wore when I was little. Mom had double-knotted them for me, and I could never untie them by myself. Mom always had to do it for me. After…when I had to tie them myself, they always came untied during games, and Dad would be mad. After…when she was gone.

I looked up over my shoulder again and into her face.

"I didn't mean for you to get hurt." I felt the sting of tears in my eyes and pressure in my chest.

"Of course you didn't, darling," she told me. "It was an accident."

"I'm sorry I forgot my gloves," I told her.

"Everyone forgets sometimes, Thomas," she told me. "And sometimes things just happen. They aren't your fault."

"He said it was."

"I know," she sighed, "but he was wrong."

"I kept my promise," I said softly. "I never forget anything."

"I know—but you don't have to remember it all."

"I don't?"

"Not anymore, sweetheart." Her hand was on the side of my face as she stroked my cheek. "You've remembered enough now."

"*One…two…three…CLEAR!*"

A sharp pain ripped through my chest and spread out like a spiderweb through the rest of my body.

"You have to go back, Thomas."

"I want to be with you."

"You haven't completed everything you need to do, Thomas. You still have things to learn."

"I want to stay!"

"Someone there still needs you."

"*CLEAR!*"

"Rumple?"

"Go to her."

"*CLEAR!*"

———— ⤞•••◐◖◗◑•••⤝ ————

I was swimming in darkness, and my limbs felt like they were trying to get though some thick, viscous substance without any strength to push it aside. I couldn't open my eyes. Someone was talking, but I couldn't make out who it was or what they were saying. They were just meaningless fragments of sentences in my head.

Extremely serious...several broken bones...kidney failure...

Flashes of pain ricocheted through my body. Nothing made any sense.

...Lacerations...shattered left scapula...spinal cord...

Where was Rumple? Was she okay? She said she was...I didn't dream that, did I?

...Scheduled surgery...his spleen will need to be removed...

Was my mom here?

...Head trauma...induce coma... best chance...

I didn't understand and let myself sink into the darkness. It was cool and safe there.

I opened my eyes, blinking.

My mouth and throat were so fucking dry, they burned.

Even through the darkness, I could see the sterile, off-white walls and bland décor of the hospital room. There was a slow, steady beeping sound from a machine on my left.

I was lying on my back, and my muscles ached. I hated sleeping on my back—I was always on either my side or my stomach. I wanted to roll to one side but didn't have the energy. I had just enough strength to loll my head to one side and notice the IV line going into my arm. Other tubes and wires for monitors and shit were sticking out from under the blanket that covered me up to my chest.

I managed to turn my head to the other side to see a small side table with a vase of faded flowers and a stack of greeting cards. Long vertical blinds covered a window, but it was obviously dark outside. The only light in the room was a small, dim table lamp in the far corner next to a reclining chair.

No one else was in the room.

There was a cup of water on the side table, and I tried to raise my arm to reach it, but I didn't have the strength. My hand twitched, and I tightened my fingers into a fist, but even that completely exhausted me.

A noise coming from the front of the room caught my attention, and the door opened to reveal a petite woman in a hospital smock with brightly colored circles all over it. She walked over to the side of the bed, reached for my IV, and looked down at me.

"Thomas?"

I licked my lips and tried to answer, but only a weird croaking sound came out of my mouth. She grasped the cup of water and held the straw to my lips. Once I managed to take a couple of painful swallows, she took it away again.

"Can you speak now?" she asked softly.

"Yeah," I managed.

"I'm going to get the doctor, okay?"

"Sure."

My head was a little swimmy. I wanted more water, but at the same time, my stomach seemed a little pissed off at the intrusion of the liquid. A couple minutes later, a guy in a lab coat, carrying a clipboard, came and sat down in the rolling chair near the bed. He came up close to me and said his name was Doctor Peter Winchester.

"Do you know how you got here, Thomas?"

Flashes of the dark Buick skidding over the ice sliced through my brain.

"Hit by a car," I replied. "Nicole? Nicole Skye?"

"She's fine," Doctor Winchester answered. "A few cuts and scrapes, but nothing serious. She's all healed up now."

"Where is she?"

"It's about two in the morning on a Wednesday, Thomas," he said. "She's probably at home, asleep."

I nodded, glad she wasn't here in the hospital and still banged up or anything. Then a single question became really fucking important.

"How long?" I asked. Speaking more than just a couple of words at a time was pretty taxing.

The doctor looked over to the nurse before fixing his gaze back on me.

"What was the last date you remember?"

"Um…January thirtieth?" I guessed.

Winchester looked at me for a bit.

"It's March fourteenth now," he finally replied.

For a moment, I panicked.

"Same year?" I asked.

"Same year."

I relaxed a little as I tried to digest some of this. That was like…six weeks. Six weeks of being totally out of it. Six weeks of lying in a bed, not using my muscles at all.

"I can't move much," I said as I looked up to him.

He nodded.

"Your body has been shut down for a while now after suffering significant trauma. You were almost pronounced dead at the scene, and we lost you once on the table as well. We had to induce coma just to keep your body in check long enough to try to fix you up."

"Did I break a lot of bones?" I asked. I wondered about my legs because they definitely didn't feel right.

"I think we should wait until your dad gets here," the doctor said. His hand patted my leg, which made it feel all tingly. Everything felt all tingly, like my whole body fell asleep.

I guess it had.

"He's on his way."

Even through the blurriness inside my head, I had the feeling this was not going to be the most pleasant of encounters. I didn't know the extent of the damage yet, but I was obviously pretty fucked up, and that certainly meant I wasn't playing soccer in the next season. I gritted my teeth. I didn't care what he would say— Nicole was okay, and that mattered more…

"Thomas?"

I awoke to someone prodding my arm. I didn't realize I had drifted off. It was Doctor Winchester doing the poking, but Dad was there, too—standing on the other side of the bed.

"Can you talk, son?" he asked.

"Yeah," I said, and then tried clearing my throat. "Kind of."

"Your vocal cords haven't been used for some time," Doctor Winchester said. "It will take them a while to get going normally again."

"How do you feel?" Dad asked with all the concern in his eyes a parent should have. His hand went to my head, and then he bent over and looked into my eyes with his little penlight.

"Weird," I answered. I didn't really know how I felt.

"You were hurt pretty bad," he told me. "I'm considering myself pretty lucky to be talking to you at all. For a while there…"

His voice trailed off, and he sighed.

"What's wrong with me?" I asked. I went into a coughing fit then, and the doctor held up the water for me to drink. My stomach lurched as it trickled down my throat.

They both looked at each other, and then Dad pulled up another one of those little rolling chairs to sit close to me. Doctor Winchester started listing all my injuries.

"The impact from the vehicle hit you in your shoulders and back," he started. "There was a rough edge near the bottom of the car, which tore open part of your left side. There was damage to your kidney and spleen, and you collapsed a lung. Your left kidney had to be removed, as well as a portion of your spleen. Your left shoulder blade was shattered, your pelvis cracked, your right arm broken, and there was some trauma to your lower back. Your spinal cord took a lot of shock with the impact."

"Shit."

Doctor Winchester chuckled, but my dad's eyes narrowed at my comment.

"Yes," the doctor continued as he gave me another drink of water, "you were in pretty bad shape."

"How about now?" I asked, wondering just how much I had mended after six weeks.

"Your bones have healed," he said, "with the exception of your left scapula, which had to be replaced. You're going to have a nasty scar down your side, but considering the circumstances, I would think you should wear that with pride."

I looked up at him questioningly.

"From all accounts of the accident, you most certainly saved the Skye girl's life."

I felt my mouth turn up in a bit of a smile.

Dad's eyes narrowed again.

Doctor Winchester looked over at his clipboard for a minute and then turned back to me.

"I want to talk a bit about your legs, though."

I felt cold, and the muscles in my shoulders tensed.

"Your right leg got a nasty cut as well," he said, "though not as bad as the one on your back. You lost a lot of blood there, but it's your spinal cord injury that is of the most concern."

"He'll be fine," my dad interrupted. "He's strong."

"We don't know that yet, Lou."

They didn't have to say it—I already knew.

"I'm not going to walk, am I?"

"You'll be fine," Dad repeated.

"Thomas, it's hard to say at this point. I'd like to go through some tests first and see how you're responding now that you are awake. Without those results, it's hard to say for sure, but it's going to be difficult. With extensive physical therapy, you may walk again eventually."

Eventually.

What the fuck did that mean?

"How long will that take?"

"I want to run some tests—"

"*How long?*" I asked again, raising my voice a little.

The doctor's eyes softened, and his lips smashed together.

"It will be at least a year," he finally answered. "Maybe eighteen months, if you really work hard, and there isn't any permanent damage. Even then, you may never have a complete recovery."

"What about soccer?" I asked, glancing up at my dad. He glared at Doctor Winchester. The doctor looked at him, took a deep breath, and then turned back to me.

"Thomas, it's very unlikely you will be able to play soccer again."

My stomach lurched, expelling the little water I had consumed. Pain shot up my back as I tried to lean over to get the water out of my mouth. Both my dad and the doctor held me to one side, and a nurse came in to help as well.

I still saved Rumple.

It was still worth it.

But what did I have now? If the only thing that had mattered in my life for years was gone, where did that leave me?

Dad closed the door to the room as Doctor Winchester left to schedule various tests over the next few days. As soon as the door was closed, I could feel the entire atmosphere of the room change.

Dad stayed at the door for a moment with his hand pressed against the frame, leaning into it before letting out a long breath and turning around to look at me.

Well, glare would be more accurate.

Here it comes.

"I always thought you were an idiot," he said darkly. "I never realized how big an idiot you really are."

He walked slowly over to the side of my bed, and I tried to shift around, though I didn't know where I was going to go. I could barely move at all, and I could feel a strange panic building inside of me.

I couldn't move my legs, and I could only move my arms a little. As soon as I shifted one arm over—even a little bit—I could feel the muscle fatigue from my shoulder to my wrist.

I was trapped.

"Do you realize what you've done?" His voice was still quite low and soft, and I looked over toward the door, wondering just how far away the night nurse was from my room. "You may very well have fucked up your entire life in one stupid, pointless move."

"Not pointless," I heard myself whisper and immediately regretted saying it out loud.

"What was that?" he snapped. "*What*?"

"Nothing," I mumbled.

"Not pointless, is that what you're telling me?" Contempt was evident in his voice. "You almost *died*, Thomas! It's going to be at least two more seasons before you can play again! For what, huh? For a piece of ass?"

Two more seasons?

"I thought the doctor said—"

"That moron doesn't know what he's talking about!" Dad waved a hand toward the door. "You'll play again—you just have to stop being a pussy and get the hell out of that bed as soon as you can. No more napping, you hear me?"

I looked up at him and then down at the blanket that covered my legs. I tried to moisten my lips, but my tongue was too dry, and I started coughing again. Once I got it under control, I tried to shift my legs like I had my arms.

Nothing.

They didn't hurt or feel strained or fatigued. I just couldn't make them move.

"Dad," I whispered as I looked up at him again. The panic was back. "I can't move them, Dad. They just...don't."

My heart was starting to beat faster, as evidenced by the increasing tempo of the monitor off to the side. My lungs expanded and contracted over and over, and I couldn't seem to make them slow down at all. I strained—trying to just shift my leg a little, but nothing happened at all.

Nothing.

"Dad..."

"Stop that," he said through a clenched jaw. "It may take a little time, but you're going to work through it. You're going to play pro."

I couldn't even listen to what he was saying. My head started to pound with the exertion of trying to make my leg move—or even to wiggle my toe. My breath came in gasps, and the monitor started going wild. My vision blurred, and I tried to grab onto the railing of the bed as my head started spinning, but my arm just flopped to one side.

"Dad!"

"Stop it, Thomas!" he yelled. I felt his hands on my shoulders, and then there was another set of hands—the nurse—holding one of my arms. "You are going to hurt yourself!"

"Relax, Thomas," the nurse said. "Should I sedate him?"

"No, you aren't going to sedate him!" Dad yelled at her. "He's just coming out of a coma, for God's sake. Did you even go to school?"

"Sorry, doctor."

"Thomas!" His voice made me cringe, and that, along with the combination of his hands holding my shoulders, was not helping me relax at all, but it did make me shut down a little. The muscles I could control tensed and held still.

"I want Nicole," I said as I looked up at the nurse. "Where's Nicole?"

"You just need to rest now," Dad said. He pushed my shoulders to the bed and started lowering it a bit.

"I hate sleeping on my back," I grumbled.

"It's better to keep all the tubes in place," Dad said. His voice had softened a lot. "It's just more incentive for you to work hard and get through this, right son?"

"When can I see Nicole?" I mumbled.

"I'll look into it," Dad said dismissively.

"She's still trying to get in," I heard the nurse say to Dad. "Shall I call for her in the morning?"

"Absolutely not," Dad replied. He glanced back to me for a moment. "I'll take care of it."

As my head settled against the lumpy, stiff pillow, my eyes closed without asking me if it was okay, and the voices faded.

It was light in the room when I opened them again, and I was alone.

My head hurt, and there wasn't a single part of my body that wasn't aching in one way or another. I wanted to roll over, but there was just no way to do it. I didn't have the strength, and all the tubes and shit all over the place didn't help at all.

For the longest time, I just lay there and stared at the ceiling.

A nurse came by—a different one than who had been there overnight—and checked my vitals. She leaned down and changed a bag near the end of the bed, which I realized must be attached to a catheter.

Fucking awesome.

Note sarcasm.

Once she gave me some more water, which I managed to keep down, she left me alone again. I tried moving my fingers, one at a time, just picking them up and putting them down again. It seemed to work out okay and wasn't making me tired. I tried lifting my wrists next, and that seemed okay, too.

My arms were a whole other thing. After two tries, I was exhausted again.

I fell back asleep.

Tests, tests, tests.

All fucking afternoon and most of the next morning.

Could I feel this and could I feel that? Lift this; flex that.

I wanted to punch something, but I couldn't make a complete fist without wearing myself out so much, I had to take a fucking nap.

Maybe Dad was right, and I was a pussy.

I wanted to see Nicole, but when I brought her up, he changed the subject or just told me to shut up.

I woke to voices in the hallway.

"I'm going to talk to him, Lou."

"He's not ready."

"Well, I need to talk to him anyway."

"I will not allow it."

"At this point, I have an incomplete accident report, and police business overrides your authority here at the hospital. I'm going to talk to him."

"Don't screw around with me. You'll regret it."

"Police business, boss."

The door opened, and I looked up to see Greg Skye walking into the room. I could still see Dad in the corridor outside with his hand gripping his hair and his eyes boring holes into Greg's back. Greg shut the door behind him.

He walked over to me slowly with a tentative smile across his face. His hand grabbed the rolling chair, and he pulled it up next to the bed before he sat down.

"How's my hero?"

I smiled and chuckled a little, which really fucking hurt. I tried to take a deep breath as I looked back up to him.

"How's my Rumple?" I asked.

Greg shook his head and smiled.

"Nicole is fine," he said. "She's really been missing you."

"Is she going to come here?" I asked.

Greg looked over his shoulder.

"I'm hoping to get her in here very shortly, but your Dad doesn't like the idea too much."

I thought about that for a minute. Yeah, I was pretty sure he didn't like it at all.

"He hasn't let her visit, has he?"

"She was here in the beginning," Greg said, "but she and your Dad had a bit of a…confrontation, shall we say? He's denied her access since then."

"I want to see her," I told him. "Tell her that, okay?"

"I will, son," Greg said, "but we need to talk about the accident a little so I can really say I'm here on official business and not just because I wanted to thank the man who saved my daughter's life and almost cost himself his own in the process."

"Worth it," I said quietly.

His hand lay on top of mine, and he gripped it for just a second.

"Thank you, Thomas," he said, and his voice faltered a bit on my name. "I'll never be able to say it enough, but thank you."

I looked up at him and saw his eyes were shining just a bit in the harsh, fluorescent lights. I nodded to him once, and he nodded back to me.

"Now let's get down to business before you need to rest some more, okay?"

"Okay."

"First question," he said as he pulled out a mini clipboard and a pencil. "What the hell is a *Rumple*?"

If he kept up questions like this, we were literally going to follow Shakespeare's words and "laugh ourselves into stitches." Somehow, just having him here made me feel better.

Now how was he going to get Rumple into my room?

CHAPTER TWENTY-SIX
play on

After a quick explanation of the origin of *RumplestiltSkye* and the painful laughter that occurred along with it, Greg gave me the details of the accident. As I had pretty much already figured out, the brunt of the impact from the car was on me, and the trajectory of Nicole's body and mine when we were hit resulted in her being partially shoved underneath a car parked at the diner entrance, which kept her from suffering much harm. She had to get stitches in her right shoulder from getting caught on something under the car and had a mild concussion but was otherwise okay.

The whole conversation lasted maybe a half hour, and when it was done, I was completely exhausted. The idea that just lying there and talking could wear me out was frustrating, to say the least. Greg was still talking when I dropped off.

I could feel soft, warm fingers over my cheek and temple and then through my hair. Instinctively, I turned my head toward the sensation, and when I awoke, I was met with her beautiful blue eyes.

"Hey there," Nicole said softly.

"Hey," I managed to croak out. Nicole picked up my cup and

held it up to me. With the bed lying back too far, the water just managed to dribble down my chin, and we played around with the bed controls until I was more upright.

Once I was settled comfortably, I just looked at her—taking in her appearance and noticing a lot of changes. She was thinner, no doubt, and she looked tired. I also noticed she was wearing one of my practice shirts, and I wondered where she got it. Would she have gone to ask Dad to let her take one? Maybe she got it out of my locker or my soccer bag.

"You look good in my shirt," I said with a smile.

She blushed and looked down at her hands, which held one of mine.

"It needs to be washed," she replied. "I kind of wear it a lot."

I thought about that and decided I definitely liked it.

"Thomas?" Nicole said softly.

"Yeah?"

"Thank you."

I looked from where she held my hand to her face and saw there was a tear running down her cheek. I tried to raise my hand to brush it away, but it just kind of flopped back down on my stomach. She seemed to understand, and with a small, sad smile, she picked up my hand and brushed it over her cheek.

"Anytime," I said, and I meant it. I'd do it all over again in a heartbeat.

"I knew it, you know," she said.

"Knew what?"

"That you didn't...say what you said because you wanted to say it. I knew it was *him*."

I looked away, focusing on the IV needle puncturing my skin. I was glad she knew but upset about it at the same time.

"What did you say to him?" I asked.

She let out a short, sharp laugh.

"Which time?"

My eyes turned back to her, and I shook my head a little.

"You shouldn't do that," I told her.

"Well, sometimes shit just comes out of my mouth," she told me, "and I don't control it."

I chuckled a little.

"So what did you say?" I asked again.

"The first time?"

"Sure."

"Well, it was about three days afterwards," she said. "I was in the hospital the first night—just for observation—but I had been coming back every day to sit with you in the ICU. You had already been through…um…three surgeries, I think. They were still keeping you in the coma on purpose then, and I read somewhere that people in a coma might still be able to hear you if you talked to them. So…I talked to you."

"What did you say?"

"Um…" She blushed again. "I told you I was here and that I was thinking about you. I think I thanked you for saving my life about four hundred times, kind of alternating that with being pissed off that you did it because you were hurt so bad. I told you I needed you…and that I loved you."

She said the last part very quietly.

"I love you, too," I told her.

She smiled and bit her lip.

"I know."

"So what happened?"

"Well, he had been in there, mostly looking over your chart and whatever between his rounds," she continued. "He told me there was no point in talking to you—that the whole idea you might be able to hear me was ridiculous, and I should just go home."

Yeah, that sounded like him.

"I told him I'd leave when you left, and he apparently didn't like that idea. He started telling me that if it hadn't been for me, you wouldn't be here in the first place, and maybe you would wake up sooner if I wasn't there."

She took a deep breath and let it out slowly. Her fingers

played with mine.

"I kept it together that time and just told him I was sorry you were hurt but that I wasn't going anywhere until I could thank you properly. He told me I should be apologizing to you instead and walked out of the room."

"That was the first time?"

"Yeah," she confirmed, "the second was a lot worse."

"Go on."

She sighed again.

"He was talking to the doctor…um…Winchester?"

I nodded.

"They were talking about your injuries and about your back, especially. That's when Doctor Winchester told your dad you, um…might not walk again. Your dad was really, really upset about that and called for a second opinion. When the other doctor said it was too early to tell, but that you'd definitely be going through a lot of rehab, your Dad kind of blew a gasket."

That surprised me. Dad never made mistakes like that— getting upset in front of other people and showing his temper. He was always cool in public.

"He yelled at the doctors for a bit. Then when they left, he turned on me." She gripped my hand a little tighter. "You should have come out of the coma by then. They weren't keeping you sedated anymore, and you should have woken back up, but you hadn't. When he started blaming me again, I snapped."

She went quiet for a minute. I could feel her dread in the pit of my stomach.

"What did you say?" I finally asked her.

"That maybe if he wasn't smacking you around all the time, you'd heal faster. Something like that, anyway."

"Holy shit," I murmured. I swallowed hard and wished I could run my hand through my hair.

"Yeah, he threw me out then," she said. "Called hospital security and said I wasn't allowed to visit you again. Once you were out of ICU, I managed to sneak in with Jeremy and Rachel for a few minutes, but we were caught when the nurse came in."

"You shouldn't have done that," I told her.

"He needed to know," she said. "He can't keep everything a secret."

"He has a lot of secrets to tell, too," I whispered. When she kept asking, I finally told her he had the pictures, and that's why I had to break up with her.

"You should have told me," she said when I was done. "We could have worked it out together."

"I didn't want to take the chance," I admitted. "If he found out, Nicole, he wouldn't hesitate to ruin you. I couldn't let that happen."

"Is that why you said all that shit on the phone?"

"Yeah." I cringed. "I'm sorry—I didn't mean any of it."

"He was there with you, wasn't he?"

"Yeah."

"I thought so."

I looked back at her and just stared at her face for a while, trying to figure out how I could have been so stupid. At the time, it seemed like the best idea, but now I wasn't so sure.

"I'm sorry," I said again and then yawned.

"Me too," she replied. "I think you need to rest."

I could only nod, and I turned my head so it rested against the pillow, but it was still fucking uncomfortable.

"I hate this pillow," I grumbled, and Nicole snickered.

"I don't think hospitals spend a lot of extra cash on down," she replied.

I wanted to respond. I wanted to tell her that despite all the shit we were going to have to go through, this was going to be a new beginning for us.

I fell asleep instead.

<hr>

"I want Nicole Skye to be able to visit me," I said to Doctor Winchester as he checked over the various tubes inserted into me.

"Hrmph," he replied. "I heard she was here yesterday."

"I want her to be able to come back without taking shit for it," I told him. "I'm eighteen—I should be able to say who can see me, right?"

"Theoretically, yes," he said, "though I don't think your father would agree."

"I don't care." I hoped I sounded more sure of myself than I felt.

"I'll see what I can do," he said with a smile.

Dad did not agree.

"That bitch is the reason you are here in the first place!" he said after the room cleared out. "She isn't coming in here again!"

"I want her to," I said again. I didn't look at him, just kept staring at my hands lying on my stomach.

"She'll just get in the way of your recovery," he told me. "I don't need her distracting you!"

"She's not," I retorted.

We went back and forth until he got so mad, I finally just stopped responding. I didn't really think he would go so far as to do anything here in the hospital where I was being so closely monitored, but I didn't feel like taking the chance, either. I couldn't move much at all. Even though my hands and arms were a little stronger, the feeling of being trapped when my dad was in the room continued to gnaw at me. The doctors kept saying I was already showing improvement, but this was the first day I had even been given anything solid to eat—if Jell-o and popsicles counted as solid. Not being able to get out of the damn bed to pee was annoying.

After Dad left in a huff, Doctor Winchester came in with a woman I hadn't seen before. He said her name was Danielle Richmond, and she was apparently my physical therapist.

For about an hour, she just lifted my legs up and down, telling me she had been doing this the whole time I was comatose. Though I could feel everything in my legs except for the area around the scar on my right thigh, I couldn't control the movements at all.

It was pissing me off.

"This sucks!" I nearly growled at her. "I'm not even doing anything!"

"Just think about how you would make your leg move along with what I'm doing," she said. "Focus on how your mind would control the muscles. Letting your brain re-learn along with your muscles is the first step."

"*First step*," I snorted. "Nice."

"Just an expression," she said with a smile. "It's good you had a lot of muscle tone before the accident. It should make your recovery more successful."

More successful. Like maybe someday I could make my legs move again without help.

She switched legs and started rolling my ankle around. It was the first time I had really seen my legs since I woke up, and they looked scrawny to me.

I must have fallen asleep before she left because the next thing I knew, I was surrounded by Nicole's scent.

"Can you get the other side?" I heard her whispered voice near my face. I opened my eyes and saw a nurse first, who had my pillow tucked under one arm while the other one was behind my head. Nicole was on my other side, holding my head up a little as she slid a different pillow beneath me.

"Rumple?"

"Oh, baby," she said, still whispering. "I didn't mean to wake you up."

"It's okay," I slurred, still half asleep. "You smell good."

She giggled and lowered my head onto a soft, cool pillow.

It smelled like her.

"I was going to wash the pillowcase first," she said, "but I figured you'd like it better this way."

I smiled and closed my eyes again as my head sank further into my Nicole-scented pillow. I still couldn't roll over, but this was pretty damn good anyway. Her hand twirled through my hair, and I drifted off to sleep.

Shakespeare said, "The soul of this man is his clothes." Somehow, I thought maybe Nicole's soul was in her pillow.

Now I could really rest.

CHAPTER TWENTY-SEVEN
counterattack

If anyone else were to tell me recovery takes time and I had to just work hard and be patient, I was going to find the strength to punt that idiot across the fucking room.

Four days after I came out of the coma, I could sit up for an hour before I had to lie down again. I could feed myself about three bites of something before my arms gave out, and I could move my toes if I concentrated really fucking hard. Everyone told me what great progress I was making, but I knew bullshit when I smelled it. I was a fucking invalid, as my father put it, and only Nicole's regular visits were keeping me from throwing myself out the damn window.

Well, that and not being able to get out of the fucking bed.

In other words, rehab sucked.

"You have to be able to do this if you're going to be able to get out of here," Danielle said as I dropped back down on the bed.

I took another deep breath and tried to use my arms to transfer myself from the bed to the wheelchair. My arms had improved, but holding up my own diminished body weight was still just a bit much for me. With a grunt, I strained my muscles as hard as I could and actually managed to drop into the chair. It wasn't the least bit graceful, and I probably would have tipped the damn thing over if Danielle hadn't been holding on to it, but I did it.

I glanced over at Nicole in the easy chair in the corner of the room. She had her hands over her mouth—probably to keep from squealing, which drove me fucking nuts when she did it—and her eyes were shining. I knew she was smiling under there.

"Just fucking say it!" I snapped.

"I knew you could do it!" She shrieked and then put her hands over her mouth again.

"Next thing you know, I'll be able to take a shit by myself," I grumbled.

"One thing at a time," Danielle said for the four hundred and seventy millionth time. "It's not going to happen all at once."

Nicole came over to the wheelchair and leaned down to kiss me on the forehead.

"You're doing wonderfully," she told me.

Whatever.

I sighed and looked up at her, all my pissiness gone along with my energy. Danielle helped me get back into bed—damn that chick was strong—and Nicole sat down on the edge. Danielle filled out her little charts and then left me for the day.

"I'm fucking useless," I mumbled, and Nicole shushed me.

"You're my hero," she told me. She leaned closer, and her lips touched mine softly. "I love you."

Her hands went into my hair, and her tongue reached into my mouth. I groaned against her, wanting to wrap my arms around her and hold her tight against me, but I just couldn't. It was easy enough to hate myself for it, but if I was going to be helpless, at least it was Nicole holding me up. Her hands slid down my arms and chest, then down to my stomach. Certain parts of my body were reminded of her touch and begged for more attention.

"At least I know my dick still works," I said with a grin. I tried to reach up and grope her tits, but my hand only managed to brush against them before it dropped back to the bed.

Nicole gave me a sly smile, grasped my hand, and held it up

against one of her breasts as she kissed me again.

Yeah—my dick definitely still worked.

"I've got to go babysit," Nicole said as she broke away and laid my hand back on my stomach. "Jeremy said he was going to come by later, and I think a couple other guys were coming with him."

"Yeah," I said with a nod, "Paul and Klosav."

"Clint still hasn't come by?" Nicole asked quietly.

I shook my head.

"I told Jeremy to tell him not to be such a pussy," I said. "He's not listening, I guess."

"He offered to take me to prom," Nicole said with a laugh. "To make up for all of it, you know?"

This was not news I liked.

"If he fucking touches you, I will get out of this bed and fuck him up."

"Hmm…" Nicole tapped her finger against her chin. "Are you trying to give me incentive?"

"Don't fucking think about it!"

She smiled and shook her head before kissing me again.

"Never," she promised.

"Damn straight!"

"I'll see you after school tomorrow, okay?"

"Yeah, yeah."

"Love you."

I reached out and tried to grab her hand. She placed it in my palm.

"I love you too, Rumple." I took a big breath and huffed it out. "Sorry I'm such a jackass."

"I know how hard it is," she told me. "I can see it. You are doing so much better. I know you don't think so, but you are. Danielle said you'd be out of the hospital and into the rehab center by the end of the week at the rate you're going."

"And how long there before I can even think about leaving? A month? Three? More?"

Her hand smoothed my hair.

"Fucking sucks."

"I know, baby."

We kissed a few more times, but I was too tired to beg her to stay any longer, and I didn't want Sophie to be late to work or something. Nicole walked out, and I was left on my own to think too much.

The main thing I was thinking about was something I had just noticed the previous night.

Usually I dropped right off, too tired or medicated to think about much of anything, but last night had been different. I was tired, but I didn't drop off right away. I was anxious, like I was waiting for something, but I didn't know what it was.

Then it hit me.

I knew what was missing.

What I was waiting for.

I was waiting for the day to pass by again—detailing the activities and carving them into my brain for safekeeping. I was waiting for my overactive mind to replay my life from the morning to the night in exquisite detail.

But it didn't happen.

I looked up at the new flowers Nicole had brought into the room—despite my insistence that boys didn't get fucking flowers —and tried to remember what had been there before. Whatever they were, they had been yellow, and the new ones were kind of orangey-red, but I couldn't remember exactly how they were different or what kind of flowers they had been.

My mind had no image for me to recall.

Shakespeare coined the phrase: "Make not your thoughts your prison." Somehow, even though the phrase fit me perfectly right now, not remembering everything was definitely a blessing.

Now maybe my mind could rest, too.

<hr>

"Hello, Thomas."

I looked up from my new bed in the rehabilitation clinic and saw a tall, lanky guy with blond hair and a soft, kind of effeminate voice despite the slight southern drawl.

"Hey," I said. I narrowed my eyes a little.

"I'm Justin," he said as he pulled up a chair to sit beside me. "I just wanted to introduce myself and let you know we'd be talking a bit while you're here."

"About what?" I asked.

"Well, the accident," he said, "and how you feel about the situation you are in now."

"Oh fucking hell," I grumbled as insight struck me. "You're a shrink?"

He laughed softly.

"Something like that," he replied.

"I don't need a fucking shrink."

"Well, let's talk a bit, and I'll make that call, okay?"

"No, it isn't."

"Thomas, you've been through a significant amount of trauma," Justin said. "You've been an extremely active individual with the potential to play soccer professionally. That changed drastically in a very short amount of time. You're going to have to talk about how it's affected you."

"How it's affected me?" I shouted. I set my sarcasm to annihilate. "*How it's affected me?* Really? Um, let's see: I can't walk; I've only been able to get myself to the john since yesterday; I can't grope my girlfriend, and my Dad thinks I'm a fucking failure! That's how it's *affected* me. Good enough?"

He just looked at me for a moment before nodding his head.

"Yes, I do think we'll be talking a bit more," he said before he stood up and headed for the door. He called back over his shoulder. "We'll have sessions for an hour every other day. I'll have the nurse add it to your schedule."

Fucking hell.

<hr/>

"One more time," Danielle coaxed.

I took a big breath and braced my hands against the arms of the wheelchair. Sweat practically poured into my eyes, and my lungs just couldn't seem to get enough oxygen in them. With a grunt and held breath, I lifted myself up and sideways onto the bed.

"Excellent!"

I dropped back down on my back, feeling anything but excellent, and panted like I had just finished a marathon when all I had really done was move from one spot to the other. My eyes stared blankly at the ceiling of my room as I tried to catch my breath.

"I think you've had enough for today," she said.

"Are you sure?" I growled. "I'm not quite dead yet."

She ignored my pithiness and said she'd be back in the morning. I waited until my biceps stopped burning and then pushed myself back up against the pillow.

Nicole's pillow.

Nicole had come to the center yesterday and brought me a new pillowcase—freshly unwashed. Some people probably thought it was nasty, but I loved it. The other one was beginning to just smell like me again.

I had been at the center for four weeks. I could get myself in and out of the wheelchair, to the bathroom and back without assistance, and I could feed myself. I was off the pain meds, except for some Motrin at night sometimes, and didn't need to be hooked up to anything anymore. It was better in that respect, but Nicole couldn't visit me every day, and that part sucked. She came when she could, but sometimes two or three days would go by without seeing her.

Physical therapy took up most of my days, alternating between building up the strength in my arms and just trying to make my legs work at all. I could feel them, but my mind just couldn't seem to make them work. I'd been through dozens of tests, and they kept saying there wasn't any spinal cord damage, but aside from wiggling my toes and bending my knees just a little, I still couldn't control them. Apparently, the doctors and experts on such things still thought my progress was good enough, and Danielle said I would probably be ready to go home in the next week.

I couldn't decide how I felt about that.

I would be able to see Nicole every day again…in theory. At least we would be close to each other. I was pretty sure Dad was going to make that pretty fucking difficult, though. He hadn't said a word to her in my presence, but his disdain for the girl who had cost him his soccer champion was plain to see.

He still insisted I was going to play again.

I kind of refused to think about it.

Soccer had been my life for so long, not being able to play just felt…weird—like I was in a dream or something. Well, all of this shit kind of felt like a dream, but that part especially. With the replacement shoulder blade, I didn't have full movement of my left shoulder anymore and couldn't raise my arm completely above my head. Even if I got full use of my legs back eventually, I wasn't going to be able to play goal.

Okay, so maybe I thought about it a little.

I blamed that shit on Justin Hammer—my therapist.

He seemed to think I needed to talk about it all the fucking time and kept asking me how I felt about this shit and how I felt about that shit. I didn't know how to feel and usually ended up yelling at him. He seemed to think that was all fine and dandy though. I apparently had anger issues and needed to learn to get it all out.

Fucking ridiculous.

I kind of liked the guy, though.

Dad came by later that night and started reading over my progress charts and crap. He bitched about the physical therapist, the insistence of the shrink, the price he was paying for the meals, and the doctors who continued to say my chances of walking again were about fifty-fifty.

"Fucking idiots," he seethed. "I need to get you home so you can start some real training again. They're just letting you slack here."

"My arms are a lot stronger," I told him. I tried to remember the exact words Danielle had used, but they weren't coming to me.

"And this bullshit about your left arm mobility—we have to work on that, too."

"I thought Doctor Winchest—"

"Winchester is a fucking moron!" Dad yelled. I cringed against the pillow a bit. He'd been like this more and more lately—going off in places where someone could just walk in on us and hear him. He used to be really careful to keep his voice down in those kinds of situations, but he wasn't anymore.

"I talked to Wayne today and told him how well you were doing," Dad suddenly said. I looked up at him with disbelief.

"What did he say?"

"He said the offer would still be open," Dad told me, "providing you got off your ass and got yourself completely recovered in the next year."

I had the feeling those weren't Wayne's exact words.

"What if…what if I can't?" I asked quietly.

"Don't give me that kind of shit!" Dad responded. "You see? That right there is why I need to get you out of here before that stupid PT and her nay-saying can bring you down anymore!"

"Danielle said—"

"Don't fucking repeat a word that came from her mouth!" he yelled. "Stupid bitch. She's as bad as the one who put you here."

I tensed, trying to keep myself from uttering the words that wanted to come from my mouth. No good would come of it.

"You should be training in Europe right now," he continued. "If it wasn't for that two-bit cock-sucker, you would be."

I looked down at my hands in my lap and tried to breathe normally. It wasn't really working, but I knew if I said anything, it would just be worse. It was better to let him belt it all out.

"I'm taking you home this weekend," Dad said as he threw my chart back onto the table. "I'll get you a PT who knows what the fuck he's doing and get you away from that faggot shrink and his 'Thomas needs to learn to cope with his disabilities' bullshit."

I really didn't think Justin's bread was buttered on that side, but I hated talking to him about everything. I usually didn't say much unless he was trying to get me to talk about Nicole. I didn't mind that topic.

"This weekend," Dad repeated, and then he walked out of the room.

My breath whistled between my lips in a deep sigh as I exhaled, and I closed my eyes. As my head dropped back to the pillow, I was enveloped in Rumple-smell, and my muscles relaxed.

<hr />

I didn't know what time in the morning it was, only that my head was still full of sleep when voices roused me.

"...I understand your concerns, Doctor Malone, but physical therapy is not always that cut and dried. There are a lot of considerations—"

"I am fully aware of how PT works," Dad said, cutting Danielle off. "That's why I've hired my own therapist to work with *my son* in our home."

I heard Danielle take a long breath.

"Mr. Chase is known to me," Danielle said softly. "Though I can't deny he's had some results, some of his methods are considered...questionable."

"You know what?" Dad's voice grew a little louder. "What I don't need from some barely-educated *therapist* is advice on my son's care. I actually went to medical school, you know, and I don't need *you* offering *me* advice on whom to hire. Consider yourself out of the picture."

I opened my eyes as Dad closed the door in Danielle's face. Dad turned and looked over to me.

"Get out of that damn bed," he told me, "and get whatever you want to take with you. We're leaving today."

Shit.

On our way out, the resident doctor, Danielle, and Justin all showed up trying to talk Dad out of it. Obviously, they didn't understand who they were dealing with. No one talks my dad out of anything. No one.

Justin said he'd like to come to the house to meet with me. Dad said over his dead body.

Danielle tried to give him a bunch of paperwork, which he tossed on the floor at her feet.

The other doctor attempted to talk to him about my condition in general. Dad told him to shut up.

Then his phone rang. It was obviously Doctor Winchester.

"At this point, I'm just not interested," Dad said, his voice just barely still in control. "I appreciate what you have done for him so far, but I'm not happy with his progress...I know that's what *she* says, but her opinion is really not holding much weight with me."

Dad looked pointedly at Danielle.

"Bottom line is, he's going home. Now. I'll be taking care of him from this point forward."

Dad hung up and turned to me.

"Get going," he said.

I wheeled myself toward the door, refusing to look at any of the three people who had been taking care of me in various ways since I woke up. It wouldn't do any good, and I just didn't want to deal with it. I made it out to Dad's car without too much difficulty, but once there, I wasn't really sure what to do.

This wasn't something I'd practiced.

Through Dad's bitching, I managed to get myself positioned next to the passenger seat and eventually flopped into the car. Dad grabbed the wheelchair and gave it a forceful shove toward the rehab center doors before he got into the driver's side.

"How will I get into the house?" I asked.

"I already got another chair for you," he told me.

"But the stairs..."

Dad grumbled under his breath.

"I guess you'll go through the back entrance."

I hoped the rain hadn't been too bad, because it got muddier than shit out in the back yard.

We sat in silence for a few minutes as Dad maneuvered out of the parking lot, down the street, and onto the highway. I just stared out the window, wishing I hadn't put my phone in the bag behind me or that I had at least kept Nicole's pillow in the front with me.

I was getting tired, and holding myself upright in the seat of the Mercedes wasn't nearly as easy as sitting in the wheelchair or in the hospital bed. We hadn't even been on the road for fifteen minutes yet, and there was probably close to another twenty minutes before we'd get home.

"Now that you are out of there, we're going to get a few things straight," Dad suddenly piped up.

Whatever discomfort I was feeling physically was overrun by the dread that came over me from his words.

"What things?" I asked quietly.

"The Skye girl is history," he started. I tried to speak up, but he shushed me. "History. She's not coming anywhere near our house, and you're not getting your phone back. I put up with her shit in the hospital, and I have no more tolerance for that insolent bitch."

Again, I tried to speak up, but he just started screaming.

"It's her fucking fault you're like this!" he yelled. "She's fucking coddling you, back-talking me, and if I hear one fucking word out of you about it, I will fuck her life up! You hear me?"

My breath was caught in my chest, and I couldn't draw in any air. My hands started to shake, and I tried to grip the edge of the seat for support, but my fingers weren't cooperating. When I didn't answer right away, he backhanded my shoulder, causing me to gasp.

At least I could breathe again.

"You fucking hear me?" he screeched again.

"I hear you!" I replied quickly and louder than I meant to. "Just…just leave her alone, all right?"

I glanced to my left and saw his slow, calculated smile.

"Now you're seeing some reason," he said. His hand went back to the steering wheel. "Next, your new PT is Steven Chase. He's very innovative with his ideas, and he's achieved some fantastic results. He's going to work you hard, and you're going to start making some real progress."

"I thought I was making progress," I countered.

"Bullshit. You still can't even move your legs reliably. You should be. He's going to fix that."

I honestly didn't know what else could be done, considering the hell Danielle had been putting me through over the past weeks. Though he hadn't said much about Steven Chase, something about his words made me nervous. I had the feeling I was going to miss Danielle.

"I don't want to hear any bitching or complaining from you, either," Dad said. "You're going to work your ass off, and if you aren't making progress, you're going to answer to me. Got it?"

"Got it," I said softly.

"You just need a little more encouragement," Dad said after a few more minutes of silence. We had just reached the stretch of road right before our house. "I've got everything set up for you in the guest room next to my study. Everything is on the first floor, so you can get to the kitchen and whatever. Steven is going to set up equipment right there in the living room. It will be a lot better than being at that place."

I wasn't sure if I agreed or not, but I nodded anyway.

I was still trying to cope with the idea of not being able to see Nicole. I wondered how in the hell I was even going to tell her what had happened. Dad ran his hand through his hair and then turned into our long driveway, expertly maneuvering through the tree-lined, hilly course.

"You know I'm just trying to do what's best for you," he said. His voice had gone back to calm and smooth again. "You want to get better as quickly as possible, don't you?"

"Sure," I said meekly.

"That's my boy! I knew you wouldn't be shut down by this shit. You're going to be fine."

He parked next to the house and brought a wheelchair out of the garage for me. It was nicer than the one at the rehab center; I had to give him that. It was a little easier to get from the car to the chair, but I was already so worn out by the time I had myself in it, I could barely move my arms enough to spin the wheels. The yard was muddy, and after the second time I got stuck, I couldn't get myself back out. Dad screamed at me a bit but ended up pushing me the rest of the way around the house and in through the mudroom off the back of the garage.

I barely looked at the guest room—completely outfitted with a hospital bed—before hauling myself onto the mattress and passing out.

I think Dad might have still been yelling.

Shakespeare once said "None can be called deformed but the unkind." Somehow, I didn't think Dad saw himself that way.

Now I had the feeling I was going to consider the last two months easy.

CHAPTER TWENTY-EIGHT
final minutes

Since the day Mom died, Dad had been more than one person.

I mean, he'd always assumed many roles in his play of life—even before she was gone—they just got more dynamically opposed later. The most prominent one just kind of lived his life, encouraged me to play ball, and went to work and shit—that was the one who was around more often than not. There was Mayor Malone, who was very suave and convinced everyone to vote for him—he mostly came out just at election time and during public functions. And then there was the guy who just...couldn't cope with what had happened.

The last one—that was the one who could be brutal. He'd yell and scream mostly, and sometimes he would lash out at me because I was the one who made him the way he was. He was usually only around for short periods of time, and then he'd go away for a while until some stress trigger brought him back out again.

But now...now something was different.

The way Dad was acting now was mostly like *that* guy, but there was something else in there—something unfamiliar. I wasn't quite sure what it was. I started noticing it at the hospital and the rehab center first, when he lost his cool in front of the other people there.

It was almost as if the brutal one had somehow increased his ruthlessness and maybe, just maybe, went a little off the deep end. The first full day I was home, that was most apparent.

When I woke up in the morning, my first thought was *what am I doing in the guest room*? Waking up always seemed to bring confusion, but disappeared quickly, and I was reminded that I was crippled in the same way a breadknife reminds the loaf that it's the greatest thing since itself.

I wasn't sure if that made sense, but it was what came to mind anyway.

Instead of running every morning at six, Dad had me get up and start doing a bunch of exercises with my arms. Apparently the new PT had given him a list of things for me to do for a couple of days before he arrived for the first time. The exercises weren't bad at all and were a lot like the stuff Danielle was having me do. None of it was the same, however, because Nicole wasn't there, sitting in the corner of the room and trying not to piss me off by smiling too much at my little achievements.

I had to find some way of getting ahold of her, but Dad had basically cut me off. He confiscated my cell phone, and we didn't have a landline. My laptop was up in my room, three flights of stairs away. I asked him for it and told him I really needed to get Jeremy or someone to bring me assignments so I could get caught up and graduate next month, but he said he'd arrange to get them for me.

Then I made my mistake.

"Nicole would bring it all over for me."

Dad lost it.

"What did I tell you?" he yelled. "What did I fucking tell you? That bitch isn't coming anywhere near this house *or you* ever again!"

"I want to see her!" I yelled back. Even as the words left my mouth, I could feel my body chill and immobilize more than it already was. I was on the proverbial thin ice carrying a precariously stacked set of dumbbells.

Dad's eyes went dark, and he slowly crossed the room toward me. I reached for the wheels of my chair and started pushing myself backwards, but there was nowhere to go. The feeling of being trapped was no longer just a sense of dread. There were no doctors or nurses or therapists here—it was just Dad and I.

His hands gripped the arms of the chair, stilling it completely. He leaned close to my face, his eyes blazing, but his voice was calm and quiet again.

"You want to reconsider?" he sneered. "Because you say the word, and I'll be sure you see her. You'll see her along with everyone else in this town—with some asshole's cock shoved up her drunk little cunt. Is that what you want? Say the word, Thomas. I'll be happy to oblige."

I stared back at him, unsure I could have moved even if all my limbs were working.

"You think I don't know who that kid was on the field?"

I hadn't really thought about it. That seemed to be a theme at the moment—shit I didn't think through before I acted on it.

"You smacked him around a little," Dad went on, "but that little whore deserved whatever she got. I'd be happy to show her father and the town all the dirty little details."

"Her father knows," I said softly, knowing that it wouldn't make any difference.

"Yeah, I'm sure he does," Dad said with a nod. "I wonder how many of his co-workers do? Or the kids in your school—I bet they could use a good image to jack off to, couldn't they?"

I had no doubt that he would do it and that he probably wouldn't stop there, either.

"Leave her alone," I begged. "It's not like she can hurt my game anymore…"

"No, I think she's fucked that up about as much as she possibly could," Dad agreed. He stood up straight and placed a finger against his chin. "You know…maybe that's a more fitting fate for her."

He took a few steps backwards.

"I mean, she took your legs away…Maybe a little retribution in kind would make more sense."

My panting increased. He wouldn't hurt her…would he?

"Maybe she needs to be in the middle of another accident."

"Dad…don't," I whispered. I could hardly get any words out. "Just forget I said anything, okay? I won't mention her again…I swear I won't! Just leave her alone."

"Maybe you can see a little reason," he said with an expression that was about as far from reason as I'd ever seen—even from him.

He walked out of the room while I tried to catch my breath again.

I was going to have to forget her. It was the only way to keep her safe, at least until I could get out of here.

Could I get out? I mean—I was eighteen. I didn't think he could make me stay…not legally. Of course, the legality of the matter probably didn't mean much to him. If I had said something in the hospital or rehab center, maybe I could have stayed there, but now…now it was too late.

I was here, alone with my father. I couldn't get to a phone or the computer, and though people knew I was here, none of them would be looking for me to come out and play any time soon.

I was completely and totally fucked.

Even with that realization, all I could really think about was Nicole and making sure no matter what happened to me, he wouldn't do anything to hurt her. That meant going along with anything and everything he said.

I had always obeyed him—always. Even before Mom died, I would always do what he said. Afterwards, I had to make him happy because I had taken so much from him.

I thought of Clint for a moment and wondered just what he was thinking or feeling. I wondered if he thought I hated him or if he thought it was all his fault. It wasn't, obviously. The car just skidded, and he lost control. I was the one who decided to jump in front of it. He couldn't have stopped me, and I didn't feel like any of it was his fault at all.

Just an accident.

An accident.

"It was only an accident."

"Sometimes things just happen."

"They aren't your fault."

It was Mom's voice in my head though I didn't recall her saying the words.

It wasn't Clint's fault.

I didn't blame him at all.

If it wasn't his fault I was hurt…

I felt the first hot tear run down my face.

"It was just an accident," I whispered softly to myself.

Shakespeare once said, "Do as the heavens have done, forget your evil; With them forgive yourself." Somehow, I finally grasped the meaning.

Now I understood everything in a whole new light.

⟩⟩⟩●⟨●⟩●⟨⟨⟨

For much of the next day, people kept coming to the house. I wasn't sure who had been there because Dad always got rid of them before I could get to the door, but I know I heard Jeremy and Rachel, Paul, Ben…and Nicole.

I was in bed at the time, just finishing my heat-and-eat supper when the bell rang, and I heard her voice. I dumped the tray on the side table and moved myself around until I could get in the chair. I was already tired from the exercises I had done with my arms right before eating, and I didn't get over to the wheelchair the first time. Once I managed to get into the chair, roll down the hallway, get through the living room, and reach the foyer, he had already shut her out.

The next day, Greg showed up.

We had been sitting in the kitchen with Dad looking over a bunch of papers and me picking at breakfast. All of a sudden,

Dad's head jerked up and he looked out the kitchen window. He growled under his breath, and then he looked at me, strode over to the back of my chair, and wheeled me right out of there.

"What are you doing?" I cried out.

"Shut up," he responded. He wheeled me all the way to the guest room and then actually helped me into the bed. I tried to protest—I hadn't been up that long, but he shut me up. "Don't say a fucking word, you hear me?"

He took the chair out of the room as he left.

"What the fuck?" I mumbled to myself.

Then I heard the doorbell.

I could hear muffled voices, but that was about it. I shuffled myself down to the end of the bed and peered out the window. At the end of the drive, I could just barely make out the back end of a sheriff's cruiser.

Greg's.

Then I heard the front door slam, and a few minutes later, the cruiser backed up and headed down the drive. I could just see Greg in the driver's seat with a phone in his hand. I dropped my head into my hands and waited for Dad to bring back my wheelchair.

———————➤•••◉◗◆◖•••———————

Steven Chase was a scary motherfucker.

It's not that he was a really big guy—he was muscular, but not huge—and not because he was outwardly mean; he wasn't. He was a tall and dark-haired man of maybe thirty with an Eastern European accent that I couldn't quite place, but it definitely made me wonder if he was a descendant of Vlad the Impaler.

That was what I thought before I realized what he had planned for me.

He had a bunch of equipment all over the living room, some of which I had seen before. Danielle had me use a few of the items, and there was the one predominant one—a set of parallel bars—that Danielle had pointed out to me in the rehab center but said I wouldn't be trying them out for a while. Steven didn't agree with that, I guess.

He did, however, like needles.

"We will begin with your exercises," he told me as Dad watched from the entryway. "After you have completed those, you will do them all again. There will be no change in the time from the first set to the second set. Then, if you admit you are tired or if it is just too hard for you, I have several ways to give you more incentive."

My whole body tensed. I even felt my toes flex.

He opened up a case full of hypodermic needles.

"What is that?" I asked hesitantly.

"Adrenalin in this one." Steven held up a needle. I shuddered a little. "This one contains testosterone."

I narrowed my eyes and looked over to Dad.

"Really?"

"It makes perfect sense," Dad said, "though it is the reason some whinier PTs don't care for Steven's work. Testosterone builds muscle. You need to build muscle so you can play again."

"Wouldn't there be some…um…side effects or something?"

"Nothing you need to worry about," Dad said. "Maybe your dick will get bigger."

They both thought that was pretty damn funny. I glared up at them from my chair.

"It can't possibly be any bigger," I snarked back at them. I wasn't so sure I agreed with Dad about side effects, but he was leaning against the wall with his hands crossed over his chest, and arguing with him wouldn't have been advisable. He was definitely teetering on the edge.

The beginning of the session wasn't unlike those I had been through with Danielle—hard and painful, and before it was done, I ended up with sweat pouring down my back. This was different though—we weren't done.

"Keep going!" Steven yelled. He hadn't just "spoken" since we started; he only yelled. "Ten more! And then ten more after that if you start slowing down!"

It wasn't even the pain in my arms that bothered me—I'd done enough weightlifting to understand how that felt—but my side ached where the gash was, and it was becoming harder to breathe. Needless to say, I did slow down, and about sixteen more tries later, my arms gave out, and pain rippled through my torso. The small hand weights fell to the ground.

"Is this all you can do?" Steven asked, his voice filled with contempt. He picked up the weights and handed them back, one in each hand, but my right arm just dropped it again. He growled at me and then went over to his bag for a hypodermic needle.

"What is that?" I asked as I tried to sink back into the chair.

"We already went over this!" he screamed at me. "Adrenaline, so you can keep going and get the results you need! This is only your arms! Just wait until we get to your legs!"

Before I could protest, he jabbed the needle into the crook of my elbow and pushed down on the plunger.

Almost immediately, my heart began to pound.

My breath came in pants.

My head started to swim.

Steven put the weights back into my hands, and my fingers gripped them tightly, reflexively.

"Twenty more!" he commanded. "Now!"

Though my hands were shaking, my fists were closed too tightly to drop the weights again, and my arms—though in protest —did as he demanded.

As I lay in my bed twenty minutes later, my heart was still pounding in my ears. My hands were still shaking, and my mind was flying.

I wanted Nicole.

I wanted my Dad to walk into the room so I could haul back and punch him.

I squeezed my eyes shut and tried to slow down my breathing, but the gasping was impossible to control. I was dizzy, and when I closed my eyes, I felt like I was going to throw up. I turned my head a little so my nose was up against Nicole's pillow, stared out the small window, and begged the stuff to make its way out of my system.

My old buddy The Bard once said, "In time we hate that which we often fear." Somehow, I couldn't agree with him more.

Now please, please make it stop…

<hr>

"Stop your whining," Steven said. He used his head to gesture over to his little bag full of needles and shit. "Or do you need a little help?"

I shook my head and did another set of lifts as my arms burned, and my side felt like it was going to split right back open.

Could that happen?

I felt a shudder run through me but wasn't sure if it was due to the weights in my hands or the thought of ripping open the gash down my side. I pushed on because there wasn't a choice. Dad was watching from the kitchen, and as I was finishing up, he took his buzzing phone out of his pocket and walked out of earshot.

"Where are your charts from yesterday?" Steven asked as I sat like a limp noodle in my wheelchair.

"I think Dad put them in his study," I replied.

"Well, go get them! I need to do some comparisons."

I took a big breath and wondered if my workout-fatigued arms would even be able to wheel me over the hardwood floors at this point. Somehow, I managed to get myself down the hallway, slowly, and to the door of Dad's study. I reached out and turned the handle and then pushed it open so I could wheel myself inside.

I could hear Dad's voice from the kitchen rise and intensify though I couldn't quite make out his words. Something about how no one's going to try to pull that shit, and he was the goddamned mayor or something. I heard Steven responding but couldn't make out his words, either.

I went through the doorway, trying to ignore whatever the hell was going on in the other room. I just didn't have the energy.

It was rare for me to go into this room. It's not like it was ever specifically off limits or anything, it just…didn't invite company, I guess. The walls were painted to look like red leather, and one whole wall was lined with bookshelves containing medical books and journals. There was even an authentic human skeleton in the corner, enclosed in a large, glass case.

It gave me the willies.

The place was also full of all kinds of shit. There were books stacked everywhere, a couple of trees' worth of papers, and tons of dust. There were staplers and hole-punches and letters on a table next to a wing-backed chair and one small corner dedicated to Real Messini merchandise, including a little Real Messini garden gnome.

Okay, the gnome was actually creepier than the skeleton, if you asked me. The skeleton didn't have any eyes, but that gnome always seemed to be watching me.

Ignoring the peering black eyes of the plastic figure, I maneuvered the chair around the side of Dad's desk and grabbed the file sitting on top. I flipped it open to make sure it was the right one and then closed it and started trying to back up around Dad's desk chair and the desk itself.

Dad and Steven were definitely yelling at each other now. I still couldn't make out the words. I hoped maybe Dad was going to be pissed off enough to fire him.

I should be so lucky.

I held tight to the file folder so nothing would fall out as I tried to get out of the small space. It wasn't easy—the space was too tight for the chair to fit, and I wanted to make sure I didn't come close to bumping into the skeleton. That would just freak me out. I backed up and pulled forward and eventually turned myself part way around so I could get out.

Well, almost.

I knocked right into the side of the desk, and three books fell off from where they were stacked. They knocked into a bunch of papers, which fell on the floor. I tried to back up to reach them and banged right into the desk again. More books fell, taking more papers with them.

"Dammit!" At this rate, I was going to wear myself out picking up all this shit before Steven even got round two started on me. I heard the front door open and slam shut and half prayed he was getting fired right now.

I reached down and grabbed at the stack of papers. It put a bit of strain on my side to reach down like that, but I managed. I stacked them up along with the books and reached over to fully close the desk drawer that had been jarred open in the process. Something very familiar caught my eye as I reached for the drawer's handle, and instead of closing it, I opened it a little more.

It was my sketchbook.

I glanced over at the door, but there was no one there, so I reached in and grabbed the sketchbook. I turned it over and over in my hands and then flipped through it. All the sketches of Nicole were gone, but the ones of my mom were all still there as well as a couple soccer sketches. I looked around my chair to see where I might be able to hide it when an envelope fell out from between the pages and landed in my lap.

I reached for it and flipped it over, noting my Dad's name and our address on the front and that the stamp had been cancelled in Chicago, Illinois. There wasn't a return address, and my curiosity got the better of me.

I reached in and pulled out the letter.

Dr. Malone,

When we last met, it appeared Thomas would be playing soccer professionally. At that time, I agreed I would not reach out to him even though it is my right since he is now eighteen. Since then, I have heard of his accident and injuries.

You have to let me contact him. I have never even seen him, since that's how Fran wanted it, but he is my biological son. Our understanding was always that if he played professionally, like you wanted, then I would not approach him. If he is no longer walking, it makes sense, now more than ever, for him to know who I am and to learn that he has other options.

You can't keep me from him forever, Lou. You said he was still sketching, which means he already has possibilities there. He can't play soccer if he can't walk, and I can offer him a whole different path in life.

Contact me before the end of the month to arrange this, or I will reach out to him myself.

Thomas Gardner

I stared at the paper in my hands.

I read it over and over and over again as Shakespeare's words echoed in my head: "The voice of parents is the voice of gods." My heart was beating as if Steven had just given me another shot, and I knew—I just *knew*—from the words on the unassuming piece of paper in my hands, I had found my salvation.

My arms felt as if someone were running ice cubes down them, and my toes seemed to be flexing involuntarily. I realized I wasn't breathing when my chest started to burn, and I took a quick breath to fill my body with oxygen.

I read the letter again.

Little tiny clicks seemed to be going off in my head, and like the tumblers of a complicated lock, the combination of events slowly fell into place.

"What the fuck are you doing?"

I jumped and practically threw myself out of the wheelchair altogether. Dad was standing in the doorway, and his eyes went from my face to the sketchbook in my lap and the letter in my hands.

I just stared at him like a dumbass.

"I asked you a question," he repeated.

"I was…getting my chart…" I stammered. I looked down at the letter in my hands and then slowly raised it as I looked at him. "Dad…?"

His eyes seemed to glaze over as he stared at the paper in my grasp. He licked his lips and slowly inhaled.

"Give me that," he demanded though his tone was not as full of anger as I would have anticipated. My chest tightened as he reached out his hand, but I didn't offer him the letter.

"You're not…" My breaths started coming faster as I tried to figure out what to say. "You're not my…"

"Shut up!" he yelled. He took a step toward me, and I gripped the letter tighter. "I am your father! I'm the one who raised you— sacrificed for you! I gave up my fucking career for you! He did nothing for you! Nothing! It was all me!"

The words tumbled around in my head—*I am your father*. I couldn't help but hear them in James Earl Jones' voice. I watched Dad's face turn red in anger but couldn't bring myself to feel any guilt or fear from his rage. I just felt numb toward him. When had he ever been a father to me? Before Mom died, maybe he could have made the case, but now? No. Definitely not now.

"You never told me," I said quietly. "Why?"

"Why should we have?" I realized it was the first time he had referred to both himself and my mother together for a long, long time. "He was nothing—nothing to her and nothing to me. He is nothing."

I remembered years ago, when I was a very young child, wondering why I only looked like Mom. I remembered her public memorial service—held a month after her death—and the lines of people who stopped to pay their respects. I remembered seeing Dad with a man who had the same color hair as mine and wondering if he was one of Mom's relatives. I had asked Dad about him, and he had blown off my question.

"He was at her memorial service," I stated. I wasn't asking.

"He had no right to be there!" Dad screamed in response.

"You should have told me!" I yelled back. I tried to move forward and raise myself up—knowing I was taller than him when standing on my feet, but of course I couldn't. I was still partially trapped by the desk drawer. I slammed it closed and tried to move the chair with one hand.

Dad's foot reached out and kicked at the wheel, shoving me backwards.

"Where the fuck do you think you're going?" he screeched.

"You think you are going to him? Huh?"

He kicked the wheel again.

"No fucking way! You are my son! Mine!"

"I'm not!" I yelled back. My mind flashed through every push, every shove, every punch to my gut, every broken rib he had given me through the years. "That's why you treated me like you did! That's why you hate me, isn't it? It has nothing to do with Mom dying! It's just because I'm his kid, not yours! You always fucking hated me!"

This time his foot hit the wheel at another angle and with much more force.

The wheelchair toppled, and as I grabbed for the desk to hold myself up, I ended up with my fingers on a stack of books. The chair, the books, and I all tumbled down and smashed against the floor. The pain from my side nearly crippled me as I smacked my jaw on the edge of the chair, and my breath was knocked from me.

"You are not going to him, you hear me? You will not! I forbid it, dammit! I'm the one who raised you—ME! She left me, and the only thing left of her was YOU! I did what she would have wanted —I made sure you became the best fucking soccer player you could be! *I* did that! There's no way in fucking hell he's going to get his fucking hands on you now!"

I pulled myself with my arms, trying to get out of the chair so I could attempt to set it upright again. Dad was still screaming, but my head was pounding, and my ears were ringing, so I couldn't understand what he said. I shook my head a few times, trying to get rid of the dizziness.

"You're my son! My son!" he was yelling over and over again. "He's got no claim to you! None!"

I reached up to my mouth and looked at my fingers, covered in blood from my busted lip. There was a shift in my mindset that I could almost hear in my head. I wiped at my mouth and turned my glaring eyes to him.

But my look faltered when I met his eyes.

There was something there—something in his eyes I had not

seen before. The look was cold, and it was heartless, and it sent a shiver down my back. It wasn't just anger or determination.

He looked…resigned.

"You weren't supposed to know," he said, his voice calm and cool again. "She never wanted you to know. She didn't even tell him. She said you were mine. You *are* mine, and no one's ever going to change that. Not him. Not you."

He turned abruptly and yanked open the top drawer of the filing cabinet, stuck his hand inside, and turned around to face me. His arm reached out to its full length, and I looked to the end where his hand gripped a gun.

Pointed at me.

King Lear's words from Shakespeare's writing came to mind: "Come not between the dragon and his wrath." Somehow, I was pretty sure the warning had come too late.

Now that I had this knowledge, would I even survive the outcome?

CHAPTER TWENTY-NINE
offside trap

"Steven!" I screamed toward the doorway.

Dad just shook his head.

"Gone," he told me. "He's not coming back today."

Not today, which meant Dad hadn't fired him. Why had he kicked him out? I looked from the door back to his face, and the only sound I could hear was his breathing.

We were alone in the house.

"You took her away," he said. His hands were shaking as he spoke, and even when I tried to push myself farther away with my arms, there was nowhere I could go. My ankle was caught between the footrests of the wheelchair and the bottom of the desk. "You're just like him. He tried to take her away, but he couldn't. He had nothing to offer her—nothing. I could support her—support you. I told her I'd go to med school, forget about soccer, and help her raise you. He couldn't do that because he didn't have shit, and she knew it. He couldn't take her from me, but you...but *you did*!"

"It was an accident!" I cried.

"That you caused!" There was barely a heartbeat between my words and his. "If you hadn't been so forgetful, she would still be here!"

377

"It was an accident," I said again. My chest felt tight, and my head was hurting behind my eyes. I tried to shuffle back again, shoving some of the fallen books out of my way, but that fucking skeleton was right behind me.

"You took everything that meant anything to me that day," he said. His hand steadied a little, and I cringed, flexing my shoulders. "I still raised you. I was still your father."

I thought about Greg and how he talked to Nicole, how he cared for her and protected her—and the ludicrousness of his words struck me full force.

"You've never been a father! I took care of myself! You didn't do anything a father is supposed to do! How could Mom even love you?"

"She did love me!" he screamed. He took a couple steps toward me, pointing the gun toward the floor where I was lying.

I pushed myself back, forgetting what was behind me, and the skeleton in its case toppled to the side, smashing the corner table full of Real Messini merchandise. The garden gnome shattered, and I jumped again.

"Don't you dare say she didn't!" Dad kept yelling. "She loved me! I know she did!"

"Then why are you doing this to me?" I cried. My mind was spinning completely out of control. I kept moving from one thought to the next—Lou Malone wasn't my father; we were alone in the house; I needed to see Nicole just one more time, before anything else happened.

He's going to kill me...

"She wanted you to be successful!" he yelled again. "She always said she wanted more for you...I could have given you that!"

"I can't do it anymore!" I looked down at my legs as if he hadn't noticed yet. He ignored my comment, turned to the side, and grabbed his hair with his fist as he growled incoherently.

"You just need more drive!" he said through clenched teeth. "I just need...need to push..."

His voice faltered, and his words trailed off into nothingness. I watched his shoulders slump as he faced me again. His eyes were heavy.

"Don't you see, Thomas?" His voice cracked as he spoke, and he turned away from me to lean against the bookshelf, his arm across his forehead. "You're all I have of her. I can't lose you…I can't."

He turned to face me and then began to pace back and forth.

I knew I had to keep him talking. As long as he was talking, he wasn't shooting. The longer I could keep him going, the better the chances were for me to come up with some way to get out of this. I had to, because I had to see Nicole again. I just fucking had to see her one more time.

My mind raced. How could I get a message to someone? Anyone. I glanced at the small window in the room and knew I couldn't just throw myself out of it—it was too high up. Even if I did, how would I get away? I did the only thing I could do and said the first thing that came to my mind.

"You named me after him?" I asked. "You gave me his name. Why?"

"She never told me!" he screamed, and his face contorted with rage again. "She never fucking told me his name! I didn't find out until…until…she was gone…and he showed up. Motherfucker!"

Shit, maybe this wasn't the right thing to do. Dad rubbed his face with his free hand, and I pushed myself a little farther from the chair, dislodging my ankle.

"He figured it out…but I told him it didn't matter." Dad went on. "You had been through enough, and I wasn't going to let him disrupt your life any more than it already was. I was protecting you! You were mine…the only thing of hers I still had. No way in hell was he going to take that from me!"

He looked back to me again with his eyes blazing. He raised his hand and pointed the gun at my face.

"No one is taking you from me! You've lived as my son, and goddamn it, you'll die as my son!"

My body was shaking, and I couldn't stop hot tears from cascading from my eyes. I squeezed them shut because I didn't want to watch and covered my head with my arms as if that was going to make any difference. I waited for the shot.

But no shot rang out.

I peeked through my arms and saw him still standing over me with his chest rising and falling quickly. His hands dropped back to his sides, and the gun pointed toward the floor. My eyes followed the weapon, waiting to see when it would rise again and end me.

"I just wanted you to be the best," he said quietly, and when I looked back up at him, he was crying. "I didn't know what to do. She was the one who took care of you. I just wanted her to be…to be…*proud*. Proud of me, because I…I took care of you…made you a star."

"Dad…" I could barely hear my own voice. I coughed, cleared my throat, and tried again. "Dad…you didn't have to…to do all that shit. I would have played anyway…"

"But I made sure you were the best," he told me. His eyes suddenly went dark again, and his voice turned into a snarl. He raised the gun once again to my head. "Until you let *pussy* get in your way."

"Don't talk about her like that!" I yelled. I remembered wondering years ago whether or not I had a breaking point. Apparently I did, and it had just been reached. I had nothing else to lose. If I was going to die anyway, I wasn't going to put up with any more shit talk about Nicole. "That's not what she is, and don't you fucking talk about her like that again!"

Through my own labored breaths, I watched him watch me. He stood for a while and just stared, not moving and without changing his expression at all. When I couldn't stand it anymore, I spoke again.

"I love her," I whispered. "Just like you loved Mom."

"No one ever loved anyone like I loved her," he said with a shake of his head. "Not possible."

"I love Nicole," I repeated.

His gazed dropped to the floor.

"She was all I ever had," he said as he backed against the filing cabinet and slid to the ground. The gun was lying across his lap, still pointed toward me. "She was the only thing that made any fucking difference in my life. She left for school…and it hadn't been that long…and then she went with him. But I was the one who loved her—not him! She came back with me…"

He scratched at his forehead and sighed heavily.

"She was everything," he said again. "What do I have now, huh? Not you—you'd rather go find some idiot who doesn't fucking know you. And now…now they say I'm not treating you right. What the fuck!"

"Who says that?"

He didn't answer.

"No one tells me how to raise my son. And you are my son, dammit."

He looked back at me and then laughed.

"If they came, you'd tell them to take you away, wouldn't you?"

"Who?" I asked again.

"Doesn't fucking matter," he said and shook his head. "None of it does anymore."

With his eyes still on me, he raised his gun hand higher.

"All gone," he said. "Everything."

His expression went blank as he looked at me. The tears on his cheeks were drying against his pale skin, and his chest rose slowly as he inhaled. He let the air out again without looking away from me. I couldn't move. My heart seemed to stop beating, and my breath got caught in my throat, threatening to suffocate me. I couldn't bring myself to do or say anything. I only stared as he turned the gun around, placed it against his temple, and fired.

I startled at the sound, and my throat started to burn. I couldn't close my eyes, but I also could not comprehend what I was seeing. The ache in my throat got worse, and I realized I was screaming. I couldn't stop.

"He that dies pays all debts."

Curled in a ball, my body shook and shook and shook.

I couldn't stop it. I had to bite down on my tongue to make myself stop screaming. I knew he was dead…There was no doubt. He wasn't moving at all…and his head…

I swallowed hard, trying to keep myself from vomiting. I looked at my hands in front of my face, not allowing myself to peer around the room and see anything else. I had no idea how long it had been since he…since he did that. It could have been a few minutes or hours, as far as I could tell.

One thing was certain—I had to get out of there. What time was it? I glanced at the clock on the wall and saw it was only a quarter past noon. I wasn't sure what time it was when Steven sent me to find the chart, but it was definitely after ten. Steven wouldn't be back until tomorrow at the soonest, and no one else was scheduled to be here at all. The idea of Steven coming back before I could get ahold of anyone else was enough to get me to move.

I forced myself to straighten out as much as I could, which meant picking my legs up and pushing them off to the side. I could make them move a little, bend at the knee maybe an inch or so, but that was it. My hips worked okay, so I could move them from side to side. The rest I had to do with my hands.

Twisting and turning, I got myself in position to lift the wheelchair off the ground, but as soon as I looked at it, I knew there wasn't any point. Where the wheel had been kicked, the frame was bent. There was no way it was going to spin even if I did manage to get it back up and pull myself into it.

"Fuck!" I grunted. It would have to be all me, then. It was a good thing my arms were basically back in shape, but where was I going to go?

There was no way I was going to make it out of the house and down the mile-long driveway to the highway. Even if I did, I'd probably be run over before anyone saw me. I looked out the window and watched the rain pour down. There was a flash of lightning and thunder in the distance.

Yeah, no way.

We didn't have a landline, so I needed a cell phone.

Dad's was probably in his pocket.

Fuck.

I rolled over and sat up, splaying my arms behind me to lean against them. My back was to Dad's body, and that was just fine with me. I took a few breaths to prepare myself, focused my mind on the single goal of getting his phone, and used my arms to maneuver myself backward across the floor while my legs dragged uselessly.

I knew I was close—I could smell it. I swallowed and then held my breath as I reached behind me and touched his leg. With a shiver, I first ran my hand up to one pocket and then the other. Nothing. Not in his back pockets, either. I forced myself to look at his shirt, but there wasn't a pocket there at all.

"Fuck!" I yipped as his hand dropped from his leg to the floor. I quickly pushed myself away—across the study and right out the doorway, where I lay panting for several minutes.

Okay, no phone on Dad. He must have left it somewhere. I pulled myself the rest of the way into the hall, glad for the smooth hardwood floors, and could have cried when I saw a small black rectangle lying on the floor near the entrance to the kitchen. With a couple of breaths to get me going, I pulled myself across the floor until I reached Dad's phone.

Well…part of it, anyway.

The screen was cracked and dark, and no matter how much I poked at it, nothing happened.

"Shit, shit, shit!" I screamed. I banged my fist on the floor and stared at the shattered screen. I looked around quickly and saw a small, black mark on the wall where he had obviously thrown it.

What was I going to do now? He had hidden my phone. It could be anywhere in the whole fucking house. I had to call someone…Nicole, Greg, 911…anyone. How else could I tell someone that I was here? That Dad was…Dad was…

Laptop.

I lifted my eyes to the stairs leading up to the third floor where my laptop was waiting for me in the closet.

Three flights of stairs.

There was no fucking way in hell.

I would never make it.

I was nearly exhausted just from dragging myself from the study, down the hall, to the kitchen, and that was all one level. Upstairs? Using just my arms? I might be able to make it halfway, but then I'd have to sleep for a freaking day before I could go on. I just couldn't last that long without help, unless…

A small black doctor's bag caught my eye where it sat next to the PT equipment in the living room. Steven must have left it here when Dad threw him out. Again, I wondered what their argument had been about, but it didn't matter. What mattered was he left it behind in his haste. From my experience the previous day, I already knew the collection of hypodermic needles full of testosterone and adrenaline was inside his bag.

Fifteen minutes later, I was at the bottom of the stairs with a shot of adrenaline in my hand.

As I looked up to the top of the first flight and contemplated the length times three, I couldn't help but conjure images of Julius Caesar and hear Shakespeare's words through his lines: "Men at some time are masters of their fates: the fault, Dear Brutus, is not in our stars, but in ourselves."

I was going to have to get myself up those damn stairs, no matter what.

I was going to contact my Rumple.

At the bottom of the stairs, I tried to get my breathing under control, calm myself, and figure out just how the hell I was going to shove a needle into my own arm. I mean, really, how does somebody do that? Just shove it in, or does it have to be in the right spot? Did I have to hit a vein or muscle?

I had no fucking clue.

I tried to remember exactly where Steven had placed it, and when I looked over my arm, I could still see a slight bruise there.

Well, that settled that. I would go for the same spot.

I took another deep breath.

Damn.

I wasn't sure if I could inject myself or not, so I decided to see just how far I could get first. Then I'd do it if I needed it. I was only wearing a pair of sweats and a T-shirt, though. I didn't have any pockets, so I stuck the damn needle in my teeth and started up the first set of stairs.

The first three were okay. Once I got to the point where my whole body was on the stairs, it got harder. My legs were kind of in my way because I didn't have enough control over them to keep them from holding me back. Not only was I pulling my body weight up, but I was also trying not to get my feet caught on the stairs as I advanced. Slowly.

I knew from years of traversing them that there were nine stairs for the first set, then what would have been two strides to get around the landing, then six more to get to the second floor. After another landing, there were thirteen more steps to the third floor. By the time my arms had reached the first landing, I was completely and totally wiped out, and I still needed to pull up the rest of my body.

Sweat was pouring from my forehead and into my eyes, and I was panting so hard, it was making my head swimmy. My muscles burned with the effort to pull myself even another six inches. If the stairs hadn't been open—giving me a place to get a good grip— there was no way I would have made it as far as I had. I pulled again, bringing my shoulders up to the level of the last step, and that's when I didn't have anything else to grab in order to go any farther.

Collapsing onto the stairs with my head on the landing, I lay there and felt like I was going to pass out. My eyes closed, and despite how uncomfortable lying on the stairs was, I could have fallen asleep right then and there.

No…can't do that. Gotta get Rumple…

I took the hypodermic out of my mouth, wiped some drool off

the edge and tried to figure out what the hell I was supposed to do now.

Just shove it in there and do it, I told myself.

Easier thought than accomplished.

I looked from my arm to the needle and then from the needle to my arm. They didn't seem interested in magically joining up, so I took a few deep breaths, put the tip of the needle up against my skin, right over the previous bruise and…

… and just sat there, staring.

"Dammit," I grumbled to myself. "Stop being such a pussy."

I closed my eyes, took another breath, and shoved the needle into my arm.

"Mother *FUCKER*!" I screamed. It fucking hurt! I growled and groaned and wanted to yank the damn thing out, but I knew if I did, I would never, ever be able to get it back in. So I gritted my teeth, squeezed my eyes shut, and shoved down on the plunger.

I yelled out a few more choice words and yanked the now empty hypodermic needle from my skin. There was some blood there—but it was only a spot. I must not have done too bad a job of it.

I knew within a few seconds that it was working.

Heart pounding, blood racing, hands shaking—but definitely ready to grab hold of anything I could reach—I tossed the damn needle away and started pulling again. I grabbed the edge of the next flight of stairs and yanked up as hard as I could, muscles screaming. I scraped my chest slightly on the edge of one stair, but it just burned a little. My eyes kept blinking over and over again, and I just tried to ignore everything around me but the next stair.

And the next…

And the next…

I pulled and pushed until my legs made it to the second landing, where I had to pause and force myself not to throw up. Then I reached out and grabbed the first step of the final flight. Pull, shift, groan; pull, shift, groan…

Another step.

Another.

The top.

I could have cried in relief, but I still had to get to the end of the short hallway.

Pull, shift, groan.

Don't stop.

Gotta contact Rumple.

I flipped over on my back and tried pushing myself along the floor that way. At least the change in position was using a slightly different set of muscles, because the ones I had been using were just about done. It didn't work, though, because sitting upright was making me dizzier. I flopped back down on my stomach and used my elbows.

Pull, shift, groan.

One more pull with my fingers digging into the plush carpet brought me to the doorway of my room. I had to stop again, panting and wheezing and feeling like my heart was trying to burst right out of my chest. My hands were shaking so badly, it was getting harder and harder to propel myself along, but I didn't let myself rest too long. I was too close to my goal.

Contact Rumple.

I pulled my arms back up underneath me, braced them against the floor and pushed my body forward again, flopping down on my chest with a bit of a gasp. I did it again and again, and in this way I managed to get inside my bedroom and move myself over to the closet door.

Of course, due to my need for order, the door to my closet was closed.

I looked up at the handle and sighed between pants. I rolled myself over onto my back and pushed myself up until I was sitting down with my back against the wall next to the door. I reached up and touched the bottom of the handle with the tips of my fingers. I strained, tilted my body a bit to the side, and twisted the knob enough to open it.

My side felt like it was on fire from the stretching, but at least the door was opened up a crack. I pushed, and it opened the rest of the way. I looked high up to the shelf where my laptop was stored, knowing immediately that there was no way I could reach that high.

Was I ever, ever going to catch a break?

Break.

That's what I was going to have to do—break something to get it to fall, and then hope to God the damn thing would still work. At least I knew through my own diligence that the battery would be fully charged.

I looked around and saw my heavy winter coat dangling from a hanger. I scooted to where I could grab it, pulled it down—breaking the hanger in the process—and positioned it over my head. I was starting to get dizzy and feel a little nauseated as my heart continued to pound and my hands continued to shake. I knew I wasn't going to last much longer. Taking yet another deep breath, I closed my eyes, tightened the coat around my head, and slammed my shoulder against the set of shelves.

Some of my books fell along with a stack of school folders and one of those boxes of sixty-four crayons with the little sharpener in the back. No laptop, though I could see it had shifted a bit with the impact. I slammed into the shelves again, raining more crap down on my head, but at least the coat blocked anything from hitting me too hard.

I peeked out from under the coat and saw the laptop sticking about a third of the way off the shelf. One more hit ought to take care of it. I covered my head again, tried to ignore the pounding in my chest, braced myself and smashed into the shelves a third time. The laptop fell, landing straight on my knee, which hurt like a bitch. I really didn't care, though. I got it!

I dropped down to the floor and lay there as my fingers worked the switch on the side, opened it, and turned it on.

I could have sworn it took about seven and a half million years for the damn thing to boot up.

"Be online, be online, be online," I chanted as the little

"Starting Windows" message disappeared, and the laptop displayed my Manuel Neuer desktop theme. I waited for the IM to automatically start…

…and then remembered I had deleted my account.

"Fuck fuck fuckity fuck fuck fuck!" I screamed and beat my fist on the carpet.

I rolled to my stomach as my arms, side, and knee all protested the shift in position. I pulled up Google, found the right app, created a new account, screamed at whatever bastard had snatched up SoccerGod2014, and managed to create one called NeedMyRumple instead. With a few more keystrokes, I opened up my little hacking program to get into her account.

Again, I started with the "be online" chant.

I accepted the friend request and waited for her profile to pop up in the otherwise empty list of friends.

BeautifulSkye18's status was offline.

"Arrrghhh!!!" I screeched and dropped my head to the floor. My temples were pounding, my pulse could clearly be felt in every artery in my body, and I was really, really close to throwing up. I squeezed my eyes shut, and my vision went blurry. There were tears in my eyes, which just pissed me off. I reached out once more, set BeautifulSkye18's profile to notify me with a chime when her status changed, turned the volume to the highest setting, and passed out.

<hr/>

There was some cat screeching at me, and I couldn't figure out why.

Meow! Meow! Meow!

It was fucking loud, too, and my head was pounding.

Meow! Meow! Meow!

My eyes opened slowly, and I tried to figure out where I was and what I was doing there.

Closet…I'm in my closet…

Why?

I closed my eyes again.

Meow! Meow! Meow!

That sound was seriously annoying, but at the same time seemed somewhat important. My head continued to pound at my temples, and I pried my eyes open long enough to reestablish that I was on the floor of my closet, lying amongst a pile of crayons with the edge of my laptop up against my nose.

Meow! Meow! Meow!

The laptop was flashing.

BeautifulSkye18 is online.

Rumple!

I moved my hand from my side and touched the keyboard. I tapped the square at the bottom twice and a little window appeared. My eyes started to close again, and my head felt heavy even though I was still lying on the floor.

I had to stay awake.

NeedMyRumple: need u

My fingers kind of locked up on me, and I could taste bile in my throat. I swallowed.

BeautifulSkye18: oh Thomas—I need you too! Dad is trying to work something out. He said it could take a day or two, though.

Ugh. I shook my head and took a deep breath.

NeedMyRumple: now pls

BeautifulSkye18: I want to—I do, but your dad won't let me in the door!

My fingers shook as I tried to tap on the keyboard.

NeedMyRumple: hes ded

BeautifulSkye18: what?

NeedMyRumple: cooime now pleadse

BeautifulSkye18: Thomas—what do you mean?

Thomas?

Thomas! Answer me! What do you mean? Dead? Is your dad dead???

THOMAS!!!

I'm coming, baby—hang on. Dad too. We'll be there ASAP

I could still see the screen, but it looked blurry, and my fingers were no longer functioning. I closed my eyes and was encompassed by darkness.

<hr/>

I could hear someone calling my name, but it was like hearing something while you're under water. I tried opening my eyes, but they just didn't want to cooperate. Slowly, the sounds seemed to get closer, and then I could actually make out the words.

"Thomas? Thomas? Oh my God…Dad!! He's up here!!"

Footsteps…someone's hand on my arm. My arm jerked a little…reflexive…involuntary. More words—muffled and distant —then another voice nearby.

"Thomas? Can you hear me, baby?"

That sound…that voice. I knew that voice.

"Rumple…"

"It's me, Thomas."

I managed to open my eyes a crack, and I saw the most beautiful angel in the world—with deep blue eyes and deep, rich, long hair hanging around her perfect face. I could feel her touch on my cheek, and I had the most important realization I had ever had in my entire life.

It's over.

"Rumple!" I cried out, and my arms found just enough strength to grab on to her and pull her against my chest. Her arms went around me, too, and she whispered into my ear.

"It's okay, Thomas," she said. "It's okay—I'm here."

I felt her turn slightly and tightened my grip.

"Don't go!" I begged.

"I'm not going anywhere," she promised. "Dad!"

I felt the slight pressure of fingers on the inside of my wrist.

"His heart's beating really fast," Greg murmured. "EMTs are on their way. Five minutes, tops."

"What about…what about his dad?"

"Looks like he shot himself," I heard Greg say.

"Oh my God," Nicole said with a gasp. "Thomas…you're okay. Help is on the way. Stay with me, okay?"

"Okay."

I inhaled deeply, taking in the scent of her all around me.

"Thomas?" Greg's voice again. "Thomas, did you…inject yourself with something?"

"Uh huh," I mumbled back.

"*What*?" Rumple cried, her shock evident in her voice.

"What was it, Thomas?" Greg asked.

"Adrenaline…so I could…get up here…"

"Shit," Rumple hissed. I felt her arms tighten around me, and I think I smiled a bit.

"Missed you," I said, and I tucked my head against her shoulder and closed my eyes again.

"I love you, Thomas," she responded. "It will all be okay now."

"Love…too…"

Shakespeare had some interesting thoughts, as spoken though Richard II: "I have been studying how I may compare, this prison where I live unto the world." Somehow, I thought things would be a little better from here on out.

Now I was free.

CHAPTER THIRTY
restart

It was raining.

Drizzling, really—it wasn't hard enough to qualify as rain. It was still wet, and it made one of the wheels on my chair squeak a bit as I nervously shifted the chair forward and backwards. My eyes looked forward, blankly staring as the coffin containing Dad's body was slowly lowered into a giant hole next to Mom's grave.

Nicole was behind me with her fingers gripping the handles of the wheelchair, and Greg was just a few feet away, kind of watching me constantly. I wanted to be pissed about him hovering and being overly concerned, but I couldn't be. I wanted to be annoyed that Nicole was insisting on wheeling me around, but I couldn't be ticked off about that either because she was there—with me.

I had been out of the hospital for exactly two hours. They only kept me there for a couple days of observation, wanting to make sure my body got rid of all the excess adrenaline and that there weren't any other complications caused by either the hormone, the injury to my side from falling out of the chair, or the exertion of pulling myself up the stairs.

I had to take their word for it—I didn't remember a thing.

It was weird. *Dissociative amnesia*, the doctors called it. I remembered going into Dad's study, finding the letter from Thomas Gardner, and Nicole being in the ambulance with me and playing with my hair as we left my house and headed for the hospital. Everything in the middle was a total blank.

Apparently, that was a good thing.

Considering I had spent a good chunk of my life remembering each and every detail of each and every day, it was strange to know I had completely lost a good twelve hours.

Reverend Walsh read from the Bible as those in attendance bowed their heads. He recited a little prayer, said amen, and that was the end of Doctor Lou Malone.

Anticlimactic, to say the least.

Then again, I wasn't so sure that he deserved much more.

Nicole moved me backwards, out from under the little tent that was positioned over the gravesite, and into the drizzle. Greg was walking behind us, holding an umbrella and being all somber. We stopped on the walkway as a bunch of people gathered around to come up and pay their respects to me. I knew the faces, remembered most of the names, but everything was still a blur as they went by in droves. Teachers, people from the hospital, guys on my soccer team, Clint…

As Jeremy gripped my shoulder affectionately and Rachel kissed my cheek, Clint stood behind them, kicking at the ground. When the other two walked away, he took a timid step forward, and I raised my eyes to look at him.

"Hey," I said.

"Hey," he replied.

He kicked the ground some more.

"Come here," I finally said with a sigh and held my hand out to him. He took it, and I pulled him to me, wrapped an arm around his shoulders and hugged him. "We're good. I know it sounds totally fucked up, but I'm kind of grateful."

I let go, and he pulled back, looking at me quizzically.

"Yeah," he said, "that does sound fucked up."

He finally smiled back and promised to bring me a copy of *Shaolin Soccer* on DVD for us to watch some time. The rain stopped as he walked away, and I shook hands and nodded a dozen times as people told me how sorry they were and offered to bring food over to the house for me. After a few minutes, almost everyone was gone from the cemetery. There were just a few still remaining, mingling about in groups of two or three.

Justin and Danielle came up to me as the crowd dispersed.

"I'll call you, and we'll meet to talk about your PT going forward, okay?" Danielle asked. I just nodded.

"I'd like to talk to you, too, Thomas," Justin said, "if that's okay."

"Yeah," I said, "it is."

Nicole put her hand on my shoulder, and I looked up into her concerned eyes.

"Tell him everything, Thomas," she said softly.

I dropped my eyes to my lap and nodded. My pair of therapists —one for my broken body, one for my broken mind—walked off toward the parking lot.

"Thomas?" Greg said from off to my side. He hadn't spoken a word to me since we got to the cemetery. "I don't know what your plans are short term, but I want you coming back home with me and Nicole for now."

Honestly, I hadn't thought about it much at all. I had kind of assumed I would just go home, but even the thought of going back there made me feel a little sick.

"I can't do that, Greg," I heard myself say. "I can't impose like that."

"Bull," he replied. "You can and you will. We need to have a service come and…and clean up over there before you go back at all. Even if that weren't the case, I don't want you going to that house by yourself. No way in hell. I'm not taking no for an answer, son."

I looked up to his stern face and twitchy moustache and smiled a bit. Going home with them did sound like about the best situation

I could conjure up, except…except…how would I even get in the house?

"Greg, you know I appreciate it, but it's not like your house is really equipped for a cripple."

I heard Nicole huff at the word.

"Why don't you quit trying to come up with excuses and let me worry about that?" he replied as he crossed his arms over his chest and glowered at me.

I sighed, knowing there was no way he was going to back down, so I agreed. He nodded in satisfaction and then went to talk to the principal about getting my schoolwork to Nicole so I could graduate on time. As Nicole wheeled me down the walkway toward the car, I tried to figure out just how in the heck all this was going to work. Even once they got me and the chair into the house, there was only the one bathroom, and it was on the second floor. I could just stay in Nicole's room, which sounded mighty fine to me, but the hallway was narrow. Would the chair even fit through it?

Nicole steered me next to the passenger side of my Jeep, which she drove because the Hyundai had finally died on her. She then told me to stay put while she dragged Greg away from the school principal. I sat there feeling kind of numb and wondering just what the heck the future was going to look like.

"Thomas?"

I didn't recognize the voice, but as soon as I looked up, I knew exactly who he was.

It was like looking into some kind of fucked-up mirror that would show you how you were going to look twenty or so years into the future. Same color hair that didn't seem too interested in staying where it was put, same eyes, and he even stood the same way I did—rocking back and forth from one foot to the other. He looked nervous.

"Thomas Gardner," I said softly, and his eyes widened.

"You know who I am?" He sounded shocked.

"Yeah," I replied.

"I didn't realize…I didn't know he told you…about me."

"He didn't," I clarified. "I found a letter you sent."

My stomach felt weird, like it was all tied up, or maybe I had just been sitting too long. Thomas Gardner ran his hand through his hair, and I had to stop myself from laughing. It was just too surreal.

"Look, um…Thomas," he said, "I know you're going through all kinds of shit right now…"

He smacked his hand on his forehead.

"Fuck! I shouldn't swear in front of you!" He realized his second mistake and cringed.

I couldn't help but laugh at that point, and he smiled sheepishly.

"I just wanted to meet you…maybe talk to you?" The poor guy looked terrified, and I felt sorry for him as he stammered through his words. "I heard about…I mean, I saw the news report about… about your dad. I didn't know if…well, if you knew…shit."

He shook his head violently.

"I'm already fucking this up," he mumbled.

"It's okay," I said.

He looked at me intently for a minute.

"I didn't want you to be alone," he finally said. "We don't know each other, but I…I…I just wanted you to know…shit."

I smiled again, turning away a bit so he wouldn't notice.

"Can we talk?" he asked. I looked back to him. I was pretty sure we already were. "I mean, away from here? Maybe get coffee? Do you like coffee?"

"Not really," I said.

"Coke or something? And not now—I know not now—but I have a hotel room in town. I'll stay as long as I have to…I just… wanted to see you. Talk to you."

"Yeah," I replied, "that would be okay."

"Really?" He sounded surprised, and his mouth turned up into an all-too-familiar half-grin. He dug around in his pocket and handed me a partially crumpled business card. "Whenever you're ready, just call and…I'll come get you…oh, shit…my car probably isn't big enough…shit!"

"It's okay," I said. He looked like he was going to have a total breakdown. "My girlfriend can take me."

"That brunette?" he asked.

"Yeah."

"You guys seem…close."

"We are."

"Good," he said with a nod. "I mean…that's what I was worried about. I didn't know if…if you had anyone."

"I'm okay," I said.

"Good," he said again. He nodded briefly. "So…maybe call me in a couple days or something?"

He looked so hopeful, it was just…cute. Weird to say about a guy who had to be about forty or so, but it fit.

"Sure," I said. I looked at the card in my hand.

Professor Thomas Gardner

Chicago Art Institute

312-555-7289

An art professor? My skin felt kind of tingly, and a bunch of little explosions were going off in my head as more pieces to the Malone family puzzle started falling into place.

"You're an artist?"

"Well, yeah," he said. "I mean, I teach it, but I do sell some paintings and stuff, too. Sometimes."

"Cool," I said.

"You think?" Again, he sounded surprised.

"Yeah," I said.

He paused for a long moment.

"Do you still sketch?" he asked quietly.

I shrugged.

"Not for a while," I admitted.

"Now might be a good time…" His sentence trailed off, and he ran his hand through his hair again. He looked back down at me and took a deep breath. "I'm not very good at this."

I smiled back.

"You're okay," I reassured him.

I heard footsteps and felt Nicole's hands grip the back of the chair.

"Thomas?" she said quietly.

"Yeah, um…Nicole?" I turned slightly to look at her. "This is Thomas Gardner…my…um…my father. I guess."

Her eyes went wide, and I could see she was checking him out, looking from him to me as she made comparisons in her head. We had already discussed my biological father while we were in the hospital—Doctor Winchester had been trying to determine how much I remembered—but Nicole and I hadn't really talked about it at length.

"I guess he is," she replied.

"This is Nicole," I told him. They shook hands quickly.

"I'm glad Thomas has someone," he said. He ran his hands through his hair once more and then rubbed his palms against his legs. "I should let you go. I'm sure you have…um…things to do. I'm really sorry about your dad, Thomas."

I nodded. I'd been doing that a lot as everyone said the same words to me. I wasn't sure if I was sorry or not.

"Call me?" he asked.

"Yeah, I will."

"Thanks." He took a big breath and looked out to the parking lot. "I should let you go…um…I guess I said that. I'll be going now. I'm really glad I got to meet you."

He held out his hand and I shook it.

Our hands looked the same, too.

He said goodbye to both of us and walked around the Jeep toward the lot. Nicole's hand landed on my shoulder, and I looked up at her again.

"You okay?"

"Yeah," I said, "I'm good."

"Are you going to call him?"

"I think so," I said. I furrowed my brow. "Do you think I should?"

"Yes."

"Me too."

Greg appeared and held the door while I got myself in the car as he folded up the chair and placed it in the back. He headed to his cruiser while Nicole got in the driver's seat. She leaned over and kissed me on the cheek before starting up the Jeep and heading toward her house.

As we drove away, I looked back toward the place where my dad's body would lie for the rest of whatever. I still didn't know exactly how I felt about all of it, but I did feel like I was stepping into a new, better world.

Cassius spoke of Caesar when Shakespeare gave him the line: "Men at some time are masters of their fates." Somehow, I thought maybe I was going to finally be given the opportunity to decide my own destiny.

Now to make it come to fruition.

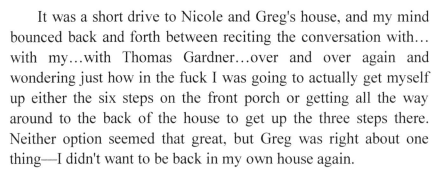

It was a short drive to Nicole and Greg's house, and my mind bounced back and forth between reciting the conversation with… with my…with Thomas Gardner…over and over again and wondering just how in the fuck I was going to actually get myself up either the six steps on the front porch or getting all the way around to the back of the house to get up the three steps there. Neither option seemed that great, but Greg was right about one thing—I didn't want to be back in my own house again.

Nicole parked the Jeep behind the cruiser, and Greg was already getting my chair out of the back when I opened the passenger door and swung my legs out. He brought the chair around and I got myself in. Then Nicole grabbed the back and started pushing me toward the side of the house.

"What the fuck?" I said as I glanced over to Greg, who was standing at the end of what looked to be a brand new walkway off the left side of the house. Nicole chuckled as she pushed me onto the sidewalk of obviously new concrete. It was narrow, but still had room enough for the wheels of my chair to have a few inches of clearance on either side. "When did you do this?"

"Oh…fairly recently," Greg said as he walked ahead of us. Nicole turned the corner to the back of the house, and I saw they had installed a ramp to get up the back steps. "The ramp's not quite permanent—I wanted to make sure the angle was right and you didn't have any problems getting up on your own. Want to give it a try?"

I just sat there and stared at him with my bottom lip getting closer and closer to my chest. They had actually had a sidewalk and a ramp made for me. My throat felt a little tight as I looked backwards at Nicole.

"You guys…had this made?"

She nodded, smiling a little.

"You have to be able to get in and out on your own, don't you think?"

"I…" I didn't know what I should say. I looked from Nicole to Greg and then to the ramp.

"Go on now!" Greg said with a big sweep of his hand toward the ramp.

I grasped the handholds above the wheels and pushed myself forward a little. The ramp wasn't too steep, and after a couple of restarts, I made it to the door without too much trouble. Nicole started clapping, which earned her a glare from me, but it was pretty quickly followed by a smirk. I reached up and tried to open the door, but since it swung outward, I had to reposition myself a bit to get it open. I had to navigate a bit of a bump over the threshold, but then I was inside.

My mouth dropped open again.

The Skye residence wasn't a big one at all with the lower floor mostly consisting of the front and back exits with a decent sized living room between them and an open kitchen off to the side. The back half of the living room had been partitioned off with what looked like the walls from cubicles you would find in an office. On the other side was a bed with rails I could use to get myself in and out, a dresser, and a nightstand. As Greg and Nicole came in behind me, they showed me what used to be a walk-in coat closet, now converted into a small bathroom.

"Holy shit," I murmured. I looked from Greg to Nicole again, and they were both all smiles.

"We got the shorter toilet and sink," Greg said, "so it would be easier for you to reach. It's still going to be a little crowded because the room just isn't that big, but I think it will work."

I wheeled over to get a better look, but I was pretty sure it would all work fine. The dresser was long but short, so I could reach all the drawers from the wheelchair, and there was even a little docking station on the nightstand for my iPhone.

I had to swallow hard to keep myself from tearing up.

"You guys didn't have to do any of this," I said quietly. I wasn't sure if I was more embarrassed or more wonderstruck. Then it hit me how much this probably cost to have it all done, and I freaked a little. Greg's salary had to be pretty much shit in this little town. There's no way they could afford this. I turned to him with my eyes narrowed. "What did this run you?"

"Don't you worry about—"

"Bullshit!" I yelled back. "There is no way—no *way* you are going to pay for all of this!"

"Thomas…" Nicole started.

"No!" I said, adamantly. "I'm going to have a big freaking chunk dropped in my lap from Dad's insurance, and there is no way you are paying for all of this!"

"Look here," Greg said with a bit of impatience, "I decided to do this, and I'll pay for it however I want!"

"Absolutely not!"

"I will!"

"Bullshit," I repeated.

"Stop swearing," Greg retorted. "You saved my daughter's life, and there is no way I can possibly ever repay you for that. You're in that damn chair because you saved her, and I'll do whatever the hell I please to make you comfortable here!"

"Dammit!" I yelled. "If it wasn't for my dad, I would have driven Nicole to school that day. All this shit is his fault! HIS FAULT!"

That was when I pretty much lost it.

"If he hadn't threatened her, I never would have broke up with her!" I cried out, and the hot tears that had been threatening to come out trickled down my face. "If he hadn't been shoving me around all that time…if he hadn't done all that shit…if he…if he…"

I took a deep breath again.

"It's all that bastard's fault! All of it! He wasn't even my father, dammit! Everything is his fault! HIS FAULT!"

My stomach lurched, and I had to swallow to keep myself from puking as bile rose into my throat. My nose was already all stuffed up, and I couldn't breathe properly at all and started hyperventilating. Nicole was suddenly there, kneeling in front of my chair and wrapping her arms around me as I bawled like a fucking baby.

I don't know how long I just sobbed with her holding me, alternating between screaming about everything he put me through and just sobbing incoherently. Eventually I quieted down and could hear Nicole's voice in my ear.

"It's okay," she whispered. "You're okay now. He can't hurt you anymore."

Once I stopped blubbering, Greg was there, handing me a glass of water and a box of tissues. I cleaned myself up, definitely fully embarrassed now, and drank the water. It felt good on my throat. When I had myself relatively composed, I looked back to Greg through still-bleary eyes.

"It's his fault," I repeated softly. "He's going to foot the bill for this."

Greg eyed me for a minute and then crossed his arms.

"We'll split it," he finally said. I knew from his tone of voice it was final, so I nodded in agreement.

With that decided, Nicole showed me around the makeshift

bedroom a little bit and told me Jeremy was going to get some of my clothes and stuff from the house so I didn't have to go back there. Again, my emotions were completely ambivalent—I was extraordinarily grateful but hated that it had to be done that way.

"Oh!" Nicole suddenly cried out. "I almost forgot!"

She left my side and went around the bed to the nightstand. She opened the top drawer and pulled out a sketchbook and a box of drawing pencils.

"It's kind of a welcome home gift," she explained as she placed them in my lap. I looked down at them with widened eyes. "I didn't really know what kind of pencils to get, but the guy at the art shop in town said these were kind of all-purpose. Lots of different types, I guess."

I opened the box and looked over the different pencils, each labeled for hardness.

"They're perfect," I whispered, trying to keep the tears from coming back again. I looked up at her. "Thank you."

"You're welcome," she replied with a smile.

Shakespeare said it best: "I can no other answer make but thanks, and thanks." Somehow, I knew that there would never be enough words to express my gratitude to both Greg and my Rumple.

Now I was about ready to fall asleep right where I sat.

CHAPTER THIRTY-ONE
goal

I wasn't sure if it was my complete breakdown or just the weight of the entire day, but my eyes burned, and I could barely keep them open. Nicole seemed to sense that and asked me if there was anything I needed before I took a nap. I hadn't actually mentioned needing one, but that's just the way it was with my Rumple—I didn't have to say it.

As I proved to myself that I could get in and out of the specialty-built bathroom, Greg decided he needed to go into the station to catch up on a bunch of paperwork or something. By the time I changed into a pair of sweatpants and a T-shirt, he was on his way out the door.

"I'll see you kids later," he announced. "Don't hold up supper for me, though. I probably won't be back until late."

Nicole rolled her eyes toward him and then shook her head.

"He thinks he's being subtle," she said.

I snickered but was too tired for a full laugh. I reached down and pushed the wheelchair over to the edge of the bed. I slid onto the mattress, immediately noticing the purple pillowcase over the pillow, and ran my nose along it, smiling. I glanced up to see Nicole smirking at me, but I didn't care. I rolled to my side, using my hands to pull one leg over the top of the other so I could get more comfortable. I wrapped my arms around the pillow and inhaled the scent surrounding me.

My eyes started to close almost immediately though I forced them open when I felt Nicole's soft touch on my shoulder.

"You okay?" she asked softly. Her smirk was gone, and only concern remained in her eyes.

"Just tired," I told her.

"Get some rest," she said. Her fingers trailed down my arm, and when they reached my wrist, I caught her hand in mine and held tight. Her head tilted slightly to the side. "You want company?"

I nodded and pulled at her hand.

Her scent and warmth enveloped me, and I realized we had not been together like this since before I had dumped her at my father's insistence. Even in the hospital and rehab center, there hadn't been room for her in bed with me. Just having someone sit on the side of the bed had jostled me in ways that hurt.

I wrapped my arms around her, and as her body melded against mine, I exhaled heavily. All at once, the exhaustion of the day, the mental fatigue of the funeral, and the explosion of everything I had held inside of me for so long seemed to seep out of my body as I sank against my Rumple.

Sleepily, I tilted my head to look at her, and her arm went around my neck. I reached forward to press my lips to hers once and then twice. I would have kissed her a third time, but the combination of her hand soothing my cheek and the warm comfort of the bed overtook me. When I closed my eyes for the third kiss, my head dropped onto the pillow instead.

<hr>

I woke when Nicole moved from the bed and tightened my grip a little bit and grumbled until I felt her lips on my temple.

"I'll be right back," she whispered. I released her reluctantly, and she climbed out of bed and headed into the kitchen. I dozed back off, and when I woke again, Nicole was sitting up in the bed with one arm draped around me and the other holding a copy of *Hunger Games*. From the direction of the kitchen, something smelled really good, and I lifted my head to tell her so.

"It's kugel made from potatoes and carrots," she told me. "It has to bake for a while, so I wanted to get it in the oven. I didn't know how long you would want to sleep, but I thought you might be hungry when you woke up."

"What's a kugel?" I mumbled as I tucked my head against her stomach and wrapped my arms around her middle.

Nicole laughed.

"I'll show you later," she promised. "You don't have to wake up yet if you don't want to. Go back to sleep."

I settled myself with my head basically in her lap and closed my eyes again. I listened to the sound of her turning the pages of her book, the sound of the rain on the roof as it began to pour, and the sound of Nicole's stomach grumbling.

Rumple's stomach was all…rumply.

I snickered against her leg.

"What are you laughing at?" she asked.

"Your tummy is noisy."

I glanced up and Nicole was glaring down at me.

"Thanks a lot!" she snapped.

I wrapped my arms around said stomach and kissed it over her shirt.

"I love it," I told her. I shifted back a bit, putting just a few inches of distance between us so I could see her better. "I love you."

"I love you too." Nicole's expression softened, and she tossed the book upside down on the nightstand. "Still tired?"

"Not as much," I said with a shrug.

Nicole slid down so we were lying beside each other again. With her hand positioned behind my head, she brought me forward and our lips met. The kisses were only soft at first, as they had been earlier in the day, but quickly turned into more. I absorbed the warmth and comfort of all of it—Nicole's body, the house, the tiny room that was really just a part of the living room, and everything they had done for me even though they really didn't have much to give.

Although Dad and I always seemed to have more money than we knew what to do with, I didn't think I had felt so…*rich*…since Mom died.

Nicole's hand moved over my shoulder and chest, her fingers digging into the fabric of my T-shirt and making me shiver. I ran my hand up her arm until I could cup her face, and I kissed her again and again, exploring her mouth and then letting her explore mine.

Nicole broke the kiss with a groan and pushed herself away from me.

"What?" I asked.

"I'm sorry," she said. "I wasn't thinking…I mean…shit, we shouldn't…"

"Nicole, it's okay." I reached up and put a finger under her chin. "I really, really missed you. Missed this."

I tightened my hold on her, bringing her closer until I could kiss her again.

"Are you sure?" she whispered. "I don't want to…push."

"You aren't," I insisted between more kisses. "I want this. I want you."

Her fingers snuck underneath the edge of my shirt, and her palm splayed out over my stomach.

"You still have fantastic abs," she mumbled into my mouth.

"Yeah?"

"Definitely." Nicole backed off and looked at me quizzically. "At least they pretty much feel the same. I think I probably ought to see them to know for sure."

"I see you get your subtlety from Greg," I commented. "You want it off, baby? You only have to ask."

I raised my eyebrows at her a couple times.

"Incorrigible," she said then pursed her lips. "Take that shirt off, Thomas. I want to see you."

"I will if you will," I offered.

"You first," she said with an eye roll.

I wasn't going to argue, and I lifted myself just enough to pull the shirt over my head.

"Mmm…" Nicole hummed as her fingers ran over my stomach. "Yep—still quite nice."

"At least some of me isn't too bad," I said and kind of cringed as the words came out. It sounded shitty, and I didn't mean it that way.

Nicole's hands captured my face as she stared at me.

"You are wonderful," she whispered in earnest, "and if your legs never carry you again, they will still be the legs that had the speed to save me. The most important part of you is here, in your head."

She took her right hand and placed it over the center of my chest.

"And here."

We stared at each other for a long moment, and when we finally moved our eyes from each other's, we had changed. At least, I thought we both had. I knew I had. My mind tried to cope with the paradigm shift that changed my outlook from being useful for nothing but my speed and my agility to…to…something else. I wasn't sure exactly what it was yet, but I knew it meant more—much, much more.

"Rumple," I whispered.

She shook her head slowly.

"Don't talk," she instructed, and her lips moved up my jaw, slowly nipping along the edge until she reached my ear. She sat up a little, and a moment later her own shirt joined mine on the floor beside the bed, followed quickly by her white, lacy bra.

I tried not to let my eyes bug out. It had been way, way too long since I had seen her tits, and I had forgotten how beautiful they were. It was as if they could become the center of a whole universe dedicated to my libido.

Even as I sat up against the pillows, and Nicole lifted her leg to straddle my waist, I knew all the physical stuff—as wonderful as it was—wasn't as important as what I felt when I just looked at her eyes and thought about having her close to me. Having her lie down next to me meant more than almost anything else in the world. It wasn't what I was once told was important, but now I knew those perceptions were wrong.

"There's a divinity that shapes our ends, rough-hew them how we will," I whispered.

"What's that from?" Rumple asked.

"*Hamlet*," I replied simply.

Drawing my hands slowly up her sides and around to the front, I wrapped my fingers around the sides of her breasts as I brushed my thumbs over her nipples. They both hardened and puckered, the little nubs pointing straight at me.

I didn't need any further encouragement.

I rose off the pillow and took the first nipple into my mouth. I circled it with my tongue slowly as I sucked and kissed at the first one then moved over to the second one to make sure it got equal attention. I mean, I didn't want any inter-titty rivalry going on, did I? My nose nuzzled them equally, and my lips nipped at them as I thought about that for a minute. If they got mad at each other, would they fight? I wondered what that would look like but had to stop because the mental imagery was distracting me from the actual imagery.

Playing around with Nicole's tits definitely could have occupied my mind, hands, and tongue for a very, very long time. The skin was soft and creamy—just slightly paler than the skin of her arms and shoulders. Her nipples were dark, rosy pink, and just the right size for me to suck into my mouth and feel the texture with the tip of my tongue.

When I did, she moaned. She wasn't quiet about it either—not like she had been when her dad was sleeping in the next room. She tilted her head up to the ceiling and practically shoved her nipples in my mouth as she arched forward and dug her fingers into my hair. I was only too happy to oblige, and I reached around her with one hand and held her against me as I alternated fondling and sucking at her breasts.

So fucking good.

I dropped my hand down to her backside, running a finger along the edge of the stretchy material of her pants. Though it wasn't meant to be one, she apparently considered it a hint and rose up on her knees. She started pushing the material off her hips, and I licked my lips as her hips slowly appeared in front of me.

"Jesus," I whispered. "You are so beautiful."

With my hands on her hips, she pushed the pants down farther, leaving just some little blue panties between my eyes and her intimae skin. She lifted first one leg and then the other, pulling the material from her legs and letting it join the growing pile of clothes on the floor. Her hands came back to my chest, and she leaned in and captured my lips with hers.

"Were you looking for something?" she asked quietly, and her hips pushed her core against my stomach. I could only moan in response, feeling not only her heat but moisture as well against my skin. I looked up to her dark eyes and grinned.

"Yeah, I was," I informed her. "I was hoping to see that beautiful pussy of yours, but it's just too far away."

"Is it?" Her eyes widened in mock surprise. "I wonder how we could remedy the situation."

I grabbed hcr backside with both hands and pulled her a little farther up my chest. She tried to position herself again, which gave me a pretty decent opportunity to hook my thumbs inside the edge of those panties and start pulling them off of her. She balanced from left to right once more, and then she was magnificently naked above me.

My eyes moved slowly from her shoulders, over her breasts, down to her stomach, and to the little mound right below. Her muscled legs screamed to have me touch them, so I did, running my hands over her thighs as my eyes took in the exposed feminine flesh right before me.

I couldn't wait any more, and pulled her up closer to me. I glanced at her eyes, making sure she knew what I wanted to do and that she wanted it, too. She only nodded, her teeth embedded in her lip.

I lifted her just a little with my hands, giving me a slightly better angle. Nicole leaned farther forward, her hands grasping the top of the headboard for balance. I glanced up at her for only a moment, raised my eyebrows and looked back to my goal. I extended my tongue slowly and tasted her sweet, sweet skin. I kissed down between her lower lips, spread them a bit with my lips and tongue, then reached in, circling her opening first, then plunging inside.

Her hips jerked, and my hands tightened their grip to hold her steady as I licked and sucked and delved. I licked her from the top of her sex to the bottom and then back again. I licked and sucked at her clit, rolling my tongue over it and pressing against it. I wrote "MY RUMPLE" in big capital letters with my tongue as I heard her breaths turn to pants and felt her hips starting to rock into me rhythmically. I released her ass-cheek from one of my hands and ran my fingers between her legs. I slipped the middle one inside and felt her tense a little. I quickly looked to her flushed face.

"You like that, don't you, Rumple?" I hummed against her skim. "Makes you think about how my cock is going to feel, driving into your tight little pussy. You still think about my cock, don't you?"

"Mmph…" she groaned, and I smiled as my index finger worked its way inside of her, too.

"I bet you think about it all the time," I said as I flicked my tongue over her clit between words. "You want my cock so bad, don't you, baby?"

She moaned incoherently again.

"Say it," I told her. I pushed my tongue against her as my fingers moved faster. I could feel the tension building in her legs. "Tell me how much you want my cock!"

"I do…" she mumbled. Her eyes were closed tightly and her

warm breath brushed the top of my head.

"You do what, Rumple? Tell me. Tell me what you want."

"Your cock," she whispered, and as she said it, my fingers and tongue drove against her—inside and out—at the same time. I kept my eyes on her as her head angled back, and she cried out over and over again.

"Louder!" I commanded.

"Oh God! Thomas! I want your cock! I want your cock! Thomas! Thomas!"

She shuddered, and I moaned at the taste of her as it rivaled the sweetness of her words to my ears. I slowly pulled my fingers from her and pulled her back down until her head was against my shoulder, and the rest of her body was splayed out over my chest.

"Fucking right, you want it," I said with a cocky half-smile.

I heard her soft laughter against my shoulder as her body relaxed into mine, and even though my cock was still looking for a lot of attention, I felt sated.

Nicole's breathing slowed against my shoulder, and I was content just to run my hands up and down the smooth skin of her back. She lifted her head to look at me for a moment, and I didn't understand her expression at first. Then she grabbed my chin and kissed me deeply.

"That was fucking incredible," she said. She licked her lips, and I knew she was tasting herself. That thought made my ass clench as my cock pressed up against my sweatpants.

"I couldn't agree more," I said. I ran my tongue over my bottom lip. "I don't think I need dinner anymore."

Nicole just gave me a grin in return and then kissed my lips softly. She moved down to my neck and then to my chest. Her tongue flicked one of my nipples, and I gasped a little. No one had ever done that before, and it felt really weird but in a good way. It tingled, and the sensation went straight to my dick.

Then she started moving lower, sliding down my body as she kissed down my sternum and then licked my navel. She drew a line of kisses across the waistband of my sweats, and then glanced up at me.

"I think these are in the way," she announced and started pulling them off my legs, boxers along with them.

As I realized her intent, my heart started beating faster, and the muscles in my backside clenched, making my dick jump a little as she pulled the fabric away. With the remainder of my clothing tossed off to the side, she positioned herself over my hard cock and stared into my eyes as she gripped the base with her hand.

"Rumple," I gasped as she lowered herself a little more and licked across the head. "Oh…fuck…"

She wrapped her lips around the end and sucked as she pulled back, making an audible popping sound as she released me. She went right back down again, running her tongue over the edge as she took me into her warm, silky mouth.

"Oh God…baby!" I cried out, and my head snapped back against the pillow. That only managed to wrap me up in the scent of her and cause my hips to buck a little. I felt the tip of my cock touch the top of her mouth as she moved back and forth over it.

I reached down and put my hand on the back of her head, running my fingers through her soft hair. I didn't do it to push at her or anything—I let her set her own pace. She licked the underside of my shaft as she pulled back up and then circled the head with her tongue again.

"You like that?" she inquired with bashful eyes.

"Oh, fuck yes, I like it!" I replied in earnest.

"You like my mouth on you?"

I could have come just from hearing her say that.

"Turning the dirty talk around, are ya?" I said with a grin.

"You don't like it?" she asked, her eyes narrowing a little in confusion.

"Oh, I definitely do!" I reassured her. Her eyes gleamed back up at me, and she smiled as well.

"Do you want my pussy, too?" Her eyes literally sparkled. My little kitten-minx had definitely gone all mischievous on me. My breath caught in my throat, and I couldn't respond at first, so she pushed it further. "Do you want to feel your cock in my pussy, Thomas?"

She moved then, releasing my cock from her grasp and straddling my thighs. My mind started spinning when I realized she wasn't just speaking metaphorically. Before I could become too elated, reality tried to bite me in the ass.

"Nicole," I whispered, "I…um…don't have any condoms or anything."

She bit down on her lip.

"I'm on the pill," she replied with a shrug.

My father's words echoed through my head, pounding against my temples like a pile driver.

"Don't fuck a chick without a condom. They'll tell you they're on the pill, and they're lying through their fucking teeth about it. They all say that. They're all just trying to trap you into something. Don't ever fuck without one, you hear me?"

I blinked a couple of times, and in my heart, I knew she would never lie to me about something like that. Even if she did…or even if something happened anyway…

I thought about the moment I saw her holding little baby Timmy in her arms and how I had wondered what I would do if it were hers. That thought immediately transformed into what I would do if her baby was *my* baby, and the thought didn't feel like being trapped at all.

"We don't have to," she said softly when I didn't respond.

"I want to," I said, and my hand caressed the side of her face. "If you want to, and you're okay with it, then yeah…I want to."

She gazed at me for a long minute.

"Are you sure?"

"If you are," I replied. "There isn't much of anything I could want more."

She lowered herself a little, and her wet pussy ran along my cock. As I groaned, she leaned forward, pressing her lips to mine as I felt her hand grasp me again, angling the tip of my dick so it was positioned at her opening. She reached into my mouth with her tongue, and she slowly started lowering herself over me.

I was pretty sure there was no better way to heaven.

As my cock slowly spread her open, my entire body went stiff, and my mind went completely blank. I was nothing but the slow sliding sensation of her heat wrapping around me, guiding me inside of her, pulling me in and hugging me tightly.

Safe.

I took in a single sharp breath—more of a gasp, really. I opened my eyes slowly, and I looked up at her—the beautiful angel above me with her hair shining on one side where the light from the bedside lamp made it shimmer. I wanted to speak—to tell her how much I loved her—but nothing would come out of my mouth.

I was inside of her.

Inside my Rumple.

And it wasn't just my cock shoved up in her pussy.

It was much, much more than that.

It was as if she was everywhere around me, and her warmth and scent and everything that she was had wrapped around my body and completely encompassed me. It was as if she was in my head—in my soul, if there was such a thing—and I was in hers. It was the single most incredible sense of elation I had ever felt in my life.

There must have been something strange in my expression because Nicole's hand ran across my cheek and held my jaw.

"Are you okay?" she asked, breathless.

"More than," I managed to say. I closed my eyes as she shifted her hips a little and the feelings ran up my body again, making me gasp. My cock was throbbing inside of her, and we weren't even moving. "God, you feel good."

The words were totally inadequate, but there weren't any words to describe it, so maybe it didn't matter too much. Nicole placed her hands on my shoulders and pulled up a little. I groaned and grasped her hips.

"Stay still a second," I begged. "Jesus…baby…you feel

incredible."

After a moment, I gathered myself a bit and opened my eyes again. She was still looking down at me with her lip mashed by her teeth. I could see her breasts rising and falling a little as she tried to steady her breaths.

"Okay," I whispered, "but go slow."

She moved slowly, pushing up with her legs and pulling me about halfway out before she sank back down again. I dug my fingers into her hips, holding her still for a moment before loosening up so she could do it again. Warm, wet, silky resistance covered me, and the same thought went through my head again.

Safe.

This…this was where I belonged.

With her.

I let out a long groan as she moved up a little farther and came down with a little more force. I took a deep breath and tried to control myself as she found a slow, torturous rhythm.

"So good, Rumple…"

"Thomas…" Her hot breath hit my ear as she leaned over and nuzzled her nose into my hair. "Never felt like this…never…"

"Me too." It was all I could say. I knew it wasn't just because there wasn't a condom between us—it was so much more intense than that. It was because it was us. Just us.

She moaned softly, ending in a bit of a grunt as she brought us completely together again. I brought one of my hands around her back, running over her skin in slow circles as the other one reached for the back of her head. I brought her face to mine, taking her lips and sucking on them as she kept moving on me. I reached my tongue into her mouth, capturing her cries as she moved again.

Up and down, she moved a little faster, and I could feel tension in my thighs even though I couldn't do anything about it. It seemed almost automatic. I wanted to dig my heels in and thrust into her—meet her movements—but my body was unable to cooperate with the notion. I wanted to buck my hips up against her, and I did—a little. I couldn't get the leverage I wanted without the use of my legs to assist, which probably would have pissed me off more if I could have thought about it. I couldn't though—my head was full of her, and there wasn't any room for self-pity. I had more important things to do.

I wanted her to get off again.

The hand on her back moved around to the front, and I slipped a finger between us, finding her clit and circling it with the tip. I latched onto the side of her neck and then slowly moved up toward her ear.

"Oh!" she cried out, and her hips angled forward a bit as I rubbed.

"You like that?" I whispered huskily into her ear. "You want me to touch you while you ride my cock?"

"Thomas! *God...*"

"My Rumple likes to hear talk about my cock, don't you baby?"

"Y...yes!"

"It feels so good...buried in your pussy...so tight and warm..."

"Unngh!" Her hips thrust forward a bit more, and her legs increased the rhythm of my penetrations. I shoved the back of my head into the pillow to get a little more lift with my hips, trying to match her pace as much as I could.

"So good..." I moaned. "Fuck me, Nicole...that's it! Oh yeah —harder, baby! Fuck me!"

She obliged, practically jumping up and down on me as her tits bounced all over the place and made me want to try to play a game of *capture the nipple* with my lips. I rubbed my finger harder against her clit, and I could feel the muscles in her legs tighten against my sides.

"Oh yeah—baby! Come on my cock!" I strained my stomach muscles trying to push up harder against her. I felt her clamp down on me as she cried out in one, long moan. That was all it took to send me over the edge. I felt my balls tighten up, and the sensation rippled through me and up into her. My cock spasmed as it filled her deep inside, coating us both with thick semen.

"Nicole! Oh...oh *God*! Nicole!"

With my eyes squeezed shut, I wrapped my arms around her and tightened my grip until her chest was right up against mine. I tucked my head into her, practically hiding my face in her hair, and just held on to her like she was driftwood in the open sea.

There were tears in my eyes.

"I love you," I said quietly, but my voice still cracked. "God, I love you so much, Rumple."

"I love you, too, Thomas," she replied. She wrapped her hands around my head, and she softly kissed my neck. "Always."

As Romeo spoke of Juliet, so I felt about Nicole. "Come what sorrow can, it cannot countervail the exchange of joy, that one short minute gives me in her sight." Somehow, as long as she loved me, I knew everything would work out.

Now I really, really needed some sleep.

CHAPTER THIRTY-TWO

new play

I looked into my Rumple's eyes.

We had been on our sides, just looking at each other for the longest time. She looked at me as her fingers traced back and forth over my jaw, and I looked at her while my fingers drew little geometric patterns on her back. It wasn't the least bit awkward or anything, either. I could have stayed like that forever.

Until some obnoxious beeping noise came from the kitchen.

"That would be dinner," Nicole said quietly as her cheeks turned pink. I had no idea why dinner made her blush, but it was fucking adorable. She broke out of my embrace and pulled her T-shirt and pants back on before running to the kitchen. I kind of wished she had just run naked so I could watch her ass bounce around as she left the room.

Maybe next time.

Next time.

Yeah.

There was definitely going to be a next time.

I had heard the term post coital bliss before, but I had never experienced it. It wasn't just due to an orgasm. I'd had plenty of those. It was more about holding her afterwards, knowing her rapid heartbeats and quick breaths were all my doing.

Well, and her doing.

Whatever.

It was awesome. That was for sure.

She walked back around the little dividing wall, asked if I needed any help or anything, and asked if I wanted to come eat in the kitchen or have her bring it to me. I was seriously tempted to just lie there, but Danielle's voice popped up in my head and told me to get off my ass, so I did. I did let Nicole hand me my clothes, at least.

Getting pants on was a bitch, but I could manage. It just took fucking forever, which pissed me off. It wasn't just that my legs didn't move at all—they did, a little. I just couldn't control them enough to have them do what I wanted. When I tried to get my legs to help—like bending a knee a bit so I could reach my foot and get the pant leg over it—they ended up jerking around and generally being in the way.

After wrestling with my pants, I pulled my shirt over my head, shifted myself back into the chair, and wheeled into the kitchen.

Vroom, fucking vroom.

Not.

I sighed and tried to bring myself back to the bliss I had been feeling just a few minutes before. Seeing Nicole dishing out… whatever the fuck she had made…onto plates and pouring dressing over a salad as she smiled up at me helped to bring back the mood.

We ate relatively quietly, just kind of glancing at each other and smiling a lot. Sometimes we snickered, but again, it wasn't uncomfortable, just…happy.

It was weird.

And I loved it.

After dinner we went straight back to my bed. Since we didn't know just when Greg was going to get back, we kept our clothes on and just made out a little bit. We did a lot of staring at each other, and Nicole tried to keep my hair behind my ear. Eventually I just closed my eyes to the feeling, and before long I drifted off.

For a day that included burying the only father I had ever

known, it was a damn good one.

⊰•••◉◍◉•••⊱

I woke to my phone ringing and tried to grab it off the nightstand before it could wake Nicole. The dim light coming through the window told me it was morning already, and we had obviously completely zonked out. As I hit the answer button without looking at who was calling, I wondered when Greg had come home.

"Hey, Malone," a fairly somber voice said.

Fuck.

"Oh...um...hi." I glanced over at Nicole and saw her looking up at me. I took a deep breath. "You want something?"

"Yeah, we need to talk," he said. "Now a good time?"

"Not really," I replied.

"Well, yeah –I figured." He was quiet for a moment. "You need to come into my dad's office. He's got some shit to go over with you—you know, will shit."

I didn't respond and heard him take a deep breath again.

"Fuck, Thomas—I'm sorry," he finally said.

"It's okay," I replied, deadpan. "I'll give him a call and make an appointment."

"Can you get in tomorrow?"

"Yeah, probably."

"Ten o'clock?"

"Fine."

"Do you need me to pick you up or anything?"

"No," I said. "I'm good."

"Okay...I'll...um...I'll be there if you want."

"No, it's okay."

"You sure?"

"Yeah."

"Okay. Later, Malone."

"Later."

I hung up and put the phone back on the nightstand. I glanced at Nicole again, who was looking up at me with her eyes full of

423

questions.

"I need to go see Dad's lawyer," I told her.

"Oh," she replied as she looked away. "Yeah, I guess that makes sense."

"He's in town," I told her.

"I can take you."

"Shouldn't you be in school tomorrow?"

"Not if you need me," she replied. "I was planning to take a couple days off—just until you're settled in."

"You don't have to do that," I said.

"I know." She shrugged her shoulders. "I want to."

She played with the collar of my T-shirt.

"Are you going to…to call…" Her voice trailed off and she bit her lip.

"My real father?" I asked.

"Yeah."

"I guess I should," I answered. "He's in a hotel in town, too."

"I heard."

"Right." I sighed and ran my hand through my hair.

"Do you want me to go with you?" she asked. "I mean, actually *go* with you? I'll drive you either way, but I'll also, you know, stay with you, too. If you want."

I thought about it for a minute, and it was seriously tempting. I knew I couldn't take her into the lawyer's office, but to talk to Thomas Gardner? Yeah, that was tempting.

But I also knew I had to do it myself.

"Thanks, Rumple," I said with a half-smile. She probably didn't buy it. "I'll definitely take the ride, but I think I have to talk to him on my own."

Her hand came up and brushed my cheek.

"It'll be okay," she whispered. "I just know it will."

I nodded slowly, not nearly as convinced. Regardless of the outcome, I knew I still had to do it. I had to see him, hear him out, give him the chance to tell me why I spent my life with Lou Malone instead of him.

Once I was out of the car and back into my wheelchair, I looked up over the door to the sign: Lucas and Lucas, Attorneys at Law.

Yeah, right.

"You want me to come in?" Nicole asked. "I can just stay in the waiting room or something."

"It shouldn't take long," I said. "I guess I'd rather you just, I dunno…hang out here for a bit? If it looks like it's going to take longer, I can call you."

Nicole narrowed her eyes a little as she looked me over.

"All right," she said. "I'll be in the car."

"Thanks," I said. I tried to give her a bit of a smile, but I wasn't feeling it. I rolled far off to one side of the entrance to get up the wheelchair ramp, then pushed hard to make the angle. I still wasn't used to going up inclines, and that shit wasn't easy. Once I got to the door, there was one of those buttons you could push to make the door open up. I made my way into the waiting room and looked up to the counter.

I recognized the chick there but didn't know her name. She was chewing gum noisily and smiled down at me as she hung up the phone.

"Good morning, Mister Malone," she said. "Mister Lucas is expecting you."

She walked around the counter and escorted me down a hallway, opening the door and holding it for me as we got to the end. P. Lucas—I couldn't even remember what the *P* stood for— was sitting behind his desk with stacks of documents all over it. He waved me in, and the receptionist was kind enough to move one of the office chairs out of the way so I could roll up across from him.

"Max said he talked to you," Lucas said. "Sorry I didn't make the funeral. It seemed more prudent to stay away."

I just nodded.

"He's still at your service if you want to keep him handy," Lucas informed me. "We still have a contract, but we can work all that stuff out later."

He smiled, and the corners of his eyes tightened a little when he did. I thought about the slight, unintentional movement, and I knew it didn't exactly indicate honesty. There was nothing about the Lucas family that was on the up-and-up. Max Lucas had been my go-to person for shady dealings and information since I got my first cell phone.

"The will?" I prompted. I didn't want to be here any longer than I had to. I almost wished I had let Nicole come with me. Almost. I didn't want her around Lucas. He was a seriously underhanded character and used to dealing with all kinds of nasty shit. Once, Dad said that Lucas was connected to bigger crime in Portland but only as one of their informants or something.

"Very basic, actually," he said. "I'd been trying to get your father to update it for some time, but it hasn't changed since your mother passed. No trust fund, nothing complicated—you are the only offspring. You are over the age of eighteen, and you get it all."

"What's *all*?" I asked.

"The bank accounts, stock portfolios, house, the three cars— one of which is already in your name—the summer place in Michigan, the island…"

"Island?"

"Yes," Lucas said with a short nod, "your father bought an island some years ago. Just off of Saint Thomas."

"I have an island?" I was a little taken aback. How could I not know he bought a fucking island?

Lucas chuckled and went on, tallying everything that was worth mentioning. The assets came up to about nine million, plus the stock portfolio, which was another six and a half. Lucas continued to babble.

"Give me the bottom line, Lucas," I snapped, interrupting him. He bristled a little, but he seemed to remember whose son he was dealing with, at least. I knew how to be an asshole. I'd learned from the best.

"Your father had three insurance policies," Lucas said. "One from the hospital, one through the mayor's office, and his whole-life insurance through Arden Mutual. They are all still valid since they've been in place for several years. The suicide clause has elapsed, so you'll get it all."

"How much?"

"Well, the mayor's policy isn't very big, and it will take a while for them to get off their asses and write a check. I did get a copy of the death certificate for them—I didn't want you to get delayed. The hospital will be more of a nightmare than the city—their administrators are kings of delay tactics—"

"How much, Lucas?" I said through clenched teeth. I did not want to be here all day, listening to him babble.

He looked across the desk at me and wiped the back of his sweaty neck with his hand.

"Combined, once they've all gone through and you pay a bunch of taxes on it, about twelve million. Twenty-seven mil with everything else."

"Damn."

Lucas smiled, and I was reminded of great white sharks with their rows of threatening teeth.

"That's a lot for a kid to deal with, Thomas," he said. His voice got soft, like he was trying to buddy up to me. "My retainer is already paid through the end of the year, and I'm going to make sure you and your money are taken care of properly."

"I bet," I said under my breath.

He tilted his head to hear me better, but I didn't repeat myself.

"Is that all you wanted to tell me?" I asked.

"There are a few other points," he said. His voice dropped a bit. "How much do you know about your father's other businesses?"

I shrugged. I knew he did other shit on the side, but I never really paid much attention to it. I didn't have the details, but considering it tended to be done at very strange hours, I knew it wasn't legal.

"The vultures have already descended on some of it," he said. "I could…set things up for you. You and I could continue to do business as your father and I had. I know what's involved. I know the contacts. That twenty-seven mil will look like nothing if we play this right. The gambling and bookkeeping alone will double that if we're careful."

The gambling. Of course. A couple more puzzle pieces clicked together. No wonder he was so hell-bent on me playing for Real Messini. All the people he would meet, the inside information he would have access to—the gambling ring he ran on the side would become huge. I ran my hand through my hair and tried to take it all in.

Twenty-seven million dollars.

Fuck me hard.

I didn't even have to wait until I was twenty-one or anything. It was mine now. I closed my eyes for a moment, rubbing my fingers into the sockets. I thought about the tiny room Greg and Nicole set up for me. I thought about their little house and Nicole's dead Hyundai. I thought about Jeremy and how his father had to file for bankruptcy after his mom had a heart attack. Dad could have helped them, worked something out with the hospital, but he wouldn't. I thought about the kid Nicole babysat for—Timmy—and the shitty prospects his mother faced for her future. I thought about how Sophie had to hide him, completely because of money.

And when it came right down to it, despite all the shit they struggled with regarding bills, they were all pretty happy.

I looked up at Lucas and smiled.

"You are a shifty little bastard, aren't you Lucas?" I kept smiling.

He chuckled softly, and I saw his posture relax. He thought he had me.

"When should all this go through?" I asked.

"By the end of the month."

"Good." I pushed my chair back away from his desk. "Once the transactions are all completed, you're fired. I'll give you the information on my new lawyer before then so you know where to send everything. Max is fired *now*—tell him not to contact me again. If I hear any more about this shit, I'll turn you in. There's plenty of evidence in Dad's study to fuck your whole agency about six times over. I bet you'd do jail time."

I had no idea if that was true or not, but I figured it was. I continued to smile as I watched Lucas go pale.

"I buried my father's body two days ago," I told him. "Today I bury the rest of his shit."

He only stared at me with his palms flat against his desktop.

"Are we clear, Lucas?"

"I suppose we are," he replied.

I left.

Shakespeare advised: "Neither a borrower nor a lender be." But I was more intrigued by the idea of giving the shit away. I had the feeling a lot of people were going to resist it, but I also knew I could be pretty convincing. I'd win in the end.

I always did.

I wheeled myself out of the office and back to the car and my Rumple.

It was time to meet my real father.

"How did it go?" Nicole asked as she helped me back into the car. I shook my head.

"Can we save it for later?" I asked. "I'm kind of overwhelmed right now. If you want, though, you can warn Greg that I just won the fight over the bills."

"What does that mean?"

"Forget it," I said. "What time is it?"

"Almost noon."

"Shit—will I be late?"

"I don't think so."

Nicole drove us over to the little restaurant where I was supposed to meet my biological father. I called him yesterday evening and set it all up. Nicole told me to take as much time as I wanted. She was going to the bookstore in the next block, and she could pretty much stay there all day without getting bored.

Nicole took me into the restaurant where we saw my newly-revealed father dancing from one foot to the other next to the hostess's station. Nicole kissed my cheek and told me to call whenever I was ready to head home. I nodded and looked up into Thomas Gardner's eyes.

Like a fucking mirror.

"Hey," he said, and his hand went for his hair at the same time mine did. We both paused, smirked, and dropped our hands.

"This is kind of weird," I said with a shrug.

"Yeah," he agreed. His chest expanded with a deep breath, which he then let out through his nose. "Should we get a table?"

"Probably."

The hostess came over and sat us down in a corner near the windows. She moved a couple of chairs out of the way, and I ended up looking right at the window with Thomas Gardner across from me. It gave him a surreal glow around his head and shoulders, and I tried not to read anything into it.

We spent about a minute and a half talking about the weather, ordering two waters, and then finally gave up on the small talk.

"So, uh…how did you know my mom?" I finally asked. However, the server returned, took our lunch orders, and walked off. I sighed and tried again. "You met her in college?"

"Yeah," he replied. His brow furrowed and he twisted his fingers together around the water glass.

"Well…?"

"I guess I should start at the beginning," he said. He took a sip of his water and looked down at his hands. "I met Fran at school. It was my last year, her first. I was into all the art stuff then—drawing, painting, theatre—and I even played guitar in a band. We weren't that great, but we had a decent local following. We performed mostly covers of whatever was popular at the time. We played at local bars for the most part, and almost every weekend, we had a gig."

He took another quick drink.

"There were four guys in the band," he said. "We ended up with…um…a bit of a…um…well, there was this group of girls… shit."

He coughed into his hand and sat up a little straighter.

"We called them our groupies. They were basically there every time we played. Fran was one of them."

He glanced up at me for a second, probably wondering what I

was thinking. My mom was a band groupie? For some shit college cover band? It didn't fit my image of my mother at all. I shook my head, trying to clear it of the very idea.

"I was…kind of shy," he said. "I would never talk to them, really, but sometimes after we played a set, they'd buy us drinks. We were actually about to break up the band. The semester was almost over, and two of us were graduating. It was about over, you know? That last night, I had a couple extra…It was my birthday—and uh…Fuck! I don't know how to say this!"

"You and my mom hooked up," I said. My voice was way too calm, even for my own liking.

"Yeah," he replied softly. "It was just that one night, and school was almost over. I left a couple weeks later. I went to Chicago Art Institute to start my master's program. I was going early to get settled in. About a week after I got there, she showed up."

"And she was pregnant?

"No," he said. "At least, I don't think so. She said she just had to see me again. I couldn't…fuck…I couldn't even remember her name right away! But there she was, claiming I was the only man for her and…and…shit!"

He slammed his hand down on the table, making me jump. He leaned forward and pushed the heels of his hands into his eyes.

"I was…flattered. She told me how much she loved my art… and how she had come to every performance of *Hamlet* when I played the title role. She thought the band's music was awful, but she just wanted to see me. I didn't know what to do. She had come all the way from the west coast and didn't even have a way back. I let her stay with me…it was only a couple of weeks. I knew it wasn't going to work out. I was going to be in school constantly. I wasn't looking to have a relationship…"

He paused, dropped his hands to his lap, and leaned back against the booth.

"I told her she needed to get on a bus home, and she started crying. I think….I mean, looking back…I think she wanted to tell me…but she didn't. We fought, and she left. I didn't see or hear from her again."

"How did you…? You ended up at her memorial service. How?"

A sharp pain ripped through my temple all of a sudden, and I rubbed at the spot. How did I know he was there? My mind raced…the letter…I read it over and over again, but it didn't say anything about the memorial service. In my mind—in the far reaches of my memories, I saw a flash of light brown hair and my father…Lou…blocking my view…leading him away.

"I was in Portland," he said. "I was an adjunct professor for a semester. My mentor was out on maternity leave, and she asked me to take over her classes. It was a class in how to teach art, and one of the students was from here in town. Class was over, but we were still talking about…I don't even remember what. Charcoal versus ink…something like that. Somehow she got on the topic of having to return home for a memorial service. She told me the name, and I knew it was her."

He stopped and looked into my eyes, his gaze running all over my face.

"I just went to pay my respects," he whispered. "But when I saw you…when I saw you—I knew. I *knew* you were mine."

"It is a wise father that knows his own child," I muttered.

"Yeah," he agreed with a chuckle. "Exactly."

I crossed my arms over my chest and held on to my biceps with my hands. I was cold even though it was really pretty warm out that day. Maybe the restaurant already had the AC on or something. I shivered.

Thomas Gardner—my father—never knew anything about me.

"She never told you," I said quietly. I tried to picture my mom —the woman who tucked me in at night and played the piano when I couldn't sleep—as a band groupie who got pregnant with me after a drunken one-night stand. I shook my head. The picture didn't fit who I knew at all.

"I'm sorry," he said quietly. "I couldn't decide if I should tell you how it was or not. I toyed with the idea of telling you we were madly in love or something, but I thought maybe you've been lied to enough."

I rubbed my eyes and shook my head again.

"I want the truth," I told him. "No more bullshit."

"Right," he said. He cleared his throat. "Is that…um…enough for one sitting?"

His voice cracked, and when I looked up at him, I thought he was going to lose it or start crying or something. He looked totally distraught, and I didn't know what to make of it.

"Are you okay?" I asked, confused.

He laughed, but there was nothing humorous in the sound. He dropped his head into his hands again.

"I swear, Thomas," he said, "I swear if I had known before then I would have done something…I would have insisted…but what your dad said made sense, at least at the time. I didn't want to hurt you. I *don't* want to hurt you or make any of this worse. I don't know shit about kids…but you're not really a kid now anyway…but I wasn't there for you. Not for any of it. Shit."

"What did he say?" I asked. "What did Dad say to you?"

"You sure you want more?"

I could only nod. My throat felt tight, and I had to keep swallowing over and over. I sipped at my ice water and stared at my own hands for a bit.

"When I saw you, I didn't know what to do. I mean, you had obviously just lost your mother, and I was in shock as soon as I laid eyes on you. I remember walking toward you—you were sitting on an overstuffed chair—and then stopping. I didn't know what I could say to you. I was at a total loss. I think I had pretty much planned on leaving at that point and maybe trying to reach out to you later, when your…your dad came up to me."

"He must have known…recognized me somehow...or just saw the resemblance and drew his own conclusion. I don't know. But he stopped me from getting any closer to you, said he knew who I was and not to upset his son any more than he already was. I remember just kind of looking up at him—at Lou—and I think I asked him if you were mine. He made it pretty clear that he was the one who had raised you and that I needed to leave. I wasn't about to make some sort of scene at a funeral home, and as I said —he had a point. I didn't want to upset you. He took my number and said he'd call me in a few days."

"He didn't call. It was about two weeks later when I ended up calling him instead. He said you didn't know anything about me and that frankly, neither did he. That's when he asked what my name was, which I thought was weird since he said he knew who I was before. I told him, and he flipped. Then I figured it out—Fran never told him my name, but she…she named you after me. He lost it—just for a minute. Then he started laughing and then calmed down again pretty quickly. I knew he had to be…to be grieving. I figured maybe that was just his way."

I had my own opinions about that.

"After a while, he agreed to meet with me," Thomas Gardner said. "I flew back to Portland, and we met for dinner. He told me a lot about you—how much you…"

He paused and looked away for a minute.

"What?" I prompted.

"How much you loved playing soccer," he finally said. "How you were some kind of goalie prodigy or something and that you wanted to play pro. He said your mother didn't want you to know me—that she never wanted me to know about you. He said if I came into your life, then it would just make everything harder for you. You had just lost your mother—your life was in enough turmoil."

"I couldn't really argue with that," he continued. "I didn't want to be a disruption. We communicated every few months, and he'd mostly tell me about your soccer playing. He even said once that you had a sketchbook and you liked to draw, but I think that was kind of a slip on his part."

I met his eyes for the first time in a while. He offered me a half grin, which was just another opportunity for me to freak out. Every time I looked at him, it was like looking into the mirror.

"I felt really…proud," he said quietly, "when he said that. Like…maybe you got something from me besides hair that won't stay where it's put."

I chuckled a little and ran my hand through my unruly hair.

"It's not as bad if you keep it shorter," he said.

"Nicole likes it a little bit long."

"She seems really good for you."

"She is," I said. I immediately felt defensive. If he even tried to hint that I shouldn't have her in my life...

"Easy," he said as he held his hands out in front of him. "It was a compliment. I'm glad you have her and that you're staying with her and her father."

I relaxed a little, but my thoughts and emotions were still all over the place. He knew nothing about me, and my mom didn't want me to know about him. Then why would she name me after him? Why?

I'm the product of a drunken hook up.

I swallowed again.

"Anyway," he went on. "As time went by, I kept asking him when the right time to tell you would be. He kept putting me off. There was always something big going on with your life—a tournament, a scout, and then this...um...*Reel Messys*, or something?"

I laughed.

"Real Messini."

"Yeah—that was it." He nodded vigorously. "There was always something important, and he didn't want you to have your life turned upside down right before something big was about to happen. He told me how playing pro was your dream, and he said if you eventually made that team, it would be huge. If something about your parentage came out then, it would be a scandal or whatever."

He sighed.

"I didn't want to agree, but he...he convinced me it was the right thing to do. I agreed that if you went pro, I'd back off—stop trying to see you. I trusted his judgment. I mean, he knew you and lived with you. He was your father, really. I knew that. I know that. I'd never try to replace him, Thomas—I swear."

He looked up at me then so intently, I didn't know if I should laugh or cry. My real father....real father...real father. What the fuck did that mean? The guy who hit me? The one who told me everything was my fault and wouldn't even let me touch the piano because it had been hers? The man who smacked me every time I dared mention her name? For a long moment, we just looked at each other. Maybe he couldn't take any more of the silence, because he eventually spoke.

"Lou was your real dad. I know that. I would never try to take his place."

My mouth opened without any consultation with the cognizant parts of my head.

"He abused me," I said quietly.

I kept my eyes on his as I watched his eyes go from hopeful insistence, to mild confusion, to slow comprehension, to absolute, cold fury.

"He what?"

The knuckles of his hand turned white as they put pressure against his water glass. A moment later, the glass broke.

In *Julius Caesar*, Shakespeare told us: "The evil that men do lives after them." Somehow, I thought it was going to be a long time before some of the scars Lou Malone left were healed.

Now how was...um...*Dad*...going to take it?

CHAPTER THIRTY-THREE
clean sheet

I just sat there while a busboy cleaned up the broken glass, and the server tried to wipe all the water up from the table. I wasn't sure what to think, and I was on edge. My toes kept twitching on my right foot, which they did sometimes. It was something reflexive, Danielle had told me. Though she said it was a good sign, it drove me nuts when it happened. I couldn't make it stop.

My...father...Dad...Thomas...I didn't know how I should address him or think of him. In my mind, I had just started calling him Gardner. That seemed to work as well as anything else. Gardner was just sitting there, too, with his hands balled into fists and his sandwich almost untouched. He didn't say anything until the server left.

"How?" His voice came out in a harsh whisper. "I mean... what? What did he do?"

"Blamed me," I replied solemnly. "He blamed me for Moms' death. He hit me sometimes."

"Did he...is he why you're in...that thing?" He waved a hand at my wheelchair as his face went deathly pale.

"No," I said with a single laugh. "I did that one myself."

"You saved that girl," he nodded, remembering. "Nicole."

"Yeah."

"He hit you?" Gardner repeated.

"Yeah," I said again. I looked down at my hands and used one finger to smear around a missed droplet of water. After a minute, when he hadn't said anything else, I looked back at him.

He was, for lack of a better term, shaking. He was taking in deep breaths—like I sometimes do to calm myself—but then as he let them out, his whole body shook with the effort.

"Are you okay?" I asked quietly.

"Yes," he breathed and then quickly changed his mind. "No! Shit! I have to get out of here…"

He stood up and slammed his legs into the bottom of the table, which knocked over my water and brought forth some more cursing. I might have found it funny, except for what he had said.

He had to get out.

Get away from me.

I felt my shoulders slump as my body tensed up.

"Shit! Thomas…I just…I didn't mean…fuck!"

"It's okay," I whispered.

"No! I didn't mean…I just need to get outside a minute… um…to smoke? I really need a cigarette right now."

"Oh," I said as I glanced up at him. He was pulling a pack out of his pocket. "Okay."

I looked down at our plates, both really about as untouched as they could be, and didn't really feel like eating anything.

"You had enough of this place?" he asked.

I nodded.

"Come outside with me?"

"Yeah."

He shuffled around until he was out of the booth and then stood there for a second with his hand in his hair.

"Do you, um…need some help? I could push you…"

"No, I got it."

He followed me as I made my way around the other tables, trying to ignore the stares. I wasn't sure if my perception was accurate, but I felt as if they all knew exactly who I was. All the people there knew what I used to be.

Gardner ran around me to open the door. Once we were outside, he lit up.

"Do you…um…smoke?"

"Nah," I replied. "I used to, sometimes. Nicole would kill me."

"Gotcha." He took a long drag and started to pace a little. "I didn't…I…shit."

I kept looking down at my hands. Eventually he stopped in front of me and bent at the knees so he could look up at me.

"Thomas…I had no idea."

I shrugged.

"No one did," I said. "It's okay."

"It's not!" he said then sighed and ran his free hand through his hair again. "I should have…I should have pushed. I should have just come here. I wanted to—I did. I was just…Shit, Thomas! I was scared. I was such a pussy about all of it. I didn't even know about you, and then what he said—it made sense…at the time. Now…now…shit!"

He took another drag and tossed the butt into the street.

"If I had known…if I had gotten ahold of you, you could have told me—I would have come for you."

"I wouldn't have told you," I said.

"I might have…might have seen the signs."

"I would have denied it," I told him, finally meeting his eyes. "No one knew. I passed it off as soccer injuries. Tape up my ribs—go on with it. No one knew."

"Tape up your…? Holy fucking shit!" Gardner stood up, nearly ripped his hair out, and then lit up another cigarette. He was really making me want one. "He broke your…ugh!"

He threw his cigarette out into the street and dropped down beside my chair again. A couple of people looked at us sideways as they came out of the restaurant.

"Fucking idiot…" Gardner was mumbling under his breath. "Should have fucking noticed something. Should have come here…should have…done something. Anything. Too fucking selfish."

He looked up at me, his eyes flaming.

"God, Thomas—I'm so sorry."

"You don't have to apologize," I told him. "You didn't do it."

"Yeah," he barked out a laugh. "I didn't do it. I didn't do jack shit."

He lit up another one.

"I was so fucking selfish," he said after a minute of hot-boxing the smoke. "I was almost relieved when he said I couldn't see you. I don't know how to be a father…I thought maybe it was best. I mean…sometimes I thought it was best not to be in your life."

He looked back to me.

"I'm sorry, Thomas." He reached out and touched the arm of my chair. "Really fucking sorry. I should have been here. I should have been here for you as soon as I knew."

I didn't know what to say to him. Would it have made any difference? Would I have ever told him anything? No. Not a chance. Before Nicole, I had never told a fucking soul, and there's no way I would have told him.

"I never would have said anything," I told him again. "Lou Malone was an upstanding citizen. No one would have believed any of it."

"I would have," he said quietly. "I would have done something. Fuck, right now I want to dig him up and beat his fucking corpse."

I chuckled and then stopped myself. It wasn't funny…well, it kind of was.

"I'm serious," he told me.

"I know," I replied. "I feel like doing it myself."

We sat in silence again, him smoking while I just tried to make the whole conversation fit into my brain. It was so much all at once, and I wasn't sure if I was ready to hear it.

"Do you want me to grab your lunch?" he asked.

"Not really hungry," I replied.

"I'll go pay the bill."

"I can get it." I started to maneuver back toward the door, but he stopped me.

"I got it," he said as he walked through the door.

I sighed, knowing I couldn't have caught up with him anyway. Instead, I tried to process all this information. He wanted to see me, which was something, at least. He wanted to beat up my dad, which made me feel a little better, but I wasn't sure where that left us now.

My dad was dead, and I had just met my father. That shit was fucked up by anyone's standards. I guess I'd just have to figure out a way to sort it all out.

Gardner came back out, and we ended up on a bench at the park across the street. Well, Gardner was on the bench. I just moved myself next to it. I could see the bookstore where Nicole was hanging out from where I sat, and I wondered if she even knew how long she had been in there.

"So, where do we go from here?" Gardner asked.

"I don't know," I said with a shrug. "I'm kind of living in the moment right now, really."

"Yeah, I can understand that," he replied. He turned toward me. "Can I help you in some way? I mean, do you still have insurance for rehab? I should be able to put you on my insurance though we might have to have a paternity test first. Did you want to have a paternity test? Fuck...I'm babbling..."

I chuckled into my hand, trying to pass it off as a cough. He *was* babbling. I was discovering that my biological father babbled a lot, and I realized it was something I did as well.

"I'm sorry," he said quietly. "I really don't know how to do this. I don't have any…any *other* kids. I've never been married. I haven't even been in a serious relationship for over a year. I do want to help you, though. I, um…I don't have a lot of money, but I should be able to help out with the rehab bills, and—"

"No," I cut him off. "Don't."

He looked over to me.

"I'm not trying to buy you," he said. "I just want to make sure if you need anything, you know you can come to me. I wasn't around before, and I really regret that now. I don't make a lot of money by any means, but I'm comfortable enough. If I can help you, I will."

"My inheritance is pretty big," I admitted.

"Oh…yeah…" he babbled. "I guess that's probably true, isn't it? I mean, doctor and all. What about the house?"

"I don't know," I said with a shrug. "I don't really want to go back there."

"Is that where he…um…"

"Yeah."

"That makes sense, then." His leg bounced up and down as he pulled out another cigarette. I wondered if he was always a chain smoker or if it was just because of me.

"Do I make you nervous?" I asked.

He let out a short laugh.

"Yeah, definitely."

"'Cause of the chair?"

"No." He shook his head. "I've got a colleague in my building at the university who's been in a wheelchair all her life. We used to share an office, so I'm kind of used to that."

"What, then?"

"Um...guilt?" He gave me a lame half-smile, which he dropped pretty quickly. "I keep thinking about what I should have done. Starting with Fran, I should have at least made sure she made it back here okay. Maybe she would have told me if I had called her. Then I should have insisted on getting to know you, or at least...I dunno...maybe hired a private investigator to check on you...Shit like that just keeps popping into my head. You're... you're my kid, and someone was hurting you. It just...makes me feel sick. I should have done something, and I didn't—hence the guilt."

He flicked ash into the wind and sighed.

"With all of that, and you being so quiet, I'm trying to figure out just how much you hate me."

"I don't," I told him. "I don't hate you. I don't...I don't even *know* you. I'm just trying to figure all this shit out, you know?"

He nodded and finished his cigarette.

"You're a pretty smart kid, aren't you?" he said.

I only shrugged in response.

"So, um..." He coughed into his hand a couple times. He took a deep breath. "Do I, um, get a chance, then? I mean, with you? I'm not going to push—I swear I won't—but I'd like to...to have something with you. Whatever you're up for."

"I guess so," I replied. Everything he said was swirling around in my head again. He really seemed like a pretty good guy, and I didn't think he was feeding me any bullshit. What would it hurt? "Yeah, okay...um...What did you have in mind?"

"I have to go back to Chicago after this weekend," he said. "I could probably make it back here about once a month or so. You could come out to Chicago any time you want. I have a ranch house over in Evanston, so no stairs. I've got a guest room, and there's a great view of Lake Michigan."

I hadn't really thought about traveling at all. How would I even get on a plane? It's not like a wheelchair would fit through those tiny aisles. That would be a damn long drive, though if Nicole went with me…

"Maybe," I finally said.

"Maybe?"

"I mean, maybe to Chicago. The other stuff would be okay."

"It would?"

"Yeah." I looked up at him, and for the first time since I met him for lunch, he was smiling.

"Thanks, Thomas," he said.

"You're welcome," I replied. "So, um, what should I call you?"

His forehead scrunched up.

"Um, what do you want to call me?"

"I don't know," I admitted. "I always called…um…Lou, *Dad*. I don't really want to call anyone else that."

"I'm not so sure I'd be completely comfortable with that, either," he admitted.

"I've been just calling you Gardner in my head," I told him.

He laughed.

"Well, no one's really called me that since I played in the band, but that would be okay with me."

"Cool," I said. I reached out and shook his hand. "Gardner it is."

Shortly after that, I had pretty much had enough of sitting in the fucking wheelchair and gave Nicole a call to tell her where we were. She came out to find us laughing since Gardner had been telling me about his co-worker going off on a construction guy who had taken her handicapped parking spot and how she just about had the poor guy in tears.

"I take it things are going well here," Nicole said as she approached.

Gardner and I glanced at each other, chuckled, and ran our hands through our hair. Nicole blinked a couple of times as she looked back and forth between us.

"O…kay. That was a little freaky." She took a step away from us. She shook her head and asked if I was ready to go. Gardner followed us back to the Jeep, and after I got situated in the passenger seat, he leaned in toward me, holding the top of the door.

"Hey, Thomas?"

"Yeah?"

"I'll be back in four weeks, okay?"

"Yeah, that'll be good," I told him.

"You can call me anytime you want," he reminded me again, "and if it's okay, I'll call you sometimes."

"I said it was." I rolled my eyes. He seemed to think I was going to change my mind and tell him to fuck off.

"Cool!" He stood back up and closed the door.

Nicole and I both waved, but as she started the car, he knocked on my window. I rolled it down for him.

"Would you do something for me?" Gardner asked me.

"What is it?"

"Before I come back, would you, um, maybe think about doing a few sketches? I'd really like to see them."

My heart started pounding in my chest a little as I looked down to my hands in my lap. I just stared at them and thought about all the times I tried to show my drawings to Dad. While I lost myself, Nicole covered my hand with hers to get my attention.

"Thomas?"

I looked over to her and then back up at Gardner.

"Yeah," I finally said, "I can do that."

He smiled and nodded before backing away from the car so Nicole could pull out and take us home. We drove in relative silence though I did tell her about the inheritance money and what Gardner had told me about my mother. She freaked out a little over the money thing but not as much as I thought she would. Mostly, my mind kept coming back to sketching, and I wondered if I'd really have the nerve to show Gardner anything I had drawn. I just wasn't sure though I did feel pretty relaxed after talking to him for a while.

Nicole got us back home, and she and Greg started going over their plans for the rest of the week, which mostly involved Greg working nights so Nicole could go to school. They didn't want me left alone though I told them I didn't need a fucking babysitter. Regardless, they were talking about doing all this shit that was going to cost a lot of money, and I was about as pissed off as I could be about the whole thing. I knew I was going to have to change the arrangement, and they were both going to be really, really pissed.

I was pissed, too.

Except, when I wheeled myself out of the kitchen and went to my tiny not-quite-a-room, I still had this smile on my face that wouldn't go away. Everything was clicking with me, and I knew this was exactly how families were supposed to act. Between Nicole and Greg, I still had as much family as I had ever had before.

I had the feeling Gardner would someday feel like family to me, too. Shakespeare once said, "One touch of nature makes the whole world kin," and I couldn't argue with that.

But first, it was time to face some harsh realities.

I asked Nicole and Greg both to come into the living room to talk to me after dinner. Greg was in his chair, and Nicole was sitting on the couch. I sat in my wheelchair between them.

"What do you mean, you're leaving?" Nicole asked.

I kind of figured this was going to be her reaction.

"I talked to Danielle this morning," I told Nicole. "It makes sense for me to go back to the rehab center for a while. You and Greg shouldn't have to look after me so much. He's got work, and you have school—"

"That's bullshit! I want to do it, Thomas!"

She was getting choked up, like I figured she would, but there just wasn't any easy way to bring this up.

"I…I know you do…" I stammered. I looked over to Greg, honestly hoping he'd see reason here.

He shook his head at me.

"You don't have to go anywhere," he said. "We can get you to rehab when you need to go, and—"

"No, Greg," I said. "I have to…to do whatever I can to recover as much as possible. I need to figure out what my life is like now, who I am, who I want to be…and I can't do that here. You know I appreciate what you've done, but I'll make more progress at the center."

"Danielle can come here," Nicole said.

"Rumple, baby," I sighed and ran my hand through my hair. "There isn't enough room here for all the equipment."

"What about…at your house?"

"I don't want to go back there," I said quietly. "I think I might just want to sell it."

"Then sell it!" she cried. "But that doesn't mean you have to leave! I just got you back, dammit!"

"Nicole—" Greg and I said in unison.

I let him continue.

"It sounds to me like Thomas has thought this through," he said to her.

"No!" Nicole stood up and took a step toward him. "He's not leaving! What if…what if that other therapist comes back, huh?"

"We're still looking for him," Greg reminded her.

Steven had apparently skipped town, maybe even the country. No one had heard from him since the day Dad shot himself. Greg had some feds trying to look for him in LA, where he had lived before coming to town, but no one had been able to find him. Once Dad's suicide and the "alternate medications" Steven had used on me were discovered, he just disappeared. The feds seemed to think he was afraid of having charges pressed and fled.

"He's not going to come back to the rehab center," I told her.

"You don't know that!"

"Look," Greg said as he stood up from his chair. He put a hand on Nicole's shoulder and guided her back to the couch. "I'm gonna go and let you two work this out. I've got some paperwork crap to do at the station, and I'll be back in a couple of hours."

So much for having my back.

Nicole put her face back in her hands as Greg got his shit together and left the house. I wheeled over as close as I could get to her without running over her foot and reached out to put my hand on her leg.

"Why are you leaving me?" she whispered through tears.

"I'm not, Rumple. I swear." I took a deep breath. "I'm doing this for you as much as for me. If there is any possibility that I might walk again, I have to go back there and work on it. I can't do that here. You haven't been back to school since the funeral, and I know you want to…to take care of me, but I have to learn to take care of myself."

"No, you don't," she said. "I'll do it. You…you saved me, and I want to…"

"I know you do," I said. I tried to hold back my own tears as she got off of the couch and crawled into my lap. I held on to her as she wrapped her arms around my head.

"I don't want you to go."

"I know," I told her. "I don't want to go, but I have to. I have to do it for both of us."

I held her. She cried. I cried. Eventually, we crawled into my bed together. We didn't get kinky or anything, just held on to each other for the longest time. We talked more about how she would still come up to the center to see me as often as she could as well as to bring me my assignments so I could finish school on time. I'd have sessions with Danielle and Justin and work my own shit out so I could be here for her when I got back out.

It wasn't what my heart wanted, but in my head, I knew it was the right thing to do.

"Rumple?" I whispered into her hair. I was half afraid she had fallen asleep. It was getting late, and Greg hadn't come home yet.

"Hmm?"

"I don't know how long I'll have to stay there," I admitted. "If I...if I'm there too long...I mean...would you...you know...wait for me?"

She turned her head up to look me in the eye.

"I can't believe you would even ask that," she replied.

I shrugged.

"You wouldn't have to," I said softly. "But...if you did..."

"I would," she said. "I will. You know I will—for as long as it takes."

I closed my eyes and sighed. I didn't realize how tense the thought made me until my body relaxed after hearing her words.

"Thank you," I said. "Because I'm pretty sure even if I do walk again, I'm still going to need you."

"Anything," she replied as she placed her lips against mine.

If nothing else, Shakespeare taught me "tis not enough to help the feeble up, but to support him after." Somehow, I knew Nicole would have plenty of opportunities to help me in the future.

Now I had to, as it were, stand on my own two feet.

CHAPTER THIRTY-FOUR
three points

"This is fucking *bullshit!*"

At that moment, I would have done just about anything to be able to jump up out of my chair and slam my fist through the wall of Justin's office at the rehab center. Instead, I only sat there with my hands balled into fists against my eyes.

As it seemed to do these days, my anger at *him*—Lou, my *Dad* —turned back inside of me and came out in tears.

I fucking hated it.

I looked up at Justin, who was sitting in the chair across from me, leaning back in the seat and making the front legs come off the floor a little. He never had a notebook or a clipboard or anything with him when we talked, and I always wondered a little if he just remembered it all or if he wrote it down afterwards.

Sometimes I hated him, too.

I wiped the back of my hand across my face and grabbed one of the tissues out of the box Justin kept on the table. Once I had wiped my eyes and nose, I crushed the tissue into a little wet ball inside my closed fist.

"I hate him," I said when I calmed down.

"That's not the problem," Justin reminded me.

I looked at him again, and I knew exactly what he meant.

"I love him, too."

"Yes, you do."

"And that's bullshit," I snapped back. "How can I feel both? He beat me and made me feel like shit. I never did anything right. I shouldn't love that shit."

"He still raised you," Justin said. "He did a crap job of it, but you still had a connection."

"It wasn't even real," I said. "He wasn't my father."

"How is Gardner? You still talk to him every day?"

"Not every day," I said. "Most days. He wants me to come out there."

"What do you think of that?"

"I don't want to until I can get on a plane," I said.

"You could do that now."

"I don't want to fuck around in an airport in this chair."

"So is this something I should add to your goal list? Get on a plane to Chicago and visit Gardner?"

"Yeah, I guess."

"Will do," Justin said as he stood up. "And on that note, it's about time for your PT. Nicole coming today?"

"She got a job at the library in town," I said. "She'll be running a little late, but she'll be here."

"Tell her I said hi."

"Sure."

I rolled out of Justin's office and down the hallway to the elevator. I glanced at the stairwell—another bullet point on my goal list—and pushed the down button. I was only seeing Justin once a week now, which I guess was supposed to be progress. Some days I felt like I was getting somewhere—like I could almost forgive Dad for treating me the way he did—and other days I still wanted to take Gardner up on his offer to pile a bunch of pictures and shit that belonged to Lou Malone and burn it all in a big-ass bonfire.

Nicole was up for that, too.

An hour and a half later, I was holding myself up by my arms with sweat pouring into my eyes and Danielle chanting encouragement at me from one side of the parallel bars. I kind of wanted to punch her, too. Just like the conflicting feelings I had about my dad, some days I loved my physical therapist, and some days I hated her.

My legs burned.

It was a weird sensation. I could feel them just fine, and some of the muscle tone was back. It was just the motor control that seemed to be missing. I could push with my feet and lift weights if I was sitting, but holding up my own body weight was a whole different thing. My legs just didn't seem to have the coordination to both hold me up and move me forward at the same time.

I could take a couple of steps at a time and had been able to for a month. I just couldn't seem to make any more progress.

"Come on, Thomas!" Danielle said. "One more step! Push!"

"I'm not having a fucking baby!" I bellowed at her.

I really don't know how that woman puts up with her patients. She says I'm not even the worst.

"Don't give me that! Concentrate!"

"You can do it, baby."

I looked up and saw Nicole at the end of the row of bars. I hadn't heard her come in. She had a big smile on her face and looked so fucking beautiful I wanted to run the six feet it would have taken to get to her just to wrap my arms around her.

Instead, I focused on moving one foot just a few inches in front of the other one.

More burning in my thighs and my left calf—like I was running a fucking marathon or something. More sweat in my eyes, and my lungs felt like they were going to go all *Alien* on me and pop out some nasty little critter.

I stopped and put my weight back on my arms.

"I can't do any more."

"We're not done yet," Danielle told me.

If I hadn't been holding myself up with my arms at that point,

I just might have slugged her.

"I'm fucking done, okay?" I yelled back.

"Ten more minutes," she insisted. "Then you can take a break and hang out with Nicole."

"Fuck you!"

"Ten minutes!"

"Danielle," Nicole called out, "may I take over?"

Danielle smiled and laughed softly.

"Be my guest," she replied. "Ten more minutes."

"Fuck you both," I mumbled. Nicole was a worse slave driver than Danielle.

"Only if you reach me," Nicole said coyly, and my head jerked up to where she was standing.

I hadn't really paid any attention when she came in, but she was wearing one of those tight fitting V-neck sweaters that showed a lot of cleavage. Her hair was over her shoulders and down her back, and she was using one finger to slide down the V-shape and over the rise of her breast.

"Fuck me hard," I mumbled.

"Come and get it," she suggested.

My foot almost moved without me asking it to.

The burning was still there, but watching Nicole's fingertips as they ran over her skin had me in a fucking trance or something. We hadn't had sex in over a week—since she stayed over last Friday night in my room at the center—and now she was practically fondling herself right out here in the open. My right foot slid slowly over the floor.

"Not so much weight on your arms," Nicole reminded me. She wasn't any easier to fool than Danielle was.

I scowled but released my death grip on the bar.

More sweat in my eyes.

More itching and burning in the muscles of my legs.

My hips started to ache.

My left foot managed to actually rise off the ground to move forward.

"Shit," I mumbled then looked up at Nicole. It fucking hurt. "I can't anymore…"

"Yes, you can, baby," she said. "I know you can. Come on now!"

Then she pulled her sweater out, away from her tits, and looked down into her own shirt.

"They're just over here waiting for you, you know."

"Fuck…you don't play fair…"

She cupped herself, and the sweat pouring down my face probably mixed with drool.

Another step.

I fumbled but grabbed onto the bar and managed not to fall over.

Another step, and I could see down into her shirt a bit as she leaned over. She stuck her finger between her cleavage, and I groaned.

"Three more steps, baby," she whispered.

I closed my eyes for a second and tried to stop panting. My legs hurt, my feet hurt—my whole lower body fucking hurt. I pushed on anyway.

Left foot.

Right foot.

Lunge.

I grabbed onto Nicole as I pushed myself forward one last time, ended up grabbing onto her, and we both fell onto the mat. My heart was pounding in my chest, and I could hardly breathe, but I did make it to the end of the bars.

"You did it!" Nicole screeched.

She was laughing and crying all at the same time. Her arms wrapped around my head, and I couldn't decide if I wanted drugs to make me pass out or if I wanted to rip her sweater off and suck on her tits.

I did stick my face between them and give her a good motor-boating.

Shakespeare told us, "Our remedies oft in ourselves do lie,

which we ascribe to heaven." Somehow, I was pretty sure my heaven was right below me, laughing and kissing the sweat off my face.

Now maybe this remedy would stick.

"Oh…yeah…baby…"

"That's it…" Nicole panted into my neck. "Fuck me back...fuck me back!"

According to the Divinyls, there is a fine, fine line between pleasure and pain. Pushing up with my hips and using my heels for leverage was kind of like that. My cock felt so fucking good in her; it overrode whatever twinges I felt in my legs.

"You like riding my cock?" I hummed into Nicole's ear. "You like it, don't cha?"

I grazed my teeth over the skin of her throat, and she shivered above me. I was still very gentle, though. My Rumple liked the illusion of getting it rough, but she wasn't into any kinky shit at all.

"Fuck me harder!"

Well, she did still say that kind of shit.

I loved it.

"That what you want, baby?" I asked, pushing up against her with as much strength as I could. I gripped her hips with my hands and pulled her down to meet me as she groaned and ground down, pushing me deep inside of her. "Yeah, that's what you want…my cock sliding in and out of you…You love it, don't cha?"

"Oh, God…Thomas…"

"That's it…" I strained to push up against her, but I was losing strength. I went back to using my hands to pull her down instead. She leaned forward and moaned loudly as I felt her pussy clamping down on me. "Oh yeah! Come on my cock! Come all over me!"

"Thomas!" she gasped as she collapsed on my chest. I lifted her up and down a couple more times before I lost it, growling and groaning as I came deep inside of her.

"Holy shit," I moaned as my head dropped back down on the

pillow.

Nicole giggled.

"You're gonna kill me," I told her.

"You love it," she replied.

"I love you."

She raised her head up and pecked my lips.

"Love you more."

"Not a chance."

We just lay there trying to catch our breath for a while as my dick softened and eventually slipped out despite her protests. She liked it when I stayed inside of her afterwards. I wasn't about to argue.

My heart rate returned to normal, and I tucked my face against the top of her head, inhaling the scent of her hair and smiling to myself. I ran my hand up and down her back a couple of times... and dozed off.

"Thomas? Baby?"

"Hmm?" I blinked a couple of times, realizing I had fallen asleep.

"I gotta go," Nicole said.

"Already?" I whined.

"Yeah...sorry."

Nicole came to the center as often as possible after high school graduation, through the summer, and even after she enrolled in community college on a soccer scholarship. Between my rehab and her schooling, we kept ourselves occupied between visits, but I lived for the times we were together.

Rumple did too.

I hugged her tight against my chest and then released her. I knew she had to get back to town in decent time today since she had classes in the afternoon. She wouldn't keep her soccer scholarship if she didn't show up for practices.

"When can you get back?" I asked as she started gathering her clothes off the floor. She tossed me my boxers and T-shirt, and I pulled them on.

"There's a game this weekend," she told me. "First one of the season. Greg said he'd pick you up and take you, if you want."

"If I want?" I snorted. "Wouldn't miss it for anything."

She pulled her shirt over her head and looked at me.

"Are you sure?" she asked quietly. "I mean…if it makes you… uncomfortable, I understand. You aren't obligated to go."

"Rumple…" I sat up and pushed myself back against the head of the bed. "I mean…it's a little weird, and I can't say it doesn't… well, make me miss it…but it's not all about me. I want to see you play. I've never seen you play in an actual game, ya know."

I smiled, hoping she believed me.

"I know," she said with a shrug. "I just don't want you to feel bad. It should be you…"

"Bullshit," I replied. "I'm going to walk again—Danielle even said I would. It'll probably be another couple of months, but I will walk. I'm not going to be able to play again…not like I did. I know that. I've accepted it."

"I know you say that," she said as she walked back over to the bed and took my hand in hers, "but I also know it still has to get you down."

I shrugged.

"Sometimes," I admitted. "But I also know that despite what my dad always said, it's not my whole life. I hope I'll be able to…I dunno, at least run around and kick a ball again sometime, but if I don't, I'll live with it. Maybe I'll coach or something. If I weren't like this, I wouldn't have you. Losing soccer is pretty fucking minor compared to that."

Nicole reached over and placed her hands on my cheeks and kissed me softly.

"My hero," she said quietly as she pulled away. I wasn't having any of that, though, and dragged her back to me, kissing her deeper on her mouth before nibbling up her jaw.

"Hear my soul speak. Of the very instant that I saw you, did my heart fly at your service."

"Smooth talker." She giggled as she pulled away again. "See

you Saturday, then?"

"I'll be there."

"Love you," she said as she headed out the door.

"Love you more."

"Not a chance."

I snickered and lay back against the pillows, still smiling and still surrounded by her scent.

I knew I would never, ever regret how I ended up the way I did. I just needed to figure out exactly what I was going to do with my life now.

———◆◆◆◆◆———

I placed the walker a few inches in front of me and shuffled my feet behind it.

I had just barely gotten used to the thing at all, and now that there was snow on the ground, I was completely paranoid about falling. Nicole and Greg were both hovering, and though in the back of my head I knew they just wanted to make sure the walker didn't slip out from under me and send me flying down the driveway, part of me was still feeling claustrophobic and generally pissy.

"I put salt on the ramp," Greg said for the tenth time. "I'll make sure there aren't any slick spots."

I tried not to sigh out loud as Gardner gave me a big grin.

"Got enough fathers in your life now?" he asked.

I just sighed and looked toward the ramp.

It was supposed to be a happy homecoming after all, but I was still insanely nervous. I had grown comfortable during the six-plus months I had spent in the rehab center, and though I had been back to Nicole and Greg's house a dozen times between then and now, this was different.

I was here to stay.

Well, somewhat.

The house I had shared with Lou Malone never sold. I guess when someone kills himself in a place, word gets around, and even though I'd dropped the price on it three times, I hadn't had a single offer. Justin made the original suggestion, and Nicole seemed to like it as well, so the place was going to be torn down and a new house built there instead.

It would be a house that I hoped Nicole and I would share when she was done with college.

I managed to get up the ramp with the walker about an hour and a half later. All right, it wasn't really that long, but sometimes I still missed the wheelchair. It was a hell of a lot faster. Nicole scooted around me, claiming she needed to get dinner in the oven so it would be ready on time. I loved her enchiladas and had gone on about them to Gardner until Nicole told me to shut up about it. She said it with a smile on her face, though.

"Where do you want all this?" Gardner asked as he held up my duffel bag.

"Over there, I guess," I replied. I pointed over to the sectioned-off part of the living room that still had everything ready for me. He helped me unpack while Nicole fucked around in the kitchen, and with a beer, Greg made himself comfortable in his recliner.

"I like these," Gardner said as he flipped through my latest sketchbook. "The detail you capture is incredible."

"Thanks," I mumbled. I still didn't like hearing people talk about my drawing, especially an art professor. I just couldn't get used to it.

"Do you still see everything so clearly in your head?"

"The old stuff, yeah," I admitted. "I still remember everything before the accident completely, and when I think about it, I can remember almost everything else, too. It's just not as…as overwhelming as it used to be."

"These are particularly detailed," he said.

I looked over and saw the drawings I had done of Nicole at her games. I could draw her legs for hours without getting tired of the activity. There were other sketches of her, but they were in another book that I never shared with anyone.

"She's particularly interesting to look at," I grinned.

"I see that," he said, and he smiled back at me. "Are you going to reconsider letting me show these off? You know, I put that one you gave me up in my office. Several people have commented on it."

"You weren't supposed to display it!" I said with a scowl.

"You told me to do whatever I wanted with it," Gardner reminded me, "so I framed it and put it in my office. I never had the opportunity to…well, you know. Lots of professors have their kids' artwork up on their walls. It made sense to me, but…I can take it down if you want."

I took a deep breath and looked up at him. I could tell by his expression that he wanted it to stay where it was. I finally just shook my head.

"Leave it there," I grumbled.

"So…what about the other stuff?"

"Who would you show it to?"

"Well, the person who showed the most interest was actually from around here," he told me. "Her name is Kathrine, and she runs a gallery in Chicago, but she has one in Portland as well. She's heard of you."

"How has she heard of me?"

"You were in a lot of articles last year."

"Oh…yeah, I guess."

Local soccer star saves girl, loses ability to walk.

It had been all over the place.

"When she put the pieces together and figured out you were, um, my son…"

He trailed off.

It had only been a month ago when I finally went to Chicago to visit him, and he had almost had an anxiety attack over how to introduce me. After I told him to tell people how it was—he was my father, but I had been raised by my mom and step-father—Gardner practically had a melt-down, even started crying, which freaked me out a little. Once I figured out they were "happy tears," I calmed down, but it was still weird. He took me all over campus at my usual snail's pace, introducing me to everyone as his son.

"It still feels weird to tell people that," he said. "I love it, but it's weird."

"I know."

We worked in silence for a bit, me propped up next to the dresser and putting clothes away while Gardner organized my sketching materials on the nightstand.

"Oh shit!" he suddenly exclaimed. "I forgot something!"

He dashed out of the house and came back a minute later with a tackle box. Greg's eyes went wide.

"You want to do some fishing?" he asked.

"Um…no…" Gardner brought the tackle box over to my bed and opened it. It was full of pencils, pastels, paintbrushes, and acrylic paints. "This is for you. I like keeping my drawing stuff in a tackle box—it just makes it easy to organize. I have some canvas and an easel back in my hotel room for you since you said you'd like to give painting a try."

"Damn." I whistled as I looked through all the supplies. "Thanks! Maybe this way I won't drive Greg too nuts when Nicole goes back to school."

"Yes, you will," Greg replied. "You always drive me nuts. Just next time you and Nicole are having one of your 'moments' in the bathroom, give me some damn warning!"

"Dad!" Nicole screamed from the kitchen. "You swore you were never going to mention that again!"

The lock on my bathroom door at the rehab center didn't work. Greg thought we were down in the exercise room or something and…um…walked in on Nicole and me in the shower. Right as he opened the door to take a piss, Nicole was yelling out something a little on the colorful side.

He chuckled and covered his eyes.

"Sorry," he said, "but I think I was scarred for life."

"Tell me about it," Nicole grumbled in response. "Dinner in ten!"

"Um…well…" Gardner babbled as he turned red and tried to

divert the conversation. "Um…so anyway…I was talking to Kathrine, and she'd like to see more of your work. I think she might even be thinking about showing it in her gallery. What would you think of that?"

"I'd think no fucking way," I responded.

"Thomas…"

"Don't give me that," I snapped. "I told you before…it's just a hobby."

Gardner sat on the edge of my bed and stared at me. It still made me feel all funky when he did that—it was too much like looking in the mirror.

"It doesn't have to be a hobby," he said—*again*. "You have talent—a lot of it. I'd like to think it came from me, but you are far better than I, despite my PhD in art, and you haven't had any formal training at all."

"I'm not going to move to Chicago," I told him, because I knew that's where this was going—*again*. "Nicole's here. Greg's here. When Nicole graduates, it's not like she's going to be able to do marine biology in Chicago."

Gardner sighed and ran his hand through his hair. I mentally stopped my hand from doing the same.

"What if…what if you went to school here, too?" he asked.

"What? For art?"

"Yes."

I frowned. I hadn't really thought about it too much.

"I have an offer," Gardner said.

"What are you offering?" I asked.

"No, no," he corrected, "that's not what I meant. I mean I have received an offer—to come and teach at the community college. You'd get free tuition with me there, and you'd be close to Nicole."

"Are you crazy?" I asked him. "You didn't tell me anything about that."

"I didn't want to say anything until I had the actual offer," he said with a shrug. "I just got it last week."

"You're going to leave Chicago Art Institute to teach at a community college? Really?"

"Yeah, I think I might."

"Gardner, that's nuts."

"Why?"

"You already have a great position at a great art school. Why would you trade down? That doesn't make any sense!"

He looked down at his hands in his lap for a minute and shrugged again.

"I'm just getting to know you," he finally said. "I know you don't want to move, and I understand your reasons—they're valid reasons. I want to be part of your life. If I have to change jobs to do that..."

My chest clamped up on me, and I had to sit down. I had no idea how I was supposed to react to this news. He was going to move all the way from Chicago just to be closer to me? Why would he do that?

"I don't understand," I finally said.

"I just...I..." He stopped and started fucking around with his hair again. He finally took a deep breath and blew it out. "You don't want me to."

My chest felt heavy again.

"That's not what I meant," I said. "I just don't understand why you'd give that up."

He turned his eyes to me again, and they were warm under dark brows that knitted together.

"I already missed so much of your life," he said quietly. "I don't want to miss anything else."

I still had no idea how to react. Thoughts of my dad—Lou—went through my head as I tried to think of something he had ever done that even came close to this. Though he had constantly reminded me of how much he had sacrificed for me, none of it compared—not even close.

"You don't have to do that," I finally said.

"I know I don't have to," he responded. He stood up then and walked around to the other side of the bed where I was sitting. He dropped down next to me before speaking again. "I want to do this, Thomas. I want to be closer to you. This way you wouldn't have to deal with a plane again—I know how much you hated that—and I'd be able to see you a lot more often. I want to get to know you better. Nicole, too."

I looked into his eyes, and there was no doubt about his sincerity. His mouth turned up into a familiar, lopsided grin.

"Speaking of Nicole…did you ask her yet?"

"Not yet," I admitted, and my face felt hot. "I don't know how to bring it up."

"I don't think I'd be much help in that department," Gardner said. "Just ask?"

"I haven't had a minute alone with her yet."

"Judging from the way you two are, I can't imagine she would say no."

"But she might," I said quietly. I quickly glanced toward the kitchen, but I couldn't see her. I could hear the sounds of plates and silverware being placed on the table. "I'm not sure how I'd handle that. She told me how her mom often says marriage shouldn't happen before you are thirty or something."

"Nicole isn't her mom."

"True."

We didn't say anything for a minute, and I just stared down at my hand, which covered the pocket containing a small, black satin box.

"So…you're okay with me moving closer?" Gardner asked.

"Yeah," I said. "That would be great."

"Will you consider going to the same school for art?"

"I'll think about it."

"Good." His hand touched my arm, and I looked up at him just as he wrapped his arms around my shoulders and hugged me to him. I hugged him back, trying to sort out all the emotions running through my head.

Gardner's voice became soft.

"I love you, son."

"I…I love you, too, Gardner."

His words had touched me more deeply than I ever would have imagined.

I guess now I'll become an art major.

"Will you marry me?"

Fourteenth time's the charm, right?

"No."

I sighed and pulled Rumple close to my chest. I guess post-coital proposals didn't work, either.

The first time I had asked, she thought I was joking. I kind of played it off that way, too, not wanting her to know how serious I really was and how her saying no had torn at my heart. I knew we were too young, but I still wanted to…I don't know, stake a claim? We were already living together off campus, so what the hell was the big deal about a piece of paper?

Her hand ran over my stomach, causing me to shiver a little and my cock to twitch. Little bastard never got enough of her, it seemed. She didn't mind though. If anything, she was ready to have another go before I was. Not today though, because Greg and Gardner were coming to take us out to dinner and celebrate.

Nicole honestly thought it was weird, but I wanted to celebrate having saved her life exactly one year ago today. She saw it as the day I got hurt, but to me, the important part was all about her being okay. Besides, I was walking again, even if I did still have to use a cane to keep my balance.

I hated the fucking walker so much, I nearly hurt myself pushing the PT and ended up in the hospital for a weekend. Danielle tore me a new one and put me on a very strict regimen after that. No more pushing myself into exercises my body wasn't ready to tackle.

Nicole made sure I only did what I was allowed to do.

"Why do you keep asking?"

It was the first time she had even attempted to speak about it after I asked. Usually she just told me to stop it or shut up or something.

"I want to marry you," I said as I shrugged my shoulders. "I know there will never be anyone else who could ever compare to you. I don't see any reason to wait."

"What about school?"

"What about it?" I asked. "We're both here, and we'll both graduate. It'll take me a little longer since I got behind, but I thought I'd take some summer courses or something to make up for it. If I can, I'll still graduate with you."

"But...to be in school and be married, too? How is that going to work?"

"How will it be different from now?"

"People will think it's...weird," Nicole insisted. "Married at nineteen?"

She snorted.

"So we wait a little longer," I said. "I just..."

I stopped. After a minute, Nicole raised her head and looked up at me.

"Just what?" she asked.

I ran my hand through my hair and cringed a little. Seeing Gardner do it all the time made me self-conscious about it.

"Guys look at you all the time," I finally said. "When you're training and whatever—they're watching you, and I can't beat the shit out of them like I want to."

"Thomas! Don't be ridiculous."

"I'm not." I shook my head. "Every time I'm there, I hear other guys, other soccer players, talk about how good you are, and I just wish..."

I stopped again, looking away from her and over to the wall next to our bed. I felt her hand on my cheek, slowly turning me back to her.

"I'm yours," she said softly. "I don't care about those guys or what they say."

SHAY SAVAGE

"They can...they can do all this shit I can't..."

"Thomas Malone!" Nicole yelled, and I cringed against the pillow. "Don't you dare talk about yourself like that! You have made so much progress in the last few months, and I will not listen to you sell yourself short!"

"It's true!" I insisted. "They could run around a field and kick a ball around with you. They could hold your fucking books between classes instead of needing a damn cane to get around."

"Stop it!" she said. "Don't make me call Justin! He said if you started feeling sorry for yourself again, I could, you know!"

I took a deep breath and blew it out my nose. Most of the time, that kind of shit really didn't bother me, but when I saw those guys looking at her and talking about her, and I knew I no longer had what they had, it just about killed me.

"Sorry," I finally said. "It doesn't get to me that much, just... sometimes."

"I know," Nicole said as she sat up and tucked my hair behind my ear. "I don't like hearing you talk about yourself like that. Sorry I yelled."

"It's okay," I told her, and she placed a light kiss on my cheek. She kept her hand in my hair, twirling it around her fingers before tucking it around my ear.

"Does it really mean that much to you?" Nicole eventually asked.

"Getting married?" I clarified. She nodded. "If we were at least engaged...I mean, we wouldn't have to set a date or anything. If you just had my ring on your finger..."

My voice trailed off.

"Let me see it," Nicole said with a huff.

"See what?"

"The ring you think I don't know about."

Damn. I really couldn't hide much of anything from her.

"No," I said, scowling. "You don't want it."

"Don't make me get it myself, Thomas."

She pushed herself off of me and made a grand gesture with

468

her arm toward the other side of the room and my desk. My heart started beating faster, and I swung my legs to the side of the bed and carefully stood. My balance was still a serious problem, especially when I first stood up. I took the four steps across the room without the cane, though. My right leg, the one that had been gashed, did suffer some nerve damage and dragged behind a little.

I opened up the top drawer and reached into the back where I had been hiding the little black satin box. I brought it back over to the bed, stumbling a bit but not falling, at least. I hadn't actually fallen in a week. I balanced the box on Nicole's knee.

She looked at it as if a ref was going to pop out of it and red-card her.

After staring at it for an eternity or two, she finally reached out and ran her fingers over the smooth top. Her thumb played over the front edge for a moment before she popped it open, and her eyes went wide.

It wasn't huge or anything, but it was pretty decent-sized. There was a large diamond in the center with smaller ones on either side.

"Do you like it?" I asked softly.

"It's...it's beautiful," she breathed. Her fingers traced lightly over the center stone.

I placed my hand on the side of the bed and lowered myself down on my left knee.

"Nicole Skye," I said softly as I gazed up at her. "I promise I will always be yours. There will never be anyone else in my life but you. In my existence, I have never known anyone who has the capacity for love and compassion like you do, and you give them to me freely. You've made me a better person, and I love you so much, I can't even put it into words. Will you please, please be my wife?"

I watched her eyes widen, and then they seemed to glisten a little in the light from the bedside table lamp. Her throat bobbed as she swallowed, and I realized I was actually holding my breath. The silence in the room was starting to hurt my ears until she finally whispered the only word I wanted to hear.

"Yes."

My face started to hurt from my grin. Air finally filled my lungs again, and I reached out to take the ring from the box and slip it over her finger.

"Fuck, that looks good!" I murmured, and Nicole laughed. She wiggled her fingers around, and the light caught the diamonds.

"Feel like you've claimed me, don't you?"

"Fuck yes."

Using the bed for support, I pulled myself back up to stand and grabbed her face in my hands.

"My bounty is as boundless as the sea, my love as deep; the more I give to thee, the more I have, for both are infinite."

"I love you," Nicole whispered.

"I love you more," I told her and placed my lips against hers before she had the chance to argue the point.

Dinner was awesome. Greg turned six different colors when Nicole and I told him the news but finally relented and said he knew it would be coming sooner rather than later. Then he made Nicole call her mom and tell her the news. Like Nicole, Greg thought Yvette Skye would throw an absolutely fit, but they were both surprised when she didn't.

We spent the next hour arguing about who was going to pay for the wedding. That conversation ended when Nicole said if we didn't shut up about it, we'd be going to Vegas for the weekend.

Gardner just grinned and congratulated us.

That night, I drew a picture of Nicole's hand with the ring on her finger. It made her cry though she said they were happy tears. I held her, and we agreed to wait until we had graduated before we actually did the deed.

Words from Shakespeare I had never considered before found their way into my head: "When this ring parts from this finger, then parts life from hence." Somehow, just knowing it was there made all the difference to me.

Now I would be willing to wait.

"Are you okay?"

"No," I said. I laughed, but the sound was a lot of nervous and not much joyful. "Do I really have to be here?"

"It's rather customary," Gardner said with a nod. "They aren't just coming to see all this."

His hand swept around the gallery—the gallery belonging to his girlfriend, Kathrine. It was filled with my sketches, drawings, and even a couple of paintings. Painting was still a little new to me —I preferred black and white. The whole show was titled "Spiral," and it included images I painted from the memories of being trapped in my father's house.

The whole thing was kind of freaking me out.

I would graduate at the end of the summer, and this was supposed to help me get my foot in the door when it came to the art community. My first showing in May, graduation in August, and wedding in September. It was a wonder I hadn't pulled all my hair out.

Nicole just shrugged it all off, saying it would happen, perfectly or not, but it was all going to happen. Eventually it would be behind us, and we'll wonder why the heck we ever worried about it. Of course, that came from the woman who already had her diploma in hand as well as an offer from the Portland Aquarium.

I still had to graduate, and I had no job offers.

Nicole's "come what may" attitude sounded a lot like Justin. I didn't see him regularly anymore, but we still talked on the phone sometimes. He and Danielle were both supposed to come to the opening tonight.

"Relax," Gardner whispered. "We open in five."

"How can you say *relax*, follow up with five minutes, and expect me to actually calm down?"

He chuckled.

I glanced out the window at the line of people outside and started freaking out again.

"I can't do this!"

"Yes, you can," Gardner said sternly, "unless you don't want anyone to take your art seriously. If that's the case, and you want to go back into 'hobby mode,' you're going to have to change your major."

"I graduate in three months!"

"Well then, you'd better get yourself together!"

Warm arms wrapped around my middle, and as soon as her scent hit my nostrils, I could feel the rest of my body calm down. I felt Nicole's hands spread out along my stomach as she pulled me back into her and rested her cheek against my back.

"Have you come to kidnap me and save me from this?"

"Nope," Nicole said. "What happened to the guy who loved to be the center of attention?"

"Not the same," I said with a shake of my head.

It wasn't either. When I played soccer, people looked at my body and what my body could do. They focused on my hands as my fingers plucked balls out of the air or my feet as they pelted the muddy ground to fight for possession. When people looking at my drawings though—it just felt so...so *raw*. It was personal. Soccer was strictly external, and when people watched me play, they were just staring at my outsides, not seeing who I was.

Now they were all going to peek at what was inside of me.

"Are you sure I shouldn't take those two down?" I looked to Nicole in earnest, which meant I had to turn most of the way around and crane my neck to one side. She had talked me into putting them up, and though Greg had nearly choked out his beer, Gardner said they absolutely had to be included in the show even if they did feature Nicole's tits.

It didn't show her face or anything. No one would know who it was. Nicole even told Greg there were nude models at the university all the time, and it could be any of them. I think he decided to believe her lies even though it was pretty damn obvious exactly who it was.

Well, I thought so, anyway.

"Of course not," Nicole said. I turned my head back to glare at

Gardner for talking me into all of this, and Nicole held me a little tighter, placing her chin on my shoulder. "Everyone is going to love all of your work. Those are two of your best."

"I'm not selling them," I said for the hundredth time.

"You can put them up in the piano room at home after the show is over."

"Okay."

Her presence relaxed me a little, and when Kathrine opened up the gallery doors, I managed not to run and hide in the bathroom.

Well, not exactly.

A back door led to the alley behind the building, and I did go and hide out there for a little while when the people and the questions became too much. By then, I had already gone through three rounds of media interviews, asking more about the accident and my father's suicide rather than art, but Kathrine said whatever got my name out there would help.

Greg was already outside. When I opened the door, he coughed and hid his hand behind his back.

"Oh...um...Thomas! How's it going in there?"

"Don't bullshit me," I snapped. "Give me one of those."

He narrowed his eyes, and I glared right back at him until he pulled a cigarette out of his pocket and handed it to me.

"She's gonna smell it on you."

"And I'm going to blame you!"

"Fine! Fine!" He held his hands up in the air, palms out. "All of this getting to you?"

"Yeah, it is," I said as I took a deep drag. It was the third cigarette I had had since Nicole caught me and Greg smoking behind her house so long ago. I had one after the first month of rehab and another one when they told me about the nerve damage to my leg, that no amount of PT would ever heal it completely.

Nicole knew about the other smokes, and I'd eventually tell her about this one, too—just not today.

"It feels like they're all looking at my guts," I told him, "or like I'm lying on a table in there with all my skin peeled off or something."

"That's kind of gross," Greg said. He put his cigarette back up to his lips and took a long draw. I followed suit. "It would only be worse if your daughter's boobs were on display for a bunch of strangers."

"Oh…um…I thought Nicole told you…"

"Yeah, and I didn't believe a word of it. Why do you think I'm smoking?"

"Heh…yeah, I guess that explains it."

We went back in together, and I was accosted by Jeremy, Rachel, Maria, and Ben. Maria was holding baby Jonathan, and Nicole was going gaga over him. It probably would have made me nervous if it weren't for all the people trying to sidle up to me. I surrounded myself with people I knew and tried to avoid everyone else.

I sold eight of the drawings that night, two of which went for over a thousand dollars each. Kathrine wrote me a check for everything that was sold, which totaled almost five grand. I couldn't believe it. Nicole jumped up and down when she saw how much they went for, and Gardner gave me a hug.

"My first show netted a whopping seventy-five dollars," he said with a laugh. "You just might make a living at this after all."

"It's amazing what a little publicity surrounding a local can do," Kathrine said with a nod. "The ones that fetched the most were bought by some big-name collectors—they're hoping you'll become very popular, and they think they got a deal. One of them offered me five thousand for the woman's torso."

"No." I glared at her.

"I know," Kathrine said with a roll of her eyes, "but those are the ones that would have fetched the most. Just saying…"

"They're hot," Jeremy said, and his eyebrows danced up and down a little. Rachel smacked him before I got the chance.

"I have to agree," Ben said. "You should have put those up for sale."

"No way in hell," Greg said, coming to my defense. "It was

bad enough having them on display!"

I nodded in agreement.

"Time to celebrate," Gardner said as he took Kathrine's hand. He was a master of diversion. We all headed out to eat, and everyone toasted my success. Both Gardner and Kathrine seemed pretty sure that's exactly what it had been, and I had to admit—making my own money felt pretty cool.

As I tipped the glass of champagne to my lips, I was reminded that being an artist wasn't going to be an easy living. Tough work didn't bother me, but I was determined to be able to hold my own and provide for Nicole as best I could. I knew money would never really be an issue for us, but that didn't stop me from wanting to provide for my Rumple anyway. Was that sexist? I didn't know and didn't care. I knew one thing for sure: I loved drawing and was even starting to enjoy painting as well. If this was something I could really do—and support Nicole as well—I was going to be satisfied.

But it wasn't going to be easy.

In *The Scottish Play*, Shakespeare wrote, "I have no spur to prick the sides of my intent, but only vaulting ambition, which o'erleaps itself, and falls on th'other." Somehow, I was going to have to gather both my ambition and my strength if art was going to be my calling.

Now to turn it into something more than just a dream.

EPILOGUE
onside

"Come on! Come on! Come on!"

I half jogged down the edge of the field, yelling at the seven first-graders who ran up and down the pitch in a little clustered formation—like they were all worker bees and the ball was the queen. It didn't matter what position they were supposed to be in, they all ended up within three feet of each other.

"Spread out!"

"Stay on your side!"

"Jonathan! You're on defense! Get back!"

Jonathan Walsh continued to trail after the ball until he saw his mother on the sidelines, holding his little sister and a pouch of Capri Sun. He stopped right in front of her.

"Can I have a juice?"

"Here you go, sweetie," Maria said as she held out a bag of sugar water for the kid. He stood there, staring blankly at the ball and sucking through the straw as the other team went right past him and made a goal.

I covered my face with my hands as I groaned.

Fuckity fuck, fuck, fuck, fuck, fuck!

At what age would I get to swear at them?

The final whistle finally blew, and I tried to give the peppiest pep talk I could before sending the kids back to their parents. I don't think any of them actually heard me—they were far more interested in what snack had been provided by the Oliver family. Sighing, I gathered up the extra balls, abandoned water bottles, and various other crap and hauled it all off the field.

"Why did I agree to do this again?" I asked my Rumple as I tossed all the shit into the back of the van. I rubbed at my right thigh as I walked off the field—some days it still bugged me after running around.

"Because Ben asked you to," she responded, "and because you love it."

I grunted, put all the gear into its bag in the back of the van, and turned back to my wife.

"Maybe I'm too old for this," I said with a shrug.

"You're twenty-six!" She giggled like one of the six-year-old players.

"I feel ancient," I replied. "Too much crammed into those years."

"Well, you still look like a Greek god," Nicole told me, "while I look like a beached whale."

"You're beautiful," I said as I kissed her forehead. I pulled my right leg back a bit so I could bend over and place my lips on the soccer-ball-shaped protrusion that was Nicole's stomach. "Especially this part."

I glanced back up to Nicole's face.

"You sure you didn't just swallow a ball? Looks like a size five to me."

I swear you couldn't even tell she was eight months pregnant from the back. She only grew in her stomach and her tits, which I fucking loved.

"Shut up!" Nicole laughed and swatted my arm. "You did this to me, and you know it!"

"How's your back?"

"Sick of carrying your son around," she complained. "Just

remember, I carry him for the first nine months. You get the next nine."

"Like Gardner and Kathrine are going to let either one of us hold him," I snorted. My father and stepmom had gone totally grandbaby crazy. Kathrine never had any of her own children, and…well…Gardner didn't know me as a baby, so it was like they were both planning on making up for it with their first grandchild. From the way they went on about it, you would think *they* were having their first child instead of us. "I think Kathrine's planning on kidnapping him from the hospital and raising him herself. She's got more baby shit over at their house than we do in the nursery."

I opened the passenger door and helped Nicole in before I circled around and got in myself. I pulled out of the parking lot just as the rain started up again. At least the fields were dry long enough for the game.

"Did you see Gardner going through a catalog of swing sets? He wants to put one of those great big climbing ones in their back yard."

"The baby won't be able to use it for years!" I exclaimed.

"I know."

"And their back yard is almost non-existent! One of those things would take up all of it!"

"I know," she repeated.

"They're crazy!"

"Yep."

"What do you have going on tonight?" I asked.

"I'm heading out with Sophie to pick up the crib and changing table," Nicole said. "You're at the gallery all evening, right?"

"Yeah, Kathrine's putting up the pieces I finished last week," I said as I ran my hand through my hair. "I really need to get those other paintings done this week before the buyers all bail on me."

"That only happened once," she reminded me.

"I know, but I ended up losing about five grand on the sale." I shook my head as I backed up and turned around. The gravel drive crunched under the van's tires.

"You still made a decent sale."

"Yeah, just not as much," I said. "I don't want to live off of the insurance money forever. I'd rather save it all for the kid's college and what-not. I want to provide for you and the little guy myself, so you don't have to go back to work until you're ready."

Frankly, we had a shitload of money; I just didn't want to use it. It was his money—Lou Malone's money. I really didn't want it and gave a good portion of it away the first year we were married. I set Sophie's son up with a college fund because the kid's dad never did shit for him and made sure I paid Greg back for renovating the house for me.

I might have built a soccer stadium at the high school, too. It always pissed me off that we had to run around in the football stadium.

When Nicole had to have knee surgery and couldn't play soccer any more, either, I paid for the renovations needed at the rehab center, and they hired the best PT for knee injuries on all of the West Coast.

"You do just fine," Nicole said.

I shrugged, not really feeling it. Nicole's making more money than I did wasn't a problem for me; it was just that what I made was so random. One month I brought in twenty grand, then the next—nothing. I had made a bit of a name for myself as an artist, but even so, it was hard to really make a living just drawing and painting.

No wonder Gardner became a professor.

I shook my head and merged onto the highway. As much as I liked living in the hometown on the weekends, I was anxious to get back to Portland. I had four commissioned paintings to finish up and an interview with a journalism student at the university on Monday. Apparently, I was going to be featured in their newsletter next month. With any luck, it would bring me more business.

When I thought back to how I got to where I was, I always ended up feeling a little strange. I didn't know how I was supposed to feel. People always asked me if I resented my accident since I still had a limp sometimes when I was tired, and I had to take stairs pretty slowly. My answer was always no because shit happens for a reason, and everything that had happened to me—my mom's death, my dad's abuse, the accident that damaged my body, but saved my soul—all of that brought me Nicole.

My Rumple.

I reached over and let my fingers draw little circles over her rounded belly as I drove down the highway, and she gabbed on the phone to Kathrine about crib bumpers. I smiled as I felt a little push back from my son. Just a little fist bump, I imagined, just to say "Hi," and "I'll be out soon."

Sometimes, I felt like the first part of my life had been played offside—like every move I made was pointless because I could never score from where I had been. Now things were in perspective, and though it wasn't what I thought it was going to be, I knew I had the chance to make something of myself.

For myself and for my family.

Shakespeare said: "The course of true love never did run smooth." Somehow, despite everything we had been through and how hard we had to run, we had come out onside—maybe not unscathed, but still better for what we had endured.

Now the true goal of my life was evident. It was my game, my life, my dream.

Not my father's—mine.

OTHER TITLES BY SHAY SAVAGE

THE EVAN ARDEN TRILOGY

OTHERWISE ALONE - EVAN ARDEN #1
OTHERWISE OCCUPIED - EVAN ARDEN #2
OTHERWISE UNHARMED - EVAN ARDEN #3

SURVIVING RAINE SERIES

SURVIVING RAINE - SURVIVING RAINE #1
BASTIAN'S STORM - SURVIVING RAINE #2

STANDALONE TITLES

TRANSCENDENCE

WORTH

FIC SAVAGE
Savage, Shay.
Offside

OCT 2 5 2016

CPSIA information can be obtained
at www.ICGtesting.com
Printed in the USA
LVOW04s1503131016
508637LV00016B/1298/P

9 781500 737887